A MAN OF HER OWN

When Hank talked of his home, he relaxed, describing it so well she could almost see the ranch with its endless sunsets and room to breathe. From the train window the land turned flat, but he painted the beauty in it with his words so clearly she could almost see it through the night.

Somewhere between Fort Worth and home, Aggie fell asleep on her new husband's shoulder, dreaming of a life where her time was her own and no one ordered her around.

from "Amarillo by Morning" by Jodi Thomas

BOOK YOUR PLACE ON OUR WEBSITE AND MAKE THE READING CONNECTION!

We've created a customized website just for our very special readers, where you can get the inside scoop on everything that's going on with Zebra, Pinnacle and Kensington books.

When you come online, you'll have the exciting opportunity to:

- View covers of upcoming books

- Read sample chapters

- Learn about our future publishing schedule (listed by publication month *and author*)

- Find out when your favorite authors will be visiting a city near you

- Search for and order backlist books from our online catalog

- Check out author bios and background information

- Send e-mail to your favorite authors

- Meet the Kensington staff online

- Join us in weekly chats with authors, readers and other guests

- Get writing guidelines

- AND MUCH MORE!

**Visit our website at
http://www.kensingtonbooks.com**

GIVE ME A TEXAN

JODI THOMAS
DeWanna Pace
Linda Broday
Phyliss Miranda

ZEBRA BOOKS
Kensington Publishing Corp.
www.kensingtonbooks.com

ZEBRA BOOKS are published by

Kensington Publishing Corp.
850 Third Avenue
New York, NY 10022

All Kensington titles, imprints, and distributed lines are available
at special quantity discounts for bulk purchases for sales promotion, premiums, fund-raising, educational, or institutional use.

Special book excerpts or customized printings can also be created
to fit specific needs. For details, write or phone the office of the
Kensington Special Sales Manager: Attn. Special Sales Depart-
ment. Kensington Publishing Corp., 850 Third Avenue, New
York, NY 10022. Phone: 1-800-221-2647.

Zebra and the Z logo Reg. U.S. Pat. & TM Off.

ISBN-13: 978-1-4201-0103-4
ISBN-10: 1-4201-0103-X

First Zebra Mass Market Printing: February 2008

10 9 8 7 6 5 4 3 2 1

Printed in the United States of America

Contents

Amarillo by Morning

JODI THOMAS

This story is dedicated to a real Amarillo hero.

Happy birthday, Hank.

Chapter 1

Fort Worth, Fall, 1889

Hank Harris squared his shoulders, forcing himself not to slump as he passed through the doorway of the Tucker dugout. He stepped into the one-room home with dread settling around his heart like sand.

At six-foot-six he knew he was destined to hit his head any time he ventured indoors. Seemed like houses all got too short about the time he started growing whiskers. Now, at thirty-one, he'd spent half his life watching out for low rafters.

He caught himself wishing that was all he had to watch out for tonight.

"Welcome, Mr. Harris!" a female bellowed as if he wasn't standing within reach of her. "Trust you made the five miles from Fort Worth without any problem. That north wind has sure been howling all day." The woman winked boldly. "I'll bet you think it's calling you home to that mound of dust folks call Amarillo."

Hank removed his hat and nodded, not wanting to encourage conversation. Dolly Tucker's shrill voice could strike kindling in a dry stove. He only prayed that her tone wasn't hereditary.

He couldn't stop the smile that wrinkled his normally hard mouth. Maybe he should be praying for himself. After all, he was the one fool enough to agree to meet Dolly's little sister. Most folks would say he had no right to be criticizing others. He wasn't the kind of man anyone would mistake as good looking and, with the price of cattle dropping, any wealth he had lay far in the future.

I'm a hard worker though, he reminded himself. And honest. If I ever get a wife, I'll never mistreat her. That should be worth something in this world.

"You're looking all cleaned and pressed," Dolly yelled as she patted his arm. "You must have stopped at the creek." She waddled around him like a round little toy. "Your hair still looks wet."

Hank didn't know how to answer. He had no intention of discussing his bathing habits with the woman. In truth, he could never remember discussing anything but the weather with the fairer sex.

When he'd seen Dolly's husband, Charlie Tucker, at the stockyard in Fort Worth a few hours ago, it had seemed simple. Dolly's sister was visiting from Chicago and Charlie said they'd like him to meet her. He had even insisted that Hank stop by around suppertime.

Hank knew what that meant. They were introducing her to all the single men in West Texas. He'd played the game before a few times in the ten years he'd been ranching. He was respectable enough for a brother-in-law to introduce. He owned his own spread, was single, didn't drink to excess. But Hank also guessed that if Charlie was rounding up prospects, he might as well take his place at the back of the line.

On the bright side, he'd get a home-cooked meal for his trouble and Hank figured that made the ride out worthwhile.

"Would you like some coffee, Mr. Harris?" Dolly didn't give him time to answer before shouting, "Charlie Ray, pour him a cup while I go to the barn and find Agnes. It's almost dark. She should be able to guess it's about time for supper. The world can't always run on *her* schedule."

Hank swallowed hard. Agnes was close to the ugliest name he'd ever heard. That must be why they keep her in the barn. Either that or the girl talked like her sister and poor Charlie would be deaf if he heard the voice coming from two directions at once.

Another thought crossed his mind. What if Agnes wasn't bright enough to know the time of day? Some men in this part of the country weren't too particular, but knowing the time seemed a necessary skill.

Dolly's husband moved to the iron stove and burned his hand grabbing the pot. Hank fought down a laugh. What was it about some men? They seem to live perfectly well by themselves for years. Then they get married and act like they've never been near a stove.

"I appreciate you stopping by," Charlie mumbled as he finally managed to pour a cup.

Hank nodded, knowing he was just doing a favor for a friend. Men like Hank lived alone. No woman would have wanted to start out with nothing like he'd had to and, by the time he could afford more than a three-room house, he'd be too old and hardened for a woman to be interested.

Before Hank's coffee cooled enough to drink, someone tapped at the door.

Hank stood ready to offer his hand as more guests arrived. He wasn't surprised to see the young banker most of the cattlemen used while they were in Fort Worth. William J. Randell always seemed fair and wore clothes that looked like he must have ordered them from somewhere up north without bothering to take his measurements. He had a habit of playing with his watch fob when he was nervous, which would have made him easy pickings at a poker table. His hair curled in thin waves over his head making him look older than Hank guessed him to be.

The man behind Randell looked almost the same age, only

Hank had never seen him before. He was stockier and stood with his feet wide apart as if expecting a fight to break out as he entered the dugout.

"Potter," the stranger said as he shook hands without waiting for Charlie to introduce him. "Potter Stockton at your service." His smile never reached his dark eyes.

Hank felt like counting his fingers to make sure they were all still there when the handshake ended. Something about Stockton didn't seem right. He was too friendly, too eager, too forward for a man not running for office. Hank found himself thinking a little less of the banker for keeping company with Potter.

Charlie Tucker didn't seem to notice. He offered the two men a seat and grinned. Before he could pour more coffee, Dolly returned alone from the barn. Her little marble blue eyes sparkled as she counted the bachelors at her kitchen table.

Within minutes, Hank was forgotten, which suited him fine. Dolly made over first the banker, then Potter Stockton, who explained he worked for the railroad. As Dolly served the food and insisted they eat, she kept the questions coming in rapid fire.

William J. Randell told all about the big family he came from in Ohio and Potter Stockton said he had relatives in Tennessee who were related to the royals in Europe. Hank kept quiet. As far as he knew he had no living relative. His mother left them when he'd been three and his father worked their small farm around Tyler, Texas, until he died before Hank turned twenty. The sale of that farm had given Hank his start near Amarillo.

They were halfway through the meal before Charlie got a word in to ask about his sister-in-law Agnes.

"She'll be along," Dolly scolded her husband as if no one would have remembered the reason they'd all been asked to dinner if Charlie hadn't mentioned it. "We'll be eating at midnight if we wait on her."

Hank pushed food back and forth on his plate, feeling like

the walls were closing in around him. He'd always hated dugouts. Everyone said they were warm and protected from the weather since they were built half into the ground, but he felt like he was half buried in them. Even through the cooking odors, he could smell damp earth.

When he stood, mumbling something about taking care of his horse, no one in the room noticed him leave. He felt cheated. Though he had no hope of finding a bride, he had thought Dolly could cook. He would have had a better meal at the café by the train station.

Once outside, he stepped into the blackness between the two small windows and took a deep breath, wishing he could ride back to town. Waiting on the platform for the midnight train north would be better than going back inside. But if he just left, it would be an insult to both Charlie and the invisible Agnes. There was an unwritten law that said the girl, no matter how homely or dumb, had the right to turn away any man who came calling.

And he'd been dumb enough to come calling, even if it was wrapped in a dinner invitation.

He knew he'd be leaving alone. Both men inside were better looking, better dressed, and probably had more money than him. Potter said he could dance and was a crack shot. Hank had never shot at anything he couldn't eat. William Randell bragged about building a two-story house in town and said he was up for a promotion at the bank. Potter swore he'd be in the cream of Fort Worth society in five years. They were dueling braggarts and Hank wanted no part of it.

"It's bad in there, isn't it?" a voice whispered from the blackness on the other side of the window.

Hank jerked away, almost knocking himself out on the low-hanging roof. He had no doubt the voice belonged to the missing sister, but she'd scared a year off his life when she spoke. In the night, he couldn't make out even an outline of her. "Yep," was all he could think to say.

"Dolly and Charlie Ray mean to marry me off," she whispered after a long silence. "Dolly's been planning it all day."

He wasn't sure if she talked to him or herself. "You Agnes?"

Dumb question, he thought. Who else would be out here this time of night?

"Yep," she echoed him, but without the accent it didn't sound natural. "I'm the old maid sister who's being passed around. If I don't get married here, I'm due in Austin at my oldest sister's place next month. Kind of like a traveling sideshow. Dress me up and put an apple in my mouth."

Hank couldn't stop the laugh. "I'm sorry," he quickly added. "I never gave much thought to the other side of this game."

"Sorry for what? For laughing or for me?"

"Both, I guess."

"My poppa sent me west before I rotted on the vine in Chicago. You see, I'm the last of five girls. The only one not claimed. As soon as I'm married, my poppa plans to take another wife. There's not room in the little apartment behind his shop for two women. I'm delaying his plan. I'm as much in the way in my home as I am here."

Hank smiled. He knew how she felt. "The runt of the litter, last to be picked," he mumbled, then thought he might have offended her.

Before he could say he was sorry again, she laughed. "That's right. I'm only half the woman my sister is."

Hank glanced in the window and watched Dolly waddle past. He couldn't say anything without insulting Charlie's wife so he changed the subject. "Don't you want to get married?"

"Not really. Do you?"

"No," he said honestly. "I like living alone. Running on my own clock."

"Me too."

His eyes had adjusted to the night enough that he could

make out her shadow. She appeared short, like her sister, but not as round.

"But why not marry? For a woman, it seems like the best life." He couldn't help but add, "Unless you hate the cooking and cleaning part?"

The shadow lifted her head with a snap. "Women do more than cook and clean."

He'd said the wrong thing. She couldn't even see how homely he was and she was still rejecting him. "I know, but it helps if they can cook a little."

Agnes laughed suddenly and he liked the sound.

"You've been eating Dolly's pot roast, haven't you?"

"Trying to." He wished she would step into the light. "What *do* you like to do . . . Agnes?" Her name stumbled off his tongue.

"Back home, I helped my father in his workshop. He was a gunsmith. Sold the best weapons in the state and repaired the others."

"You liked working in his shop?"

"No," she answered. "I liked repairing guns in the back. I wish I'd been born a man. I'd love working on my own little workbench all day and coming home to a hot meal. It's always appeared to me that a wife was more an unpaid servant than a partner. I'd hate that, so I don't see much point to marriage. If I could, I'd open my own repair shop, but I have no seed money and none of my family thinks it would be a respectable kind of place for a woman to have. So, I'm cursed to circle my sisters' houses looking for a husband."

Hank leaned against the building. He could hear Dolly's voice asking if anyone wanted more pie, but he didn't glance toward the window to see if any victims had volunteered.

"Would you marry someone if it was a true partnership? Each taking care of himself, taking turns with shared duties. Each supporting the other in whatever work."

"No one bossing the other, or controlling?" She leaned closer, almost crossing into the light.

Hank had no idea where his thoughts were going, but for once he wasn't talking to a woman about the weather, so he decided to keep talking. "Right. Just two partners sharing the same house. Both bring in what they can as far as money goes. Both respecting the other's privacy."

"No wifely duties? No children coming every year?"

Hank thought he knew what she was talking about. He shook his head, then remembered she couldn't see him and added, "None. They'd each have their own room, their own things, their own lives." He'd seen men who ordered their wife around as if she were a slave. On the other side, he had watched a few women bossing their man in the same tone. In truth, he couldn't remember ever seeing a couple stand as equals.

The one memory he had of his mother circled among his thoughts, not quite substance but more than dream. A tall woman sitting by the window, ignoring all the world around her, including him. Long after she'd gone, Hank remembered asking his father why she'd left. His father had only mumbled that she didn't want children. They'd never spoken of her again.

Hank glanced across the darkness, pushing the image aside, trying to understand the woman only a foot away.

They were both silent for a few minutes, then she whispered, "I'd marry like that. A partnership. In fact, I'd consider it heaven. But even if I found a man willing to follow those rules, what's to make him keep his word? He could lock me in the house and beat me, and no one would stop him."

"You're the gunsmith, Agnes. You should be able to figure that one out. Ask for his guns as a promise. No man but a fool would stand in front of a barrel, even in the grip of a woman."

She laughed then offered her hand across the light of the window. "It was a pleasure talking to you, but I have to go in and turn those two down before they die of food poisoning."

He took her tiny hand in his. "I wish you luck, Agnes," he said, realizing how much he meant it.

Just before she shoved at the door, she whispered, "My friends call me Aggie."

He placed his hand above her head and added his strength to hers. "Aggie," he said so close to her that he could feel her hair brush his face as the door opened. "I like that name."

Chapter 2

Hank blinked at the light as he stepped inside. Aggie walked ahead of him and stopped just over the threshold as if too afraid to go on.

He looked at the two men at the table. They both glared open-mouthed at her as if she were some kind of creature and not human. His fist clinched, and if she hadn't been in front of him, he might have closed their mouths with one blow. He didn't care what she looked like; she seemed a kind person who had a right to some degree of respect.

"I'm sorry I'm late," she said as if she hadn't noticed the way they stared. "One of the calves Charlie brought home from the stockyard is sick, and I had to make sure he'd eat before I came in."

Charlie smiled a lopsided grin and shrugged as if taking the blame for his sister-in-law's tardiness. "Once in a while they cull out the little fellows too weak to make the trip north. If I don't bring them home, I have to bury them behind the lot."

No one but Hank seemed to be listening.

Potter and William bumped heads trying to stand at the same time. Both were stumbling over words.

Hank stood behind Aggie, proud of her. She timidly offered her hand to each as if these two idiots made sense. The banker started playing with his watch chain and Potter talked even faster than he had at dinner. They were both "honored" and "privileged" to meet her.

The banker pumped her hand up and down so fast Hank feared he might break bone.

Potter kissed her fingers while he mumbled something in French. Hank would bet even money that he learned the phrase in Fort Worth's rough section called Hell's Half Acre.

If Hank didn't know better, he'd swear both men had been drinking.

"And Agnes, I believe you must have met Hank as you came in." Charlie sat down, adding only, "He often does business at the stockyard when he's in town."

Aggie turned to offer her hand to Hank.

"Nice to meet . . ." was all he got out before he saw her face. He'd braced himself for a plain girl, maybe one with pockmarks or scars, thick glasses or a birthmark. But what he saw almost buckled his knees.

She had the face of an angel, with perfect skin and curly auburn hair tied into a mass of curls at the base of her neck. And, he noticed, the devil twinkling in her blue-green eyes.

"Nice to meet you, Mr. Harris," she said shyly. "Would you like a slice of my sister's pie?"

There it was again, he thought. The sparkle in her gaze— daring him—challenging him.

"If the others left a piece," he managed to say. "I'd love one."

He sat down and watched her as she talked with the others. He ate the pie Dolly passed him without tasting it.

Aggie asked the other two men questions, as if she'd been coached, about their life and what their plans were. Hank didn't try to speak up. His life on a ranch would look pretty stale compared to Potter Stockton's travels and parties, or the magnificent house Randell planned to build in the center of town. She'd probably be bored to hear the details of raising cattle in West Texas.

He *was* proud of his house though. She might consider it

plain with the high ceilings and wide uncovered windows. But if Hank could have gotten a word in, he would have told her how from every direction she could see for miles, and how when the clouds hung low, close to the ground, his home seemed suspended between heaven and earth.

The banker and Potter found their footing on her questions and begin to compete for her attention. They said pretty things to her, flattering her with words Hank could never hope to put together. Within minutes both men were hinting that she should consider marrying them. William Randell seemed good-natured with the competition, but Stockton's bragging carried an edge. He seemed a man who was used to fighting for anything he wanted, and he claimed Aggie was the prettiest girl he'd ever seen.

Aggie listened politely, without comment. It crossed Hank's mind that she'd probably heard such talk all her life. For a woman who said she liked working alone, the idea of entertaining and the dinner parties that Randell talked of must seem frightening. Potter boasted of traveling with his work and staying in hotels across the country.

Hank seemed the only one who noticed she didn't smile. In fact, if he was reading her right, Aggie was one step away from bolting out of the room.

Hank also noticed that the more she drew everyone's attention, the sharper Dolly became. It must have been hard on four sisters with the baby being so beautiful. That might explain why the father kept her tucked away in the back workshop. Hank wondered if she'd stayed in back because she was naturally shy, or if the sisters had forced her to remain in the shadow. Whichever, one fact was obvious to Hank. Beautiful Aggie was afraid of people.

He watched her carefully. She wasn't believing a word they said. She kept her hands laced tightly together over her frilly dress. He felt her loneliness more than he saw it. She was on display, something to be sold to the highest bidder, and no one stood by to help her. In fact, her sister made it plain that if she could decide for Agnes, little sister would already be packing up her things.

After an hour, Dolly ended the torture, not for her sister's sake, but for her own. Dolly complained that her feet were tired and it was time for bed.

As the banker moved to the door, he held both of Aggie's hands and kissed them. "I'll dream of you this night," he said with practiced flow. "Think of me also."

Potter was bolder. He swore he'd fallen in love at first sight and asked for her hand in marriage. He said she was the first woman he'd seen in Texas who would be perfect on his arm, and now that he found her he saw no need to hesitate. Without waiting for her answer, he began listing his qualities and continued to do so as Charlie showed him the door.

Aggie politely said she'd consider his offer.

Both men stood at the doorway and waited to see what Hank would say, if anything. Obviously, neither considered him a threat, but they had no intention of leaving him inside with the prize.

Hank stood and put on his hat. When he walked past Aggie, she seemed so small. He hoped his height didn't frighten her. She didn't look up, and he wondered if she was embarrassed by all she told him in the darkness. After all, her family had made her options limited and for all her brave talk outside, she might still have little choice but to marry.

"Thanks for the meal." Hank nodded toward Dolly. "And for the invitation," he added to Charlie. "It was a pleasure to meet you, Miss Aggie."

She still didn't look up. He leaned and unbuckled the gun belt he always wore when he traveled. "There's a train leaving Fort Worth about midnight. If you're on it, you'll be in Amarillo by morning." He lifted her hands and placed his weapons in her grip. "If it's a partnership, equal and forever that you want, I'll pledge my Colts that it will be true."

The silence in the room was complete for the first time that night.

Finally, Charlie whispered what everyone was trying to believe. "You're giving her your guns?"

Hank nodded once.

When William Randell and Potter Stockton finished laughing, they yelled things like, "You don't give a woman a gun, you give her flowers," and "Give a ring." One of the men even suggested that maybe this girl was the first woman Hank had ever been around. Both seemed to be rehearsing the story that they planned to tell many times over.

Dolly swore at Charlie, calling him a fool for inviting someone so crazy to their dinner. "Waste of good food," she yelled as the men mounted.

Aggie stood in the doorway, gripping the Colts and looking up at Hank. He saw the fear in her eyes, the uncertainty, but he also caught a hint of a smile on the side of her lips.

They were all laughing, except her. As he turned his horse, he caught a glimpse of Aggie buckling his gun belt around her skirts, and he knew as sure as he knew the sun would rise that she'd make the midnight train.

Chapter 3

Aggie didn't say a word on the ride into Fort Worth. She sat on the bench of Charlie's old buckboard feeling like she was waiting for her life to start. She barely noticed the cold wind whipping from the north, or the rustle of brittle leaves that still clung to the live oaks along the creek. Her brother-in-law made this trip each morning and evening, so he knew the road well even in the darkness. Five miles was a long way to travel to work, but between her sister and the cattle auctions, she guessed it might be the only silence he knew.

Hank Harris had asked her to marry him, or at least she thought he had. It wasn't like any proposal she'd ever heard. He'd offered a partnership, equal and forever. Then, he'd un-buckled his gun belt and handed it to her. And, for the first time in her life, she found she couldn't say no.

She smiled to herself. Her sister had argued all the while Aggie packed. At one point Dolly even insisted Charlie Ray stop Aggie from going with the crazy cowboy who thought a proper engagement gift was a gun. But Charlie, for once, spoke up and said he'd had enough. He claimed Hank was a good man and if Aggie wanted to go with him the only duty he saw as his was to see that they were married before the train left the station.

Hank and Aggie might be in Amarillo come morning, but they would be wed tonight.

The night air cooled Aggie's tears as she gripped her hands together in her lap. She'd never been brave, she reminded herself, but the fear of everything remaining the same was worse than the fear of the unknown. She had to go. She had to take Hank's offer. She had to end the torture of being passed from house to house.

"I never heard Harris swear," Charlie interrupted as the lights from town blinked on the horizon. "That's one good thing about him, I reckon."

Aggie took a breath. "Yes." She had one brother-in-law in Kansas who thought "damn" should serve as an adjective to every noun he used. Not swearing was definitely a good trait, she decided.

"Though I don't think he has much money, he always pays his bills at the stockyard. Some ranchers, even after they have the cash for the sale, try to slip by without paying." Charlie spit a long stream of tobacco into the night. "Paying your bills is good."

"Yes." Aggie guessed Charlie was trying to calm her. Maybe he thought she might jump out of the wagon and run away wild into the night. But, to be honest, if he didn't hurry she was more likely to bolt and run toward the station. Charlie Ray Tucker was the best of her brother-in-laws and he was barely tolerable. After being passed from sister to sister she'd noticed that all their husbands had bad habits.

Closing her eyes, she tried to guess Hank's.

"If he goes to the whorehouses he ain't one to brag about it." Charlie interrupted her thoughts again.

"That's good." Aggie tried to forget all the lectures her sisters had given her, as though each man she'd turned down had been her flaw. She grinned, realizing that accepting a proposal hadn't halted the lectures. If Dolly had had the time she would have ranted for hours.

All her sisters thought Aggie was weak-minded. Poor,

beautiful, slow-witted Aggie. She can't cook, can't sew, can't remember the time of day when she becomes interested in something. The only way she'll find a man, they claimed, was to remain silent until the wedding. They barely noticed what she *could* do, all the things she fixed, how dearly she loved animals. All they saw was the way she hid in corners at socials and refused to talk to strangers.

Charlie didn't seem to notice her silence as they passed the pens of cattle waiting to be shipped. He was on a roll praising Hank. "And he's clean. I swear some of them boys come in smelling worse than the cattle."

Aggie nodded as she watched the station draw closer. She had no trouble making out the tall man standing with his feet wide apart at the end of the platform. He must have been waiting for her for over an hour. She thought she saw a slight nod when they drew close enough for him to recognize Tucker's wagon, but his expression was hidden in the shadow of his wide-brimmed Stetson.

"What's your bad habit, Mr. Harris?" she mumbled to herself. "What will I have to put up with?" With a slight nod, she greeted him, realizing whatever his shortcomings were, they couldn't equal hers. He'd be the one shortchanged tonight.

Charlie pulled up to the platform and tied the reins around the brake handle. "I'll go wake the preacher. He don't live but a block from here," he shouted so that Hank could hear him. "You two might as well get acquainted."

She watched her brother-in-law disappear into the clutter of homes behind the station. For a while she just stared into the darkness wondering what she'd say to this man she was about to marry. Getting acquainted wasn't easy when neither liked to talk.

When she finally turned, Hank Harris looked as nervous as she. He offered his big hand and helped her down from the wagon. As his sleeve slipped a few inches up his arm she noticed a white bandage.

"Are you hurt?" If he'd had a bandage on his arm at dinner, surely she would have noticed.

Hank pulled his shirt over the wound as he shook his head. "It's nothing really. Right after I bought our tickets, some fellow I've never seen before thought I should have a drink with him. When I said I was waiting for someone he pulled a knife." Hank brushed his coat sleeve as if the wound could be dusted away. "The doc in the saloon across the street stitched it up for me. He was well into his whiskey, but he did a fine job. He wasn't much of a doctor and it wasn't much of a cut, so he only charged the price of a bottle. I was more worried about not being here when you drove in than the blood."

She frowned.

Hank continued, "I think the fellow mistook me for someone else. He was drunk enough that, by the time he realized his mistake, he decided to be mad at me instead of himself."

Her smile returned. "I can see how he'd take you for another." She scanned the length of him. "There must be quite a few men your size catching the midnight train."

Hank hated comments about his height, but somehow he didn't mind her teasing. "Be careful or next time I'll tell the guy to stay around until my wife arrives to shoot him."

"Did he try to rob you?"

Hank shook his head. "No, just a drunk wanting company."

Aggie brushed her fingers along his arm, lightly feeling the bandage beneath layers of shirt and coat. When their eyes met, they both turned away, embarrassed at her boldness.

He quickly stepped to the wagon bed. "This all of your luggage?" he asked as politely as if she were a stranger he'd offered to assist.

She glanced at the carpetbag and two boxes tied with twine. "I've a trunk my father said he'd ship once I settled. That's all." She knew it wasn't much. Most brides came with all the necessities for setting up housekeeping, but without a mother to help her, Aggie had neither the skill nor desire to quilt and stitch a dowry.

He picked up her belongings and loaded them on the train. When he returned, she whispered, "Thank you."

"You're welcome," was all he answered.

They just stood, side by side, as mismatched as any couple she'd ever seen. Her fingers twisted together, she shifted in place, straightened her skirt, retied the bonnet Dolly had insisted she wear.

Hank could have been made of stone. He didn't even seem to breathe. They both stared at the few lights of Fort Worth. On the breeze she thought she heard the tinny sound of a piano and guessed the only thing open this time of night would be the saloons.

"You cold?" He startled her with his question.

"No," she lied, pulling her cotton dress coat around her. She wasn't about to complain or tell him this was the only coat she had. Her father had bought her three new dresses to "go on her courting journey." Only, when she'd left for her first sister's house, it had been late spring. Now, in another month it would be Thanksgiving. Her three fine dresses were worn from washing and pressing, and no brother-in-law had offered to loan her money for winter clothes. Not that she would have taken a single coin from them. All any of them wanted from her was her absence. She was another mouth to feed and something for their wives to complain about. Nothing more.

She watched Charlie hurrying down the platform. A chubby young man, trying to pull on his long black coat, rushed behind him.

"I finally found a preacher," Charlie grumbled. "We can get this done now."

The preacher introduced himself as Brother Philip Milton. He shook Hank's hand with a strong pumping motion. "First," the young man said, straightening to his full height, "I have to ask if you're still wanting to marry this lady." He looked nervous, as if this might be his first ceremony. "I don't push nobody down matrimony road that don't want to go."

Hank swallowed, then nodded. Aggie wished she could see his face and know for sure that he wasn't having second thoughts. She wanted to warn the lean cowboy that all she'd ever been was trouble. Her mother died giving her birth. Her sisters had to take care of her when they were little more than babies themselves. Her father carted her to work with him until she'd been old enough to go to school. She didn't like, or trust, people, and she smelled of gun power and oil most of the time. If this man had any sense, he'd run now while he still had the chance.

Brother Milton patted Hank on the shoulder and turned to her. "You feel the same about him?"

She fought down a scream as she managed to whisper, "Yes."

While the preacher continued, she told herself nothing could be worse than being passed around. At least she'd have a home, no matter how small or plain.

Brushing the Colt at her waist she remembered his offer. A partnership. If he was fool enough to offer, she was crazy enough to take him up on it.

The preacher asked them to join hands as the first whistle to load sounded. Hank's fingers closed around hers and she tried to hear Brother Milton's words over the pounding of her heart. She was doing what her father had ordered. She was marrying.

Steam filled the night air, fogging the lights on the platform as travelers rushed by, unaware that two people were joining their lives together, forever. Aggie gripped Hank's hand and breathed in the damp air. Silently, she said good-bye to all she'd ever known, and hung her hopes on his promise.

The preacher pronounced them man and wife as the second whistle sounded. Hank reached in his pocket and handed Brother Milton two dollars.

Charlie yelled for them to hurry and suddenly they were running—her hand still in Hank's—toward their new life.

Hank paused a few feet ahead of her as the train began to

move. Then, without warning, he reached for her and lifted her up to the second step as the train picked up speed. A moment later, he jumped aboard.

Aggie backed up another step, giving him room, and found herself at eye level with the stranger she'd just married. She should have been afraid, but all she saw was a pair of walnut-colored eyes reflecting the questions and uncertainty she felt. She knew without asking that he hadn't come to dinner planning to leave with a wife. He didn't even seem all that happy with the turn of events. He looked more confused and worried.

He might be clean and not swear, but for all she knew he'd murdered and buried several wives out on that ranch of his. No one, not even her brother-in-law, knew Hank Harris well enough to pay him an honest compliment. He might be a raving maniac living way off in a town she'd never heard about. But then, who was she to question his sanity. She'd married a giant she'd talked to for five minutes in the dark.

The wind tugged a strand of her hair free. She turned away from his stare and tried to push it back beneath her bonnet. When she looked back, he was still staring at her as if she were the first woman he'd ever encountered. He had a strong face, made of all plains and angles. Not handsome, but solid with character.

Aggie let out a breath and told herself that a man's face didn't lie.

One corner of his mouth lifted. "How are we doing so far?"

She couldn't help but smile. "Well, I haven't shot you yet so I guess the marriage is lasting."

"You think we might try sitting down? It'll get mighty cold out here in the next eight hours."

Turning around just as the car shifted, Aggie lost her footing on the narrow step.

Hank's hand touched her waist only long enough to steady her. When he pulled away, she thought she heard him whisper, "Sorry."

They moved inside and found an empty seat. While she slid close to the window, Hank tugged at the top half of the bench in front of them, shifting the back so it made the seat face them. He sat his saddlebags on the empty bench. The tiny square he'd created offered them space and the hint of privacy. With an almost empty train, no one would be close to them for the journey.

He stood, halfway between the seat next to her and the one across from them as if debating where to sit.

"Do you like to ride facing backward?" she asked, thinking he looked so cramped having to lean forward to keep from hitting the top of the car.

"No," he said but didn't move.

She pulled her skirts close against her leg, making room for him.

When he sat, his knee brushed hers and he apologized again.

Relaxing, she almost giggled. Any man who'd said he was sorry twice in ten minutes of marriage couldn't be as bad as her fears. "It's all right," she said. "We're married. We're bound to touch now and then."

He nodded and tossed his hat and coat on top of his saddlebags. "We probably need to talk about the rules of this partnership. I'd sure hate to do something to make you think you'd just as soon be a widow."

She patted the gun belt at her waist and smiled. "It's a long way to Amarillo. Maybe we should set a few rules so we both know what the other expects."

And they did. He told her of his house and how he'd change one room to be hers. She said she only knew how to fix breakfast, but she'd do that every morning if he'd cook dinner. He explained that his land was less than a mile from town so they could manage to eat at the hotel café some nights.

When he talked of his home, he relaxed, describing it so well she could almost see the ranch with its endless sunsets and room to breathe. From the train window the land turned flat, but he painted the beauty in it with his words so clearly she could almost see it through the night.

Somewhere between Fort Worth and home, Aggie fell asleep on her new husband's shoulder, dreaming of a life where her time was her own and no one ordered her around.

Chapter 4

Hank put up with her wiggling beside him, trying to get comfortable, for as long as he could stand it, then he shifted and circled his arm around her shoulder. Her head settled against his heart. She sighed softly in sleep and stilled as if she'd found the place where she could relax.

He thought back over everything he'd done or said all evening, and for the life of him he couldn't figure out how he'd ended up heading back home with a beautiful woman sleeping on him. Not just a woman . . . his wife. He'd always said he liked his solitude, but he looked forward to seeing what tomorrow would bring for the first time in years.

He felt like a miner who'd been breathing stale air for so long that a fresh breeze made him dizzy. Everything in his life had seemed fine until he met Aggie, then he noticed the emptiness. And, it had happened in the darkness outside, before he'd seen her face. He admired her honesty, her spirit, but her beauty made him nervous.

For a while he worried about what she'd think of his house, then he remembered Charlie's dugout and decided she'd like his place just fine. She wasn't his real wife, he reminded himself. Not in the true sense of it. But to the town, to his friends, she would be. Somewhere in their discussion of the rules for this partnership, they'd agreed to keep the arrangement between them. Which suited him fine. He wasn't sure anyone would believe him even if he tried to explain. She'd told him that he could touch her in any way that would be acceptable in public, but that she'd not be ordered around anywhere. He grinned, guessing she'd had enough bossing with four older sisters.

Her determination to work surprised him. He hadn't missed the way, after telling him of her dream to be a gunsmith, that she'd waited as if she expected him to argue.

He'd told her Amarillo had several places that sold guns, but no gunsmith to repair them. He offered to speak to Jeb Diggs at the mercantile and ask if he'd put out a sign.

Hank smiled again, realizing he'd smiled more tonight than he had in months. Once he mentioned the sign, she'd asked questions, wanting to know all about the possibilities of her working. Aggie told him about her small box of tools and said she could mail order more with the first money she made.

For a few moments her shyness had disappeared. She'd promised him she'd pay her way, buying her own clothes and paying for half the food. The last thing she'd said before falling asleep was that she'd be no trouble to him at all as if by agreeing to marry her he'd somehow taken on an extra burden.

Touching her hand with one finger, he wondered how such a delicate creature could want to work with weapons. Her blue-green eyes had sparkled at the thought though, and if that was what she wanted, he'd do his best to see it happened. He had a feeling, trouble or not, great changes were coming in his life, and all he could think was that it was about time.

He rubbed his chin against her auburn hair. She'd been asleep an hour. They'd be pulling into Wichita Falls soon. He knew all the noise would wake her, but he wasn't ready to have her pull away. They might be strangers, but she felt so right against his side.

The whistle blew as the train slowed. As he knew she

would, Aggie straightened and replaced her bonnet. "Are we close to your home?"

"No," he managed to answer while thinking how ugly her hat fitted her face and hid the color of her hair. "We've only made the first leg, but there's a café here that stays open for this train. You hungry?"

She nodded.

"Twenty-minute stop," the porter yelled as he passed. "We don't wait for anyone."

Aggie's hand slid around Hank's arm as they rushed from the train. "Does the wound pain you?"

He covered her cold fingers with his. "I'd forgotten about it." He guided her into the café.

After they ordered, Hank decided to voice his thoughts. "I've been thinking since I just sold a few cattle that you should go ahead and order those tools you need right away. There's a mercantile across from the station." He added in almost a whisper, "We could also pick up any clothes you might need and maybe a hat to protect your face from the sun."

She looked up from her coffee. "I'll keep a record and pay you back."

He nodded, guessing she wouldn't accept the money any other way, and was thankful she didn't take offense at his suggestion of a new hat. "I could build you a bench in the barn to work. I have a bench out there where I'm always intending to build a few pieces of furniture, but I never seem to have the time. You could work with me on warm days, then when it gets cold you could use the kitchen table as a work area."

"You wouldn't mind?"

"I wouldn't. If we're to truly have this partnership, then half the barn, as well as the kitchen, is already yours."

"Thank you," she said as the cook delivered two bowls of chili with cornbread on the side.

When they were alone she added, "Mr. Harris, would you consider telling me why you married me?" She'd talked freely of her work and the rules, but she must think this question personal for her shyness returned.

"Don't you think you should call me Hank?"

She shook her head and looked down at her hands. He finished half his chili before she spoke. "My father told me once that my mother never called him anything but 'dear.' Would you consider it too bold if I did the same?"

No one had ever referred to him as dear. "I wouldn't mind." He wanted to add that she'd just made this bargain worthwhile even if she didn't do another thing, but all he said was, "I married you because you needed me."

She looked surprised. "Not because you wanted me or because folks say I'm pretty or because you needed a wife to help out?"

He shook his head. "You know you're pretty. In fact, I think you may be the prettiest girl I've ever seen, but I wouldn't have offered if that were all there was to you. In the dark, when we met, I saw your dreams, your hopes and, when we went inside, it didn't take much to see that those two fools would never make them happen."

She laughed, but her eyes studied him as if searching for a lie. "And will you?"

"Nope," he answered between bites, "but you will."

They ate the rest of the meal in silence with him wondering if she believed him. When they left the café and ran for the train she huddled close to him. The wind blew hard from the north. Hank could feel a storm coming and he hoped he made it home before it hit.

When they settled back into their seats, the car was empty except for a drunk snoring on the last bench. Aggie tugged off her shoes, doubled her legs beneath her skirts, and shifted so that her back rested on the window. Hank folded his leather coat and made a pillow for her to lean against.

"Thank you, dear," she said as casually as if she'd said the endearment all her life.

"You're welcome," he managed.

Hank had been an only child raised by a father who seldom said more than was necessary to anyone, including him. He was totally unprepared for Aggie. As the train pulled away from Wichita Falls and moved into the night, she began to talk, shyly at first. She told him of her home and her father, then she described all four of her sisters and how they'd married one by one and moved away.

Hank listened.

Tears bubbled in her eyes when she talked about how lonely her father seemed with all the girls gone except her. She loved working beside him and he'd taught her all he knew, but there still seemed to be this big hole in him that didn't fill until he began stepping out with Widow Forbes.

Hank liked the sound of Aggie's voice and the way emotions reflected in her face. He saw pride when she talked about her skill, and sadness when she told of leaving home and knowing if she ever returned she'd be a visitor in another woman's house. Anger also danced in her blue-green depths when she described how her sisters passed her from one to the other, each adding another layer of reasons why she wasn't married.

He could read in her eyes far more than she told. He'd bet the five hundred dollars in his pocket that she'd been her father's favorite and her sisters had resented it. He'd also bet the sisters hadn't wasted much time looking for the best man for Aggie.

Like a top spinning down, she finally said all she had to say. She must have waited a long time to find someone who would listen.

"You tired?" he asked.

She nodded.

"Turn around and lean against me." He shifted.

She pressed her back against his chest and he pulled his coat over her, resting his arm over her to keep the coat in place. "Trust me," he whispered against her hair. "I'll wake you before we get there."

"Yes, dear," she answered, already almost asleep.

Chapter 5

With the dawn came a downpour that seemed to be trying to wash the small town of Amarillo off the map. As the train pulled into the station, Aggie tried to catch her first glimpse. She stared out the foggy window at gray skies blending with the brown landscape.

"This is it." Hank stood as the engine braked. He crammed on his hat as if preparing for a fight. "We're home." Slinging his saddlebags over one shoulder, he moved toward the door. "I'll take your carpetbag now and come back for the boxes when I fetch my horse."

She sat motionless realizing he expected her to follow him.

"You have to be joking," Aggie mumbled. "I can't go out in that." She pointed at the rain pelting the windows. "There are tree branches blowing by bigger than me." She twisted her hands until her fingers turned ghostly white. "I can't go."

Hank laughed. "Train's moving farther north in half an hour and my guess is the storm only gets worse from here. We have to get off now."

When she didn't move, he added, "I'll carry you to the mercantile across the street. It's not far. You'll still get wet, but at least you won't get muddy . . . or blown away. Don't worry. I'll hold on to you."

Neither option seemed possible. Even if she had an umbrella, using it would be like fighting a bear with a twig. Much as she hated it, the only choice might be to run for the nearest shelter.

Hank moved down the aisle as if their discussion was over and she followed, her hands worrying in front of her. Marrying a stranger might have been reckless, but stepping out in that wind bordered on suicidal in her mind. No wonder there were no people in the Panhandle of Texas. They'd all blown into the Oklahoma Territory.

She watched as Hank crossed onto the platform, his legs wide apart and solid against the wind.

Before she could say anything, he swung her up and jumped from the train. Aggie wrapped her arms around his neck and held on for dear life as he ran into a wall of gray rain.

Shivering against him, she was too frightened to make a sound. Once they were off the platform, the street turned more river than road. He slowed, picking his steps. As tiny hailstones joined the rain, she felt his heart pounding even through their clothing.

His face lowered and his hat protected them both. A rough brush of whiskers touched her cheek.

"It's all right," he whispered, his lips near her ear. "We're almost there."

Aggie managed a slight nod and felt her cheek touch his once more. She tightened her grip. He did the same.

When he stepped onto the porch of Diggs Grocery and Hardware, she didn't lessen her hold. Now the rain wasn't hitting them, but the sound of it seemed deafening against the tin roof.

Hank pushed into the store. "We made it," he whispered with a laugh.

Aggie realized she hadn't been nearly as frightened as she thought she would be. She'd felt safe in his arms.

Placing her hand on his jaw, she turned his head slightly so that their eyes met beneath the shadow of his Stetson. "Thank you." She silently mouthed the words as she studied his face. A strong face with honest eyes, she decided. This tall man held far more than her at the moment. He held her future.

Warm air circled around them. Hank took a deep breath and raised his head.

When she looked up, a colorful mercantile greeted her. Everything from clothing, blankets, and food supplies to farm equipment and furniture seemed haphazardly piled around them. One man with a wide smile stood in the center of it all.

"Aggie." Hank cleared his throat. "I'd like you to meet Jeb Diggs."

Jeb Diggs, as round as the potbellied stove he stood beside, hurried toward them. "Well, well, Hank Harris. I didn't expect to see a soul today, much less you. What you got there?" The fat little man wiggled his eyebrows at Aggie.

Hank's hat dripped water as he looked down. "My wife," he answered as if the two words were all that needed to be said. Leaning, he set her feet on the floor.

"Mary Carol! Get out here!" Jeb bellowed. "Hank just found him a wife."

A woman matching Jeb in size waddled from the back. They both stared at Aggie as if they'd never seen such a strange creature.

Aggie straightened slowly. "Nice to meet you," she managed between shivers.

Hank's hand spread across her back, steadying her as though he sensed her fear.

Jeb motioned for them to come closer to the stove.

Hank circled her shoulder as if to draw her forward, but she didn't budge. All her life she'd hated meeting strangers. Her father had never made her wait on customers in his shop as her sisters did. Now, everything and everyone about her was a stranger, and she longed for her quiet days spent in the back of the shop.

She glanced up at Hank. He smiled slightly, but didn't say

a word. He looked like if she planned to remain rooted at the front door, he'd stand right beside her.

Mary Carol misunderstood Aggie's hesitance. "Don't worry about getting this floor wet, we'd outlast Noah, and don't pay no mind to that basket of cats. I found them out on the back porch without no momma to look after them. I couldn't stand them newborns getting soaked in this rain, so I put them as close to the fire as I dared."

Forgetting her own worries, Aggie looked at the basket by the stove. Wet, crying kittens wiggled about. She crossed and knelt, seeing that they were newly born and shivering. Blindly, they searched for their mother.

"If you have a cloth," she asked the lady staring at her, "I could wipe them dry."

Mary Carol smiled down at her. "I'll get one for them, and one for you too."

Aggie removed her ruined bonnet and wet coat, then sat beside the basket to began rubbing each kitten down.

"She's a pretty one," Jeb Diggs said as he watched Aggie. "An angel you got there, Hank."

"She needs dry clothes and a warm coat. Just put whatever she picks on my bill," Hank said as he shoved back on his hat. "I have to get my horse unloaded."

Aggie looked up, hating that he had to go back out in the storm.

"You be all right here?" he asked, studying her.

She nodded.

Mary Carol waved Hank away. "You hurry right back. Jeb will put on a fresh pot of coffee and it'll be waiting for you. I'll see to your new missus." She studied Aggie. "I'll bring out the few choices of clothing we have to pick from, and you can change in the storage room when you finish with them cats." As she walked away she mumbled, "You'll be needing boots as well."

The woman disappeared behind the stacks of clothing, but her voice continued, "You're lucky, we got in a huge shipment last week of winter wear. Nothing as fancy as what you have on, but good sturdy clothes."

Aggie looked down at the wrinkled violet dress she wore. Two of her sisters had picked it out, saying she needed something elaborate to attract a man, but the frills and buttons weren't comfortable and hadn't worn well.

Mary Carol tossed clothes over the stacks. A dark, rich, blue wool skirt landed at Aggie's feet, and a blouse cut like a man's, except for the collar and cuffs, followed.

Aggie ran her hand over the outfit. Growing up, her clothes had always been hand-me-downs. Pale yellows and washed-out pinks. She'd never worn anything in dark blue and couldn't wait to try it on.

"I got just the right vest to go with that," Mary Carol shouted as she hurried into sight. She held up a multicolored vest that looked like it had been made from an Indian blanket. "What do you think?"

Aggie grinned. It wasn't like anything she'd ever worn. It was perfect.

Twenty minutes later, when Hank stomped back into the store, Aggie sat by the stove drying her hair. He almost didn't recognize her. From her black boots to her western vest, she put any model he'd ever seen in a catalog to shame. He felt his mouth go dry. How does a man tell a beautiful woman she's just improved on perfection?

Tiny gray kittens, now fluffy and dry, were at her feet wrapped in a towel. Hank tried to concentrate on them as he moved closer, but five feet from her he made the mistake of looking up and froze.

"What's wrong? Is the storm worse?" She stood.

"No, I think it may be letting up a bit," he said, studying the way the mass of curls danced around her shoulders. "I just didn't know you had so much hair."

She frowned. "I'm afraid it curls when it gets wet. I'll . . ." Lifting her hands, she tried to pull it back.

"It's nice. Real nice," he said, wishing he could think of something more descriptive than "nice." He should have told her that the beauty of it took his breath away, but words like that would never make it past the lump in his throat. She must truly have no idea how beautiful she looked.

Something wiggled in his shirt, demanding Hank's attention. "Oh," he said, pulling a gray cat out before she permanently scarred his chest. "I found this under the porch. Hope it's the momma."

Aggie laughed and took the cat from him. "Of course it's the mother cat. She's probably been frantic looking for her babies."

As she sat the cat in the middle of the towel, the little mother began licking each kitten.

Hank watched. "Guess she didn't think the storm got them clean enough."

Aggie shook her head. "More likely she's cleaning off my scent."

Before either could say more, Jeb entered with a round of coffee. "I was just askin' Mary Carol," he bellowed, unaware he was interrupting a conversation, "how did Hank manage to leave a week ago with cattle and come back with a wife?"

Hank ignored the store owner and moved closer. "I like your choice of clothes," he whispered before Jeb reached them. "They look right on you somehow."

She leaned nearer, almost touching him. "Thanks for bring the mother cat in."

"You're welcome," he said, liking their whispering game.

Jeb tried again. "When did you two get married?"

"Last night, before we boarded the train," Hank answered without taking his eyes off of Aggie. "And as for how, I asked her, and she said yes."

Jeb laughed. "So that's it. We was figuring she must have

held that gun she's wearing to your head and made you marry her—her being so homely and all."

Aggie lifted the Colt from its holster as if she hadn't heard the backhanded compliment. "Hank gave me his gun because, like my father, I'm a gunsmith."

Hank took one of the hot mugs from Jeb and almost laughed at the man's surprise.

When he found his voice, he asked, "A gunsmith?"

Both men stood silently as she opened one of her boxes. She pulled out her tools wrapped in oil cloth, then sat on the stool by the stove and used the checkerboard as her workbench. While they watched in amazement, she disassembled the Colt and cleaned it. She then dried the holster and rubbed the leather down with saddle soap to keep it soft.

Jeb stared at Hank. "Let me get this right. She's not only beautiful, she can fix guns too." He raised both eyebrows as if piecing together a puzzle. "And she married you?"

Hank laughed. "That's about the size of it, except she wants to practice her craft. Do you think you could hang a sign in the window and take in any work folks might need done? We'll come by every few days and deliver back and forth if she gets any business."

"And I'll give you a percent of all I earn, Mr. Diggs," she added.

Jeb shook his head. "Don't want a percentage. It's your work. I'll make any money for my time by selling more from the extra customers the sign will bring in. My guess is when word gets out that you're here, you will have all the business you can handle."

Aggie rolled up her tools. "Thank you. I have a list of tools I need." She pulled a slip of paper from the side of the box.

Jeb took the list. "I could probably get most of them from a supplier in Fort Worth. Wouldn't take more than a few days." He tapped the paper with his finger. "I'll send this order with the afternoon train." He glanced at Hank. "And, of course, I'll put it on your bill."

Hank agreed but didn't miss the surprised look she gave him. He couldn't help but wonder how long she'd carried the slip of paper with her small box of tools.

She accepted a mug of coffee and went back to her seat beside the cats. "Thanks for the coffee and for letting me watch your kittens."

Jeb shrugged. "In a few weeks you can have your pick of the litter."

She grinned at Hank.

He nodded his agreement.

"We'll take the runt," she said and went back to watching the animals while the men talked about the weather.

When his cup was empty, Hank pulled on his slicker over his coat and asked if she was ready to leave. He slipped a new slicker over her shoulders and covered her hair with the hood, unable to resist touching the curls.

Her hand gently brushed his forearm and she whispered, "Should I change this bandage? It must be wet."

Hank shook his head. "It'll just get wet again. Wait until we're home. I've got a good stash of medicine there."

She agreed and Hank heard Mrs. Diggs mumble something about lovebirds.

Before they realized there was nothing between Aggie and him but a partnership, Hank waved good-bye and held the door open for his wife. "I didn't bring the wagon into town. I thought I'd be coming back alone. You mind riding double?"

Surprisingly, she giggled. "I've only been on horseback a few times. My father always drove a wagon."

Hank bumped his head against the door frame, too busy watching her and not where he was going. "I won't let you fall," he mumbled, thinking that if he didn't stop staring at her and start paying attention, he'd have brain damage before the day was over.

Chapter 6

The rain launched an assault to keep them inside, pelting at full force when they cleared the door. Hank motioned for her to wait while he climbed onto his horse and tied her bag and the boxes in place behind the saddle. He rode close to the porch so he could lift Aggie up in front of him.

She might be shy, but her willingness for adventure surprised him. He'd half expected her to refuse to go with him. He'd bluffed her into following when they'd left the train, but he had no idea what he would do this time if she refused. He didn't know her well, but he didn't think Aggie would take too kindly to being tossed over the saddle against her will.

Mary Carol rushed out with two bags. "Here's her wet clothes," she said, pulling her shawl around her head. "I also packed a few supplies—bread, milk, and coffee just in case you don't have any out at your place."

"Thank you." Aggie accepted both bags.

"No problem. I put them on your account."

Hank's arm tightened around his bride as he turned the horse toward home.

"Maybe you should stay and wait out the storm?" Mary Carol yelled as they pulled away.

"Want to wait?" he whispered near Aggie's ear.

She shook her head. "I want to go home."

Hank no longer cared about the weather. He'd been so many years without a family, without anyone, heading home with Aggie seemed almost too good to be true. He had a feeling any moment he'd awake from this dream and find some other man had won her hand. The thought brought to mind Potter Stockton's frown last night. The railroad man had made fun of the proposal almost all the ride back to Fort Worth. Hank hadn't missed the anger in Potter's remarks. He'd hinted twice before they split near the depot that Hank would be smart to go on back to Amarillo alone and leave the courtship of Aggie to a man who knew how to treat a woman like her.

Hank couldn't help but wonder, if he'd missed the train last night, would she have agreed to meet Potter Stockton again, or would she have turned both men down and moved on to the next sister's house? Hank remembered how Stockton talked about her beauty and how he'd laughed and commented that shy ones always "take the bit" without too much fighting. Hank didn't even want to think about what Stockton meant.

If Hank hadn't already asked for her hand, he would have turned around and ridden back to Aggie just to warn her not to see the railroad man again.

If she wasn't cocooned in her slicker, he might have tried to tell her where his land started, but with the rain she could see little. He wished he'd had time to telegraph ahead and have his hand, Blue Thompson, light the fire in the house and put lamps in the windows to welcome her.

When they reached the ranch, even though it was late morning, all was dark. He leaned down to open the gate. She twisted in front of him, holding tightly to his slicker.

He straightened and pulled her close once more. "It's all right, Aggie. I won't let you fall."

Her hood slid back enough that he could see her nod, but she didn't turn loose of her grip on him. When they reached the long porch that rounded three sides of his house, he lifted her with him as he stepped from the saddle and carried her up the steps. Old Ulysses, his guard dog, barked from beneath the porch.

"Hush, Ulysses, it's just me," Hank mumbled.

The dog growled, but quieted.

When they were well out of the rain, he sat Aggie down beside the only piece of furniture he'd brought north with him when he'd homesteaded—his father's rocker. "Don't worry about Ulysses. He's mean and hates everyone, including me, but he's a good guard dog. He keeps snakes away and warns me if anyone gets near the place."

Hank straightened and gripped the doorknob. "If I'd known you were coming, I would have . . ."

He didn't finish. It was too late for explanations or apologies. "Welcome home," he managed as the door creaked open.

Aggie walked in ahead of him and didn't stop until she was in the center of the polished floor. The storm's gray light shown the open area in layers of shadows. He stood at the threshold and stared at her back. The big main room looked empty with its two chairs and one long table. The fireplace was cold and dusty. The curtainless windows were stark, letting all the rage of the storm inside and holding no warmth.

"There's a kitchen and mudroom behind the fireplace. My room is to the left and yours will be to the right once I get my tack out of it. I'll move my bed in for you until I can build you what you need."

She hadn't moved. Her back was so straight he decided she must be in shock. To him the house had been great, but to her it must look cold and bare.

"The kitchen ceiling is only seven feet. I built an attic above it." He almost said "for kids." "I haven't been up there in a while, but it would make a good storage room if you need one. All that is up there now is an old trunk someone sent back to my father after my mom died."

"You weren't there when she died?"

He shook his head. "She left my father and me when I was barely walking. Never heard from her. There must have been nowhere to send her trunk. Our address was still written on the top so they shipped it home to my father. We never opened it." His words sounded hollow, even to him, but better that, he decided, than angry, which is how he'd felt most of his childhood.

He watched Aggie closely. "I could move it to the barn if you need the space. I don't even know why I lugged it from East Texas when I moved."

He had no idea what Aggie needed to feel at home here, but he planned to make sure she had it. "We could order more furniture if you want. I never had much use for it until now."

She took a step toward the archway leading to the kitchen.

Hank had to keep talking. "You can't see them for the rain, but there's a bunkhouse and barn about a hundred feet to the north, and we got a windmill and a good well. In the spring the view is a sight to see from every window."

She'd reached the kitchen and still hadn't turned around or said a word.

"I hire hands to help with the spring calving and branding, but during the winter, Blue Thompson and I do all the work. He and his wife, Lizzy, have a place down by the breaks halfway between here and town." Hank felt near out of information. If she didn't say something soon he wasn't sure what to do.

Without warning, she twirled suddenly, her arms wide, her head back, her hair flying behind her.

He watched, hypnotized by the sight of her. If angels ever touch ground they could look no happier than she did right now.

When she stopped, she faced him, a smile lifting the corners of her mouth. "I love it," she said.

"You do?"

She nodded. "All my life I've lived in tiny little rooms crowded with too many people. Here I can breathe."

Hank relaxed. "Then I can bring your stuff in and you'll stay?"

Tugging off her slicker, she answered as she disappeared into the kitchen. "Yes, dear, I'll stay."

Chapter 7

Aggie explored her new home while Hank brought in her boxes and bag. Like the main room, the kitchen was twice the size of any she'd seen, and her bedroom had enough space for all four of her sisters to join her. The windows everywhere were tall. She laughed, deciding Hank built them that way so he could see out without leaning down. Her father was short, only a few inches taller than she, and always fidgety in movement. Getting used to Hank would take some time. His strides were long and easy, graceful in a powerful way. But when he was still, he was perfectly still.

While Hank moved his bed into her room, she inspected the area above the kitchen and was surprised there was nothing in it but the battered old trunk he'd mentioned. She couldn't imagine a house with so much space that there would be an empty room. It also amazed her that he seemed to think it should be her room to do whatever she liked with. She moved around the attic, touching each wall, each window—silently saying hello to her new world.

"Aggie?" Hank called from below. "Come down and meet Blue."

She hurried to the kitchen and nearly collided with a gray-haired man almost as tall as Hank and twice as wide.

The man shuffled out of her way. "Pardon me," he mumbled, then laughed and added, "I didn't know you'd be flying down from above. Truth is I'd forgotten that room was up there."

Even with his slicker covering most of his body, she could tell his right shoulder was twisted, but there was nothing weak or soft about him. His frown seemed tattooed across his face and mistrust danced in his eyes. The big man looked as afraid of her as she was of him.

She fought to keep from running to Hank.

As if he sensed her fear, her husband moved to her side and looped his arm around her shoulder. "Aggie, I'd like you to meet my friend, Blue Thompson."

She knew Hank wouldn't use the word friend lightly, but Thompson looked like a man who hadn't trusted anyone since birth.

The big man stiffly offered his left hand while Hank continued. "Blue was shot up pretty bad at Williamsburg. When they found him in the cold, he was so near dead he looked blue." Hank offered him coffee.

"I've been called Blue ever since," the big man said. "I kinda like the name too, since I lived."

Aggie's fingers disappeared in his as they shook hands. "Nice to meet you, Mr. Thompson." She didn't miss the way he glanced down at Hank's gun around her waist and nodded once, as if he understood that Hank wouldn't have given his Colt to any woman unless she mattered to him.

"Just Blue," he corrected. This time when he returned her gaze she saw acceptance and maybe a little respect.

"Just Blue." She smiled. "And I'm just Aggie."

The old soldier relaxed. "Hank said your daddy taught you about guns."

"That's right," Aggie said.

"I got a French LeMat I carried in the war. Haven't been able to fire it since that day I was shot, but I keep it anyway. Do you think you could have a look at it for me?"

"I'd be glad to," she answered, realizing Blue was accepting her a few inches at a time. "I've worked on one of them before. Bring it by when you have time."

Blue frowned. "I'd go get it now. Our place isn't that far away, but there's a fence down." He looked at Hank. "We gotta get to it, boss, or there will be hell to pay by morning."

Hank agreed. "Help me get the tack in the barn, then saddle the paint."

Blue tipped his hat to Aggie and followed orders.

"You'll be all right here?" Hank sounded like he hated leaving her.

For a moment she thought of arguing. This was their first day together. All her life her father never minded postponing work. He'd even stop working to enjoy his pipe, or a conversation. Aggie knew ranching wouldn't be like gunsmithing. Problems couldn't wait. "Go," she said. "I'd hate to pay hell in the morning."

Hank smiled. "I might need to talk to Blue about his mouth." Hesitantly, he leaned and kissed her on the forehead. "I'll be back as soon as I can. If you run into trouble, just fire three shots. If I'm not close enough to hear, Lizzy, Blue's wife, will come running."

Aggie moved to the window and watched the two men disappear into a curtain of rain. It occurred to her that she should feel lonely and abandoned, but even with the storm raging, she felt protected in Hank's house. She needed the time here to settle in.

The walls glowed honey colored with each lightning flash as she ran from room to room loving the open feel to it. Space was a luxury she'd never known.

A hundred yards from the house, Hank realized he'd almost run out of the kitchen. He'd known that if he looked at her a moment longer he wouldn't be able to leave. As he lowered his hat and rode into the rain, he wondered at what point his mind had turned to oatmeal. How could a woman he hadn't even known twenty-four hours matter to him? When had she crawled under his skin and become a part of him?

Within an hour, he and Blue were riding the fence line looking for breaks. Compared to most of the ranches, his herd was small. Hank couldn't afford to lose any cattle. The cows he'd saved back from the last sale were all good breeding stock and he'd need them come spring. Last year he'd finally made it to the black after ten years of scraping by. He'd bought more land when the Duncan ranch next to him failed, and still managed to put some in the bank for a rainy day.

His plan had been to build enough to finally sell this spread and buy another, bigger one, farther from town. But, now, with Aggie in his life, he might have to rethink that plan. If she wanted to work, they'd need to live close to town, and the way Amarillo was growing it would overtake his ranch one day. The thought of being so close to town didn't interest him, but he couldn't see himself moving so far away that he made Aggie unhappy.

Smiling, he remembered the way she'd twirled around, her blue skirts flying.

Hank was so deep in thought he almost missed the downed fence. If Blue hadn't yelled at him, they might have ridden passed a hole so big his entire herd could have moved through by morning.

As they worked, the storm played itself out. The wind settled to a breeze and the rain to a drizzle. The red Texas mud clung to their hands and boots. By the time they finished, both men were covered in caked dirt. The watery sun blinked its way between clouds, baking the earth to their clothes like shingles on a roof. Hank pushed hard, trying to keep his mind on his job and not on the woman who waited for him at home.

Blue, as always, worked beside him. For a man with little use of his right hand, he managed to earn his wages. Over the years the two men had learned to work as a team, but they rarely talked.

Late in the afternoon when they headed home, Blue turned off along the breaks with a wave and Hank followed the stream. He was bone tired after not sleeping the night before on the train, but he pushed his horse, wanting to reach the house long before sundown.

While he washed and put on his good white shirt in the mudroom, Hank noticed the bandage on his arm was spotted with blood. Sometime during the afternoon one of the stitches must have pulled loose. He wrapped it with a towel so he wouldn't get blood on his clean clothes, then entered the house as quietly as possible.

He found Aggie curled up in the middle of his big bed, which he had moved into her room when he brought her boxes in. The guard dog, Ulysses, slept on the rug beside her. The moment he sensed Hank, he raised his head and growled.

Hank chuckled. "Protecting the lady, Ulysses?"

Aggie awoke with a smile and touched the dog's head. "We had a long talk on the porch. Ulysses promised to be good if I let him come in for a while."

The old dog lowered his head, but continued a grumble as Hank walked to the bed. "How about we see if together we can't find something to eat." He offered his hand to Aggie. "I'm starving and Ulysses is always in a better mood when he's eaten."

Aggie's feet slipped to the floor as she accepted his hand. "First," she said, staring at the towel, "I'll check that wound and put a fresh bandage on it. I may not be able to cook, but I'm a fair nurse. My father was a walking accident looking for a place to pause. I hope Widow Forbes keeps her medicine kit handy."

"We'll send them one as a wedding gift." Hank laughed as he accompanied her to the kitchen.

To his surprise, she raised her hand to his shoulder and pushed. For a second he didn't understand what she was trying to do, then he realized she was attempting to push him into a chair.

He sat.

"I found the medicine box when I went through the cabinets." She pulled the box forward and stood in front of him. "I also found a full stock of beans and peaches." She hesitated, then added, "and nothing more."

Hank watched her clean the wound. "Most nights I come in too tired to fix anything else. Lizzy brings over a good meal every Monday when she comes to do the laundry and clean." He watched Aggie closely. "I pay her twice a year in beef. If it's all right with you I'd like her to still come. They depend on the meat."

Aggie nodded, but Hank wasn't sure she really listened. She worried over the cut.

"You're lucky this isn't showing signs of infection." She poked at the skin around his cut. "I think if we wrap it correctly the wound will stay closed, but I'll want to clean it and put medicine on it twice a day."

"It'll be all right." He shrugged, thinking he'd had far worse cuts.

She let out a huff of impatience and worry. "I'll clean this twice a day if I have to tie you to the chair."

Hank smiled. "Yes, ma'am. I had no idea I was marrying such a bossy wife."

She raised her gaze to his and wrinkled her forehead. "I never thought I would be, but it seems so. You'll just have to put up with it, I'm afraid."

Loving the way she'd lost any fear of him, Hank put his hand at her waist, steadying his arm as she bandaged his wound. His gun belt was missing from around her hips and he wondered if she simply removed it while she slept, or if she felt safe enough with him not to bother with even the pretense of the Colt.

"How are we doing?" He repeated the same question he'd asked on the train steps twenty-four hours ago. "Any complaints, so far?"

She worked silently, her nearness affecting him more than

any poking she was doing. Taking a deep breath, he let the scent of her fill his lungs. He'd smelled perfumed women in the saloons, and a few proper ladies who bore the scent of starch and talcum, but Aggie was like neither. She reminded him of spring water just when the land turns green, all fresh and new.

When she didn't answer, Hank waited, figuring out that something bothered her. If he were guessing, he could think of several things—he'd left her their first day, the storm, no furnishings in the house to speak of, no curtains on the windows, none of her family close.

"There is one thing," she finally said as she tied off the bandage.

"What?" He wouldn't have been surprised if she said she changed her mind and wanted to go back to Fort Worth. Maybe the banker or the hotheaded Potter Stockton weren't looking so bad after she'd spent the day here alone. He remained still, his hand at her waist.

"When you left, you kissed me on the forehead."

If she was waiting for him to say he was sorry for *that,* she'd wait a long time. Finally, he managed to mumble, "You'd rather I hadn't been so informal?"

She shrugged. "No, actually, I was thinking that if you are going to kiss me good-bye, I'd rather you didn't do it on the forehead. It makes me feel like a child. I may be over a foot shorter than you, but I'm not a child. I wish never to be treated as such again."

Now he said, "I'm sorry," and meant it. "That was not my intent." He watched her closely, unsure where the conversation was going. "Where would you like me to kiss you when we part?" He thought of mentioning that couples do kiss one another politely when saying good-bye, but in truth he could never really remember seeing any husband do so except at the train station.

She placed her hand on his shoulder and leaned slightly

toward him. "The cheek would be all right, I guess, or even the lips would seem appropriate. After all, we are married."

Hank had that feeling of walking on ice. One misstep and he'd disappear. He wondered if he'd ever be able to read this woman. She'd made it plain she wanted a partnership marriage and nothing more, and now she was telling him where to kiss her. It crossed his mind that if all women were as hard to read as Aggie, no wonder the saloons were packed with married men.

He dove into deep water. "Like this," he whispered as he tugged her near and brushed his lips lightly along her cheek.

She leaned away, considering. "That would be acceptable, I think." She smiled. "Your whiskers tickle."

His arm slid around her waist once more but this time when he pulled her, she stumbled, landing on his knee. Before he could change his mind, Hank kissed her soundly on the lips.

When he raised his head, her eyes were open wide.

"Is that acceptable, Aggie?" he said, preparing himself for any answer.

Standing, she whispered, "Yes, dear." She turned, suddenly giving all her attention to putting up the supplies.

Chapter 8

They ate their dinner of beans and peaches at the kitchen table without saying much. Hank would have thought he'd upset her, only her last words still sounded in his mind. She'd said the kiss had been acceptable.

He was thinking of when he should do the acceptable again when she asked, "Where'd you get your dishes?"

Glancing down, Hank noticed the mismatch of china. "I bought them in the discount bin a few months after I came here. When my dad died, I sold the farm and packed up what I could in a wagon. Somewhere between East Texas and here, the box of his china fell off the wagon." He lifted one bowl. "This was the only piece that survived."

Aggie smiled. "This makes me feel right at home. When my first sister married, she took Mother's good china with her. The second packed away the everyday set. Papa bought more, but they left after the third wedding. After that he just bought odd pieces." She lifted the china teacup she'd been drinking coffee out of. "As near as I can remember, my mother's best set looked like this one with the tiny blue flowers around the rim."

Hank had never noticed the flowers, but he was glad he'd chosen the tea set. He bought them because he thought the pieces somehow made his place appear more like a home. Now he thought the cup looked right in her tiny hand.

"After dinner," he said when he realized he'd been staring at her for a while, "we could walk over to the barn. I'll need to measure how high you want your bench. I'm guessing you'll want to do some of the gunsmithing in the barn."

"It's late," she said, glancing out at the night, "and it looks like it might rain again."

"I know, but I want to get started on it at first light tomorrow morning." He grinned and added, "While you're cooking breakfast."

She finally looked at him. "Let's hope I'm better at it than you are at supper."

Hank didn't argue. She'd only eaten half the beans he'd served her. "Blue, before he got married, used to come over for meals from time to time. He said I made a good stew and in the summer I can fry up fish and potatoes regularly." He'd already decided that if the mud wasn't too bad he'd take her in for dinner at the hotel tomorrow night, but he wanted her to know he wasn't going back on his offer to cook. "I plant a garden in the spring. For half the vegetables and a case of jars, Lizzy will can all we can eat next winter."

"What about this winter?"

"I told her all I'd need were potatoes and carrots. They're in a root cellar. I'm not real fond of the green stuff, even floating in stew, but if you like them, I'll barter for black-eyed peas and green beans. Soon as it dries out, we can pick up all the canned goods we need at the Diggs' place."

She pulled a small tablet from her pocket. "I've been making a list of things I need. If you'll loan me the money, I'll pay you back." She looked down at her new clothes. "I'd also like to buy a few more sets of clothes like these. I don't think I want to wear my old dresses. They don't seem to belong here."

He couldn't agree more.

Hank stood and pulled a coffee can from the top shelf. "I

have some money in the bank, but this is what I planned for winter expenses. There's a little over five hundred dollars here. You're welcome to however much you need." He started to return the can to the top shelf, then reconsidered and shoved it between the spices so it would be within her reach.

"I'll pay you back. Once we're square, I'd like it if we both put the same amount into the can each year. Then whatever else you make on the ranch or I make working will be for each to decide."

He wanted to argue that it wasn't necessary, but she'd said each year like there would be many. Figuring he'd have time to talk out expenses later, Hank asked, "Did you decide if you want to use the room upstairs?"

"I thought I'd make it my indoor workroom, that way the kitchen won't get cluttered. The light's good up there and on cold days the kitchen fire will keep it warm."

"I could frame you up furniture tomorrow. The good thing about winter on a ranch is there's time to do all the chores I couldn't get to in the spring and summer. The bad thing is I never seem to finish the list before calving." He stood and lifted a lantern from the peg by the back door. "You want to walk with me to the barn and tell me where to put that bench?"

She nodded and followed him out of the house and along a path of smooth stones. Ulysses tagged along as far as the barn door. He growled and barked at the shadows, but before Hank could tell him to quiet, Aggie touched his head and he moved to her side, standing guard as if something were just beyond the light waiting to hurt her.

They spent ten minutes walking around the barn, determining where would be the best place for a bench, and finally decided on a spot near the door. There she'd get the breeze, the morning sun, and anything left on the bench overnight would remain protected from the weather once the door was closed.

"I'd like to start tonight." Hank knew it was late, but he wouldn't sleep anyway. Too much had happened today, and

Aggie would be too close, even three rooms away. "I'll turn in before midnight."

She looked up at him. "All right. I think I'll turn in now. I feel bad taking your bed though."

"Don't worry about it. Somehow it wouldn't be right if you were the one on the floor. I'll talk Blue into helping me string another frame this week, but for now a bedroll will be nothing unusual for me to sleep on."

She hesitated. "Well . . ."

They stood in the circle of light staring at each other. As he guessed she would, she broke the silence first. With her fingers laced together in front of her, she said suddenly, "It's not fair."

Hank fought down a smile. She fired up fast when something bothered her. "What's not fair?"

She fisted her hands on her hips and looked up at him. "If I want to kiss you good night, I have to ask you to bend down first."

A slow smile spread across his face. He grabbed a milking stool from the first stall and set it firmly in the center of the light, then he lifted her atop it.

They were equals. He stared straight into the devil dancing in her blue-green eyes.

He waited as she leaned forward and kissed him lightly on the cheek. When she straightened she said, "Good night, dear." Her hand rested on his shoulder. She made no effort to remove it.

"Good night," he said as his mouth touched hers. This time his lips were soft and slow. He fought the urge to pull her against him. He knew where a kiss could lead, but she was innocent. If he moved too fast, she might be frightened.

Too fast! his mind shouted. When had he crossed some invisible line from accepting her as a partner and nothing more to thinking of what came after the kiss?

Gently pulling away, he smiled when she pouted. "I'll put a stool in every room so all will be fair," he whispered, so near he could feel her quick breaths on his cheek.

He couldn't resist; his lips found hers once more. The kiss remained gentle, but his hands at her waist tugged her slightly so that their bodies touched. He felt her soft breasts press into his chest each time she inhaled, and the feeling was so right.

His fingers relaxed. Aggie could have stepped back if she'd wanted to. But she didn't break the contact. Feather light, she placed her other hand on his shoulder and continued the kiss.

She was learning, exploring, he realized, and he had every intention of being her guide.

Ulysses barked at a shadow somewhere beyond the barn and Aggie lifted her head. For a second their eyes met and Hank didn't miss the fire in her shy gaze a moment before she looked down.

"Aggie," he whispered, ignoring the dog's barking. "Aggie, look at me."

Slowly she raised her head.

"There's no need to ever be embarrassed or shy with me. I'm your husband."

She nodded. "I know, dear. I'm not."

"Then what is it?" Even in the shadowed light he saw the blush in her cheek and felt her fingers moving nervously over his shoulders.

"I . . ." She looked down again, then forced herself to face him. "I just didn't expect it to feel so good."

"The kiss?"

"Yes, that, but also the nearness of you. Even last night on the train I liked you holding me close. And the kissing part, I always thought it was something a man did to a woman. I guess I never considered it as something they did together."

Hank had no idea how to answer. He should have stayed with talking about the weather. He'd never be able to explain what was happening to her. Hell, he couldn't put his own emotions into words most of the time. "Would it help any if I told you I feel the same?"

She smiled. "Not much." He saw it then, that twinkle in her

eye. That warning that one day soon she'd understand him better than he did himself.

"Good night, Aggie." Hank decided he'd be wise to stop this conversation while he could still form reasonable thoughts.

As he settled her on the ground, he knew beyond any doubt that he'd be wasting his time building another bed. They'd share the same one soon. It bothered him that he wasn't sure if it would be his idea, or hers. And worse, he didn't care.

Part of him decided it had to be impossible for such a beautiful woman to know so little, but then with four older sisters she must have always been chaperoned. And, for some reason, she trusted him.

He grinned. The perfect wife, a preacher once said, was a woman who made a husband want to be a better man. Hank stared out into the night and silently promised he'd be that and more for her.

He watched the old dog follow her back to the house. She looked like she belonged here. Turning, he set to work on the bench, his thoughts full of Aggie. She was shy, and probably more than a little spoiled. He'd have to tell her that putting her fists on her hips and demanding something wasn't fair might not always work with him.

Suddenly, he laughed, realizing it had.

He heard the back door close and Ulysses run around the house barking at the darkness. Probably a rabbit, Hank thought. That and snakes were the only invaders the place ever had.

Thunder rattled several miles away. He looked up in time to see the next round of lightning. Across the flat land it was easy in the blink to pick out the black outline of the windmill, the bunk house, and a lone rider on horseback waiting just outside the yard light.

Hank froze. No one but trouble would be riding up behind the house this time of night. He reached for his Colt and realized it was with Aggie.

Blowing out the lantern, Hank stood perfectly still and

listened. Someone was out by the windmill. Someone who wasn't a friend or he would have yelled a hello.

Ulysses had climbed on the porch and was barking wildly now, standing guard, Hank decided, protecting Aggie, just where Hank would have wanted the dog. Whoever moved in the moonless night would not step on the porch without being attacked. Aggie would be all right for now.

The only problem was, the shadow lay between Hank and home.

Chapter 9

Aggie washed and slipped on her nightgown with a blue ribbon at the throat. She'd bought it in Chicago and kept it wrapped in paper in the bottom of her bag. Smoothing the cotton, she told herself this wasn't her real wedding night. But she had to wear it. Dolly had demanded she leave her old one behind. Somehow, even though she'd sleep alone in her bed, it seemed right to start her new life in all new clothes, even a nightgown.

She'd almost finished brushing her hair when she realized Ulysses hadn't stopped barking. At first she'd thought he'd just been running the night like guard dogs do, but now the sound he made was different. Angry, fierce.

Hank was outside with the dog. Surely he'd silence him with a yell soon.

But minutes ticked by and nothing. In fact, if anything the dog's growls sounded near panic.

Her mind began to think of all the possibilities. What if Hank were hurt? What if a wild animal had charged him? She'd heard there were mountain lions and bears in this part of Texas. Her father had often said he'd never go west because it was full of mad animals and crazy people. Her sister told her the Indian Wars had been over for a few years, but what if . . .

She couldn't stand guessing anymore. Grabbing Hank's gun belt, she strapped it around her waist, then pulled on her robe without bothering to tie it. If something was outside, she had no intention of hiding indoors.

Without a lamp, she felt her way though the main room to the front door. The barking sounded like it was coming from the back of the house. If she stayed in the shadow of the porch she might see trouble before it found her.

As she slipped outside, the cold, wet boards felt slippery beneath her, but she couldn't take the time to go back for shoes. Slowly, her fingers sliding along the painted walls, she moved toward the side of the house where she'd be able to see the barn.

Lightning flashed and she froze, knowing that if there was someone, or something out there in the night, they would be able to see her for a few seconds.

But nothing moved.

She continued her progress, one small step at a time. When she turned the corner and saw Ulysses—still barking—facing the barn, she silently pulled the Colt and readied it.

"Easy, Ulysses," she whispered, not wanting to surprise him from behind. "I'm here now."

Ulysses lowered to a growl, but didn't move. Something between the dog and the barn held his full attention. It took her brain a moment to recognize the outline of a man on horseback with something held high in both hands, like a warrior of old wielding a sword.

Aggie waited for the next flash of lightning.

Seconds passed. She and Ulysses stood vigil.

With a sudden flash of lightning, Aggie saw a man again, closer now to the opening of the barn.

As thunder rolled, Hank shouted, "Aggie, get back inside."

He'd seen her, but she hadn't had time to find him in the moment's flash. The blackness that followed swallowed all light. Aggie strained, trying to make out any form, struggling to hear any movement.

The whack of board against bone thundered across the yard. Once! Twice!

Ulysses went wild.

The sound of a horse stomping rumbled near the barn. The animal screamed as a man's voice shouted a curse. A moment later the horse broke into a run. Aggie raised her Colt and fired as a rider blinked past her. Before she could draw aim again, the horse had taken his dark knight out of range.

Suddenly, Ulysses and she were running toward the barn.

"Hank," she cried, not sure if she were screaming his name or praying. "Hank!"

Stepping into the barn reminded her of falling into a cave. Velvet blackness on the moonless night. She clambered for the lantern she'd seen Hank set on a shelf just inside the barn, hoping he had only turned it out and not taken it down.

The lantern was there along with an almost empty box of matches. It took three tries before Aggie brought the match to life and lit the lantern. When she turned, spreading light, she might have missed the heap on the ground beside the stall if Ulysses hadn't been right beside him. At first she thought it might be rags, then she recognized a white shirt.

"Hank!" He lay face down and far too still. Blood dripped from his head and one of his long legs twisted just below the knee at an unnatural angle. A long two-by-four lay beside him, harmless though spotted with blood.

Aggie sat the lantern a few feet from him and ran for the barn door. As soon as she cleared the roof, she lifted her gun and fired three quick shots. Then she ran back to her husband.

By the time Blue Thompson and a woman who had to be his wife arrived, Aggie had wrapped the belt of her robe around Hank's head and was applying pressure where blood dripped with each of his heartbeats.

"What happened?" Blue asked as he jumped from the buggy.

Aggie couldn't stop the tears. "I don't know. I heard some-thing. Someone. Then he rode off and I found Hank."

"Who would want to hurt Hank?" Lizzy demanded as she knelt beside her husband. Her voice was low, but her hands moved skillfully over Hank's injuries.

"I don't know." Aggie fought panic. "I don't know."

Blue slowly straightened Hank's leg, shaking his head as he worked.

"It looks busted," Aggie cried. "Oh, God, what if it's busted?"

Lizzy grabbed Aggie's chin with bloody fingers. "Don't you worry none, we're going to take care of your man." She forced Aggie to look at her and not Hank. "But we're going to need your help. You understand?"

Aggie pulled in the frayed strings of her emotions and forced herself to take a breath. "All right. We can take care of him. We can."

The no-nonsense directness of the older woman had helped and she allowed Aggie no time to think of what might be beyond this moment, this crisis. "First," Lizzy said in her low, southern voice, "we get him to the house."

Aggie looked back at Hank. "We can do that." She raised her chin.

Lizzy smiled. "Right you are."

"His leg probably is broke." Blue voiced what they all knew. "We'll have to be real careful moving him. Once he's inside and the blood's cleaned off, we can see the damage. If he's still breathing, I'll ride for the doc."

It took all three of them to lift Hank without moving his leg more than necessary. He moaned once, telling Aggie he was still alive, but his normally tanned face looked almost as white as his shirt.

Aggie held his head while Blue and Lizzy removed his boots and trousers. There was no doubt the leg was broken; a jagged bone had ripped the flesh from inside out. Blue straightened it as best he could, then tied both legs together with a strip of bandage. He explained that he'd seen doctors do that in the war when there was no time to look for splints.

With only a nod toward his wife, Blue left to get the doctor.

Lizzy brought cold water from the well and handed Aggie bandage after bandage for his head. Each time they switched, blood covered the cotton. They talked, trying to convince themselves that his being unconscious was better than if he were awake and in pain, but Aggie could tell Lizzy didn't believe their reasoning any more than she did.

In what seemed like minutes, Blue was back with the doctor, a man who barely looked old enough to shave, much less finish medical school.

To Aggie's surprise, the doctor asked her if she wanted to stay while he examined her husband. Part of her wanted to run as far away from the smell of blood as she could get, but another part knew she belonged here. She was bound to this man she'd known less than two days. Bound by honor as well as the law.

As the doctor worked, stitching up the long gash in Hank's hairline, Aggie gently held his head in her lap. The wonder that she could care for a man so quickly danced in her mind with the grief that would come if she lost him.

In the few hours they'd been together she'd taken him into her heart, and there he would remain whether she loved or mourned him for a lifetime. Closing her eyes, she tried to remember the moment she'd known he could be someone to depend on and trust. Though she liked his laughter and the way he gently teased her, it had been something far more basic that drew her even during their conversation outside the dugout. Hank listened. He really listened to her. Could something so simple form a bond that would weather them through hard times?

She looked down at his lean body. Strong and tan from hard work. It occurred to her that she'd never seen so much of a male body before and she should be embarrassed, but she wasn't—somehow this man belonged to her—was a part of her.

"Keep his head as still as you can, Mrs. Harris," the doctor ordered. "I don't want him thrashing about when I set this leg."

Aggie placed her hands on Hank's cheeks and noticed her tears were falling across his face, but it didn't matter; nothing mattered but Hank. She could not, would not, lose him.

When the doc and Blue set the leg, pulling the bone back in place, Hank groaned in pain. Aggie pressed her face close to his and whispered over and over, "You're going to be all right, dear. You're going to be fine."

Aggie watched, feeling the pain with him as they sewed up the cuts and strapped his leg to a board that ran from his knee to his foot. She washed his face and chest, keeping him cool as the doctor checked his head wound again and again.

Finally, a little after dawn, the doc packed up his things, saying all that was left to do was to wait and see. Hank seemed to be resting comfortably, which was the best medicine.

An hour later, Aggie heard Blue talking to the sheriff. The lawman insisted on speaking to her, but she wouldn't leave Hank's side to go into the main room. Her new nightgown was spotted with blood and she didn't remember when she'd removed her robe or where. Hank's Colts hung on the headboard, within easy reach if she needed them.

Finally, Blue opened the door and asked if it would be all right if the sheriff came in for a minute.

Aggie pulled a thin blanket over her shoulders and nodded. The sheriff walked in, took one look at her, and didn't waste time with small talk.

"Did you see the man who did this?"

"One man." Aggie tried to focus on something besides Hank's breathing. "I only saw his shadow. He wasn't tall but he seemed thick, barrel-chested, or it may have been his coat that made him look so. His horse was dark, black or brown and bigger than most. I don't remember any markings. I heard him swear as he rode from the barn, but he was only in my sites for a moment."

The sheriff looked up from his notes. "You fired at him?"

"I hit him," she said.

"How do you know? He didn't stop. How can you be sure, Mrs. Harris? Maybe you only thought you hit him?"

Suddenly too tired to keep her eyes open, she curled beside Hank. "I hit him," she mumbled, "because I always hit what I aim at."

"And where did you aim?"

"Left shoulder," she answered as she rested her head on Hank's arm. "Look for a man wounded in the left shoulder and you'll find the man who attacked my husband."

She fell asleep without seeing the look the sheriff and Blue gave each other.

Chapter 10

Hank came to one painful inch at a time. His leg felt like he'd left it in a campfire. His head throbbed.

He turned slowly. Something soft bushed his chin.

Opening one eye he recognized Aggie's hair. She was curled up in a ball, sleeping beside him. The thin blanket barely covered her.

"She's been asleep like that for a few hours." Blue's voice sounded from the doorway. "Stayed up with you all night. Refused to leave your side even when the sheriff wanted to see her this morning."

Hank forced through the pain and moved his head enough so that he could watch his friend cross the room. "She okay?"

Blue chuckled. "Sure. Says she shot the guy who clubbed you." The older man added, "Said it as calm as if she weren't doing nothin' more than shooting rats in the barn. Just from what I've seen today I'd say she might be a tiny thing, but there ain't nothin' frail about her."

Hank closed his eyes, trying to remember what had happened in the blackness of the night. Someone had been outside of the barn. He remembered stepping to the door. Then he'd seen Aggie on the porch, her white gown billowing around her, waving danger her direction. His last thought had been that he had to get to her.

Slowly, he lifted his hand and felt the bandage across half his forehead. He must have been hit, but he couldn't remember the blow. The only thing in his mind had been panic that Aggie was in danger.

"What's the damage?" he asked as if he were talking about a machine and not his body.

Blue shrugged. "Not as bad as it could have been. Four stitches in your head. Left leg broke about three inches below your knee. Doc said it should heal clean."

Hank mumbled as Blue offered him water. "Any idea who or why?"

Blue shook his head. "Didn't know you had an enemy in this world, boss, but one thing is for sure, whoever attacked you meant to hurt you. The second blow broke your leg, not the first. A man planning to rob you wouldn't have done that. No need. You were already out cold."

Hank tried to reason as he cobbled together all that had happened. Maybe the traveler was afraid he'd shoot him for being on his land. Or maybe he was an outlaw running from the law and wanted to make sure no one followed. Why else would the stranger break his leg?

"Get some rest." Blue pulled a heavy quilt over Hank. "It looks like it's going to rain the rest of the day. Lizzy and I are going home to get some sleep. We'll be back long before nightfall to check on you and bring some soup. My guess is that little wife of yours won't leave your side to cook any more than she would for other reasons."

Hank touched the gun belt on his bedpost. "We'll be fine." He forced his voice to sound stronger than he felt. "Let the mutt in before you leave. He'll warn us if anyone tries to get into the house."

Blue nodded. "I'll find you a stick to use for a cane. The doc says you can climb out of that bed as soon as you feel up to it, but don't put any weight on that leg for at least a week."

Hank nodded, hating the idea that he'd lose days of work. The cane might get him around the house, but he wouldn't be able to go outside until the mud dried out, and even then he couldn't ride. Being laid up was going to cost him dearly.

"I'll keep an eye on things until you're getting around better." Blue's face seemed to have added a few new wrinkles in the past hours. "Lizzy or I will check on you two a few times a day just to see if we can help, and I'll go in for any supplies you need." He glanced at Aggie. "Hell of a first day for the little missus."

"Much obliged." Hank hated needing help, but he knew he'd offer the same to Blue if need be.

Blue disappeared out the door.

Hank stayed awake long enough to hear them leave. They let the dog in and Ulysses hurried to the side of the bed where Aggie slept. The old dog laid his head on the edge of her blanket and waited for her to pat him.

"Lay down, Ulysses," Hank whispered as he drifted off. "She'll pet you when she wakes."

An hour later, Hank moved slightly and pain brought him back from a dream. He rolled his head and faced sleepy blue-green eyes watching him from a few inches away.

He didn't move. Their heads rested on the same pillow.

"Do you need anything?" she whispered.

"Sleep," he answered. "How about you?"

"I'm cold," she admitted as she crawled off the bed.

Her crimson-spotted nightgown was stiff in spots with Hank's dried blood, and so wrinkled it looked more like a rag.

He lifted the side of the heavy quilts covering him. "Climb in," he offered. "We can go back to sleep. With this rain it seems like twilight outside."

She shook her head as she tried to straighten her gown. "I can't sleep in my clothes and I have no other gown. Maybe if I get dressed and wash this it will dry in a few hours."

Pointing toward the door, he ordered, "Grab one of my

flannel work shirts from the mudroom. It'll be warmer and probably as long on you as that gown."

She hesitated, but the night without sleep must have won out. She disappeared.

Hank relaxed as he listened to her bare feet run across the main room floor. He should have told her to grab socks as well.

A few minutes later, she stepped back into the room, buttoning the last button of his favorite shirt.

The flannel clung to her body and stopped at her knees. Though the shirt covered almost all of her, the sight of it on her warmed Hank more than the cotton warmed her.

Without a word, he lifted the corner of the quilt and she slipped in beside him, careful not to touch him.

When she shivered, he raised his arm and pulled her close. Her feet brushed his uninjured leg with the shock of an icicle sliding across his skin, but he forced himself not to flinch.

Her hand pushed against his bare chest. "I'm too close. I'll hurt your leg."

Hank couldn't help but laugh. "Believe me, Aggie, your nearness isn't affecting my injury at all."

When she wiggled, cuddling, Hank fought down a groan. His left leg was about the only part of his body not reacting to her.

"Go to sleep," he said more harshly than he meant to.

"Yes, dear," she answered as she settled beside him.

Hank lay awake and listened to her breathing slow. If he'd known all it took was a few blows from a two-by-four to get the most beautiful woman he'd ever seen in his bed, he might have taken the hits earlier. She felt so good next to him. As her body relaxed in sleep, her softness melted against him, alive and comforting like he'd never known.

Moving his face against her hair, he took a long breath, pulling the scent of her deep into his lungs. Blue had said she'd refused to leave him last night when he'd been out. Hank curled a strand of her hair around his finger, wondering

how he could matter so much to her. One look at her and
anyone could love her, but how could it be possible that she
cared even a little about him? He was nothing special to look
at and he sure couldn't offer her much. Even his own mother
hadn't stayed around.

But Aggie had. She'd stayed by his side.

He knew he had been little more than her way out of a bad
situation. For a shy woman traveling around, being put on the
marriage block for first one group and then another to offer
for, must have been torture. Why had he been the one she
went with? The one she wasn't afraid of?

He watched the storm play itself out, then finally drifted to
sleep with his hand resting at her waist.

Around sunset, he awoke to find her gone. He took her absence like a blow even before reality fully registered on his
aching brain. Glancing at the side of the bed, he noticed the
mutt had also vanished. Wherever Aggie was, Hank would
bet his saddle the dog would be with her.

He didn't have long to wait. Five minutes later, she backed
her way into the room carrying a tray of food. Seeing her
fully dressed made him frown. He'd give up food altogether
if she'd crawl back in bed with him.

"I brought you some of Lizzy's soup and bread. They
headed home, wanting to be settled in before it got dark." She
didn't meet his gaze. Her shyness had returned. "Do you want
me to feed you?"

Hank pulled himself up until his back rested against the
headboard. "I can feed myself, Aggie," he grumbled. "My leg
is broke, not my arms."

She nodded without looking up as she carefully sat the tray
beside him. "The doc said I'm to check the bandage on your
head at sunset. If there is no new blood, I can leave the dress-
ing off."

Hank lifted the bowl of soup and drank it down without
taking his eyes off her. He couldn't believe, after how they'd
slept together all day, she could go back to being so shy again.

She busied herself getting everything ready while he ate, but not once did she look at him.

Finally, he could stand it no longer. "What is it, Aggie? What's wrong?"

"Nothing," she said as she removed the tray and began tugging the bandage on his head away. "How do you feel?"

"Fine." He returned a lie for a lie.

"The stitches are holding. I don't think you need a bandage again." She brushed his hair away from his forehead and moved to the wound on his arm. "The cut looks good. You heal fast."

Hank didn't want to talk about his injuries. He wanted to know what had changed between when she'd cuddled next to him this morning and now. Until this moment he'd thought he missed little by not having a mother around. Now he realized how much he had to learn about reading women. No. Not women, he corrected. Aggie.

When she tucked the blanket around him, his fingers gently closed over her hand. "What's wrong?" he asked again, his tone more demanding.

When she tried to tug her hand away, he held fast. He'd never learn if he didn't start right now.

Finally, she looked up at him, her eyes filling with unshed tears. "We've only been married two days and you've been injured two times. At this rate you'll never last a week." Her chin rose slightly as if she were forcing herself to face facts. "My sisters were right. I'm nothing but trouble. Dolly said once that having me around is no different than having the plague circling. All my sisters were glad to help my poppa get rid of me."

Hank laughed then realized she didn't see the humor. "Aggie, it wasn't you who had a knife at the train station, or who wielded the board in the darkness of the barn." He tugged until she sat beside him. "But it was you who took care of me. And the reason your sisters wanted to marry you off had nothing to do with you being bad luck, trust me on that."

She nodded once, obviously not believing him. She pulled her hand away.

He fought the urge to reach for it and hold on tightly, but she had to come to him on her own time if there was ever to be anything more between them.

The rain tapped on the windows again, drawing their attention. Aggie turned up the lamp by the bed, then watched gray streaks run down the long windows. "Tell me about the beauty of this land again, dear. I'm having trouble remembering."

Hank laughed, realizing this time of year it would be hard to see any beauty, but she seemed to need calming. Worry wrinkled her forehead, so if she needed to talk of something besides what had happened, he'd give it a try.

He told her of the first day he'd ridden over his land. How spring turns the world green and the colors in the rock walls of the canyons seem to wave and billow like the skirts of Spanish dancers. He described a summer shower that came up all of a sudden like a phantom riding the wind, dumping a bucket of water that sparkled like diamonds over the wet grass. He told how a dust devil seemed to chase him over the open range, following behind no matter which way he turned his horse.

He caught her glancing out the window from time to time as if she didn't quite believe his tale. The tapping grew louder as the rain turned to hail. The tiny balls of ice hit the ground and bounced almost like popcorn jumping in a skillet. Within seconds the ground was white as snow.

Hugging herself, Aggie asked, "Should I light the fire in the main room?"

"No." Hank chose his words carefully, knowing there might be a long way between what he wanted and what was about to happen. "We'll be warm enough under the covers." He kept every word level, without emotion, as if he'd said the same words many times before.

She nodded, and to his surprise picked up the flannel shirt. "I'll wash up in the kitchen and change."

As soon as she left, Hank grabbed the stick that Blue had left to serve as a cane. Slowly, he moved off the bed. Without putting any of his weight on the broken leg, he crossed the few feet to the washstand and chamber pot.

Aggie might be his wife, but there were some things Hank had no intention of asking her to help with. By the time he was washed up and back to the bed, sweat covered his forehead. He sat down with his back resting against all the pillows and pulled the covers up to his chest. He wished he'd had the sense to buy a nightshirt sometime in his life. Having lived all these years alone, he'd seen no need. But Aggie might find his bare chest shocking.

Hank smiled suddenly. She hadn't commented on it earlier. Maybe she didn't notice. One leg of his long handled underwear had been cut off at the knee just above where the splint started. The other leg was spotted with dried blood, but he'd wait until morning to put on a clean pair. He wasn't sure he had the energy tonight.

Aggie appeared wearing his shirt. "I washed my gown earlier," she began, "but it didn't get dry."

"You look fine," he said, and then wished he'd thought to say something more. In truth, she looked adorable.

She sat on the end of the bed and folded her legs beneath her. "I was hoping, if you're not too tired, that we could talk a while."

Hank didn't move. Bedtime conversations were totally new to him and he had no idea what to talk about. She, on the other hand, looked like this was part of her nightly routine, and with four sisters it may very well have been.

She placed her elbows on her flannel-covered knees and rested her chin in her hands.

He swore she looked twelve years old.

"Blue and I have been talking and we don't think the attack

on you was an accident. No one would be just riding by this place. It's too far off the road."

"So, what are you saying?" Hank watched her as he tried to follow the conversation. She had shifted and now the soft roundness of her left breast molded against the shirt. Suddenly, nothing about her seemed childlike. There was no doubt she was all woman.

"I'm saying . . ." She moved again and Hank closed his eyes so his ears would work. "I'm saying," she repeated, "that someone wants you hurt . . . or dead."

Hank shook his head then regretted the action. "I don't think so. I don't make a habit of crossing folks if I can help it, and it's been years since I even had a heated discussion with anyone."

"Try and think," she coached. "Who lately would benefit from your being hurt or dead? Who has threatened you?"

"Nobody but Potter Stockton on the way back to town the other night. He told me I'd be wise to get on the train and forget about you, because I must know you'd never come." Hank told the account in passing, nothing important, he thought . . . until he saw Aggie's face. "You can't believe Stockton would send someone to hurt me? Sure, he was probably disappointed when he learned you left with me, maybe even mad. But mad enough to try and kill me?"

Aggie nodded. "On the way to the station, Charlie told me he was glad I didn't pick Potter even though Dolly thought he was the best choice. Charlie said he heard Potter beat a man near to death one night after losing a few dollars in a poker game. He said the railroad man had gunfighter eyes—cold and hard as casket wood."

Hank raised a doubtful eyebrow. "But Charlie still invited him to dinner?"

Aggie shook her head. "He only invited the banker and told him that if he knew a man looking for a wife, to bring a friend along."

That explained Charlie's coldness to Potter Stockton, but

Hank still found it hard to believe any man would try to kill another over a woman he'd just met.

Then he looked at Aggie with her beautiful hair and shining eyes and he knew it must be true.

"When did the man insist on having a drink with you?" she asked.

Hank tried to remember exactly the order. "He was standing behind me when I bought our two tickets."

Aggie frowned. "So he knew you were expecting me?"

"He also knew I didn't have time to wander over to the saloon."

She leaned closer. "Do you think, when the offer for drinks didn't work, that he pulled the knife thinking one way or the other he'd make sure you missed the train?"

Hank didn't want to admit it, but she made sense. The fellow hadn't acted all that drunk at first, then as soon as he'd slipped the knife over Hank's arm, he'd run away. "Maybe," Hank admitted. "He knew if I wasn't at the station you wouldn't be going anywhere that night."

Aggie finished the thought. "And if you weren't there, I would have turned around and gone back to Dolly and Charlie's place."

Their eyes met. Hank felt like he could read her thoughts. There was no need to continue piecing the puzzle; they'd both seen the picture it made.

Lacing her fingers together, she leaned an inch closer and whispered as if saying her words too loud might make them come true. "Do you think the hired gun might come back?"

Hank wished he could say no, but he didn't want to lie to her. "He might," was the best he could do.

Aggie swallowed and nodded. "Then, would you mind if I slept in next to you? I'd planned on making a pallet in the kitchen, but I'd feel safer here."

Hank wouldn't have trusted any words. He simple lifted the covers beside him.

She smiled and joined him.

When he stretched and turned out the light, she whispered, "Thank you, dear." As if he'd done her a favor.

Hank wouldn't have been surprised if lightning came through the second floor and struck him any moment. He wasn't worried about anyone trying to kill him; his shy little wife was going to give him a heart attack by doing something as simple as trusting him.

This time she didn't wait for him to pull her next to him. She snuggled against him and laid her hand on his bare chest.

Then, before he could think to breathe, she laughed.

He covered her hand with his. "What's so funny?"

"Your chest hair tickles."

"Aggie?" His fingers stilled her hand.

"Yes, dear?" she answered.

"Kiss me good night," he whispered as she looked up.

This time, when his mouth covered hers, he couldn't hold back. He had to kiss her the way a man kisses a woman . . . the way a man kisses his wife.

His arm pulled her against him. The thin layer of flannel did little to mask the feel of her. He kissed her long and hard, drinking her in, needing to end the drought in his life, needing to need another.

When he finally let her go, Hank rolled an inch away and tried to think of something, anything to say, but no words would come.

He could feel her tugging at the covers, pulling a blanket over her shoulders, snuggling into her own pillow. "Good night, dear," she said in almost a whisper.

"Good night?" he answered. "Don't you have anything else to say after what just happened?"

She rose to one elbow. "What just happened?"

Hank closed his eyes and swore beneath his breath. She was going to make him say it, then there would be no doubt what he was apologizing for. "About the way I kissed you. I didn't plan it, but I'll not say I'm sorry."

"All right," she said as if she'd given it no thought.

He had the feeling she was staring at him in the darkness. Probably thinking of ways to kill him herself since he was stepping way over the line of being partners.

"You're not mad about the kiss?"

She laughed again. "No, dear," she answered. "I rather liked it. I'm surprised that something I've given little thought to in my life could be so pleasant."

He was back to step one of trying to understand Aggie. "Then you wouldn't mind if we did it again?"

This time she rolled toward him. "I wouldn't mind at all. I rather like the feel of you." Her lips lowered above his before he had time to move. With her mouth brushing his, she whispered, "I find I like kissing you very much."

This time he didn't try to hold her to him. He let her lead. Her kiss was softer, sweeter than his had been. But the weight of her breast resting on his chest drove him mad. "I love this shirt," he whispered against her mouth. "I love the way . . ." She didn't let him finish. She was busy learning.

When she finally raised her head, she stared down at him. Even in the darkness he could see the devil dancing in her eyes. She shifted, using his chest to lean on and propped her head on one elbow. "What comes next, dear?"

"You really want to know?"

She nodded. "I didn't think I ever would. I thought things between a man and a woman were for the man's pleasure, never the woman's. Since you kissed me I've been reconsidering."

"I'll show you," he said, wondering how she could possibly want him to be her teacher. "But how fast we go down this road, and when we stop, will be up to you."

"Fair enough." She nodded as if they'd made an agreement. She waited.

He hesitated. "Aggie," he finally said. "What do you know about how it is between a man and a woman?"

She shrugged. "Mostly what my sister told me. About how it's something to be endured. I wanted no part of that.

But your kisses don't seem that way." She looked down, embarrassed by her own boldness.

Hank placed his hand on her waist. "And my touch? Would you welcome my touch?"

She nodded slowly.

"Aggie," he whispered, "look at me."

She raised her head and he saw her eyes in the moonlight. Nervous. Shy, but not afraid.

His hand moved slowly up her ribcage, a light touch against soft material and softer flesh beneath.

Her eyes widened, but she didn't move.

His first finger touched the bottom of her breast and gently pressed against its weight. Then, as slowly as cold molasses, his fingers moved over the fabric covering her breast. The full mound ripened beneath his caress, and he explored.

Hank's breaths came faster as if there were not enough air in the room to fill his lungs. He cupped her in his big hand and thought he might die from the pleasure the feel of her brought. His fingers moved gently across her and she closed her eyes for a moment and smiled.

He'd never wanted a woman the way he wanted Aggie. For the first time he understood why men of old fought dragons for their women. The need for her was a physical ache so deep within him he thought his blood must surely be heating to boiling level. He stared at the cotton covering her breast as his hand twisted the material into his fist.

She pulled a few inches away. "You'll rip the cloth."

"Then take it off." He spoke his thoughts in a voice so low he didn't recognize it as his.

She rose, stood there, and stared at him. If she decided to walk away, he couldn't even follow. With his leg, he would never be able to catch her if she ran. And he had a feeling that if he frightened her and she ran, she'd run all the way to Dallas or Austin or Chicago before she stopped.

Hank closed his eyes and groaned. What did he think he was doing? A man with a broken leg doesn't seduce his wife.

He'd almost passed out moving to the washstand and back. If he even tried to make love he'd probably succeed only in making a fool of himself.

When he finally opened his eyes, Aggie was still sitting next to him. She'd unbuttoned two of the buttons of the shirt.

"If I get to pick when we stop," she whispered, "I pick one touch tonight. I know there is more, but I have to think about it first."

Hank took a deep breath, almost saying thank you. He wanted their first time, if there was to be a first time in this partnership, to be perfect.

"One touch," he agreed. "Only, if you've no objection, I'd like to do so while we kiss good night once more."

She nodded and moved off the bed so he could lift the covers. When she scooted beneath the quilts, another button had come loose.

Chapter 11

Aggie lay on her back and waited while Hank shifted onto his side without moving his broken leg any more than necessary.

Her heart pounded faster then a sparrow's as she unbuttoned the entire shirt and spread the soft material away from her chest. She didn't move when Hank lifted the covers away to her waist.

"Are you cold?" he asked, staring at her body in the shadows.

She shook her head, too afraid to speak. In truth, her skin felt hot and she was sure he would notice when he touched her. She told herself she'd agreed to one touch, even wanted it, but she hadn't thought ahead to realize that he'd also look at her. Not just look—study.

Before she lost all courage, she turned her face toward him and his lips gently met hers. She'd thought he'd touch her breasts first, but he took his time tasting her lips. She liked the way the hard line of his mouth turned soft when it touched her. His rough cheek brushed against hers as he moved slightly. His tongue slipped across her tender lips and pushed inside. Her cry of surprise blended with his sigh of pleasure.

When she didn't pull away, his kiss softened once more, offering her paradise, but still, his hand remained at her waist.

With his coaching, she opened her mouth wider, enjoying the newness of her husband's kiss. She thought that marriage was so much more than she'd imagined it would be. Nice, she decided; marriage was nice—then his hand spread across her abdomen. And nice moved to pure bliss. The warmth of his mouth, the slight weight of his fingers on her skin, made her whole body warm with an awareness she'd never experienced.

Her fingers reached up and brushed the hair just above his ear, liking the way the thick coarseness of his straight hair felt to her touch. He was her man, she thought, hers. She liked his strong body and his gentle ways. She liked his voice and the way he worried about her. She liked everything about him.

Just when Aggie was reaching a flat plateau of shear enjoyment, he broke the kiss.

Gripping his hair in her fist, she tried to tug his mouth back to her, but he'd already found somewhere else he wanted to taste. As his open mouth moved down her throat, she let out a sigh of delight. Roughly, he pushed her chin aside so that the length of her throat lay open to his exploring.

His hand pressed gently into her middle, anchoring her to earth while she floated toward the heaven of his kisses against her skin. When he brushed his lips across her ear, he whispered her name then added softly, "Aggie, my love."

She thought he'd return to finish the kiss, but slowly she realized his mouth planned to play along her skin until he had his fill of the taste of it. He opened wide and touched his tongue to the spot where her pulse pounded, then dipped low until the whiskers of his chin brushed across the top of her breasts.

She lay beyond words, beyond thought as his mouth took hers once more, giving and demanding fire all at once. As if her body had a will of its own, she arched, pushing against his hand, fighting to get closer to him.

He held her fast to the bed, but his mouth told her of his pleasure at her attempt. He was tasting deep of her now, taking all he wanted from the kiss, and giving more than she'd ever known to ask. His fingers gently stroked her stomach, and she felt the light embrace all the way through her body.

She grew dizzy with wanting, all shyness, all hesitance shoved from her mind by the taste of him.

When she thought she could stand no more of paradise, he gentled the kiss, bringing it back to soft and loving, almost pure, almost chaste. Only slim memory of its former fire, but the memory forever seared across her mind. Now, even his light touch stirred her blood.

With his lips whispering against hers, he began to move his hand across her flesh and this time there were no boundaries just below her throat or at her waist.

At first he circled her breasts, pushing lightly at the under-side of each with his thumb—letting her know and long for what was to come.

The circles made her skin tingle with tiny points of joy, and her breasts ache with need. When he stretched his fingers over her fullness she was ready, arching toward him. This time, he let her move, filling his hand, pressing hard into his palm.

She felt his laughter against her lips as his hand took its time molding her softest flesh to his will. He knew he was pleasing her just as she knew her soft moans pleased him.

Without warning, he deepened the kiss once more. When she responded in kind, he tightened his grip over her, branding her forever with his "one touch."

Chapter 12

They didn't say a word when he finally pulled away with one last tender kiss on her cheek. She buttoned her shirt. He straightened flat on his back once more. Both knew the other was awake. Both were too lost in their own thoughts to talk.

She stared out the window. A sliver of a moon was slightly visible between two clouds. She could still taste his mouth on hers. She could still feel his hand over her breast. He'd kept his word. He'd kissed her good night and he'd touched her once. A kiss that had taken her to heaven. A touch that she felt all the way to her very soul.

How could the gentle, quiet man do such a thing? Why had he?

A smile slowly spread across her bruised lips. Because, she answered herself, I asked him to. She felt a power build inside her, a power she'd never known. She'd always been the little sister, the daughter who obeyed, who would have been the old maid taking care of her poppa in his aging years if he hadn't found the widow to marry. No one had ever let her set the rules for anything in her life, and now this strong, powerful man did just that.

She couldn't stop grinning. She might have set the rules, but he'd made full use of his one touch.

"Aggie," he said low near her ear. "Are you asleep?"

"No, dear," she answered, seeing no reason to pretend.

"Why me?"

"What?" She knew what he was asking, but she wanted to make sure.

"Why'd you marry me? There must have been men at every house you visited. Men with more money. Men better looking."

"There were." She wished she could tell him how many had made fools of themselves, promising her the moon and stars as if they could deliver. Promising her that life would be one endless party when all she wanted was a quiet place to be happy.

"Then what made you meet me at the train?"

"Because," she whispered as she relaxed into sleep. "You saw me. The inside, not just the out. And you liked me—just me—even before we"—she yawned and mumbled the last few words—"stepped into the light."

Hank heard her breathing slow and knew she was asleep. "You're wrong," he whispered. "I loved you—even before we stepped into the light."

Chapter 13

Dawn slowly spread across the sky. Aggie shoved her hair out of her eyes and lifted her head.

Hank lay beside her, looking like he hadn't moved all night. His jaw had darkened with whiskers and his hair covered his forehead.

She smiled, thinking that he was handsome in his own way. Her poppa used to say that most folks "ugly up" after you get to know them. But Hank hadn't. In fact, the opposite had happened. The rest of the world might think him strong, and big and rough, but he'd been gentle with her from the first, and funny. Even when he tried to be stern, she could see through the act.

Laughing, she realized he was more afraid of her then she'd ever be of him. She'd known it even in the darkness when he'd jumped at the sound of her voice.

Without warming, he opened one eye. "Where's breakfast?" he mumbled.

She shrugged and pulled the covers over her. "I think I'll be one of those wives with the nature to sleep 'til noon."

He pulled the blanket off her head. "I don't think so. I'm starving. You agreed to cook breakfast." He frowned, but she could see the cracks in his armor.

She climbed out and stretched, then laughed at the way he stared at her. She was learning to read this man, and if she was right, he'd just forgotten all about breakfast.

"On second thought . . ." He opened her side of the covers. "We could sleep a while longer."

"Oh, no." She laughed. "I'll put on coffee and bring you hot water. Then I'll cook breakfast while you shave."

He groaned.

She grabbed her clothes and disappeared before he had time to argue. Ten minutes later, when she brought him a cup of coffee, he'd managed to sit up but he looked like he'd been thrown by a horse a few times.

"Do you need any help?" she asked.

"I'm fine." He frowned. "Could I get you to bring the washstand over here?"

"Sure." She leaned close and kissed his cheek. "Good morning, dear. Always wake up on the wrong side of the bed?"

"Yep," he answered. "It's my nature."

She moved the nightstand so that he could reach the pitcher and bowl without standing. "Where is your shaving cup and razor?"

"In the mudroom," he answered.

When she returned, loaded down with everything that had been by the back sink, Aggie studied him. Hank was pale and the pain still reflected in his eyes, but he looked better than he had yesterday.

"How do you like your eggs?"

"Any way you make them," he answered as he brushed hot water into the soap cup and began to circle. "Just make it an even dozen."

She nodded and turned toward the door.

"Aggie?" He stopped her with one word.

"Yes."

"Last night was really something."

She grinned, not allowing his fancy words to sway her. "I agree," she whispered, and vanished before he saw her blush.

Thoughts of how he'd touched her filled her mind as she made breakfast. Thanks to Lizzy and Blue, the milk and eggs were in the cold box along with butter. Bread and apples sat on the table. Aggie mixed up a fine breakfast.

Hank had dressed by the time she checked on him.

"Can you make it to the table or shall I bring it in here?"

"I can make it." He stood, then swayed like a tall pine about to tumble.

She moved to his side and helped all she could as they slowly crossed to the kitchen. The stove she'd lit already warmed the room. He sat at the table while she poured him another cup of coffee and served her first cooked meal to him.

He ate as if he'd been starved for days, downing the bread almost as fast as she could spread butter and jelly on it.

They were just finishing when Blue stepped through the back door with a box on his shoulder.

Aggie stood. "Wonderful." She nodded at Blue. "You brought supplies. Hank's already eaten through a week's worth this morning."

"Nope," Blue said setting the box down on the far end of the table. "The supplies are still in the wagon. Jeb sent this box over for you."

Aggie wiped her hands on the towel she'd been using for an apron and looked inside. Guns, more than twenty of them, all different brands and sizes, each with a tag tied to the handle.

She lifted the first one. "Firing pin broke." The second said, "Trigger jammed." The third read, "Needs a good cleaning."

"Jeb said he has never seen anything like it," Blue mumbled as he poured himself a cup of coffee. "Folks started coming in as soon as the rain slowed yesterday. He told me to tell you that he knew you probably had your hands full with taking care of Hank, but he thought he better have me bring out the first box."

Hank said, "I don't need to be taken care of," at the same time Aggie mumbled, "First box?"

Suddenly, she was too excited to finish her breakfast. She wanted to get to work. While Blue brought in supplies, she carried the box of weapons up to her little attic room. Sitting in the center of the floor, she examined each project. Always before, in her father's shop, she'd been the helper. Now, she was the master.

She had almost finished looking over her work when Blue bumped his way upstairs. "Hank told me to rig you up a table." He carried two six-foot boards. "It won't be perfect but it will work until he can climb the stairs and make you a proper desk. He won't brag on himself, but that man of yours is quite a carpenter."

That man of mine has many hidden talents, she almost said aloud, but all she could manage to say to Blue was, "I know."

The older man made three more trips before he put the boards over empty barrels. Between his loads she managed to slip down and carry up her two boxes of tools. On the second trip, she noticed Hank sitting in the big old rocker on the porch.

She walked to the door. "Will you be all right if I work a while?"

He looked lost but said, "I'll be fine. I'm just not used to staying in the house. I'm usually out by sunup." The mild day didn't reflect in his mood. "When Blue finishes with your makeshift benches, he said he'd carry the leather work up from the barn. I can do it as easy here as there. Maybe tomorrow the ground will be dry enough for me to hobble out there."

Standing just behind his chair, she moved her fingers through his hair. "Hank," she whispered and waited until he looked up. "You make me very happy."

He looked puzzled. "Do I?"

Heat spread into her cheeks. She'd been thinking about her attic room, but realized he thought she meant their good night kiss. "Yes," she answered, meaning both. The room was a grand place to work, but last night's "one touch" had been a slice of magic, pure and unreal.

His eyes darkened as if knowing she was thinking the same thing he was, but he didn't move to touch her. Both knew it wouldn't be proper in the daylight. Both knew they'd wait.

When she returned to her work space, she decided the stool Blue had brought wasn't high enough for the makeshift bench, so she tugged the old trunk over. Surprised at how heavy it was, Aggie looked inside the one thing Hank said was sent back home after his mother died.

Layered between tissue paper and smelling of cedar were several finely made quilts.

Odd, Aggie thought. The paper looked as neatly pressed as it must have been the day Hank's mother packed away the quilts, and Aggie couldn't help but wonder why Hank, or his father, had never bothered to look inside. Maybe the chest was simply something Hank didn't want, but couldn't leave behind for strangers to discover.

She spread the quilts out, realizing each was a work of art, made with great care. They transformed the tiny attic room into a field of flowers and plants, each reflecting a different season.

Finally, she folded them away—all but one. The last, a beautiful spread of blue-bonnets, she couldn't make herself fold. If she put it away the room would go back to being colorless. On impulse, she reached for two small tacks among her tools and hung the quilt on the wall. When she stepped back, she couldn't help but smile. One wall with windows framing a view of winter across Hank's land. The other wall now showed a spring field with all the warmth of a quilt made with love. She'd found the perfect place to work.

Time flew as she practiced the skills her father had taught her. In a strange way she felt at home with her hands moving over the weapons that belonged to strangers.

She checked on Hank several times during the day, but his mood never lightened. He was a man used to action who didn't take to doing chores from a rocking chair. When she came down for the last time, she found him already in bed, asleep.

am happy, dear. I hate that he broke your leg and somehow I'm probably to blame, but you must know that I'm happy— here on the ranch—with you."

He looked up at her then as if he wanted to believe her, but something deep inside stopped him. She thought he was about to argue, but he only said, "I want you to promise to wear my Colts today. Don't take them off."

She nodded.

"I can't just sit here and wait for trouble to come, but I can work in the barn. I'll have Blue move my workbench so that I can keep an eye on the house and my rifle will always be within reach."

"I'll bring my tools out. It's warm enough for me to work in the barn."

He pulled her into his lap and held her gently. She thought of a hundred things that needed doing, but it felt so good to have him holding her. She'd almost woken him last night to ask if he would. She knew he liked her here but didn't completely believe her when she'd told him she was happy. Maybe it was the way they married with no promises of love. Or maybe it was more deeply rooted in his past, when mother left him and never returned.

Aggie kissed his throat and Hank stilled as if returning to reality.

"We'd better get to work," he said.

She nodded and stood, wishing he'd kissed her back just once.

An hour later Blue returned with another load of broken revolvers and a few rifles from Jeb, and a box of new tools shipped in from Wichita Falls. Aggie was so excited she went right to work, hardly noticing Blue moving Hank's bench to the other side of the barn doors.

They worked all morning, their backs to one another. Hank sat on a stool with his leg propped on the crossbar of his workbench. She preferred to stand when she worked with rifles. He asked her to pick up a hammer he dropped, and once she asked if he'd help her pry a jammed cartridge shell out. Neither talked of anything else.

At noon Aggie went to the house and brought back leftover meat and cheese for lunch. She insisted he rest his leg while he ate. She talked about a few of the problems with the rifles, but he said little. His eyes were always looking beyond the barn.

When Blue returned that evening, Hank asked if the hired hand would lend him a shoulder to brace against so he could make it to the house.

Aggie almost cried. He'd worked too hard. He should have turned in hours ago and gotten all the weight off his leg. She grabbed her tools and ran for the house. "I'll work upstairs for a while," she said as she passed the two men. "You rest, dear."

"I'll want no supper," Hank answered. "I think I'll call it a night."

She wanted to argue that he needed to eat, but she didn't want to nag in front of Blue. Instead, she went to her little space above the kitchen and worked, telling herself tomorrow would be better.

She worked until the box of guns was repaired. When she finally crawled into bed, she wished there was something that could make Hank happy, or at least make him believe that she was happy. At some point, when he'd been little, he'd stopped believing he could be loved. That's why he could offer the partnership—it had been safe, there wouldn't be a disappointment, for love wasn't part of the deal.

Shoving a tear away, she silently scolded herself for crying, then she realized why she couldn't stop. Hank didn't believe in love and she loved him. She might never be able to say the words or make him believe, but she loved him.

An idea struck her. Slipping from the bed, she ran back upstairs. Within minutes another quilt was hung, this one on the blank wall of their bedroom. Tomorrow, no matter what the weather, Hank would wake to a sunny day filled with sunflowers and morning glories.

Laughing to herself, Aggie slipped out of her nightgown and into his flannel shirt. Then she crawled in beside her husband. As she moved close to his warmth, he circled her and pulled her against him. His slow steady breathing told her that his action was more instinct than thought. She molded against him and whispered, "Good night, dear," a moment before she fell asleep.

Chapter 14

In the darkness Hank came awake one pleasure at a time. Aggie's hair tickled his nose, her cheek lay against his heart, and her breast pressed into his side. For several minutes all he could manage was breathing. He'd been in a bad mood all day yesterday, battling pain and the fear that someone might try to hurt Aggie. After an hour of berating himself, he'd decided she probably didn't want to come to bed with him.

But she had. She'd not only shared the bed, she'd curled up against him. He'd managed to live another day without her running out on him.

Finally, he slipped his hand along her back and cupped her round little bottom. She wiggled with his movement, then settled against him. Hank smiled, thinking he'd try harder. "Aggie," he whispered.

She raised her head, her hair wild around her. "Is it morning already?"

"No." He shoved her curls away from her face. "But close. The horizon is already beginning to glow."

"Are you all right?" She rose to her elbow.

"I'm fine. I'm sorry I woke you. I hadn't meant to say your name out loud."

Aggie fell back against the pillow and pretended to snore.

Hank laughed. "Don't you want to stay awake and watch the sun come up?"

"I'll catch it tonight, then turn it over in my mind."

He scooted up and propped the pillow behind his back. "Come on. Wake up and watch. Sunrise is the best part of the day."

Like a grumpy groundhog, she crawled out of her warm hole and sat beside him.

After a few minutes, he asked, "Are your eyes open?"

"Is it here yet?"

"Almost."

"Just let me know and I'll open them then."

Hank couldn't resist—he tugged her to him. He wanted to pull her shirt off and repeat all they'd done before, but for now, he had to let her set the pace. Just because he couldn't advance physically with making her his, didn't mean he couldn't move forward.

"Listen, sunshine, I've been thinking."

She was busy settling atop his chest.

"Are you listening?"

She made a slight sound, half yes, half yawn.

"I don't think I'm going to build another bed. If you've no objection, I think we should just share."

He felt her nod.

"I mean from now on, not just while I'm laid up with this leg."

She nodded again. "I understand. Except for the few months I had after all my sisters left, I've always shared a bed. It has advantages. Someone to cuddle with on cold nights. Someone to talk to when you can't sleep."

"Aggie, sharing a bed with a man is different."

She stilled. "I know."

He waited for her to say more. The easiness between them was gone. She lay stiff at his side. "You know," he whispered, "I would never hurt you."

"I know," she said again. "This isn't what I thought it would be like between us."

He understood. When he'd handed her his gun, he'd thought he was making a partnership that at best would keep her safe and offer him company. But now, it was already more, far more.

Without a word, he leaned down and brushed his lips over hers, loving the sweet dawn taste of them. She wrapped her arms around his neck and held him to her as she turned the kiss to liquid passion.

Hank fought to keep it light, but his hands slipped back over her bottom, tenderly gripping each hip and holding her close.

She broke the kiss and shoved away, and reason fought its way into his brain. He tried to find the words to say he was sorry for something he wasn't, but before he could speak, she unbuttoned her shirt.

"Touch me again, dear." She opened the flannel and in dawn's first light he saw her beauty.

All reason vanished as he lowered his mouth to her breast.

She cried out in surprise, then arched her back and allowed him his fill of her flesh.

By the time sanity returned, the sun had cleared the horizon. He kissed her long and hard, letting his hands continue caressing her breasts, now moist and full from his careful inspection. She'd complained only when he pulled away.

In the lazy stillness while they each remembered to breathe, Hank spread his hand across her stomach and made lazy circles over her flesh. "There's more," he whispered, loving the rise and fall of her abdomen as she breathed.

"I figured there might be." She moved her cheek against the side of his head.

"You'll let me know when you're ready." He didn't bother to say 'if you're ready.' After the way she reacted to his second touch, there was no doubt where they were headed.

She sighed.

"It might mean children." He'd heard of a few ways to prevent pregnancy, but doubted any one would work all the time. "You wouldn't mind children?"

She frowned. "I wouldn't mind your children. I think I'd love them dearly."

He tried to keep the sadness from his voice. "That's more than my mother did."

"That's not true." She shoved away, unaware how the sudden sight of her beauty stopped his heart.

He shrugged. "I'm afraid it is. My mother left me before I could talk and never looked back."

"No," Aggie shouted as she scrambled off the bed. "No!"

As she backed against the wall, he saw the quilt for the first time. "Where did that come from?" He knew nothing of crafts, but he could see that he must be looking at a work of art. No clumsy blocks, no crazy designs, but an intricate picture painted with tiny bits of fabric and fine stitching.

"Your mother. She loved you and must have spent years making these."

"These?"

"Didn't you know they were in the trunk? Beautiful masterpieces of the seasons. The finest work I've ever seen."

Hank shook his head. "I never looked. I figured it would be her clothes and I didn't want to see them. I didn't want to be reminded of a mother who never touched me." All his old feelings of being abandoned washed across his thoughts. "Besides, quilts in a trunk mean nothing."

Aggie had reached the edge of the quilt. Without a word she turned the fabric over and he saw a small square in the corner. Even from five feet away he could see the stitching. Three words: "For my son."

He sat staring at the quilt as Aggie buttoned her shirt and ran upstairs to get the others. When they were all spread out on the bed, Hank could no longer deny they were for him. Each one had the same three words carefully embroidered on the back. She might have left him, but she hadn't forgotten him.

A knock sounded a moment before they heard the front

door creak. Aggie jumped like a rabbit at the sound of gun-fire, and in seconds she was dressed.

"Hank?" the sheriff's voice boomed. He opened the bedroom door while Aggie stood behind it finishing buttoning her shirt. "Oh, there you are. I didn't think you'd be in bed. You all right?"

Hank tried to think of some reason he'd still be in bed after sunrise. He knew a very good one, but he wasn't about to tell the sheriff. "I was just getting dressed."

Aggie slipped out behind the sheriff, then managed to act like she was just walking in. "Oh," she said, "good morning, sheriff."

"Morning, ma'am. I got some good news. They found that other fellow in Fort Worth who Stockton hired to bother you. He was still drunk in the same saloon, claiming he thought the offer was a joke. So you can stop worrying."

"Good." Hank drew a long breath. "How about some coffee?"

The sheriff nodded. "I wouldn't mind if I do. I saw Blue in the barn. I'll run over and tell him the news and be right back."

He disappeared. Aggie ran to put coffee on and Hank dressed. When the sheriff returned they were both at the kitchen table.

After a cup of coffee and small talk, the sheriff stood. "I best be getting back." He lifted his hat. You folks have a good day." He took a step toward the door, then added, "That sure is a fine little rocking chair you're building out there, Hank."

Hank smiled, remembering how he'd worked all day on it and Aggie had been so busy she'd never asked what he was making. "It's for my wife. The one on the porch is too big for her."

The sheriff looked at Aggie. "You'll like that, Mrs. Harris."

"I'll need it," she said calmly. "I'm going to have a baby."

For a moment Hank thought he'd be embarrassed, but suddenly he couldn't stop smiling. He shook the sheriff's hand and limped to the door to say good-bye.

Aggie moved beneath his arm to steady him while they waved the lawman away.

When they were alone once more, Hank whispered, "I think I'm falling in love with my partner."

"I'm afraid I am too." She smiled up at him.

"But, Aggie, you're not pregnant."

She frowned. "We'd better work on that, dear, before the sheriff finds out I lied."

Hank looked up at the bright morning sun. "Lucky for us it's almost sundown."

They turned toward the house and stepped inside. For the first time since he'd built the place, Hank locked the door and they made love beneath each season of quilts.

A Shade of Sunrise

DeWanna Pace

Chapter 1

Wind rattled the pane, warning that winter might stage a final battle before giving in to spring. Briar Duncan stared out the window at the variety of humanity that had arrived in Amarillo daily since the new year. Strangers strode along the depot's platform, tipping their straw boaters and Stetsons to the ladies disembarking. Lingering wisps of frontier gunsmoke made Amarillo a meeting place for past and present these days. The city sprawling golden across the Texas Panhandle had suddenly become host to an influx of men posed to fight—a back-porch base to El Paso where other fortune hunters, adventurers, and doughboys positioned themselves for Pancho Villa's next move.

Seeing no sign of his coworker among the new arrivals, Briar decided Nathaniel must have chosen to stay in St. Louis longer than expected. If he didn't get back soon, the telegrapher would miss his opportunity to be part of the excitement. William Randolph Hearst had used every telegraph and teletype machine west of the Mississippi to keep him informed of the security of his cattle herds and silver mines. Briar had been so busy with taking care of Nathaniel's job that he'd had little time to do his own as station master. That left even less time to waylay his daughter's latest shenanigans.

"If you don't hurry home," Briar admonished the train as if it were his longtime friend, Nathaniel, "Violet will outgrow those dresses you're bringing back."

Thoughts of his seven-year-old daughter's latest growing spurt made Briar focus his attention on the hobbled skirts and new ankle-length war crinoline worn by some of the women. Wind whipped at the crinoline, making the fuller skirts billow. Parasols dipped to block dust and soot from blasting the feminine faces.

A dull throb started a rhythmic beat across Briar's brow and threatened to become a full-throttled brain buster. Blazes. Choosing clothes for Violet was worse than shoveling coal to feed the firebox. He had as much fashion sense as a cow had wool. Still, it was his duty to see that his daughter was accepted into genteel society one day. If that meant reading ladies's catalogues and taking heed of the latest feminine finery, then he'd do so until he could tell bustle from bonnet.

Briar watched as a tall, slender figure suddenly stepped off the train, set down a valise, and faced the wind. "Well, who the high plains are you?" he asked aloud. The stranger wore a lampshade tunic with baggy trousers gathered at the ankle and a matching yellow turban that offered an exotic halo to a mixture of doe-shaped eyes, high cheekbones, and full lips. A woman?

She bent to retrieve something laying on the platform, studied it, and turned the item over in her hands. With a quick flick of the wrist, she deposited the article in a pocket.

It was then he noticed her watching him. His first impulse was to back away from the window and pretend that he hadn't been staring at her. Instead, something made Briar stand his ground. Meet her gaze.

He longed for something different in his life lately, something other than his repetition of duties and responsibilities. He loved Violet and didn't resent a moment of his time with her. She was all he had left. But when the world seemed active and he felt trapped in monotonous duties, he longed for a change . . . for anything that would bring some sort of adventure to his days. Something in the gaze that stared back at him now whispered that this strange-looking woman might have brought it with her. A muscle in his jaw tightened as his spirits threatened to dampen. He knew with certainty that it would bother him if she looked away as if he'd been mistaken in her interest.

When she smiled and retrieved the treasure, holding it out toward him in silent question, blood surged hot within him. "No." He shook his head as if she could hear him from the distance that separated them. "Not mine."

She shrugged and put it away, grabbing her valise while letting her gaze linger on him once again. Just as suddenly as she had exited the train, she turned and joined the stream of passengers heading toward town. He watched until the yellow of her clothing blended with the myriad of newcomers rushing to find transportation to their next destinations. The other women and their fashions now suddenly seemed plain or even frivolous.

"No wonder you didn't want to wear the blamed thing this morning," he mumbled as he eyed the crowd for sight of his daughter among the stifling skirts that made the wearers's steps more difficult. The little minx had argued that no "suffer-gette" would let herself be hobbled like a horse. When he asked where she had heard such nonsense, she told him that one of the doughboys who'd gotten off the train told another soldier that a "suffer-gette" was a woman who had a mind of her own and the gumption to walk in a man's shoes.

As odd as the woman in the turban had looked in her harem pants, he'd bet she had no problem moving in any manner she chose. Was she a suffragette? The idea of getting to know her well enough to discover her capabilities appealed to Briar just long enough to quickly dash it from his thoughts.

If Violet caught sight of the stranger, he'd never hear the end of letting *her* wear pants!

Tumbleweeds, buggies, and touring cars fought for supremacy over the roadway that transferred visitors from the train station to places of lodging elsewhere in the city. It was almost impossible to get a hotel or boarding room lately. Doughboys heading south to El Paso were even pitching their Sibley tents if lodging proved unavailable.

Sand flicked the thick glass, sounding like angry insects committing suicide against the depot. The sun would be setting in a couple of hours and he hadn't seen Violet since she had gone off to fly her kite. Frowning, Briar reprimanded himself for allowing the strangely dressed woman to distract him. His gaze wandered to a group of boys wrestling farther down the platform. The militant atmosphere that pervaded Amarillo the past few weeks had roused most of the citizens in some form or fashion. He'd bet today's wages his daughter would be somewhere nearby. She tended to herd with the steeds and leave the mares to their grazing. If only Katie Rose were here. She'd know how to work through this little revolution Violet seemed so insistent upon.

"I'll black your eye and knock you two days into next Tuesday," a tiny, familiar voice shrilled sharply through Briar's thoughts.

Behind him Briar heard a *tick-tick-tickety-tick* begin in earnest, signaling an incoming message. Yet, he was forced to ignore it. "Stop that," he demanded, throwing open the door to the telegraph office and rushing down the platform to stop the group of boys. A tangle of hobbled skirt flipped end over end with a melee of trousers. Heads turned as others noticed the fight and stopped to see what had caused the ruckus.

Exasperation filled him. Wasn't someone else going to do something about the situation instead of just standing there? Was everyone so ready to fight that they'd stand by and gawk as the children went at it? Well, the wire could just sing for the moment. Preserving his rowdy daughter's dignity was of more importance.

"You boys stop fighting." He peeled one lad off another. "Violet, get up from there before you lose a tooth or . . . Now look at you . . . you're going to have a black eye."

All the children stood as if someone had aimed a rifle at them; everyone but his daughter, who avoided a direct gaze at Briar. Black brows arched like check marks over eyes that had inspired her name. One gloved fist came to rest on her hip, the other shaking vehemently at the red-haired, freckled-face boy standing opposite her. *Just wonderful,* Briar thought. One of the Corbetts' grandchildren. The newspaper moguls weren't over Violet's last jumble.

"He said you're a desk dandy, Daddy, so I went and hit him." The eye that was not swelling and showing signs of bruising narrowed. "I told him I would, but he said it again. You said we should give one warning, and I gave it. It's his fault he got the licking, not mine."

"Well, I'm gonna tell my daddy." The boy started crying. "I didn't tell no lie. You *are* a desk dandy."

"Don't tell your daddy, Jim," one of the other boys advised. "He'll take a switch to ya for letting a girl whip ya."

"A suffer-gette girl," Violet proclaimed as she lifted her chin proudly.

The other boys started chanting. "Violet whipped Jim. Violet whipped Jim. Beat the fire out of him, he-um, he-um."

Violet giggled, setting off another scuffle. Fists went flying and legs kicking. Violet lunged forward. Briar spread his arms, blocking his daughter's fist from joining in again. "You kids get out of here or I'm going to talk to each of your parents. Take this battle elsewhere, unless you want some explaining to do."

They scattered like rabbits chased by a wolf.

"Come inside," he insisted. "It'll be suppertime soon, and you look like you could use some cleaning. We'll go home early—"

"I didn't do nothing." She stood her ground. "He laughed at my dress and called you a name. I told you I shouldn'ta worn it, but you made me. So it's your fault."

Briar bent so she didn't have to crane her neck to look up at him. He knuckled her chin gently and lifted it. "Honey, his words didn't hurt Daddy, and he's too young to know the value of a pretty dress." Ripped at the empire waist, the garment would never be fit to wear again. Not that he would let her wear another one like it. It played too prominent a part in tangling her feet and, consequently, blacking her eye.

The ticking of the telegraph persisted. Briar glanced toward the machine as if willing it to answer itself. "Come inside for a minute, pumpkin. I'll answer the machine, then we'll get you cleaned up and talk about this at—"

"I gotta go get my kite. I left it," she said, stepping away and pointing past him. "You said proper ladies take care of their things."

"Don't be long, then." Briar gave in, knowing she had used his own sense of propriety to take her leave. A momentary wave of parental ethics engulfed him. "But don't think this has ended," he warned and gave the top of her head a quick pat. "We'll talk about this at supper."

Violet took off abruptly and turned around to wave, babbling that indecipherable chatter she and the other children used when they wanted to keep adults at bay. It irritated him to no end that he couldn't understand a single word of the child-speak, but she refused to include him in its meanings. He wouldn't put it past the little firebrand if it was some sort of secret code used to mount an insurrection against parents. Briar laughed despite the seriousness of the possibility. He dearly loved everything about her, including her obstinate attitude.

Tickety, tick, tick. "All right, all right," Briar complained to the impatient instrument. "I'm coming." His long-legged gate closed the distance in a few steps.

No rest for the totally outmaneuvered, he told himself, silently warming to his daughter's sweet manipulations. She was personality to the hilt and headstrong as her mother. The only thing she'd inherited from him was his dark hair and twilight-shaded eyes. Everything else was Katie Rose. How could he find fault in that?

Briar listened intently to the incoming message. Relief flooded him. Nathaniel. Lord, but he was glad to hear from him.

Have answer. Stop. Arriving Amarillo by morning of Feb 20. Nathaniel.

Briar's smile wavered. Though his friend would be home tomorrow, the partial message was unclear. Have what answer? The only problem they'd discussed before leaving was whom they could get to look after Violet while they worked. Surely, Nathaniel hadn't gone and hired a governess in St. Louis. He wouldn't do that without consulting him, would he?

"You're supposed to be bringing *dresses*," Briar told the machine as if it were Nathaniel. "I can find somebody *here* to help us."

Heaven knew there were enough new people in town lately to choose among. Trouble was, he preferred hiring someone he and Nathaniel knew well. Someone they could trust to teach Violet about silk and sashes and show her the delicacies of becoming a well-bred young lady. Someone not easily daunted by a feisty seven-year-old. Briar knew that Violet needed a special magic, a social polish that he had never found within himself. Maybe the telegram meant just what it said. Interviewing a governess would certainly explain the telegrapher's long absence.

Briar watched the engine's steam billow and swirl away with the gusts of air. "Blow some magic in with you, wind, will you?" Briar whispered. "If Nathaniel's bringing someone back with him, make her an angel. One who has a will strong enough to do battle with a devilish, little imp."

One with a heart not as easy to win as mine, he added for good measure.

Chapter 2

"Are you an angel?"

Mina grabbed the branch above to stabilize her perch atop the limbs of the large Chinese elm tree that held her, then peered down to catch a view of the voice's owner. A little girl.

"I couldna say that I've ever been called that, sweeting." Mina laughed, shifting her position so she could finish what she'd set out to do. Perhaps the kite that had tangled in the elm belonged to the lass. "But if I do enough good deeds while I'm on this earth," Mina continued, freeing the obstinate tail at last, "then ye might call me that one day."

The little girl's eyes rounded and flashed like two amethysts dazzled by the sun. "I know a really good deed you can do."

Was that a bruise beneath one of her eyes? Mina made her way down, moving one branch then another to see better. Why, the poor little thing sported a bruise as dark as coal pitch. "Do me a favor first," Mina insisted, wanting to investigate the child's injury further, "then I'll be for granting any deed ye wish. Catch this kite so I can jump down, will ye now? No, come a wee bit closer. There now, lassie, that would be the spot. Ready. Set. Ahh, 'tis a good hand at catching ye have!"

Mina swung from the lowest branch and landed with only

the slightest breach of poise. She quickly dusted off her clothes and thanked the lass for helping her.

The girl giggled. "Do all angels talk like you?"

Mina joined in her merriment. "Theirs would be a wee more refined than me own, but I'd like to think I could give the Lord a good laugh now and again, doncha know."

The ebony curls that graced the sweet child's head bobbed, making Mina even more aware of how the eye injury would soon match the shade of its owner's hair. She gently reached out to touch the lass's cheek and was warmed by the fact that the little girl did not move away and trusted her to add no further harm. "How did ye come by this?"

"Got into a fight." The child's lips lifted into a grin as she rocked back on her laced boots. "But I won."

I just bet ye did. Mina admired the winner's pluck as she quickly surveyed for further damage. Only a torn dress that was definitely not anyone's hand-me-down. The garment showed no signs of long wear, so the assumption that the girl might be a street urchin instantly evaporated. "Are ye father and mother aware of these fisticuffs?"

"Daddy is."

Mina's attention averted to their surroundings and the people walking in and out of the shops along the roadway. None of them seemed concerned that this child was talking to an absolute stranger. "Is he nearby?"

"Huh-uh." The girl looked away for a moment, then faced Mina again, her brow wrinkling. "Will you do that good deed you promised me now?"

Whatever concerned the child seemed terribly important. "Of course, lassie. Ye caught the kite for me ye did."

"Will you come home with me?"

A twinge of longing swept through Mina so sharply that it nearly took her breath away. How long she had waited to hear those words? How often had she dreamed they would be offered in such kindness? Just as many times as there had been nights spent huddling behind tarps or hiding in secret nooks along the wharfs of St. Louis. The lass had no clue how deeply her request touched Mina. "What is yer name, sweeting?"

"Violet. Violet Duncan."

Duncan? "Are you related to Briar Duncan, the station master?"

Violet nodded. "He's my papa, but then you probably already knew that, being an angel and all."

"Angel-in-training," Mina corrected, not seeing any harm in going along with the child's insistence for a moment. "Is yer father still at work or is he somewhere about?"

"He's always working."

The way the lass said "always" told Mina everything she needed to know. Her mother obviously did not care where the child played, not providing adequate supervision and allowing her to run the streets. Saints and begorra, what if someone with less moral decency had found her? She knew what it was like to be a child without the security of a parent or guardian. At least she knew where to take Violet, and once she did she would give the man a good tongue lashing. Employment be hanged. She would just have to find another way to pay back Nathaniel.

"Is that yer kite?"

Violet nodded. "You want it?"

Mina shook her head. "I will fix it for ye, then 'twill fly again, it will."

The child handed the toy to Mina. "No, you keep it. I don't need it no more."

She accepted the offering, deciding Violet would change her mind once it was repaired. "Did ye walk here?"

Violet pointed to the approaching streetcar. "I rode that. Come on, it won't cost no money. I get to ride free."

But I canna, Mina worried silently as she grabbed her valise from the base of the tree where she'd set it. She would need to preserve the few coins she possessed until she found other employment, now that it was sure and certain Violet's father would not be hiring her.

Much to Mina's surprise she also rode for free. Violet seemed an apt manipulator of boosterism for Amarillo. The conductor agreed with the child's reasoning that it made good sense to give a stranger a lift now and then just so the stranger could tell others about the pleasure of the ride.

"Whew! I thought we'd never get here." Violet started running for the depot. "Daddy's already turned up the gaslights."

The child was not looking where she was going. Mina noticed a touring car coming at an incredible speed. Violet would not reach the platform in time. "Watch out, lass!" she yelled, dropping the valise and kite. She dashed after the child, grabbing Violet's hand and jerking her backward to safety just as an obnoxious honk emanated from the passing motorized Flivver.

"Violet!" a masculine voice shouted. "Are you all right?"

The tiny heart beat fast against Mina's hip, nearly drumming through the child's back. Mina turned her around and surveyed her face. "Ye okay, lassie?"

"I'm a-all right, angel," Violet finally managed and hugged Mina tightly.

"How can I thank you, ma'am?" asked the man who came running up to check on them. Mina looked up and stared into a familiar face. His eyes were a shade deeper than his daughter's but the Duncans had the same lock of hair that curled just over the peak of their brow. The same full upper lip. The resemblance was unmistakable. Briar Duncan was the man in the window. Mina's breath did not slow despite her effort to ease it.

The station master's chest swelled as he tried to catch his own breath, making him seem even broader than earlier sight of him suggested. Anger and disappointment rose to battle with the attraction kindling inside Mina. How could such a fine-looking man be such a cur of a father? "Ye can thank me by not letting yer child walk the streets on her own. She could have been hurt."

"You're right, of course," he said, though the friendliness

in his gaze narrowed into purple slits that glinted like stone. "It's almost dark and I should have had closer watch on her. Violet, thank Miss—?"

"McCoy. Mina McCoy."

"Tell Miss McCoy how much you appreciate her help, and we'll be on our way."

"She's coming home with us, Daddy." Violet's hold on Mina tightened. "She's my angel and I found her. I'm gonna keep her."

"I suppose I should be explaining." Mina's anger began to ease because of his obvious concern for his daughter.

"No need, Miss McCoy. I'm sure it has everything to do with the kite."

Mina glanced back at the kite then up at the handsome man. *Stop it,* she told herself. *He's married and ye've no right to think him the devil's own temptation.* "The kite? How could you know—"

"Violet?" The station master gently reached for his daughter. "What are you up to? You know this lady can't stay with you."

Violet went willingly into her father's arms. "Uh-huh, Daddy. She said she would."

"I said I would take her home, and that I've now done, sir. Kite or no, my promised deed is finished." Mina retrieved her bag and the toy, offering the latter to Violet. "I canna stay, lass, but I will come to see you now and again while I visit Amarillo . . . if yer father and mother are of a willing mind."

"But you're *my* angel. You're supposed to stay with *me*." Tears welled in Violet's eyes as she refused to take the kite. "You're supposed to stay *here*."

"Don't cry, honey." Briar patted his daughter softly while she hid her face in his neck and began to weep.

When Mina gave him a puzzled expression, he sighed deeply. A sound filled with regret and something else. "Turn the kite over, Miss McCoy, and I'll explain."

Mina set down her valise and turned the kite as instructed.

On the back of it, scrawled in childish letters were the words, "Come Home."

"She lost her mother almost four years ago, and she's flown that kite every day since. I told her that her mama went to be an angel in heaven."

Mina's heart clenched, feeling as if a hundred-pound weight had dropped upon it. Violet had known a mother who loved her once. The wee one had suffered a terrible loss. Mina could search the world over for her own mother and never experience the same hurt. *Her* mother had never wanted her. Mina's voice became whisper-soft with compassion. "So she thinks she's caught her angel?"

"I'm afraid so."

Maybe refusing the job her friend had offered was no longer an option. It seemed everyone else on earth was trying to reform the injustices of the world at the moment. Maybe she could start on a smaller scale by reforming one father. Maybe being the little girl's angel for a while was just the good deed she needed to do to set all their lives on a better course. "Well, I may not be the angel she bargained for, but I can stay. That is, if ye'll give me the job Nathaniel promised."

"Nathaniel?" Surprise registered across the man's face. "You know Nathaniel?"

"Ye received his telegram, telling ye I was on me way?" She saw that he had even before he admitted it.

His gaze swept over her from head to hem, making him frown. "You don't look like a governess."

"A governess? 'Tis a telegrapher I am. Nathaniel said that I would be a replacement telegrapher until he returns. The man did me a favor once, and I came here to pay it back. I just arrived a day earlier than planned."

"A telegrapher? You can't—"

"I certainly can," she argued, her fists balancing defiantly against her hips. "And quite good at it, I am."

"I meant, the usual in-office housing accommodations won't do. There's only a cot separated by a silk screen and that affords little privacy if we have to keep the office open overnight. And we've done that more often than not lately."

"There are worse places than a cot to rest, sir."

Violet sniffled. "She could sleep in Nathaniel's bed since he won't be there, Daddy."

"No, honey, she can't." Briar Duncan looked suddenly uncomfortable as he explained. "Nathaniel and I share a place close to the station since we work so much. Two bachelors, you know. Violet has her own room, of course, but Nat and I share the other. One of us is usually working when the other isn't so that someone is able to watch over my daughter. He's been gone for a while, and I've had my hands full with . . . That's neither here nor there. I can't see any logic in hiring you as a telegrapher, miss. There'd be too many complications."

She should insist for Violet's sake. It would be a way to spend some time with the lass, maybe even make sure her da did the same. But the truth was, she really needed the work. "Then I have no way to pay him back the favor."

"Can't you get employment somewhere else and do the same?"

"Most likely, but Nathaniel insisted that I help ye. By helping ye, he said it would be helping him." *'Tis a clever man ye are, Nathaniel Rhodes. Always lending a hand to a friend in need. Looks to me like ye had three friends in mind, this time.*

"Yeah, I'll just bet it would." Briar looked genuinely sorry. "I've got to say no to this scheme of his, Miss McCoy. I'm afraid you've traveled all this way for bad news."

Mina picked up her valise. She couldn't go back. She was nearly out of money and certainly out of ideas to go about getting more anytime soon. "I'll be seeing what Amarillo has to offer, then. Maybe when he returns, I can finish the deed in some other way." She patted Violet on the back. "I'll see ye a time or two before I go, lassie."

Violet's sobs began in earnest.

Though the man attempted to calm his child, the lass refused to be appeased. Finally, he conceded to her anguish.

"Maybe we should at least ask her to take supper with us, don't you think?"

The sobs stopped as abruptly as they started.

Briar's gaze met Mina's. "It's the least I can do to thank you for rescuing my daughter."

Violet lifted her head from her father's shoulder and pleaded, "Will you, angel? Even angels gotta eat, don't they?"

Everything inside Mina warned that she should listen to the man's wisdom and run as fast and as far away as she could, but the hunger of existing on very little suddenly voiced itself as a rumble in her stomach. The need to reform a parent and the beguiling voice that had been the first to ask her home joined forces, convincing her to accept the devil's own temptation.

Chapter 3

Briar had never seen a woman eat so slowly in his entire
life. It was as if she had never tasted roast beef and potatoes
before. Not that he really minded. She was a sight worth
studying. Just as he suspected in that short glimpse he'd had
of her when she first exited the train, she was not a traditional
beauty but rather a strange mixture of imperfections that made
her striking in her own way. The sun-bronzed tone of her skin
hinted that she seldom used a parasol. Still, she looked health-
ier than some of the women in the restaurant who appeared
lily-white in the gaslights's amber glow. Her nose was not the
pert little stub and her mouth not the Cupid's bow that he usually found appealing, but rather a length he could only describe as royal and a spanse of plentiful lips. Wisps of blond
curls lacing her turban hinted that she probably could boast
some Nordic heritage, despite her Irish brogue.

But it was her eyes that intrigued him most. Eyes that
slanted slightly at the corners and looked the color of dew-
moistened wheat. Eyes that stared at him directly now.

"Is something wrong?"

"Excuse me." He grabbed his napkin and wiped his mouth.
"I'm afraid I was staring. I'm sorry."

She dabbed at her own lips. "Did I drop something on me?"

"He thinks you're pretty," Violet interrupted. "Me, too."

The little imp. Just wait until he got her home. "I was wondering how an Irish woman happened to be blond and . . . What exactly do you call that color of eyes?" Briar refused to deny his attraction to her. She was beautiful.

"Me da said they be the color of honey, the first of the season fresh from the comb. Full of sting and sticker, they are." She laughed until she snorted, then laughed even louder at the unladylike sound. When several heads turned to see what had caused the merriment, she did not seem to mind their attention. Instead she looked at them all squarely and added, "Ye'll find that out soon enough about me, 'tis true."

She didn't have a shy bone in her entire body, it seemed. Certainly not the ideal woman to hire as governess, as he'd been mulling since he'd turned her down as possible telegrapher. Certainly not the kind of woman who would be a good example for Violet. "I've been thinking about your predicament, Miss McCoy." He cleared his throat. "And I've decided that we should refund the money you spent coming to Amarillo. I'll drop by the bank in the morning, then I can meet you at your hotel." When she paled at the suggestion, Briar reminded himself that she might think them too newly acquainted to allow him to call upon her in a less public atmosphere. "Or if you prefer, I'll have the money or a ticket waiting for you at the station."

She shook her head. "That willna be necessary, Mr. Duncan. I plan on staying in Amarillo, just as I said, until Nathaniel returns."

"If that's your choice." He nodded toward a table filled with rough-looking men. "It might be hard to find employment, though. There are adventurers of every kind in town lately, trying to earn their keep until war either breaks out with Pancho Villa or President Wilson goes ahead and gets us into the Great War. It's lucky that you found a hotel room."

"The luck I have today, sir, is enjoying this fine meal and

the even finer companions to share it with." She smiled down at Violet, then hastily took another bite.

Without thinking, he reached out to halt her hand. "You mean, you don't have a room yet?"

Her gaze met his and locked, her mouth stopping in mid-chew. He thought he felt her tremble just before she slowly set the fork down and grabbed her goblet. She took a long drink, as if she had been banished for days in the drought-driven plains and could only now quench her thirst.

Those glorious lips of hers shifted into a grin. "'Tis confused I am how to answer ye, Mr. Duncan. Do I say, 'Aye, 'tis what I mean, or nay, I have no room.'"

"*Briar*," he insisted, wanting to watch her lips form his given name, wondering how the Irish lilt would sound in a feverish whisper of passion. Blazes, now he felt parched.

"Well, then, *Briar* . . . 'Tis a strange name, that. Did ye mum and da suspect ye'd be a troublesome lad?"

She was avoiding an answer. "Long story I'll tell you when we have more time." He set down his own goblet. "Right now, I need to hunt you up a place to stay. That won't be easy this time of evening. I don't suppose you noticed that sign when we passed the billiard hall, did you?"

She forked the last piece of beef and sopped it in the gravy. "Ye mean the one that said they were renting beds in eight-hour shifts? I appreciate the thought, but 'twould be mighty hard on a body's back I'm thinking." She winked at Violet. "I'll not be needing a *cue* to make me look elsewhere." She chewed the beef with a flourish, staring at him as if waiting for him to object.

Briar reviewed what she said then began to chuckle. She was waiting to see if his wit was as sharp as her own.

Puzzlement etched Violet's brow. "I don't get it. What's so funny?"

Their guest nearly spit her food out as she struggled not to laugh, but the effort elicited a bigger snort. Now all three joined in the merriment. Everyone around them looked on as if she'd lost her mind as well as her taste in clothing.

"I don't know when I've had such a good meal," Briar admitted, finally yielding to some semblance of control. "Or laughed so hard."

"Since Mama went to heaven," Violet announced, abruptly causing them all to sober. "It's true." She attempted to soften the blow of her words. "You ain't laughed since I can 'member."

Briar thought back over the past few years and realized the truth of his daughter's words. Though Violet was exaggerating the length of time, he didn't laugh much anymore. He missed it and, more important, how it made him feel when Violet laughed with him. "I'm sorry, pumpkin. I'll try to do that more often."

"Maybe I can help." Their guest scooted her plate away, its empty surface a testament to the restaurant's fine reputation. "I've been thinking about what ye said earlier, Mr. Duncan. If 'tis a governess ye need, then 'tis a governess I'll be till Nathaniel returns. If 'tis transcribing messages ye want, then I'll be for doing that as well. Ye'll find me a good hand on the wire, and I would love to spend some time with Violet."

She yawned, a sound too indelicate to be anything but a combination of a full belly and sheer exhaustion. "I've no mind where I sleep, long as it offers a place to lay me head and a warm cover should the weather turn cold. Which I understand is doubtful, considering Nathaniel said the plains have seen their worst drought in years." She yawned again. "That cot is surely calling to me now."

He'd prayed for an answer to his problem. Now one had presented itself. Damn Nathaniel for not coming home. But what could he do? If the billiard hall was using its tables to sleep people, then there obviously were no rooms to be found anywhere. He couldn't leave the woman out on the streets, and he couldn't leave her alone unattended at the office. Rail crews were rough men. An unchaperoned woman in their midst would only stir up trouble. Still, he needed help. Maybe if she could relieve him for part of the day.

"I'll tell you what . . . I'll leave you and Violet here to have dessert and get to know one another a little better while I run over to the filling station and use the phone. I'll call around and see if I can find you more comfortable accommodations than the cot."

"I have the job then?"

"Most likely. But I'd like to reserve final agreement until you answer a few questions about your qualifications. Those questions can wait until I secure you a room somewhere."

A half hour and a handful of phone calls later, Briar returned to find Mina sitting alone. "Where's Violet?" He searched the room for sign of her and glanced at the batwing doors that divided the dining room from the restaurant's kitchen. "She's not in the back bothering the cook again, is she?"

If the woman couldn't control the imp long enough to keep her seated at the table, perhaps taking her on for hire was not such a good idea.

Mina pressed a finger to her lips, then pointed downward.

Briar stepped closer and leaned to see his child stretched across her chair, her head leaning in the woman's lap. "Asleep?"

"Right after ye left. The lass can sleep through a stampede, it seems."

"I'll take her."

"No, I ordered ye a pie," she whispered, "and asked them to keep it hot till ye returned. No use wasting good food or hard-earned money."

No sooner than Mina informed him, the waitress bought Briar the pie. He thanked her and decided that tonight he would give a slightly bigger tip than usual for the extra service.

Mina looked at him expectantly and he realized she was waiting for him to take a bite. He had been the commander of his own eating habits for almost four years now and he found her insistence both warming and irritating. Warming, because it felt good again to have someone care that he ate. Irritating, because that same care reminded him of the loneliness of his life.

He pushed the plate away. Better to get down to business and put their relationship into its proper prospective. "I need to open the station in the morning, Miss McCoy, sell tickets and do my daily rounds with the rest of the crew. I've decided to hire a man to watch the 'graph on the nights we need one, if you'll listen in the afternoons. That would give you the morning with Violet, and she can take an afternoon nap on the cot while you work. Lord knows she's slept through it a hundred times. The afternoon will let me finish the daily books and whatever else I didn't get done earlier. Just decide which one or two afternoons you'd like off and that will be fine. Is that satisfactory to you?"

"When will *you* spend time with her?" The honey-colored eyes took on their sting.

Briar would have told her the matter was not open for discussion, but he supposed he was now making it the woman's concern. He thought about his schedule then decided he might as well give himself a little added incentive. After all, he had thoroughly enjoyed supper. "I'll share the noon meal with you both, then after her nap, I'll make sure she and I do something together." He looked at his daughter and realized just how many months it had been since he could remember doing anything special other than share a meal or go to church with her. Months must seem like years to a child so young.

"Like we used to, Daddy? You didn't forget how?" Violet sat up, her uninjured eye suddenly wide awake with expectation.

Had she just been pretending? "I haven't forgotten, pumpkin," Briar reassured her. Shame for his own actions of late made him stand and quickly pull the funds for their dinner from his pocket and place them on the table. The need to hold his daughter compelled him to take her up in his arms.

The woman was right. He should be more attentive to Violet. He should have hired a temporary man when Nathaniel first left so that he could spend time with her. He should have been a better father in a hundred different ways. And he would be, beginning now. Tonight. "You ready to go home and rest those pretty eyes so they'll be ready for church in the morning?"

"Can my angel go with us?" She nodded, sighing softly against his shoulder.

He looked at Mina. "Most likeliest place to let a new angel in town get to know people, don't you think?"

She giggled and her head nestled into the crook of his neck. "I'll show her to the Corbetts and the McCords and, oh yeah, to Mr. and Mrs. Harris. Daddy says Mrs. Harris used to own the gun shop, but she ain't no devil. She's a real nice lady. Her boys run the shop now. I don't see them much 'cept at church. They're old like Daddy."

Mina took coins from her pocket and placed them by her plate. She laughed. "Just how old is yer da?"

Before the tattler could answer, Briar reached over and scooted the coins back to Mina. "Older than Exodus. Now keep your money. Supper's my treat, remember."

"Twenty-seven." Violet giggled, then squealed when her father poked her gently in the ribs and began to tickle her.

"Cowboy counsel, gabby-girl, remember?" It felt good to hear her sweet giggles against his throat as she tucked her head and moored herself against him. "Especially with family secrets."

"Cowboy counsel?" Mina asked. "'Tis an Amarillo saying, I'm thinking."

"A Texas saying, ma'am," Briar announced in his best Lone Star drawl. "Which means that you don't run off at the mouth about things that should be kept private."

"Angel says she's twenty-three," Violet interjected, then cupped her mouth. "Uh-oh, Daddy, it ran off all by itself."

"Violet!" Briar and Mina objected in unison.

"Well," she defended, spreading her fingers just enough to let through her explanation, "It just came right out and I was too tired to stop it."

"God help us both." Briar made a visual pact with Mina as he offered his free arm to escort her out of the restaurant. "We're going to need Him."

Chapter 4

They walked only a few streets before opening a gate to a yard that housed a handsome wood cottage painted the color of her ancestral homeland and trimmed with white gingerbread molding. Was this the Duncan home? "Ye're not thinking of putting her to bed and leaving her alone while ye escort me to the station, are ye?"

"No, ma'am. I'm not. You'll both be staying."

Her fingers unlocked from around the muscular band of his forearm and she backed away. No matter what employment he offered, she could not sleep under his roof with him. Though she had never worn a heavy cloak of propriety about her shoulders, she tried to maintain a thread of decency. "I'll not be obliged to sleep in yer home, sir. 'Tisn't fitting."

"It wouldn't be if I were going to be sleeping there with you." Though his voice reassured, the deep timbre of it enticed with the playfulness of their earlier banter. His eyes darkened to moonlit globes framed in lashes of ebony. "I'm loaning you my bed."

Mina's heart altered its beat, as if it were a tossed stone skipping along the surface of a pond. A warm bed where she would be safe from her troubles was what she had hoped for so long that now, when offered, it seemed more dream than reality. But sleeping in a place that would be filled with the sights and scent peculiar to this man seemed more dangerous than any of those nights spent hiding under tarps on the wharfs of St. Louis. He'd captured her interest with that first look they'd shared when she disembarked. The allure only deepened the more they had talked . . . when he touched her hand at supper. She must remember her anger with him concerning his daughter's welfare, lest she be swayed by his charm.

Despite the voice of reason stirring her thoughts, her feet moved forward as if they had a will of their own.

He accepted her hand again and guided her to the porch. "Bunking in at the office and letting you and Violet sleep here really is the logical thing for me to do, Miss McCoy. It's getting late, so I'll need to situate Violet for the night. After I remove a few of my things we'll have our discussion, then I'll be off to the station. No one will find fault with those arrangements."

Our discussion? She reviewed their talk at supper and realized he meant to interview her about her qualifications for employment. She was tired, and it had been a long journey. But she must remain alert. She would tell him just enough to satisfy his curiosity and nothing else. "Very well, then. If ye're certain 'tis no trouble to ye."

"I've practically been there every night this last month. One more won't make a difference."

"Ye've left that wee lass alone in the house?"

"Let's get out of the night air, shall we?" He opened one of the two front doors that graced the cottage's facade. "And yes, I suppose I did. But I checked on her hourly to make sure she didn't need me."

"'Tis a good thing ye live so close to ye work. Not that ye have to worry about strangers getting off the train and needing a warm place to stay."

"*Touché*, Miss McCoy."

He left her standing in the parlor of his home while he disappeared behind a dark-wooded door that shone like a freshly washed apple at the back of the room. She set her valise down by the armchair made of the same wood and a red velvet backrest and cushion. Side tables held kerosene lamps designed in floral bouquets. Someone had lit one of them, offering a warm welcome to those who entered. Had Briar stopped by while he was gone to make the phone calls?

She noted another lamp hanging in the center of the ceiling, its mother-of-pearl base and crystal chandelier shade not quite as fancy as those she'd seen back east. Before she could notice further details of the room, Briar returned and waved her to the chair. "Please take a seat, Miss McCoy."

"Yer home is lovely."

He glanced about as he sat opposite her on a davenport of a similar design as the chair. "It's one of the kit houses brought in from Sears, Roebuck. The family who ordered it pulled up stakes, so I was able to get it for less than the usual cost. I'm no carpenter by any means, but Nathaniel and I had a cussing good time putting it together."

Naturally curious, she wanted to know more of what made his eyes spark with such a happy memory, but he steered the conversation back to the business at hand. At least he seemed capable of providing for his daughter, and quite well from the look of it.

"I thought we could start things off while Violet dresses herself for bed." He lifted a palm. "Now don't object . . . she won't let me help her. Has something to do with her latest 'suffer-gette' doings."

Mina smiled despite her initial reaction. Violet would be the sort to latch onto the craze that had menfolk drinking deep in their cups. The lass would be more than a handful once she took on her full petticoats. "So, 'tis yer questions I'll be hearing now."

"First, how do you know Nathaniel?"

A safe enough subject if she handled it just right. She noticed the Shoninger desk organ and wondered if he or Violet played the instrument. Her fingers rubbed together in anticipation of teaching the lass a few tunes. Playing a lively jig was the one true teaching her da had passed down to her before throwing her into the streets.

She looked Briar straight in the eye, a practice she found helped to convince people of her sincerity. "I knew him when he lived in St. Louis years ago. He was acquainted with me father." She made sure she didn't say friend to her da, so it would not be a lie. Seamus McCoy had few friends and Nathaniel was not among them. "He managed to get me a badly needed job. I told him I would pay him back one day for the favor."

Lincs creased Briar's brow. "That had to be ten or more years ago. He's lived here for more than eight."

"Nine would be the whole of it."

"You worked at fourteen?"

"Lots of people work at that age." Her chin rose at the criticism.

"They do." He looked apologetic for having offended her.

He couldn't know he had touched on an embarrassing aspect of her life. She kept the reason she had been forced to take the employment secret from anyone who didn't have to know. What had he called it . . . cowboy counsel? "And for that reason, 'tis here I am. To pay him back."

"Sounds like you have a lot of experience working."

She shifted in the chair, feeling as if she were losing ground instead of gaining a firm foothold. "More than I care to admit."

"May I be blunt?"

His eyes had a way of looking at her so deeply that she could feel their searching as if it were a tangible touch that left smoke drifting in its wake. Like a blaze whose heat simmered long after the burn. "I prefer that ye speak yer mind," she whispered, feeling vulnerable and unable to hide the breathy rush of her voice. "Ye can be certain, I will."

"I need to know any reason you wouldn't be a proper teacher to my daughter."

Mina stood abruptly. "If ye mean to ask if I ever worked in an *improper* place, then ye can rest assure I have not."

Genuine regret filled his face. "I'm sorry, Miss McCoy, if I've spoken out of turn. My daughter's upbringing, no matter what it may seem, is of the utmost importance to me. I'm very careful of the women who come into her life because she *is* a motherless child. As you can tell, she's eager to attach herself."

"That I can understand." And she could, better than he would ever suspect. "So, have there been many? Women, I mean? Since her mother's passing?" The fact that other women may have been close to the Duncans bothered Mina, more than she wanted to admit.

"I've tried several governesses. Let's just say, none seemed up to the challenge."

Mina was relieved to find her good humor again. "The lass has a crafty wit about her, even at this wee age."

"I thought we were going to be *blunt*." He laughed, a sound filled with both exasperation and pride. "She's the devil's own taskmistress at times."

"I knew that from the moment I met her, but 'tis no deed yer lass has done that I have not stumbled over meself."

"Good then, you feel up to the task?"

"Aye, and qualified to see her come out the better for it, I am. I worked four long years in Mrs. Higginbotham's Lady's School. I know all the refinements she'll be needing and have taught them a time or two to others. There is, to me regret, the matter of diction. Though it doesna transfer across the wire as brogue, I'm not prepared to teach the lass proper English."

"No need to concern yourself there. School will start back soon. It was canceled so families could work their ranches to stave off the drought. But if the weather doesn't let up soon, there won't be much to save and no reason to keep the children out of school. She's taught diction there."

"Am I to cook for her, then? See to her washing and such?"

Briar moved to the two brocade drapes that curtained off

what must be another room. "The kitchen's here. If you like to cook, I'd appreciate the help. If you don't, then leave it to me. I'm more concerned with teaching her good manners and"—his gaze swept Mina—"appropriate fashion."

Traditional, Mina decided, silently latching onto a seed for change she must plant in the man's thinking. If she was expected to teach Violet how to conduct herself in the ways of the elite, then she must teach him to be more progressive. At least he had vinegar enough to know he needed help in the matter. "These are the latest from Paris, Mr. Duncan." She tugged on her pants. "Mark me words, Mademoiselle Chanel's fashions will soon fill ladies' wardrobes everywhere in America. While ye men wage yer battles these days, 'tis freedom of movement we women are fighting for."

Violet chose that moment to peek around the door. "I'm ready for you to tuck me in now."

"Want to help?" Briar motioned Mina ahead of him.

Mina remained still just long enough to let him lead. She was pleased to be included in the obvious nightly ritual. She'd been certain he would argue with her about her clothing choices, but he didn't. Instead, he'd let her comment pass. Perhaps he was just too tired to challenge her views.

Something about the way Violet's hand went trustingly into her father's and led him down the brief hallway warmed Mina's heart. She'd been too harsh in her thoughts of Briar Duncan. He might be guilty of neglect. He might even be guilty of too traditional a view in his raising of his daughter, but it was clear he loved the lass dearly. There would never be a lifelong abandonment as her own parents had done.

Mina watched as father and daughter entered a room and knelt beside a four-poster bed whose plush lavender-colored quilt had been turned down. Hand-painted clouds drifted along the sky-colored ceiling, offering a billowy white pathway to the kite that flew among them. Though the room boasted only a rocking chair, night table, armoire, and lamp, it looked like a princess's palace to Mina. Aye, this father dearly loved his daughter. Or, at least, he made a good show of it when no one was looking.

In unison, Briar and Violet cupped their palms in prayer.

"Dear God," Violet began as Mina knelt at the end of the bed. "Bless everybody we love and help everyone be good to each other. Oh . . . and don't let Jim Corbett get in too much trouble with his Pa 'cause I whipped him. He can't help it if he's dumber than—"

"Violet." Briar opened one eye to look sternly at his daughter.

"Well, okay." She peeked at him with her good eye, then shut it tightly. "I guess You might want to spend some more time on Jim, God. He needs lots of help. Oh yeah, best of all, thank You for sending me my angel." She blew out a long sigh of relief. "I guess You was too busy to hear the part about hurrying up and send her. Amen."

Briar leaned over and kissed the top of Violet's head. "Climb in there before you get yourself in trouble."

Violet leapt into the bed and pulled up the covers. She waited till her father tucked in the quilt and kissed her once more before she held her arms out toward Mina. "You gonna kiss me too, angel?"

"Wouldna miss it for the world." Mina swept past Briar to press her lips against the cherubic cheek. "Now sleep, lass, we've got lots to do tomorrow."

"Okay, but angel . . ." She wiggled one finger so Mina would move closer.

"*Mina*. Call me Mina."

"You don't have to teach me nothing, Mina," she whispered. "I already love you."

"I already love ye, too, lass," she whispered back, both surprised and pleased that she meant it. "Now rest that sore eye so it can heal."

Chapter 5

Briar lay on his back, staring out at the moon that rose over the high plains of Texas. The windows lining the eastern wall of the depot's lobby gave an expansive view of the night sky blanketing Amarillo—a view that he needed to mull the choice he'd made today. The telegraph office had felt too confining, limiting his ability to think. He had tried stretching across one of the passenger benches, but his legs extended too far over the side and the seats were just narrow enough that he couldn't curl up comfortably. There was nothing else to do but move his bed out here and set it up near the window. He shifted on the cot, threading his arms behind his head. The curious restlessness he had managed to hold at bay seemed to intensify while he waited for sleep.

Today had been eventful, to say the least. He'd never expected the strangely dressed woman to enter his own life. He'd surely never meant to allow her to take charge of Violet. Perhaps tomorrow would bring wiser thoughts. But as dinner had worn on, she'd looked increasingly tired and probably needed sleep more than he needed to determine the level of her qualifications.

Mina McCoy's presence had filled the restaurant with a spirit he found intriguing and a concern for his daughter that he could only admire—two very becoming qualities that lured his mind away from the duties at hand and made him acutely aware of her as a woman. The sight of rambunctious little Violet nestled deeply in her lap, the smile of peace written across that cherubic face, had sealed the bargain in his heart, much less his mind. He marveled that his daughter had so easily come to trust the woman, since she gave few people that honor. Despite his interest in his new employee, he felt a twinge of something he could only define as envy. He doubted that Violet trusted him so openly.

And why should she? He'd been caught up passing off his own grief as a need to make her a living and give her everything he could. But he hadn't given her the one thing she wanted most. The one thing she needed. Unstipulated love.

Oh sure, he'd made a good show of doing his duty. But the love he'd offered her always became a bargain between them—a quick fix to any time-consuming situation that arose. You do this, Violet, and I'll do that. Yet, *real* love had been buried along with Katie Rose. Love offered without expecting something back. Love given without consideration of one's own needs. Love offered without restraint. Miss McCoy was right. He had neglected Violet for far too long.

Briar bolted to his feet, needing a breath of fresh air. He threw on a shirt and boots then hurried outside, not taking the time to grab the rest of his uniform. Lantern light down the tracks reminded him that the porter was out checking the roundhouse and making sure the Eclipse was in good working condition for tomorrow. Though the windmill that pulled water to fill the steam locomotives had survived hundreds of windstorms, it was a contrary contraption at best, needing careful maintenance and plenty of patience. Nathaniel seemed the only man who could square off with the twenty-two-foot mechanical rogue and win.

Its wooden blades had taken on speed since Briar went to bed, indicating a good wind was gusting in from the southwest. The breeze would cool the yards and help the cattle

She started back toward the house. Briar hurried to fall into step beside her, afraid she would go in, yet praying that she would so that this hunger growing within him would not reveal itself. He would surely frighten her. It sure as sin scared the hell out of him. "You've been crying." He reached out to touch her. "Let me help."

Briar didn't know what to offer, what more to say. She suddenly buried her face in his chest, anchoring her arms around his shoulders, holding on as if he were a lifeline.

"Just hold me," she whispered, molding against him.

Briar's body hardened as if bracing for the blast of a furnace. Her touch stirred sensations in him that were almost too overwhelming to contain. His knees threatened to buckle. "I need to take you inside."

"Aye," she breathed.

One hand locked beneath her arm, while the other lifted her into his embrace. Her breath fanned his neck with its ebb and flow while the scent of something floral drifted from her hair. She'd obviously borrowed some of Violet's lavender soap. The image of her bathing in their tub coursed blood to every part of him.

Sanity intruded, reminding him that he'd known her less than a day and he wasn't the kind of man who took advantage of a woman's vulnerability. Thankfully, she had left the door ajar. He nudged it open, searched the dark for one of the kitchen chairs, then sat. Mina continued to cry softly against him, her tears feeling like dew upon his chest.

Finally, she stopped and unlinked her arms from around his neck. Her body jutted backward as she silently insisted upon standing. He gently released her. "Care to tell me what this is all about?"

She stared at her bare feet, then back up at him in that disconcerting way she had of looking at him. "'Tis cry I do, when happiness fills me."

"Happiness?" If he lived to be a hundred years old, he'd never understand women. "You were crying because you're happy?"

She nodded and twirled around, opening her palms. "I have a job, a wee lass to take care of, and now *this*. A roof . . . walls . . . a home . . . if only for a while. A home has got to be the best place on earth, wouldn't ye agree?"

"Are you homeless, Miss McCoy?" Briar finally asked the one question he'd not quite found the nerve to bring up in their earlier conversations.

"*Mina*," she reminded. "Aye, that I am, sir. Does that make a difference to ye now? I would think ye'd expect anyone who hired on in such a capacity to be unattached to a dwelling."

"It makes no difference to me, Mina," he assured her, though his mind was now made up about something else. He would not spend any more time looking for her a room. She would live in his home until Nathaniel returned.

Nathaniel had telegraphed that he would be home tomorrow, but he often didn't keep his word. And for the first time in months, he hoped Nathaniel didn't hurry back.

Chapter 6

The scent of fresh, clean linen and the sound of a soft sigh woke Mina. The feel of the strong arms in her dream drifted away as if it were smoke carried on the wind. She wanted to chase after it, catch it, hold it to her as she did the keepsakes she often found along the roadway, but sleep spirited the treasure away into the saffron glow of dawn.

The reality of a tinier, softer body nestling against Mina quelled the disturbing thoughts of just whose arms she'd been dreaming. She would leave that mulling for later, when she was alone.

'Tis not alone I am. The words sank in, filling her with a joy that warmed the tips of her toes and stretched her lips into a grin. She had slept in a comfortable bed, in a real home, and with no concern whatsoever to danger. Best of all, there was someone to wake up to. There could be no finer morning than this.

Sometime during the night Violet had climbed under the covers alongside her. The sigh that Mina had thought was her own came from the child curled against her. She gently pressed a kiss atop the tiny head.

"Am I awake, angel?" whispered Violet.

"Not quite, lass." Mina raised the lass's chin to study her

face. That poor little eye barely peeped open amid its circular bruise. "But ye're working on it, 'tis certain."

"I just might have some trouble doing it right this morning." Violet snuggled deeper into the covers.

"And I think ye will not." Mina threw back the quilt and tickled the child until Violet erupted into a fit of giggles. "Because I plan to help ye wake up. We have things to do, people to meet, and places to go. What do ye say to getting dressed and having some breakfast?"

"I can help cook. Daddy lets me sometimes." Violet unfurled and stood. "I'm pretty good at biscuits."

"I just bet ye are." Images of the possible volatile combination of Violet, lard, and flour propelled Mina to stand, though she wished nothing more than to linger in the comfort of the bed. She needed to dress and arrive in the kitchen way ahead of little Miss Helper. "Do ye know what ye want to wear to church," she urged, "or am I to make the choice for ye?"

"You mean you're gonna let me choose?" Excitement filled Violet's tone as she rushed from the room.

"Ye're the one wearing the clothes, are ye not?" After all, her father had allowed her to dress herself for bed. Mina followed to make sure Violet did not venture toward the kitchen first.

"I sure am. I knew an angel would understand." Violet disappeared into her bedroom and shut the door.

The child was up to something. Mina needed no celestial wisdom to understand that much.

An hour and a half later, she was wishing for some heavenly intervention. But, of its own volition, her head kept turning to view Briar sitting beside her in the pew. Light shining through the stained glass windows made her aware of how he filled the church with his presence. The pews were packed, causing everyone to squeeze in closer to allow for the influx of visitors. His shoulders and thighs touched hers, making it difficult for Mina to concentrate, much less listen to the sermon. He seemed to sense the exact moments she could not resist the impulse to look at him, his eyes mesmerizing her with their intensity as they turned to share those glances with her.

Allowing Violet to choose her own church clothes was the first transgression she'd made this morning. But now it seemed she'd made yet another. A congregant with a broach-studded hat kept openly glaring at Mina. She most likely would not have noticed the woman's glare, but the lady had no eyebrows. Had they been burned off and never grown back? Twin broaches amid a spray of silk chiffon garnished the hat's brim, looking like pearl-studded substitutes for the missing brows.

Mina wondered if she had committed some unknown sin that would cause the woman to want to exorcise her from the sanctuary.

Mina didn't plan on staying in Amarillo long enough to let anyone, much less High-Brow, intimidate her, for whatever reason. So when the woman thrust her double chins upward and looked disapprovingly at Mina again, Mina just smiled in return. It was far from the first time she'd been looked upon with disapproval. It certainly wouldn't be the last time. Wonder what would happen if she informed everyone that the woman had obviously used some of that new French Harmless Hair Wave to curl and color her hair? The price paid for such a bougainvillea-colored nest of curls would feed an overcrowded orphanage for six months or more. Could anything she have committed be worse than spending more than a thousand dollars on a permanent wave? High-Brow best loosen her curls a wee bit, if she knew what was good for her.

Finally, the service ended. With relief Mina stood, glad to put distance between herself and Briar. Waking up in his room and knowing he usually slept in the bed she'd found so appealing had been difficult enough to forget. Remembering how it felt in his arms last night and touching his thigh during the service had only kindled the fire of attraction that skittered along her senses like she was taking on a second skin. Mina gently reached for Violet's hand, but the lass pulled away instantly and tugged on her father's pant leg.

"Daddy, can we go now, please? I really need to go. Now."

"Hold your britches, pumpkin," he announced then shot Mina a stern expression. "Seems kind of appropriate, doesn't it, Miss McCoy?"

Mina shrugged, glad she'd chosen to wear her riding skirt rather than *her* trousers. "'Tis sorry I am, if I may say it again. She wanted to dress herself and ye let her do so for bed. I saw no wrong in allowing Violet to do the same a second time."

Briar took his daughter's hand. "I can't blame you too much, I suppose, when it's my own fault that I indulge her. If it hadn't taken so long waiting for the surrey, I could have picked you up sooner and given her time to change."

"The britches will go back in the drawer . . . unless ye say they can come out again. True, lass?"

"Okay," she said too agreeably, "but can we go *now*?"

"We will after Mina has a chance to meet some of our friends." Briar watched the other children gathering with the McCord family. All of the children appeared more jubilant than usual. "Today is the hayride out to the breaks, isn't it?" His brow furrowed. "I didn't remember that when I made plans for us this morning."

"Can I go, Daddy, please? You said I could last week and everybody's going."

She rattled off some of the ragtime language Mina had heard back East, and one of the boys answered back. Mina shook her finger at the pair of them. "Ye'll be wanting to make sure none of them tadpoles swim in the punch, me precious darlings, or ye'll be too sore to sit yer bottoms to a pew next Sunday."

Briar glanced from his daughter to Mina. "You know what they're saying?"

"'Tis jive or rag talk and little else. Have ye no ear for it here in Texas?"

"Apparently some of us Texans do." Briar frowned at his daughter. "What's this about tadpoles in the punch?"

"It wasn't gonna be me, Daddy, I promise. I knew about it, but I wasn't gonna do it this time."

"Have you considered it before? No, don't answer that. I don't really want to know." He shot Mina a look of gratitude. "It's a good thing you know jive or jag or rag or whatever it is she called it."

"I know seven other languages as well, and a few twists of the English version, I assure ye."

Surprise etched Briar's expression. "You'll have to tell me how you came about developing that talent, Miss McCoy, but for now I guess I better decide whether or not I'm going to let her go with the others. What do you think?"

She couldn't deny the lass a chance to be with other children and have fun, even if it meant putting off time spent between Violet and her father. "I say a hayride might be just the thing to practice her social skills."

"Well, her clothes fit the purpose, don't they? Can't say the choice had anything to do with remembering the hayride, though, can we?"

"No, sir," Violet admitted. "But I promise I'll wear a dress next time."

He ruffled his daughter's hair. "All right, you can go, but only if you follow the McCords's instructions to the letter and stay in eyesight of an adult. Remember what almost happened yesterday with that car. And I better not hear you gave anyone—boy, girl, or adult—any trouble."

"I'll be careful, I promise."

"Am I to go along with her?" Mina started to nudge past him.

"No, there will be plenty of chaperones. They've had this planned for weeks. So it seems you've been given a reprieve. Maybe there's something you would like to do, some place you'd like to visit in town while you have some time to yourself?"

His gaze averted to those leaving the sanctuary and she wondered if he wanted to go with his daughter and felt an obligation to entertain her as his guest. Well she wasn't his guest. She was his employee. "I can find something to do on my own."

"That won't be necessary, unless you just prefer being alone."

Alone was the last thing she wanted to be again. She'd had enough of "alone" for a lifetime. "What will ye do until she returns?" Mina asked, not wanting him to see how much his company had already come to mean to her.

"I usually take part of Sunday morning off so we can go to church, but today I asked Sam—you'll get to know him soon—to stay a little longer than usual so I could show you some of the town. I've got the rig until noon if you'd like me to take you somewhere particular."

Before she could answer, the woman with the pearl-studded brows and double chins waddled up beside him. "Good morning, Mr. Duncan. I assume this is Violet's new governess. I'd like to talk to you about what your daughter did yesterday."

"Gotta go. See ya." Violet rushed to join the others.

So, 'twas the lass and not meself ye were oogling all sermon, Mina decided once she heard the reprimand in the woman's tone. Mina glanced at Violet who now blatantly peeped from behind one of the pews to see what transpired between the congregant and her father. Innocence did not play well upon the child's features this morning.

Nonetheless, whatever the blessed lass had done to irk the woman, it served her no purpose to attack Violet full brow. *Best loosen those clips, High-Brow*, Mina warned silently as she abruptly faced the woman once again, *or those pearl studs will be plowing new paths in those wavy, red roots*. "Aye, that I am her new governess, madam. And I can assure ye Violet will be no trouble to ye again. She has asked that I express her sincerest apology for yesterday and begs ye to understand that she must be on her way with the others and canna tell ye herself."

"May I offer my own personal apologies, Mrs. Humphrey," Briar joined in. "And, of course, I will be glad to repay any damage you might have incurred because of my daughter's antics."

Mina glared at the woman, daring her to demand anything more from Briar than an apology. It may have been his fault Violet got away with whatever she did, but Violet needed to be the one to make amends or she'd never learn where to draw the line between prank and harm.

High-Brow must have thought she could exact any price from Duncan. She seemed to grow uneasy in Mina's presence, pressing a laced handkerchief to her forehead, daubing away a bead of perspiration that had a pinkish tint in its dew.

"Just see to it that she has appropriate guidance from now on and that will be repayment enough." She nodded at Mina. "We do hope you'll stay a long time with our community, Miss—? I don't believe I caught your name."

Mina swapped names with her.

"Do stay as long as you can, Miss McCoy. I'm sure Violet will benefit greatly from your teachings."

"My intention completely, mum."

Mavis Harper Humphrey was just the first of many names Mina learned in the ensuing bevy of introductions. By the time the sanctuary was empty, she had met so many people she thought she would never get their names straight. Still, none of them were the right name or the treasured face that she searched for any time she met someone's gaze.

The headmistress at the Lady's School where she had worked called her frank study of faces unladylike. Arrogant. Mina had said it was nothing more than curiosity and the need to search for resemblance to her own features. No woman here looked anything like Mina. No chance that any of them were her mother. After a while, she had grown tired of the disappointment and waited quietly for Briar to finish his discussion with the minister.

"You seem lost in thought." A voice stirred her from her reverie. Briar grabbed his hat from the rack where others were stored during services.

"I was thinking about where I would like to be taken," she fibbed. *To me mother*, she wished, then decided she might yet be speaking the truth if circumstances proved such. "To the graveyard, if ye have time."

"The graveyard?" Briar busied himself with walking her down the steps and getting her settled into the surrey. He commanded the horse into action and they were long past town before he spoke again. "Do you mean Boot Hill at Tascosa or the one closer to Amarillo?"

"Both, if time allows."

"We'll do Boot Hill another day." His tone was sharp. "It's several miles out."

"I can go on me day off. Ye do not have to take me today." He seemed so distant now, though he was sitting only inches away. Was the closeness she felt toward him last night, when he'd held her in his arms, a figment of her imagination or some magic conjured by the night? "Ye seem angry. Have I offended ye in some way?"

"Why would you think that?"

She stared at the robin-egg sky overhead with its lack of clouds. "Perhaps 'tis yer frowning face and angry tone that gave me the clue."

Briar looked at her like she'd lost her senses then suddenly burst out laughing. "Are you always so direct?"

"I try to be. It gets things said quicker."

"Why do you feel the need to say things quickly?" His eyes searched hers for understanding.

"It comes from moving around a lot, I suppose."

"You've lived a lot of places? Had a lot of adventures, have you?"

She heard the longing in his voice. The boredom. "'Tis one

thing I learned in me many travels, Briar. Places are not the adventures to be enjoyed. *People* are. Ye should enjoy what time ye have with yer wee one. She'll grow up and leave ye long before ye'll be wanting her to."

"That I know all too well, I'm afraid."

The spark that had shone in his eyes a moment before now faded with his smile. He was remembering his wife's passing and she had been the fool to remind him. "I seem to be saying 'tis sorry I am quite often this morning. First, for allowing Violet to wear the trousers. Now asking ye to take me to the graveyard. 'Tis where yer wife is buried, is it not?"

He nodded. "You've no need to be sorry. I'm the one who should apologize for my bad temper. I just can't seem to bring myself to visit Katie Rose's grave."

"Not since her passing?"

"Not once. I have the minister put flowers on her grave for me, but I can't. It would be admitting . . . I just can't."

"Had something come between ye?"

"Nothing like that. We loved each other as much as the day we agreed to marry."

"Then let me go with ye this first time," Mina encouraged as she threaded her arm through his to offer support, "so ye willna be alone." She knew how it felt to be alone. She was a master at being alone.

"No, and I don't want you ever taking Violet to it either." He flicked the reins to speed their journey. "You couldn't possibly understand."

"I do more than ye think, Briar." And she did. Mina decided to share the reason she visited cemeteries so that he would realize she knew sorrow as intense as his own. "I search every graveyard in every town I visit. Ye see . . ." She had never said it aloud before. Never shared the truth with anyone till now. "I study the names on the tombstones for the one name I need most to read—my mother's."

He seemed even more driven than before, his grasp on the leather straps fiercer than before. Mina placed a hand upon the reins to restrain the anger that drove them. "Stop running from it, Briar. Stop running from yer future. Some day ye'll have to look at yer own Katie Rose's tombstone and know that yer time with her is past. At least ye have her memory. At least ye know she never abandoned ye. She died, Briar. Maybe not of her own choosing, but she's gone. Ye just doona want to tell her good-bye."

The gallop slowed to a canter, and it was only then that Mina realized that her breath had been racing too. Racing to make him understand, to make him stop denying the truth, to make him start living again for himself, for Violet, and . . . somewhere deep in her heart . . . she heard a whisper that said his acceptance would affect her own future as well.

They sat in silence until he pulled up rein at the cemetery. When Briar put his hands on her waist to help her from the surrey, he quickly set her down and acted as if he'd touched something most foul.

Despite understanding his grief, she couldn't help feeling hurt by his brusqueness. "Forgive me if I ask too much, Briar. I only mean to help."

"Go do what you must, but don't ask me to participate. I find no comfort in seeing the dead's name written in stone."

She swung around in fury. "And ye've a cold heart, Briar Duncan, if ye think I enjoy looking for me mother's name among the dearly departed." Despite her best effort, tears brimmed in Mina's eyes when the depth of her lifelong anguish took voice. "'Tis easier to believe me mother died than that she actually abandoned me. Look for her I will, till I know the stone-hard fact, for sure and certain. At least ye had a past to put to rest so ye can go on."

Chapter 7

Later that afternoon, Briar watched Mina's fingers tap out the reply to General Pershing's previous telegram and had to admire the dexterity of her movements.

"Ye're being too wordy." She frowned at the note he'd scribbled down to answer the commander's questions about what news there had been concerning the Villistas in the area. "Whyna condense it by shortening these two lines. Ye're saying the same thing twice."

He nodded his approval. "You're good at editing. Go ahead and make any other changes you think necessary. I'll get us some coffee."

The battered pot heated on the stove. It kept passengers warm who waited in the lobby. The lobby was empty at the moment, the westbound long gone and the northbound not due in for at least a couple of hours. As Briar filled two cups with the steaming brew, his mind focused on the woman who'd filled his every thought since he'd met her. She seemed adept at the telegraph and knew when to offer suggestions without altering his intent. Mina was not an easy woman to read, but he'd found her fascinating. She seemed hard as a pine nut in her directness, yet vulnerable as a kitten that had been abandoned by its mother. The moment he made the comparison, Briar's gut wrenched. She was no kitten, but a flesh-and-blood woman who had been abandoned at an early age and, apparently, by a mother too little known to describe further.

Since their ride from the cemetery, Mina insisted upon talking about Violet's right to know more concerning Katie Rose—a subject that he preferred to cast off as quickly as it intruded upon his thoughts. Though he defended himself by telling Mina that he intended to wait until Violet was old enough to understand more, the truth was that it hurt too much to talk of his wife's passing. But Mina would have none of it.

The woman made him think more in twenty-four hours than he had in several years. Made him question some of his choices when he had not allowed anyone else even to broach the subject. Hell, Mina McCoy had made him *feel* like he never felt before. And that was the most startling aspect of all. It was as if she could see beyond the granite wall of reserve he'd built around his heart and decided to slam a maul against his suffering and make him acknowledge the pain, instead of chipping away at it a little at a time. Quick and constantly challenging. That's how she'd entered his life and that's how she kept his thoughts stirred.

He didn't need a suffragette to tell him he should make changes if he was ever to find contentment with his life again. He didn't need to hang on to her every word about places she'd been and things she'd done to know that he was a poor example of how to get on with one's life after an emotional storm. But what he admired, and discovered he craved, was the honesty she'd brought with her. He'd lived the lie of his life for nearly four years now, denying that Katie Rose was gone forever and that he must make a life for him and Violet without her. From the moment he met Mina, she'd sensed the lie and that same openness that radiated from her as if it were a fragrance somehow washed over him like a cleansing tide.

He may have met her questions with stone silence, but Mina's concern had awakened the roaring discomfort of his choices.

"Thanks." She took one of the mugs from his hand and sipped. "I canna remember the last time I had coffee."

"It's one of the few things I cook well. We drink a lot of it around here."

"I favor berry juice or jasmine tea, meself. Coffee will keep ye up nights."

Briar took a seat on the cot he'd moved back into the office for the day, glad that their earlier anger with each other was subsiding. "I tend to work a lot of nights, so it keeps me going."

Mina leaned closer, the honey of her eyes warming. "I can see I have a few things to teach Violet's father as well."

The look was blatantly suggestive. Provocatively inviting. He'd felt the attraction between them from the start. Wanted to give in to it when he'd held her in his arms last night in the yard. Prayed for the strength not to wrap his arms around her in church when she'd sat pressed against him. The time had come to see if what she'd stirred within him was one-sided or if she felt any attraction toward him as well. He didn't want to make a fool of himself when she might only be trying to help Violet by aiding Violet's father. Yet, the prospect of experiencing something sensual, something close, with Mina had its allure. He was rusty at flirting, wasn't even sure he had ever been adept at it. "And what would you teach me, Miss McCoy?"

She reached out, took the cup of coffee from his hands, and set it down. "First of all, I would have ye learn the value of a good vegetarian diet and healthy beverages."

Had he mistook her meaning? Was he so enamored with her that he wanted to read more into their relationship than actually was there? Briar frowned, trying to douse the fire of want that flamed any time she drew near. He needed some sort of distraction. Anything to cool his thoughts. *A joke. Say something funny. She appreciates a quick wit.* "A vegetarian diet, in the *cattle* capital of the country, and this from the woman who wolfed down a side of roast beef last night?"

She giggled, her eyes lit with challenge. "A sassy tongue ye have on ye, Briar Duncan, and I have a taste for *many* things."

God in heaven, help him! Taste and tongue. Words that sent seductive images coursing from his mind to ignite all points less rationally motivated. Her hair curled so wild and free around her cheeks, he could do nothing but reach out to caress one blond silken strand. The air between them grew thick and electric, as expectant as right before a thunderstorm. The world around Briar faded as if nothing but he and she existed, and time ceased to move. Briar could barely form the words as his heart pounded in his throat, his voice deep and low, "I want only one thing right now, and that's a taste of *you*."

Push me away, he pleaded, but her eyes softly shut and Mina leaned closer. He pulled her to him and covered her lips with his. Her mouth opened invitingly as her arms went around him, pressing her length against his. He needed no further encouragement and his tongue slid lazily between her lips to taste deeply of her. A low moan dissolved against his mouth, the kiss becoming ravenous, rough and wanton. Their rapid breaths soughed together as the attraction that had consumed him heated into exquisite pleasure.

"Open yer eyes," she whispered against his lips. "I want ye to know who this is ye're kissing."

Briar's eyes sprang open in direct challenge, the moment threatening to subside into the reality of the woman in his arms being a stranger only yesterday. Her slow lazy smile held no hint of reprimand but something more of an askance, a need to be desired; she *wanted* to be kissed for herself and not as a stand-in for Katie. "God help me"—he flicked her earlobe with his tongue, pressing hot, urgent kisses against her neck— "why did you let me kiss you?"

"Because I damned well wanted to be kissed, and by ye."

Her throaty groan vibrated against his lips, sending them urgently to reclaim the treasure she offered. He combed his fingers through her hair, loving the way it felt silky and smooth as it slid between them. Drifting over her shoulders, his fingers caressed the vee of ribs that slimmed to a sensual swell of hips. He gently slid one hand beneath her tunic to palm a warm, soft globe that peaked exquisitely against the thin material that felt like nothing more than butterfly wings. Her groan became a soft gasp of yearning, a sound so feminine he wanted only to tame, yet protect it in the same instant.

"W-What's this?" he wondered aloud at the sound of a loud rip that startled him from his revelry. She was not wearing a corset but some strange contraption to cover her breasts, now rendered beyond repair by the impulsiveness of his passion. He raised the triangular patches of cotton netting and the ribbon that held them together. "I've torn your undergarment."

What should I call it? Briar wondered, never having seen anything like it in the fashion catalogs.

"I can always find a new one." She shook her head, as if unable to regain her focus.

"*Buy* a new one, you mean." Briar took a deep breath, attempting to recover his own good sense. No, she meant *find*. She continuously collected things anyone else might have discarded. She'd been in the office one morning and already there were five new items he'd seen her pick up and place on the desk. Had she picked him up too, like a foundling who was broken and need of repair?

He stepped away from her, more to put distance between himself and his need to touch her again than for his embarrassment over damaging her finery. "I apologize, Ms. McCoy. I don't quite know what came over me."

"*I* came over ye, just as ye came over me. Plain and simple. Not the kiss, by any means"—her fists ended as balls against the lovely hips he'd admired with his hands only moments before—"at least as far as I am concerned. 'Twas one bally-hoo of a brassiere buster, in me way of thinking."

"I take it that this is a brassiere?" He held up the contraption. Despite the awkwardness of the moment and stab at his pride, Briar began to laugh. His pent-up passion needed release and the laughter allowed him to rid himself of the tension. "I've heard of them but never seen one before."

She nodded. "A homemade one, but it serves the purpose." She took it from him and laid it on the cot. "I should say *served* its purpose. I'll be for finding something else to string it together again."

Coffee. I need coffee, Briar decided, his throat now parched for anything to quell the taste of Mina. *Hell, I need a beer*. Briar searched for something to do with his hands to stave off the feel of her. Of all times for the telegraph to lay silent. What he wouldn't give to hear a ten-liner humming the wires. "Here, better drink your coffee before it gets cold," he suggested, handing her a cup and taking his own. "No telling when the messages will start up again, and Violet ought to be in soon. She'll be full of stories, I'm sure."

Challenge radiated from the golden eyes that seemed to reach straight down into him and twist his gut.

"So we're gonna pretend we didn't kiss, are we?" When he took too long to mull exactly how to answer her, her chin lifted indignantly. "I would like to know if ye're gonna be glad or sad that we did it."

"Really, Miss McCoy, you continue to amaze me." Briar stared at her over the rim of his cup. "Why is it so important that you know how I feel about it?" Yet, he could see that it did matter to her . . . greatly.

"To see if ye liked it well enough to do it again."

Do it again? Briar bolted to his feet and put distance between himself and the temptation she presented. Blazes, that's all he could think of was doing it again, and again, and again. But he wasn't sure how to handle a woman who wanted in such equal measure. Katie was . . . well, Katie just wasn't so hot a burn. "I'm supposed to be the one who . . . The man's suppose to—"

"What? Take the lead?" Her hands flung out to encompass the world about her. "I've no time for it. If ye canna tell that what we just shared was something God-golden-glorious, then 'tis my sworn duty to help ye find yer wits."

Briar didn't know if he liked her blatant, in-your-face sexuality. *Hell, admit it man, you like it too much.* "We think a little differently, you and I."

"'Tis rightly so, and 'tis different ye've been wanting. I'm just the change of flavor ye've been hungry for and yer kiss told ye so. Deny it, if ye like, but the truth is the truth."

Briar's eyes met hers. His lips still tasted like hers; the fire of her seduction still simmered in his veins. He may have made a mistake in kissing her, but he would never deny that he was forever changed by it. "I wanted the kiss. Wanted *you*. But I can't give you what I don't have to offer."

"And what is it that ye canna offer me? That ye've no ability to give?"

"A heart that can love again," he answered with more truth than any she'd demanded of him.

Till now.

Chapter 8

The afternoon had been hectic, leaving Mina little time to think about what had transpired between her and Briar. Incoming and outgoing telegrams were so frequent that she'd barely had enough time to settle Violet in for her nap. But the lass must have enjoyed the hayride. She was asleep almost as quickly as her head lay on the cot. Small wonder Briar had been swamped with all his duties, if today's activities were any indication.

The moment she thought of him, it was almost as if she could smell the wonderful essence that surrounded her any time Briar was near. A clean, musky, masculine scent that forced her attention away from the machine to see if her imagination had willed him closer.

"You okay?"

Mina wondered how long he'd been standing in the doorway watching her and hoped it had been for a while. That might mean he enjoyed what he saw and, after the kiss they shared and his certainty that she could not persuade his heart to soften, she was determined to make him enjoy being with her. She deliberately stretched her arms and yawned, hoping to define her femininity to its finest. "Tired. But 'tis a good tired I am. Got a lot done."

His gaze traced her movement, lingering at her breasts then widening as it raised and locked with her own. A grin suddenly lifted his lips as a look of acknowledgment warmed his eyes. Mina smiled back.

For a moment, she savored his grin for all it promised.

For a moment, she let him see that she was making a promise of her own.

And for a moment, she hoped that both promises might lead him to love again, if he would allow himself the chance.

"Was the imp hard to settle in for her nap?"

Mina allowed him a better view of the child that rested behind her. "No trouble at all for an even bigger imp to handle."

"You may be just what we . . . *she* needed." He moved past Mina and bent down beside Violet. "I haven't seen her rest this well in a long time," he whispered.

"I promised her if she took a long nap, I would take her on a treasure hunt after I finished my work."

"A treasure hunt?"

Violet's well eye opened. "Yeah, Daddy, and I slept real good. You gonna let her stop now? She worked real hard."

Both adults laughed.

"Tell you what I'll do. I've got about another hour of cleaning the roundhouse. That'll see the six-fifteen come and gone. I don't think Sam will mind taking the reins forty-five minutes early. He's wanting some extra hours with his oldest's birthday coming up."

Briar stood and glanced around the office. "This place hasn't looked so good since we opened it." He picked up an old boot standing on the corner of her desk. Indian paintbrush, blue flax, and yucca stalks filled the tanned leather in a colorful bouquet of red, white, and yellow. "You've added a decoration or two."

"I brung her the flowers from out at the breaks, Daddy." Violet got up and lifted the boot so her father could have a better look. "Old Joe decided to have his annual foot washing in the creek and threw away his old boots. I couldn't lift but one of 'em, so I put the flowers in it to make it smell better. Angel said it was the best thing she ever got."

She picked up what was left of the brassiere Briar had ripped off Mina. "I seen her picking stuff up like this off the ground, so I figured she'd like Old Joe's boot since he didn't want it no more."

"Ye figured right," Mina complimented, quickly taking the bra from her hands and stuffing it in a pocket. "And it is the nicest present anyone ever gave me. If not the most odoriferous."

"The most odorous?" Panic seemed to etch Violet's expression. "Can you still use it when the flowers go away?"

Mina's heart lurched. What was the child really asking her? Was she hearing something in Violet's tone that wasn't there? Was she being too sensitive? She couldn't take the chance of saying the wrong thing. After all, she'd been seven once and left behind. What would she have understood at that age? What had she needed to hear?

"I never throw anything away, lass." She fingered one of the blue petals. "If I canna keep it, for whatever reason, I fix it and give it to someone who will love it more than me. And the word is odoriferous."

Violet returned the boot to its place. "Good. 'Cause them flowers got mean stickers, and it was hard picking 'em."

The wire started humming, signaling an incoming message. Glad for the interruption, Mina turned her attention to duties and let the Duncans visit while she took the message. She needed time to quiet the memory Violet's question had evoked in her own past. Yet the more she heard of the message, the less she wanted to decipher it.

"Mina?" Briar put a hand on her shoulder. "You look pale."

"Do I?" She tried not to lay her cheek upon the back of his hand. *Doona go*, her mind screamed. "I must need some air," she whispered. "Will ye take over for a minute? 'Tis quick I'll be."

"Take your time. The roundhouse can wait."

It was all she could do not to run outside. Mina forced herself to walk as if she had no concern for anything but a breath of fresh air. Once outside, she took long strides away from the depot so that no one would stop her and ask questions. She needed time alone. Time to get hold of herself.

She chose a path alongside the roadbed, allowing it to lead her away from the hustle and bustle of the busy station. Once she felt no one could see her, she searched the ground for a rock, found one, and threw it as hard as she could against the iron rail. It shattered into tiny pieces, mirroring the way she felt at the moment.

"Why is it that Ye want me alone?" she yelled at the blue sky above, her voice taking on volume as rage erupted from her. "I did what I should have. I proved I could take care of meself. All by meself, I grew to a woman, fine and true to Yer good ways. And with no help from either father or mother." Her calls were full of breath and bluster. "I learned to wait."

She pointed at the roadbed that led to the station. "And now, just when I found someone who doesna fear me shadows and makes me light up like the dawn, Ye're gonna send him a fine message such as that! Take him from me like Ye have everyone else Ye ever put in me life? Take him from what's best for *her,* too?"

If Briar was this busy in Amarillo, no telling what would happen to Violet if he carted her off to who-knew-where. Mina picked up one of the pieces of the rock and crumbled the rest of it between her fingers, letting the wind carry it away. "Ye're gonna lead him off to somewhere in Texas or Mexico where he'll find her too much of a distraction. Where he'll not need or want me?"

The tears came now, unbidden, hot, cruel. "Am I such a tribulation, Lord? Why does no one want me?"

Two strong arms wrapped around her, pulling her back into a familiar embrace. Her eyes closed as she breathed in the essence of Briar and the haven he offered her. The sanctuary she needed.

"Don't cry, Mina."

"Ye heard?" She prayed he hadn't. She wondered if he understood.

"I knew something was wrong. I couldn't let you go without finding out. I left Violet with the wire. She's probably contacted Japan by now."

Mina laughed, grateful for a way to stop the flow of tears. Awed that he had cared enough to follow. She faced him, finding comfort in the fact that he continued to hold her. "I promise you I'm worth wanting, Briar." Her eyes met his. "And I'm willing to wait however long it takes for ye to want me in return."

"I'm not going to accept Pershing's offer, Mina. Raising Violet right is my true adventure now. It has been all along and I just was too blind to see it. I have you to thank for that. And just so you know"—his breath mingled with her own as his lips lowered to hers—"wanting you has never been in question."

She held nothing back. The first kiss they'd shared had been one to tempt him. This one meant to seal their fate so that nothing would ever keep their hearts apart. Shadows that had been so long a part of Mina suddenly vanished with the promise of a radiant dawn. The abandonment that had cloaked every fearful night of her life was now vanquished in the heated wake of belonging somewhere and to someone. The earth seemed to rock beneath her feet, as if the roots of their future had buried themselves deep within the soil.

When the kiss ended he took a step backward, looking dazed. "I vowed to love Katie forever, Mina. I just don't know if I can make such a promise again."

It wasn't what she wanted to hear, but she'd learned to be patient. To wait on life to lead her in a better direction. She knew now, beyond a shadow of any fear, that Briar was the pot at the end of her rainbow.

Forever meant different things to people, but the one thing true for everyone was that forever could always be exchanged with *now*.

Chapter 9

"Where did you find that?" Briar took the sack of flour from Mina's hand. They had been walking the streets between his house and the restaurant for an hour. The stores were closed so she couldn't have got it from the mercantile.

"Someone must have dropped it off one of their wagons when they headed home. I put a notice up at the filling station in case the owner asked about it." Mina dusted off her skirt where some of the flour had obviously leaked out of the bag. "I'll make a blueberry patch of pies if no one claims it. The preacher will be glad of it when I share the pies with his flock next Sunday."

"And look what else we found, Daddy." Violet opened the pouch Mina had given her to carry whatever treasures she found. She pulled out a cob pipe that had lost its stem, a rolled up newspaper, a silk ribbon, a piece of leather, and a tassel that could have easily been taken from the surrey he'd driven earlier.

"Looks like you found a bunch." He examined each of her prizes carefully. "Decided what you're going to do with them?"

"Angel said she'd fix 'em for me. I'm gonna give them to my friends. Angel said treasures should never be thrown away. You can always fix them up and give them a new home."

"That's mighty nice of you. I'll bet your friends would enjoy them."

"Except this ol' newspaper. Jim Corbett said he's seen enough newspaper at his grandpa's house to last him till the earth runs out of ink."

"I would like to keep it, if ye doona mind." Mina waited until Violet handed her the newsprint then uncurled it. "It says here that rainmaker, Charles Hatfield, predicted heavy rains in San Diego, California, in January and, saints and begorra, if it didna come a downpour." She held the headline up for Briar to see. "Maybe ye need to send the man a telegram and invite him to the panhandle."

"Oh yeah," Briar scoffed, "I'll just bet every family who's experienced the boom and bust of their wheat crop will go for that idea. I'd be laughed off the high plains."

Mina gently hit Briar with the paper. "Ye have any better idea how to call down the rain?"

"Maybe talk some of Quanah's kin into dancing for us. It always worked for them."

"Is his tribe still around? Nathaniel said the area was safe."

"The last battle was out in the canyon a few miles from here."

"Rainmaker or rain dance"—Mina did an Irish jig—"whatever will get the message to heaven quicker, I'm thinking."

Violet quickly returned her discoveries to the pouch and tugged on Mina's skirt. "Will you fix my kite for me?"

"Sure, but I thought ye didna want to play with it anymore."

"I got me a real important message to send."

Briar escorted them home and made supper while Mina and Violet worked on the kite at the kitchen table. He enjoyed watching her instruct his daughter, listened closely as she answered Violet's questions and guided every helpful hand the child offered. She did not criticize the misspelling of the message, but rather applauded Violet's diligent effort. Mina knew how to work with children. She would be a good mother.

The thought led his mind too easily to the kisses they'd shared this afternoon and the feel of her in his arms. He tried to will the same image of Katie, but it dimmed in comparison to what he'd shared with Mina.

"Are you two about finished?" he asked, almost too brusquely, aware that he was angry at Mina for his betrayal of Katie's memory. "I need to set the table soon."

"All done," Mina announced, handing the kite to Violet. "Go put that in yer room on top of your footrest and I'll help yer da with the plates. Be sure to slant it sideways as you go through the doors."

"You've got her believing she can call down the rain with that. Don't you think you're being a little foolish?" Briar stirred the gravy before it bubbled over. He took a bowl down from the cabinet to use once the gravy cooled.

"Is it a fool's wish to hope? Better to use yer imagination and try, than to sit back and do nothing."

Criticism echoed in Mina's tone, stirring his anger further. He couldn't let her innuendo go unchallenged. "Say what you mean, Mina. You've always been frank before."

"Okay, then I will. Ye say ye want me, but ye do nothing about it. Ye say ye canna love again, but yer lips tell me differently. Why are ye content in withdrawing from the fact that death has parted ye from Katie Rose and ye must find a way to live without her? Ye've lost yer way, Briar, and ye just need to find yer way back. I hope 'tis me who leads ye there, but if someone else is in the plan, then so be it. But ye must trust yer heart again, man, if ye want a better life than the one ye've now chosen for the two of ye. And I say chosen, because 'tis what ye've done. Ye're *choosing* to be lost. 'Tis in yer own power to change things."

He set the gravy off to cool. "My life's not so bad."

"It could be better."

"Violet, come eat," Briar called loudly, knowing Mina was right but unwilling to admit it. "You need to get to bed soon."

"And yer da needs to stuff his mouth so he can evade the

issue," Mina added before she grabbed up the skillet and poured its contents into the blue-speckled tureen.

Craackk! The gravy began to seep out the edges of the large split that rent the tureen's porcelain side.

"Ohh, 'tis sorry I am." After Mina dropped the red-hot container, she began to mop up the gravy with the hot pad she'd used to lift the skillet.

Briar grabbed an empty pan from the cabinet and quickly transferred the remainder of the mixture into the pan.

"Please let me help. I'll—"

"I've got it. Go wash that off before it burns your hands."

Apology etched her face. "I wasna thinking. It was hotter than . . . Ye can take it out of my first wages or 'tis another I'll buy ye at—"

"It can't be replaced."

Her eyes rounded. "It was Katie Rose's?"

"Our wedding bowl."

When the bowl was empty, he placed it gently in the trash. "Tell Violet to wash her hands before she comes to the table. That will give me time to make sure we didn't get any on the floor so none of us will slip on it."

"I'll send her in, but please doona set a plate for me. I-I canna eat."

Mina yawned. It had to be three in the morning, but at last she was done. It had been difficult working in the dark, but she knew if she had turned on the light she might awaken Violet. She only hoped the glue on the tureen would hold and that the mixture of flowers, flax, and candle wax was enough to hold the porcelain together. She'd used flowers and candle wax for glue before, but the idea to add some of the blue flax to hide the crack had come to her about an hour ago. She'd taken the bowl apart again, gathered some of the flowers from Briar's backyard, and altered the mixture. Just as she planned, the color of the flax blended perfectly with the bowl's design and the crack was no longer visible. Now if the glue held, she would be able to present the bowl to Briar almost in its original shape. Almost.

She decided to check on Violet before turning in. Mina tiptoed to the child's room, hoping not to wake her. The rascal had a bad habit of not really being asleep. Briar had returned to the station hours ago after doing the dishes. She'd started to help him, but then thought better of it. She'd broken one of Katie's precious belongings. If she harmed another, he would never forgive her.

Mina smiled as she saw all the treasures Violet had found now laying about her room, all with a piece of paper and the person's name to whom she planned to give the treasure scrawled across its surface. She leaned down to press a kiss against Violet's brow only to discover a wisp of hair had fallen into the lass's eyes. She smoothed it back, then gently kissed the tiny forehead.

"I 'member somebody doing that," Violet whispered. The bruised eye opened slightly as she yawned. "I think it was my mommy."

Mina pulled the covers up and tucked the child in, then sat on the edge of the bed. "Do ye remember much about her?"

"Only that she smelled nice and she sang pretty."

"Did she give you this?" Mina lifted the silver baby rattle that lay on the stand next to the bed.

"Nope. That's Daddy's. His godfather gave it to him, and he gave it to me."

"His godfather?"

"Mr. Corbett, the newspaper man. He's the one who helped Daddy meet Mommy, I think. 'Least that's what Daddy said."

"What else has yer da told ye about her?"

"Nothing. He said it would just hurt me to know. But you know what, angel?"

"What, sweeting?"

"I think *he* hurts when he talks about Mommy, so I don't ask him."

"Maybe someday soon he willna hurt anymore, then he'll tell ye all about her."

"You really think so?"

"Ye can be sure of it, love."

"Jimmy told me my mommy's buried in the graveyard, not in heaven like Daddy said. Did you see her when you went there?"

"No." Mina was glad she could answer that question honestly, but she would not lie to the child. "People who get sick and go to heaven usually go to the graveyard first."

"I don't believe you. You and Jimmy are talking jive. I want to see her."

"Yer da will have to take ye there, Violet. I promised him that I would leave that to him. Now close those sleepy eyes and go to sleep or ye'll be too tired to fly yer kite tomorrow. Ye doona want another hot, dry day, do ye? We could sure use the rain."

The child reluctantly went back to sleep. Mina waited until she was sure her steps would not reawaken the lass, then tiptoed out into the hall. A shadow shifted just as she sensed a presence in the hallway. "How long have ye been standing there?" she asked, her heart pounding in her throat.

"Long enough to tell you to stop discussing Katie Rose with my daughter."

Mina moved past him and took a seat in the parlor, needing to sit to stop her trembling. She had forgotten about his occasional check-ins to make sure Violet was all right. His anger was almost palpable; she didn't need to see it on his face.

"I didna discuss her," she countered, electing not to turn on a light. "I merely asked Violet what she remembered and, frankly, 'tis a sad lot she recalls."

"It's none of your business, Miss McCoy. I'll tell her when I'm ready."

"And when is that? When ye've withdrawn so far into yerself that ye canna teach her how it is to love and be loved? She's a little girl expecting her mother to return. She needs to know Katie's never coming back. She needs to know that doesna mean she was never loved while Katie lived. Violet has a right to know her mother fully so she can treasure that memory. 'Tis the greatest legacy ye can give her."

"How much of this is your own need, Mina?" His voice softened slightly as he took a seat opposite her. "Don't you know why your mother abandoned you? Are these all the things you need to know from her?"

Mina's back stiffened as if he'd lashed her with a quirt. "Me da told me nothing other than she left him . . . us . . . when I was two months old, and that every day of my life since then I reminded him of her. That's the sum total of what I know."

"And how long did he stay around?"

"Until I was twelve. And he was not the one who left. He kicked me out."

"On the streets?"

"A far better place than the so-called home he provided."

"Care to tell me why you were kicked out?"

"As ye said. Some things are just no other's business."

"Then we agree. You don't talk to Violet any more about her mother and I won't ask you about your father."

"I'll not lie to the child. If she asks me and I know, I'll tell her."

He stood. "Then I may have to ask you to leave."

"And that choice, Briar Duncan, may one day break yer daughter's heart as well as yer own."

Chapter 10

Nothing had gone right for Briar all day. The 8:10 was late. One of the cows broke out of its holding pen, and Violet had ignored his warning of the past three days about flying her kite too close to the Eclipse. She'd tangled it in the windmill's blades and destroyed the toy beyond repair. Violet and the windmill had been cranky ever since.

Mina's mood was no better. The woman had been curt to him ever since he scolded Violet and said she should take such nonsense elsewhere. Mina retaliated with her own reprimand, telling him to quit yelling like a banshee and take his anger out on the person at whom it was truly directed.

Damned if she wasn't right and damned if she hadn't been ever so courteous to every male who'd walked into the telegrapher's office since she'd hired on. He was glad it was time for her to be off duty so he could concentrate on what he should be doing instead of what everyone else was trying to do with her. Briar was damned mad and he didn't care who knew it.

"You two ready to head home?" he asked, irritated that three men waited in front of Mina's desk to send a telegram. Violet sat behind her on the cot, using some of the glue Mina had given her to repair the treasures she'd found along the roadside.

When had news gotten around about his new telegrapher? He never seen this much participation from male members of this community in sending wires. The men usually sent their wives or sisters to do this kind of triviality, spending their time on heavier tasks. But, if he'd watched one man go into the telegrapher's office, he'd seen twenty. You'd think they never saw a beautiful woman before.

And Mina was beautiful, the more he looked at her. The more he knew about her. The high color of anger on her cheeks had only made her eyes look more golden. The stiff arch of her back every time he walked in to check on Violet had only defined Mina's voluptuous figure.

Voluptuous. The word echoed in his brain and sent his blood coursing with heated memories. Hell, he'd been reading too many fashion books lately. No man should have to gauge the difference in buying full-figured, voluptuous, and petite clothing. That was women's work!

Mina laughed so hard she snorted.

What the hell did Harris say to her that made her laugh so hard? Briar listened closer to the conversation she was having with her current customer, irritated that his mind had drifted from the task at hand. Damned if he hadn't been unfocused all day.

He reminded himself that he usually found Brett Harris a likeable soul. Why couldn't he have inherited more of his dad's height and a little less of his mother's good looks? "I said, are you ready for us to change out hands, Miss McCoy?"

"Excuse me, gentlemen, it seems I must get off the clock." Her smile could have melted the snow atop the Rockies four hundred miles away. "Me boss is of a mind to save the railroad a few pittance. He or Sam will be helping ye now."

She stood and moved with such fluid grace that all four men's heads turned in unison to watch her. "Are ye ready for a bite to eat, lassie?" she asked, helping Violet gather her things and stow them into the pouch.

A doughboy stepped out of line behind Harris and offered to carry the pouch for Violet. "We can't have a little thing like you carry such a big old bag now, can we, miss?" He tipped his hat to Mina. "May I have the pleasure of escorting you and the little lady home or, better yet, could I interest the two of you in joining me for supper?"

Mina shook her head. "Perhaps another time, sir. 'Tis other plans I've made for the evening already."

Other plans? With whom? Briar stewed.

"Corporal Tuz, miss. You can reach me over at the Amarillo Hotel. At least until I'm called to El Paso."

"Till another day then, Corporal."

Till the caprock collapses, Briar vowed. "I'll see you home," he insisted.

"We know the way." Mina gently took Violet's hand and swept past Briar before he could object further. All three men in line doffed their hats as the females passed.

"Oohwee, I'd like to drink my fill of some of that Irish whiskey. I'll bet she can—"

Briar grabbed the man by his lapel and rammed him up against the office wall. His fist knotted the broadcloth shirt, squeezing off the foul words that might have ended the sentence. "I'll thank you not to talk like that about a lady in my company."

"I-I'm s-sorry, Duncan. I meant n-no—"

"Then watch what you say." Briar released his hold, aware that he'd allowed all the tension of the past few days to form the fury of his fist. He was ready to kill the man if necessary, all because he'd slighted the woman he cared about. And care about Mina he did, in a depth he'd let no emotion reach in years. Briar backed way, lest his opponent notice and think he feared completing the threat.

"Your machine's going off," Brett Harris announced. "Do I need to call Sam in here to take it for you?"

Briar noticed the hum of the wire, realizing it had been sounding off for a while. He'd thought his rage had taken voice and sang through his veins. *Get back to work, man, and get her out of your thoughts. Out of your blood.* "Thanks Brett. That won't be necessary. I'll take it."

Arriving Amarillo by morning of the 26. Stop. Bringing my wife with me. Stop. You read right. I said "wife." Couldn't stop myself. Stop. Nathaniel. Stop. A little telegraph humor. Stop. Get it? Stop.

P.S. Never guess who's on the eastbound headed your way. Stop. Charlie Chaplin, the film star. Stop. Heard he's heading to Europe. Stop. Might want to give Mayor Beasley the heads up. Stop.

Nathaniel was finally coming home. And with a wife!

"Bad news?" Brett asked.

"No." Briar placed the telegram to the side and reached for the message Brett wanted to send. "As a matter of fact, it's good. Things will start getting a little easier around here. Nathaniel's on his way home tomorrow."

"Does that mean you won't need your new telegrapher?" Brett's question stirred the other men into further comments.

"I hope she sticks around town."

"I think you ought to keep her on and let Nathaniel help somewhere else."

"We'll decide all that when Nathaniel gets here." Briar didn't want to hear any more. His head already began to throb with the decisions he knew he'd have to make within the next twenty-four hours. Why keep Mina on after Nathaniel returned? He could let his friend and bride have the house as long as they allowed Violet to keep her room. He could continue to sleep here at the station, until he found some other place for him and Violet. Maybe Nathaniel's wife would be willing to watch after Violet while they worked. After all, school would start up soon again, and it wasn't like Violet would be taking up most of her time as it had Mina's the past two days.

Then again, a new bride might not want to be saddled with watching a child that wasn't her own.

"Next?" Briar held out his hand for the next missive. He wanted nothing more than for Sam to finish up with that last delivery so he could take over the wire for him. He made quick work of the remaining requests and took in two more messages before his replacement arrived.

"I'm going to run this over to the mayor and check on Violet, then I'll be back."

"Still sleeping on the cot?" Sam asked, taking his seat at the wire.

Briar hadn't told his coworker that he'd not tried to help find Mina another place to stay and didn't feel like a long discussion now. "Yeah, looks like for a while now. If Nat's bringing home a wife, they're going to need a place to stay."

"That mean Miss McCoy will be looking for one too?"

Add that to another list of his decisions to make. He supposed Violet could share her room until one opened up at the hotel or boarding house. "Women sure do add a whole lot of trouble to a man's life, don't they?"

Sam grinned. "Yeah, but they're worth it."

"Shut up and wipe that grin off your face." Briar felt his mood lighten slightly and was grateful that his barrel-chested friend always easily put him in a better mood. He was a family man with six daughters and a wife who could do no wrong in his eyes. He might not have the wealth of some of the others around town, but he was richer than most in other ways. "You're just spoiled rotten to the core."

"Uh-huh, and loving every minute of it. You ought to rope that Irish hellion for yourself, laddie." Sam imitated their coworker's brogue.

"I don't need to. She's already thrown a loop herself and almost got me hog-tied," he finally admitted to his friend and even to himself. "*Almost.*"

Sam's laughter echoed over the incoming message which reminded Briar that he needed to be on his way to the mayor's house and to decide just what he planned to do with Miss Mina McCoy.

"And you say Chaplin's arriving tomorrow?" Mayor Beasley's face beamed with pleasure. The ceiling fan over the tall man's head chased the smoke away from the cigar that puffed steadily amid its mooring between his broad span of teeth. The black pin-striped waistcoat he wore nearly swelled to its seams as he puffed his pleasure. "Did Nathaniel say how he got the information?"

"No, but you know Nat. He wouldn't get you all riled up, knowing how big a fan you are. If he says Chaplin will be on the eastbound, then count on it. That means he'll arrive late afternoon." Briar watched the man grab a pen and start writing.

"We'll need to rouse the Ladies Auxilary and have them fire up their ovens." His Honor scribbled as fast as he talked. "And I'm sure the churches will allow us to borrow their tables to set up along the platform. We can put up the banners we use for the Fourth, and I'll have Silas inform the band to polish up their instruments and brush off their uniforms."

"So we're going full throttle on this?" Briar asked after he'd heard enough to keep him and the rest of the community up all night making preparations for Chaplin's arrival.

"Of course, man." Surprise raised Beasley's eyebrows almost to his hairline. "It's not every day a man of his re-known and influence graces our township. Just think of the interest Amarillo will gain once the world knows he's been given the key to our city. Yes, yes. I deem this our civic duty to make him feel most welcomed."

"The train only has a thirty-minute stop. He'll barely have time to freshen up, much less eat or anything else you've got planned."

"At least it will be available to him. Savory food, fine music, and convivial company. He can choose whichever he prefers for that thirty minutes."

"Then you best let me get started on all of this."

"My secretary will call the Auxilary. You call the others. Send me a bill for any charges you accumulate. Oh and invite that lovely young lady I've seen around town with your daughter. I hear Chaplin appreciates a handsome woman."

"Chaplin and every man west of the Mississippi, it seems," Briar muttered on his way out.

Chapter 11

Mina and Violet arrived back from Boot Hill well past sundown. She thanked the preacher for the ride and gently lowered the sleeping child onto her shoulder.

"I've never seen her so tired before." The preacher thumbed back the black slouch hat he wore. "But then I've never seen her remain quiet for that long either. She was quite the somber soul this evening."

"She had a lot to think about, Reverend. Four years of wondering in that little imagination would be an ballyhoo of exhaustion. Now she knows what a grave site looks like and what it means. The lass is too smart and she wouldna stop asking me questions. Better that I satisfied her curiosity about a graveyard than have her stumble over Katie's grave. But 'tis sure and certain I am, once I tell her da what I've done, he will send me on my way. Still, I know I did the right thing."

"Do you want me to talk to Briar for you?"

"No, Reverend. 'Tis my doing. 'Tis I who will suffer the man's anger."

The sound of hammers echoed in the dusk, urging Mina to look past the preacher's surrey. "It seems some late builders are working this fine Friday night. New kit houses going up?"

The preacher shook his head. "I don't believe so. I noticed

a lot of the striped banners we hang over the storefronts on the Fourth of July are in place. Looks like we may be having a big to-do tomorrow. Though, I don't remember being informed of such." He tipped his hat again. "If you'll excuse me, Miss McCoy, I'll see you safely inside then I'll go find out what's stirred up my flock."

"Violet and I are safe enough. Her father will be checking on us soon. I thank ye for providing the ride and the fine company, sir."

"Good evening then."

"And to ye."

Mina walked up to the porch then turned to see one last time what stirred the citizens of Amarillo before going in. The streets were alive with activity. People hustled to and fro. Model Ts and horse-drawn surreys trailed each other down the roadway, carrying colorful bundles and baskets full of items she couldn't define from here. She'd lived plenty of mean places, but Amarillo wasn't one of them. The golden city of the Texas panhandle might be drought-ridden at the moment but it was awash with a community of people who worked together to make it a happy one.

A sense of peace settled over Mina and she allowed herself a moment to savor the feeling that at last she was in a place she would like to make her home. She admired the town and its people, she adored the child she held in her arms, and she loved the man who was too obstinate to know his own heart.

Well, two could play at that game, she decided, opening the door and stepping inside. She'd shown him that he had come to mean something to her, and he brushed her away as if she were a pesky fly buzzing around his head. Pride was not new to her, and Mina refused to let him know how deeply it hurt that his feelings toward her, apparently, were not as strongly felt as hers were toward him. She didn't need him. She didn't need anyone. She'd proven herself quite capable all on her own.

But pride proved a lonely companion. She found little

comfort in being adept and capable if she couldn't share those abilities with someone. Do things for someone. Love and be loved by someone. That someone she had longed for had finally taken on a name—Briar Duncan.

And love him she did. She'd known it the minute she kissed him the second time. No, she first suspected it even before then . . . when their eyes met after she stepped off the train. It was as if whatever love she'd wanted had dared Mina to look beyond the glass surface that separated her from her future and the happiness she'd searched for all her life.

And now because Briar wouldn't let go of his past, neither of them would have the future she knew felt right for all three of them.

Maybe if she left, Briar would realize what he lost and would come after her. But the thought of leaving him, leaving Violet, nearly ripped the heart from Mina's chest. She held Violet tighter, unable to consider a life now without either of the Duncans in it.

How could her own mother have left a two-month-old and a man she loved? How could she endure the pain that weakened Mina's knees and made her feet plant themselves like roots so they wouldn't carry her away from where she belonged? How did a woman walk away and never come back?

She couldn't have unless she'd never loved them.

The cold reality that Colleen McCoy had never loved this deeply brought the tears that, to Mina's great surprise, allowed her to finally forgive the woman. How could she blame someone for what she did not know or couldn't feel?

The anger and hurt of years calmed into a quiet resolve of pity. She vowed in the morning to tell Briar of her love for him. To let him know that she would wait until he was ready to accept that love, no matter how long it took. And to let Violet know that she would remain in Amarillo and would always be near if she needed her. She would be no Colleen McCoy and run away. She would stay and fight for what she wanted.

Mina elected not to turn on the light since she saw one shining from beneath the doorways of both bedrooms. Briar had obviously been here and gone, leaving the lights on to guide them in. When she opened the door to the child's room, she discovered she was right in her assumptions. The covers had been turned down and Violet's nightdress laid out. An aroma of something delicious-smelling emanated from the towel-wrapped plate sitting on the nightstand. He'd obviously left supper for the child. Mina knew, without doubt, there would be one in her room, too.

His room. She reminded herself of the dozen kindnesses Briar had offered her the past few days. He'd made sure she was comfortable, gave her employment. He'd cooked for her and helped her hunt for keepsakes. He'd even begun repairing some of them for her. He may not love her yet, but he cared for her. That was clear in his every deed, no matter what he said to her. She just needed to stay around and let love settle in for him. It had been clear from the first, and she was quicker at determining what was right between them.

That thought brought a smile to her lips.

As she placed Violet on the bed, she noticed a note propped against one of the pillows. READ IMMEDIATELY had been scrawled across the folded front.

Mina's heart quickened and, despite her resistance to dreading anything before knowing why she should, she ignored the demand and set the note on the table. Violet's clothes needed changing and change them she would, before doing anything else.

The simple act of settling the lass into bed relieved some of the tension growing inside Mina. Some of it, but not all. *'Tis silly ye are*, Mina reprimanded herself silently and grabbed the note. She turned down the light and made her way through the dark to Briar's room.

A quick glance told her that he'd been just as thoughtful to her, but her own meal could wait. *Read immediately* kept echoing in her mind and felt as if it were branding the skin

against her pocket where the missive now rested. She took out
the note and unfolded it.

> *Received a telegram from Nathaniel. He and his bride
> are arriving tomorrow. They'll need to stay at the house
> until either they or I can make other arrangements. I
> thought you might want to clear your things out and put
> them in Violet's room. You can bunk in with her once they
> return.*
>
> *The mayor's got the whole town in an uproar making
> glad-to-meet-you preparations for some film star that's
> passing through on the eastbound, so I'll be busy deco-
> rating the depot. Don't know when I can check back
> again.*
>
> *But I know I've left Violet in good hands.*
>
> *Hope you were doing something you both enjoyed
> tonight. We'll talk about all that's gone on the past few
> days. I've been grouchy. I was just worried you'd take it
> on yourself to show Violet the graveyard. It's the one
> thing I couldn't forgive if you did.*
> —*Briar*

Mina's legs felt as if they were stuck in quicksand. She
sank onto the bed. "Saints and begorra," she whispered aloud,
"I've done it this time."

If only she could turn back the clock a couple of hours. She
stared at the note as if it were Briar and he could answer the
question that exited from her lips as little more than a squeak,
"*Any* graveyard?"

Chapter 12

Both of their duties that morning had kept them so busy, there'd been no time for Mina to find out the repercussions of the note. He'd asked her to listen to the wire all shift so that he could do the myriad of tasks required of preparing for the film star's arrival. When he told Mina that Violet could help some of the other children pick flowers they wanted to offer Chaplin, she'd almost insisted that the lass remain with her. She didn't want to take the chance of Violet telling her father where she'd spent the previous evening until Mina had time to explain it to him herself.

All day long the station filled with journalists, the mayor and city officials positioning themselves for front row view of the celebrity. Kaira Corbett, one of the women of the press, insisted that the station clock be set exactly with the one on the courthouse so all their clocks were synchronized and the band could start up a minute before the eastbound's arrival.

Much to Mina's surprise, wires started coming in from all points. Wires that had nothing to do with the constant chatter on the wire about Chaplin's impending visits along the rail line.

Briar had apparently sent a message to every telegrapher in range asking them to find out her mother's location, including visiting their local cemetery. One of them had found her.

Mina began to cry as she transcribed the dots and dashes.
*Buried in Charleston, S.C. Stop. Nothing but her name,
dates of birth and death listed on tombstone. Stop. Born, May
23, 1876. Died, May 24, 1892. Stop.*

Her mother had been barely sixteen years old, and she'd
died two months after Mina's birth. She must have been sick,
sick and scared. She must have done the only thing she could
do, leave her infant with its father. An act of love far greater
than Mina ever dreamed possible. An act only someone who
truly loved her child would be brave enough to do.

Forgive me, Mother. Mina willed her thoughts to heaven,
knowing her mother now abided with Violet's. *'Tis I who
should ask yer forgiveness.*

She would have to thank Briar for what he'd done. For setting her past to rights. For caring enough to know she could
never truly be happy anywhere until she knew.

Sam interrupted her. "Briar sent me in to give you a break.
Said you'd been at the wire long enough."

Briar. The celebration. Nathaniel. Mina's mind had to focus
on the tasks at hand. What a time for Nathaniel to bring home
a bride. The couple would arrive on the train that followed
Chaplin's and everyone in town would be so exhausted from
all the day's events to give their own a rousing welcome
home.

Mina decided she would use some of the flour she'd found
and bake them a pie. As she passed the decorated tables and
streamers that hung from the ceiling welcoming Chaplin, she
realized baking a pie would be about as useless as trying to
convince Briar to take a break. The tables were laden with
every baked good imaginable.

The least she could do was take Briar a glass of something
cold. That is, if she could find him.

She stepped out of the door and almost had to fight her
way through the surging throng of people. The brass buttons
of the constables' uniforms gleamed in the sun, pinpointing
the amount of law enforcement called in to control the crowd.

How was Briar getting anything done? she wondered, having to bite back a flair of temper that erupted any time she couldn't move as quickly as she preferred.

"Enough of that, you boys! Violet, drop that pie now or I'll send you back to Mina and you won't get to help the other children."

Mina forced her way through the onlookers so she could take the children off Briar's hands. Where were the other parents and why weren't they watching them?

A pie flew through the air narrowly missing Mina's head. The sound of several thuds warned that others had been thrown as well.

"Uh-oh," a tiny voice exclaimed and then yelled, "Scram!" and something else too quick for Mina to decipher.

All of a sudden miniature bodies sliced through the crowd, dodging in and out from adult entrapment. Mina recognized the ebony curls headed her way and grabbed just as Violet tried to rush past. "All right, lassie. That will be enough. Stand and take yer comeuppance like the suffragette ye want to be. Time to do a wee bit of suffering for a good cause."

"But Daddy's going to whoop me good this time."

Eyes the color of twilight rounded in a look so pleading, Mina had to hide the amusement that threatened to override her disappointment with the child's actions. "I've not seen him take a hand to ye in all my time here. But ye owe him an apology, and an apology ye'll give him, else take ye home I will. Ye'll march straight to yer room and think about the extra work ye've put on yer poor da in cleaning up those pies."

"Oh, all right, but I don't really want to."

"Ye really have to. So be done with it."

Despite her reluctance, Violet turned around and headed back to Briar. Mina followed making sure that she didn't veer from her obligation.

"I'm sorry, Daddy. I'll help you clean up the pie."

"Why did you throw it after I asked you not to?" Exasperation and something else filled his tone. Exhaustion.

"Here, let me help," Mina offered, grabbing one of the rags he'd been using to wipe the benches set up for the elderly. Egg whites sprinkled the backs of several of them. The platform would have to be washed clean or someone would trip.

"Answer me, Violet. Why did you throw that pie?" Briar was not letting Violet off with just an apology.

"Jimmy called me a liar, so I told him to stop or I'd hit him. You said I couldn't hit nobody with my fists no more, so I picked up that pie." Violet shrugged. "I warned him, Daddy, like you always told me. But he called me a liar, liar, has-to-mind-old-man-Briar. You ain't no old man and I ain't no liar, so I hit 'im."

Briar's eyes closed as he knelt beside his daughter as he, obviously, fought for words of wisdom. "You shouldn't let someone goad you into not behaving well, Violet. If you react to them, then they've won. If you act like it doesn't matter what they say, then it takes the wind out of their sails. He can't bother you unless you let him. Understand?"

"I think so."

"Good. Now look at me." Father stared at daughter. "Why did he call you a liar?"

Violet dared a glance at Mina. "I can't tell."

Briar's gaze met Mina's. The moment she'd worried about all night and through the day had finally arrived. He was about to learn where she'd taken Violet. She had to face it sometime, and she wouldn't forego the repercussions at the child's expense. "Tell him, sweeting. We've done no wrong."

The more Violet said, the redder Briar's face became. He stood and glared at Mina. "Give me the rag."

"I want to help. Ye're tired. Briar, 'tis sorry I am—"

"It's best you leave."

Knowing she'd overstepped some boundary he'd not been willing to remove, she asked, "May I have a final word with the lass?"

"You've told her enough."

It took everything within Mina to look one last time at the

two faces that had become so beloved. She was not even being given a chance to say a proper good-bye. Mina turned and walked away, flinching as she heard the tiny plea, "Come back, angel. Come back!"

Briar threw the rags into the wash bucket, splattering the floor he'd just cleaned. Damn, but he was mad at himself for sending her away so abruptly. Damn, but she was wrong for having taken Violet to the cemetery without his permission. No matter that it was Boot Hill and not where Katie was buried. Taking her was his choice, his right, his responsibility.

One that you've failed at miserably, he reminded himself justifiably. A glance at his child, sitting on the bench weeping her eyes out, only made him feel worse. She apparently was none the worse for the visit to the graveyard, but Mina's leaving looked like it would make her ill. Already the other eye was swelling to match the bruised one and she kept acting as if she wanted to lose her lunch.

To hell with Chaplin and anything else that needed to be done. He must find Mina and tell her he'd overreacted. That he was tired, and too stubborn for his own good, and, frankly, so in love with her that he didn't know what to do with himself anymore. When all this fanfare for the mayor was over, the three of them would ride out to Katie's grave and, together, they'd say a proper good-bye.

"Want to go find Mina with me?"

Violet stopped sobbing. "You mean you don't want her to go away?"

"I just needed time to think, pumpkin. Sometimes men don't know their own minds," *and hearts,* "as you women do."

An engine whistle blew, signaling the incoming train. The band started up, playing, "The Eyes of Texas Are Upon You." As the train pulled into the station, the waiting crowd surged forward, giving a rousing cheer.

Briar grabbed his daughter's hand and took advantage of

the opening he saw in the pathway. "Let's check the telegraph office. She knew Sam wanted to meet the man, so she's probably taken the wire back."

Sam said he hadn't seen her.

She wouldn't have left her post unmanned and wouldn't have disappointed Sam. She'd obviously left the depot and that meant she'd taken his words to mean something more.

Regret and a pain unlike any he'd ever felt before sent Briar's fist slamming against the station wall. A bloody swath colored the textured surface as he pulled his hand away and sputtered a mouthful of curses. "What the hell have I done?"

"You hit the wall," Violet informed.

Briar looked down at his child and began to laugh, her words having more meaning than she could ever imagine. "You're exactly right, pumpkin. I hit it for sure and it's all crumbling down around me. Thank God. Do you think you and your pals would want to go on a treasure hunt for me?"

"Yeah, Daddy, what are we looking for?"

"The only treasure I need other than you, little lady . . . and that's Mina. I'll check and see if she's gone to the house and you and your friends go through the crowd and see if you can spot her. Get her to go to the ticket office with you, if you find her."

"What if she won't come with me?"

"Tell her that she can't go without saying good-bye. It's not fair." He knew how Mina would react to that and once she returned, he'd never let her go again.

Briar had never gotten home so fast. Much as he feared, Mina's valise was gone, and the wedding bowl, completely repaired, had been left on Violet's bed. The sight of it made the worst of his fears possible. She had given up on him. Mina was saying good-bye.

There was only one place he could think she could go where she might believe no one would find her at the moment. The train itself. Everyone in town would be visiting with Chaplin, but the train would be empty. Briar gathered a deep breath and sprinted down the path he'd just traveled.

Minutes later, he passed Mayor Beasley as His Honor boarded the eastbound. "Have you seen the new telegrapher?"

Beasley shook his head. "No, just your daughter and her cohorts. It seems they're playing hide and seek inside the cars. Hardly the welcome to give our guest."

Violet's presence inside meant she'd traced Mina here somewhere. All of a sudden a small, frazzled-looking man appeared from around the doorway of the Pullman that Briar headed toward. "Good heavens, are those your children?"

"Was one of them a little girl with a black eye?" Briar recognized the film star from the playbills the mayor had shown him.

"Indeed."

"She's mine. They in your car?"

"Yes, and I'm afraid they're trying to, how do you say it in Texas, *lassue* a most becoming blond woman."

"*She's* mine, too," Briar informed, making sure the man whose reputation with women preceded him knew that Mina was off limits.

"Lucky man." Chaplin straightened his necktie and glanced at Briar in askance. "Do I look like a man with something profound to say?"

Briar laughed. "Don't worry. This isn't a lynch crowd. They'll love whatever you tell them."

"Good, I never know for certain what mood I'm to be met with. I rather enjoy preaching to the already devoted."

Mayor Beasley must have caught sight of his hero, for his voice came barreling over the crossover that linked the two cars. "Welcome on behalf of the children of our fair city and please be our guest at supper during your stay."

The door to the Pullman swung open. A disheveled Mina stood in the entrance, surrounded by a dozen little hands locked around her arms and legs. "Ye wanted me for something?" she asked in exasperation.

"That I do. Now if you children will leave Miss McCoy

and me alone for a while so I can apologize and tell her everything I want from her."

"Does that mean y'all are gonna kiss again?" Violet looked up at her father and grinned.

Briar's eyes met Mina's. "I hope so."

"You gonna let him kiss ya, angel?"

"Depends on just how sorry he is." Mina smiled in return.

"Oh he said he was a pretty sorry-son-of-a—"

"Violet, don't repeat that!" Briar's hand clamped over Violet's mouth until he realized it still smarted something fierce from the blow against the wall. Little ears sure had big mouths to go with them.

"Well, you said it, Daddy."

"Go play. Go toss pies at each other. Better yet, go keep Chaplin busy for a good thirty minutes or so. I think I need to repair the door to his Pullman for him."

"Aye, lass." The honey-colored eyes filled with a look that sent Briar's blood to heating. "Tell him something's wrong with the latch. And tell him 'tis an hour it might take. A slow hand is needed for *this* repair. Tell Charlie 'tis a *lengthy* time we'll be needing."

Her gaze traveled a slow path from the tip of his head, down to boldly admire places that would have to play hide-and-seek themselves if she didn't turn off that come-hither smile. Briar blushed for the first time in twenty-seven years.

When the children raced past, she swung the door to the Pullman open and laughed that all-engaging snort he'd fallen in love with the first time he heard it.

"Must be the devil's own deception. 'Tis not a bit unhinged," she teased.

Briar pulled Mina into his arms. "No, but I am, my angel, and I need you to teach me how to fix what I didn't even know was broken inside me. Forgive me. Marry me. Stay with me tonight and every night hereafter."

"I will," she whispered against his lips, "until ye show me every shade of sunrise in yer arms."

The Love Letter

LINDA BRODAY

In loving memory of my husband, Clint.
Your light still flickers inside,
reminding me to go on and
reach ever higher for my dreams.
May you have the restful peace you earned.

Chapter 1

There were two kinds of loneliness in the world—one that taunted with each breath and one that sat quietly, jabbing holes in a body's spirit. Amanda Lemmons knew a lot about both.

With a steely glint, she surveyed the rocky terrain of the Texas Panhandle. Leaning heavily on a staff, she trudged behind the sheep, her moccasins scraping earth that stretched endlessly toward the deepening pink and purple sunset.

Drawn by the scent of fresh meat, night predators threatened with the approaching darkness. She increased her pace and motioned to Fraser, her border collie, to push the flock.

Clumps of purple horsemint amid yellow buttercups dotted the landscape of the unused north pasture, becoming mere shadows in the twilight. One black silhouette caught her eye as she approached. Leaning, she picked up a worn, felt hat. No doubt the Stetson belonged to some high-struttin', bow-legged cowboy who staked ownership in the world and everything in it. Didn't take much guessing to know the saddle tramp worked on one of the cattle empires surrounding her fifty-acre strip of battleground.

"The fool must've let the wind carry his bonnet off. The hat's on my land now, and he'll get it back over my dead body."

If the cattlemen wanted war, she'd certainly oblige.

Tucking the find under her arm, Amanda beamed with pride in the way her border collie firmly commanded the modest flock she'd inherited, encompassing the sheep in a sweeping arc before driving them forward. Fraser had been with her father, Argus Lemmons, since a pup, and was raised with sheep until the animal probably thought he could bleat with the best of them.

She sighed with relief when she climbed from an arroyo and caught sight of her adobe house and sandstone corral. A sudden gust of wind flapped a piece of paper on her door. Prickles rose on the back of her neck. Someone had come onto her property uninvited again. Her gaze narrowed to the calling card tacked to her door.

"Another damnable note!" Her sudden outburst perked Fraser's ears, though his sharp eyes never left his wooly charges.

Amanda's anger simmered to a low boil.

Mysterious letters, three so far, had suddenly appeared over the last week. Each one had spoken of the brightness of her smile, the pleasing curve of her lips, and other such drivel. None bore a clue to the Lothario's identity.

She wouldn't allow them to rattle her. Whatever the caller intended, she wouldn't let it cloud twenty-eight years of judgment that kept her on firm ground thus far.

"Put the flock to bed, Fraser, and let's rest our bones."

The collie's sharp yap seemed to agree as he herded the *baahing* chorus into the pen.

"Good boy." Amanda quickly shut and fastened the gate, then bent to scratch his ears. The dog's tongue lolled to the side, his tail whipping her leg. "You're all a woman could wish for. You earned an extra treat tonight. The least I can do is feed you a meal fit for a king. Now, let's find out if the trespassing varmint who left that on our door put his name to this declaration of love."

In a way she hoped it was the cowboy looking for his hat. She'd take special delight in making sure he never found it.

A tack held the same brown paper used in any ordinary dry goods store. She ripped off the offending scrap, scanning the area again for the skulking culprit. But nothing moved except the swaying sea of wild rye and sagebrush.

"It's a good thing the miserable wretch didn't hang around to show his face. I'd make him rue the day he messed with me."

The collie scooted past her into the house and poised beside a piece of broken powder keg bearing the faded words U.S. ARMY MUNITIONS. Her father had come across the makeshift dish that the regiments had tossed aside once they finished *civilizing* the Indians. One thing about Argus, he found a use for everything except a daughter. Sudden pain pricked her heart. Even in death he could still wound. A ragged breath squeezed from her mouth.

Fraser cocked his head to the side, whined, and lifted a paw.

"Beggar." Amanda wagged her finger. "For shame."

Dropping the note on the table, she smoothed the thick fur, accepting Fraser's wet caresses. "One day I'll get you a real bowl. You deserve much better. Rest while I whip up that feast I promised. Everything is safe for tonight."

The latest missive received little more than a cursory glance. She scurried about the kitchen corner that consisted of a stove and a few half-empty crates that doubled as cabinets. She really should go to town to restock supplies.

The thought brought a tightening in her chest.

Amarillo didn't exactly throw out the welcome mat for a mutton puncher. A smart woolie had to know how to keep to herself in a cattle town. Sometimes the lines blurred, making distance all but impossible.

"To keep our bellies fed I have to pretend to like the connivers and backstabbers. Pig's foot!"

In no time, Amanda dished Fraser a good helping of

roasted leg of lamb and carrots she'd fetched from the root cellar. To top off the fare, she added a thick slice of sourdough. The collie had his principles it seemed, promptly nosing the crusty bread to the side before attacking the meat with relish.

She laughed and measured herself a smaller portion on a tin plate while she tried not to jar the rickety table, praying the legs held together a bit longer until she could save up for something better. She'd shear the sheep soon. Folks paid top dollar for wool even though they despised the animal it came from. She intended to sell a few of the flock. Many of the ewes had birthed lambs, so her number had risen. But finding a buyer had become more difficult of late. The cattlemen had the market sewn up, leaving little room for anything else. Yet they kept harping how sheep destroyed the land, making it unfit for their precious bovine. No satisfying the puffed-up land grubbers.

Amanda blinked away tears. *Damn them!*

Hell would freeze over before she let them force her out. Of the overwhelming numbers of sheepherders once occupying the area, only three stood their ground. Seemed she'd always occupied a spot someone else wanted.

Sometimes in the mist of a gray dawn she dreamed a handsome prince would pluck her from the endless despair and add his strength to hers. And, if a girl dreamed, she might as well dream large. This man wouldn't mind the bleating of sheep.

His kisses would bring light to a world that had been dark so long.

His arms would be strong enough to withstand the buffeting winds of the cattlemen's greed.

And his wild spirit would equal her cussed muleheadedness.

Words on the note she'd casually flung to the table caught her interest. She held the paper to the glare of the lamp.

"My Dearest Amanda," it began.

*I yearn to see the beauty of your face, hear the tone of
your voice, and inhale your fragrance that wafts in the
wind like a million wildflowers in bloom. Please meet
me in Amarillo by morning in the lobby of the hotel.
Then, you shall know the love I speak. Look for the crescent birthmark on my right hand and the adoration in
my eyes.*

The flowing initials P.M. graced the bottom of the letter.

P.M.? Who on earth? Longing rippled past life's disap-
pointments and sorrow. Amanda squelched rising excitement,
trying to recall crossing paths with Mr. P.M.

Not that he could truly be a secret admirer, so she'd best remember that. The motive had to be some callous attempt to
belittle her. She'd suffered the brunt of ridicule much of her
life and knew that particular sting. She wouldn't put stock in
flowery words scribbled on a piece of paper.

The swain wouldn't trick her. Her adversaries had a bag
full of low, unscrupulous practices. She knew them all.

This, however, was a new tactic, and the ruse would prove
far more damaging than the others should she buy the flattering prose.

Amanda didn't. She wouldn't entertain that for a second.

Her hand shook slightly when she held the note toward
glowing embers in the stove. The paper caught easily and
turned to ash in minutes. Like her life, it flaked into nothing-
ness and fell amid the flames.

Fraser whined. His soulful, brown eyes said he knew her
pain.

Jerking up the wayward Stetson that had come into her
tender, loving care, she threw it down and stomped until the
black felt flattened into a circle.

Now, should the cowboy come looking, she'd be oh-so-
thrilled, in fact duty-bound, to return it.

"Here boy." She grabbed a handful of oatmeal cookies

she'd baked that morning and aimed for the middle of Fraser's *new* feeding dish. "I didn't forget that extra special treat."

Quiet yearnings settled in the deepest corners of Amanda's heart. Things she hadn't revealed to a living soul. She swallowed hard. Years had passed since the abandonment, and yet the hurt haunted. If only she could take solace in the fact that each day took her further from the misery. Except it hadn't. She was truly, utterly alone.

Amanda glared at the hat. Trust could make a woman do foolish things. She wouldn't put any faith in a fiddle-faced cowboy with a vivid imagination and too much time on his hands.

Inhale her fragrance that wafts in the wind like a million wildflowers would he? She snorted.

"I trust you about as far as I can throw an iron jenny."

Amanda absently twirled the spinning wheel that was tucked in a corner of the room while she plotted.

She'd get gussied up in the new apricot dress she'd sewn from last year's finest wool . . .

Put a dab of rose water behind her ears . . .

. . . And paste on a smile that would melt a man's hardest, most cruel intentions.

The louse wouldn't expect a sheep rancher with brains.

Or a devious plan.

Yes, she'd go.

And she'd make the Lothario sorry he ever messed with her.

Absolutely, without a doubt, sorry.

Chapter 2

Cussing and yelling from across the Frying Pan Ranch's compound might've broadened Payton McCord's vocabulary, if he lived someplace more civilized than the rough Panhandle or pursued another line of work besides cowhand.

His Uncle Henry had spouted a lot of wisdom before he went on to the hereafter and, although a good portion of the interpreting changed with each telling, one parcel stood out: *Spittin' into the wind can leave you drying your face with a long-handled mop.*

In hindsight, Payton should've heeded that particular warning before playing the latest practical joke on his best friend, Joe Long. Fact of the matter, Payton had forgotten he'd planted his damn feet in the downwind position, and now had to suffer the consequences. In the dying light of a spent day he could definitely feel the fine spray of blowback drenching his mustache.

Payton raised his head when sudden silence filled the brisk, spring air, deafening him. Strands of hemp dangled from the partially braided rope in his hand.

Maybe Joe'd patched things up with his wife, Lucinda.

That glimmer of hope died when abrupt banging and clanging replaced the brief moment of calm.

He swung toward the commotion and winced.

Pots, pans, and pottery flew from the doorway like missiles from a Gatling gun, followed by Joe's hasty exit.

Hell and be damned, Lucinda Long had a temper!

A guilty conscience rolled a heaping boxcar of blame at Payton's door. He shouldn't have convinced that saloon trollop Joe would welcome her affections. In his defense, who would've predicted Lucinda would pass by the swinging doors and spy the tosspot perching on Joe's lap with her skinny arms wrapped around his neck?

While Payton recounted the scene, a skillet grazed the ranch foreman's head. Joe nursed his wound, limping toward him and safer territory inside the barn.

"Reckon Lucinda's not in the forgiving mood." Payton trained his gaze on the new rope. Blood made him a mite squeamish. Besides, he couldn't bear the misery in Joe's eyes.

"The woman's fit to lasso a trapped cougar."

"Give her a day or two. Maybe she'll take you back."

"Damn you, McCord! You've gone too far this time. Messing with a man's marriage is serious grounds for an ass whooping."

Payton planted a matchstick in the side of his mouth. "I never meant for Lucy to see that hussy. Our pranks have always been harmless fun. And I reckon the God-awful jokes you've pulled ever since I arrived three months ago conveniently slipped a cog in your memory. I recall those were none on the pleasant side."

Replacing the Bull Durham in his pouch with cow dung still stung. . . .

And filling his canteen with skunk oil? Luckily, the odor hit his nose before he tipped the container. He'd had to throw the damn thing away though. Those incidents straggled at the end of a list long as his arm. He finally raised his eyes to check for blood. None that he could see.

Joe gingerly rubbed the knot on his head. "Let's call it quits. We're even. I'm willing to let bygones be bygones."

"Shake on it?"

A fraction of a second passed before Joe accepted Payton's olive branch. The hesitation let it be known he might forgive but not forget. At last, Joe clasped Payton's hand, a small assurance they were still friends despite everything.

"Talk to Lucinda. She might listen to you, Payton."

"Sure. Might have to let her cool off first though."

"I figure that'll be sometime after next year's thaw. I ain't seen her this riled in all my born days."

Just then a pair of men's britches skimmed the air and landed on the whiplike, spiny branches of an ocotillo bush. Clusters of crimson flowers peeked from the crotch. Shirts and long johns soon littered the buttercups and black-eyed Susan landscape until the ground developed a case of measles.

Payton shifted the matchstick. "You might oughta go get your britches, Joe."

"Tarnation! Rub salt in the wound why don't you, you low-down marriage-wrecker. Add some vinegar while you're at it."

"That's no way to speak to a friend."

"You'd best talk to her soon if you want to remain one," Joe growled.

"I admit I owe you that. I'll do my best to fix the harm." Payton straightened and lowered his hat. Then, he stalked to a pair of recently pitched white underdrawers smothering a patch of winecup and began waving them as he cautiously crossed the battlefield. "Lucy, now don't you throw anything else."

The termagant stepped out. A stiff breeze tossed the mass of flaming red curls hither and yon.

"Stay out of this, Payton. I have no quarrel with you."

"That opinion may change once you hear me out. Let me come inside. I don't think a body should air dirty laundry where God and everybody can hear."

She clutched the door but moved aside. "You can talk until the saints go marching in and it won't affect things one iota."

Leaving the drawers on the stoop, he stepped across the threshold. "First of all, you know Joe and I have played pranks on each other from the moment we met?"

"I don't see how that pertains."

"Joe has no use for that saloon hussy. Won't give any woman the time of day except you." Payton ran a hand through his hair and met her wrath with frank honesty. "Truth is I created this predicament when I told the girl Joe'd welcome a little feminine persuasion not of the wifely kind. I didn't stretch or bend the truth . . . I lied."

"Kiss my foot! I could spit in your eye if you weren't so blasted tall, Payton McCord."

"Would it help knowing I didn't think it'd come to this?"

A swift blow to his shoulder knocked him sideways. Damn, the little woman carried a punch! Lucy's temper came in degrees of hot, boiling, and scorching. He'd earned the full measure though. Never let anyone say he didn't take his medicine even if it did go down backward and lopsided. Or all over his face.

His belly twisted when he saw tears swimming in her eyes. Lucy truly loved Joe despite his faults.

Not that Payton particularly knew anything about love. Closest he might've gotten was the time he raced into a burning building to save Mavis Harper and found her half-clothed. The only fire had been the grease on the stove. He'd sure had hell peeling Mavis off him though.

Ever since she batted those eyes like a cow that'd eaten a bunch of locoweed, and he ran in the opposite direction.

Maybe that was love.

Maybe it *should* scare the stuffing right out of a man.

And maybe he had no business changing his ways now. A confirmed bachelor didn't suddenly wish to wed any more than a cowpuncher developed a craving for dumb sheep. He was a single man, a cow man, and that was that.

Love and marriage . . . who needed that cluttering up things?

Those notions were for young pups with stardust in their eyes and enough courage to wrestle a pack of mangy wolves.

Payton was too old for pretending he had what it took. An achy back and bum knee tended to remind him whenever he let his thoughts get too frisky.

In light of today's events he could see the disaster a wife made of a man's life. He should probably count his blessings. Though too often, when he rode the range with the cattle, he imagined being able to wrap his arms around a woman who belonged only to him and hold her until dawn's faint light whispered "I do, I forever will" in his ear.

Those things weren't for him. He'd accepted that.

Dear Uncle Henry swore the love of a good woman could cure a man of bachelorhood, sin, and sanctimony. Payton had no doubt he needed saving, but didn't harbor any fervent desire for it.

"Come here, Lucy." He folded his arms around the woman and let her blubber and sling snot on his clean shirt. "Joe worships the ground you walk on. Always has. Always will."

"You'd defend him no matter what."

"I know he has eyes for no other woman in the world."

Lucinda dabbed at the tears. "Are you sure?"

"Positive."

Although he wasn't privy to such things, he took her wobbly smile as a good sign.

"Do you think you can find it in your heart to take Joe back?" He handed her a handkerchief. He'd always heard a woman liked a man to pay attention to tears and snot.

"You always were the only one brave enough to call me Lucy." She blew her nose. "Joe can come home . . . in time."

Visions of the uncomfortable sort swept through Payton's head. Each one brought to mind a swarm of angry bees after someone knocked down their hive and stole their honey.

"Exactly how does a man measure 'in time'?"

"When he's learned his lesson good and proper."

Which meant what? Female riddles—who could understand

them? He'd rather have things spoken straight out. That way a man knew where he stood. Looked as if Joe sat astraddle a fence and Payton couldn't advise him where to light.

Nodding as though it made perfect sense, he backed out the screen door and returned to the barn in time to catch Joe scribbling on a piece of paper. His friend hurriedly pushed the writing tools under the britches he'd retrieved from the yard, his foot tapping out a rhythm on the dirt floor.

"Well? What did Lucinda say?"

"Hell if I know what a woman means." Heavy silence followed after Payton relayed the message.

"Damn it!" Joe yelled at last. "No telling when her disposition will sweeten. I guess you did your best to make amends. You know, this forces me into your company. Can you try not to raise the roof with your snores?"

"You should talk. It's me that has to put up with your sorry hide. What were you writing?" Payton glanced at the edge of the paper peeking from the worn, blue denim. This wasn't the first time he'd seen Joe trying to hide his handiwork. Maybe letters posed the best way back into Lucy's good graces. And it stood to reason Joe would want to avoid the ribbing the ranch hands would give him.

"Me?" Joe tucked the pencil above his ear and grinned. "Nothing. Nope, wasn't writing a goldarned thing."

"Reckon I'll get my gear ready for branding then."

"I forgot to tell you . . . Mr. Sanborn wants you to meet James Wyness in Amarillo first thing tomorrow. Cattle Raisers Association business. He can't go himself."

Meeting with Wyness midweek seemed rather peculiar. Especially at the start of branding season.

Payton smelled something afoot, and it wasn't manure either.

Chapter 3

Payton eased his sore bones onto a comfortable settee in the lobby of the recently completed Amarillo Hotel and stretched his long legs. His aching knee thanked him for taking off the weight.

All right, he was here. Where was James Wyness?

An ornate grandfather clock struck eight. He searched the room, hoping to spy the boss of the LX Ranch. No luck. Again, Payton wished Mr. Sanborn had elaborated on the all-fired urgency in getting to Amarillo by morning.

The door abruptly opened and he swung an anxious glance toward it.

A ragged breath filled his lungs. The slight beauty who strode through bore little resemblance to Wyness's craggy features. High cheekbones sculptured her face into a rare work of art that belonged on some artist's canvas.

Though he really couldn't say she was the most beautiful woman in the world, given his limited knowledge of such things, she was easily the most memorable. The hotel guest could put any heifer in the pasture to shame in nothing flat. He inspected her through a narrowed gaze.

Despite her small build, the way she carried herself seemed to suggest legs clear up to Sunday.

And she had big . . .

He swallowed hard.

. . . eyes, he finished lamely. He dragged attention from the rounded curves. Yep, they were sure big.

Somewhere among the cobwebs in his brain he recalled that a gentleman shouldn't notice a woman's figure. Especially the top half—unless of course he already had before he could help himself.

A polite nod wouldn't hurt though, which he managed weakly before she sat down and propped a valise at her feet.

She'd not only captured his attention, but every last man, woman, and child's in the hotel. Whispers circled. Pointed stares flew her direction. Her presence appeared to engulf the lobby. He couldn't say he blamed the onlookers. She was a rare sight for the newly platted town.

Payton snatched up the weekly edition of the *Panhandle Herald* and whipped it open. Maybe reading about cattle prices would get his mind off the traveler's . . . embellishments.

The pretty lady must've arrived on the Fort Worth and Denver City Railway that had pulled into the station fifteen minutes ago. Perhaps she came in on one of the many excursion trains bringing prospective buyers for town lots. Beyond the hotel doors, Amarillo whirred with comings and goings. Way too noisy. One reason he stayed well removed unless necessary. Give him peace and quiet of the ranch any day. Except the Frying Pan had become littered with too many pots, pans, and prickles of late. Thinking of Lucy and Joe, he felt another rush of guilt.

Rosewater drifted around him in a lazy swirl.

Payton tried to ignore both the fragrance and the faint rustle of fabric, but his senses had stood up and taken too much notice. A hard blow couldn't slap every nerve ending back down that had popped to the surface and saluted.

"I beg your pardon, sir." The rich tones, wrapped in layers of female softness, slid over his skin like satin on silk.

So much for the expected bumper crop of odoriferous mushmelons. Payton lowered the newspaper and found himself face to face with the slight beauty who probably had to stuff rocks in her pockets to weigh a hundred pounds. She'd scooted beside him and was damn near in his lap.

"Yes?" He tried to sound unruffled, as if conversing with eye-boggling women was an every day occurrence.

"You're reading the paper upside down."

"Oh." Beads of sweat dotted his brow as he hurriedly switched it around. "Anything else?"

"I don't believe so."

"Well, much obliged."

From under the edges of the morning news he fastened his gaze on the woman's shoes . . . rather, moccasins . . . peeking from the hem of a dress the color of ripe peaches. How unusual. Payton couldn't recall anyone quite so unorthodox. Or one with feminine enticement oozing from every nook and cranny.

He felt her lean closer and squirmed.

Her breath dallied on the newspaper like a gentle caress. A ragged gulp of air couldn't save him. He knew if he lowered the shield again he'd fall into the bottomless depths of her sooty gaze. He'd wrestled many a steer and ridden ornery broncs without a speck of the panic he knew now.

"Excuse me," mystery lady's silken request further muddled his musing.

Payton reluctantly folded the paper. "Yes, ma'am?"

"Could I beg you for the time?"

"I believe it's half-past eight. Meeting someone?"

"Perhaps." She captured the tips of each gloved finger between pearly teeth and with painstaking deliberation drew off the soft kid before extending her hand. "I'm Amanda."

"Pleasure's mine. Payton McCord of the Frying Pan Ranch."

Miss Amanda had a firm grip. No limp-wrist woman.

Yep, the pleasure was most definitely his. Heat rose from his midsection and spread in sultry, scorching waves.

A curtain of dark hair the shade of thick, warm molasses cascaded from a jeweled contraption fastened at the crown instead of worn in the God-awful stiff custom of the day. Amanda evidently thumbed her nose at convention both in her choice of footwear and appearance. He was a lucky man.

"Forgive me, Mr. McCord. I shouldn't pry. But can you tell me if you wear leather gloves all the time?"

He sat up a little straighter. "What the . . . ?"

"I see I've shocked you. Too much time alone I fear. I forget the niceties."

A woman of her caliber shouldn't ever be alone. What a waste of prime womanhood. Payton glanced again at the clock wondering if it had gotten stuck on half-past eight. "If I learned niceties they didn't stick. And yes, gloves have become a permanent fixture. Helps in my line of work."

"Which would be?"

"Cattle."

"No surprise there," she murmured so low he had trouble hearing. Or it could've been the swarm of angry bees in his head that searched for stolen honey.

Amanda withdrew a lacy kerchief from her handbag and dabbed at the slim column of her throat. Blood pounded in his ears as he followed the lazy, agonizing path to hidden soft skin lurking beyond the vee of her neckline. She toyed with the top button.

Payton wanted to look higher, somewhere in the vicinity of her forehead. Dammit, he tried. But there weren't enough horses in the state of Texas to drag his attention anywhere else. Perspiration soaked through the underarms of his shirt. He prayed she'd not notice. Sweat probably offended a nice lady of her obvious breeding, the moccasins aside. She could've fallen on hard times and resorted to what she could get. He wouldn't hold that against her. He'd like to hold *him-*

self against her though. The startling idea launched another wave of heat.

Crossing his legs, he nodded at her valise. "Traveling?"

"No." Tendrils of Amanda's hair curled about her ear with the shake of her head.

Then why in Sam hell did she carry a case?

"Traveling folks usually tote one of those." He pointed to the worn leather bag.

"Oh, that." Her quick laugh washed over him in thick, indolent pulses. "I thought this may require spending the night instead of riding back to my ranch. Depending."

"On what? If you're at liberty to say, that is." Why had his throat gotten so dry all of a sudden?

"My plans depend on the person I'm meeting. If he shows up and things . . . Well, if things turn out. I'm sure you understand."

Payton's stomach twisted, resisting the fact that Amanda had a man friend and they might be doing . . . uh, never mind what they might be doing. The painful lump in his throat grew.

"No need to explain."

Absolutely no need. She didn't have to plow a whole dad-blamed field before he knew she was sowing something. He might be a bachelor but he had more than a little experience with the ladies. In fact, too much, or his mind wouldn't linger on featherbeds and social calls. Amanda rested her hand on his arm, the touch plundering the remainder of his good sense.

"Are you waiting for someone, Mr. McCord?"

"James Wyness, head of the Cattle Raisers Association."

"My goodness, your meeting must be awfully important."

"I couldn't say. I'm in the dark why the boss sent me."

Amanda twisted the handkerchief around her finger. Feathery lashes lowered to hide her burnished mahogany gaze.

It surprised him that she'd be nervous. Must be her first time. A married woman cheating on her husband? No ring weighted her hand, but she could've discarded it. He hoped she at least knew this fellow she was fixin' to let ruin her life. The bastard would make her a fallen woman.

The thought soured on his stomach.

Payton made a rule not to judge others but at the moment he could gladly whip the fellow up one street and down the other for taking advantage of such a genteel lady.

With angelic grace, she fingered a strand of warm molasses while treating him to a wide-eyed regard. Payton's heart skittered sideways.

"Your ranch, ma'am . . . would it have a name?"

The smile that teased the corners of her lush lips wobbled. "It's a small spread and I tend to keep to myself."

"How many head you running?"

"More than enough to keep me busy." Shadows lurked in the dusky gaze that swept the room's occupants. "And yes, I'm the sole owner. I do the work of several."

So the lady had no husband. Interesting.

Payton shifted. "Awful big burden for small shoulders."

"Whatever doesn't whip us into the ground makes us stronger, I'm told."

Amanda touched the outside of each eye with the tip of the handkerchief, examining Payton. He had the right initials. But he couldn't be the letter writer for the obvious reason that he'd come to meet the Scotsman, Wyness. Not her.

Flitteration!

Part of her wished he was. He had an honest firmness that made him shine above other men. Payton McCord would stand up when it came time to be counted. He would never fold or trifle with her. How she came to that conclusion she wasn't sure, or why she took to a saddle-warmer of all things.

Well, she never wanted a perfect man. Just one that would hold her when she was cold, frightened, or empty, and ask for nothing except the sharing of a life in return. This one she could learn to accept if the price were right. With him the midnight hours would hold no loneliness or despair.

McCord had a rugged strength. Perhaps he would afford her respect few others had.

Eyes the color of freshly picked mint seemed to look at the world in shades of green—perhaps not minding that she raised sheep of all things. Sandy waves, streaked by the sun, brushed his jacket collar in rebellion. And the groomed mustache added flair to features that had probably seen good times and bad in equal measure and served to forge some strong steel.

From lowered lids she imagined the gentleness of the sensual mouth. The rapid thud of her pulse seemed loud as the ache expanded.

The mustache would tickle just a tiny bit.

But she wouldn't mind. Not when he could banish the ills of the past. And she had little doubt that he could. This man held promise. She needed, desired, him to be real. Was that too much to ask?

Look for the crescent birthmark on my right hand.

Amanda shook herself and returned to the devious plan she'd hatched to turn the tables on the Lothario. She loathed plunging on but she must. She just prayed for an outcome that wouldn't break her heart.

"Would you mind terribly removing your gloves?" She flashed a bright smile, confident in her feminine wiles. And so far, Payton McCord swallowed the entire lasso, knot and all. "I know it sounds ridiculous, and I don't normally go around asking it of strangers, but I do have a reason."

"Can't imagine what or how it possibly pertains to me."

His black scowl indicated the first sign of balking. This called for a lot more sneakiness. Perhaps she should throw in a bit of candor—to a point.

"You see, I have no way of recognizing the person I'm meeting other than by a certain mark."

And the look of adoration in the swain's eyes. But she didn't add that. She'd already seen it swimming in the green stare. The intensity there made tingles tiptoe up her spine.

Payton scowled. "A mark. On his hand I take it?"

"I'm sorry to have bothered you." Amanda rose, gathering her valise and her pride. "My problems shouldn't concern you."

"No, please. It appears both Wyness and your . . . appointment . . . stood us up." He untangled his legs and sprang to his feet. "Let's hash this out over coffee? Or tea. I feel obliged to help a pretty damsel in distress."

"Very kind. How can I refuse a . . . true gentleman?"

"You can't."

She handed him the valise and accepted his elbow. Heads turned when they entered the dining room and for once Amanda couldn't tell if they stared at her, the mutton woman, or the devilishly handsome wrangler. He pulled out her chair and waited until she sat down before taking a seat.

Tiny details caught her notice—the quiver that rippled through muscles in his arm when she brushed it, the solid feel of his tall frame, and the genuine warmth enfolding her that chased away the ever-present chill in her veins for a moment.

Hmmmmm . . . Despite apprehension, she could do far worse than having refreshment with a cowboy. Not just any though. Payton seemed special.

Besides, should he turn out to be the author of the love letters, and if he had written them for the purpose of making her a bigger laughingstock, her plot would succeed. Everyone would see him keeping company with a lowly sheepherder. Nothing else would ruin a staunch cattleman's reputation faster.

But if he had and the declaration of love was genuine?

Somehow her vision didn't seem as clear now.

Strange that he hadn't mentioned the love letters once or shown an inclination he knew her. She could've jumped to the wrong conclusion from the outset. Damaging someone like Payton seemed wrong, particularly if he penned the words from deep inside. It might do more than leave his reputation in shambles. Picking up pieces of a heart . . . that was something in which she was well versed. She steeled herself against the pain and clenched her jaw. Reality was a harsh taskmaster. Better she let the chips fall.

Payton McCord had to be the one. He was the best candidate out of the gathering in the lobby—four who entered with wives and two others who appeared on their last leg, slipping fast and probably with reservations for the undertaker.

Then there was the matter with the initials. Yes, McCord was Lothario all right. And she had to protect herself. Time to get at the truth.

With the valise at her feet and napkin in her lap, she met Payton's reserved perusal and tilted forward. His gaze meandered to the rounded tops of her bosom where he lingered for a long second. His Adam's apple bobbed when he swallowed.

She let her fingertips rest on his gloved hand. "Mr. McCord, thank you so much for taking pity on me."

"Payton . . . I insist. I'm not one to stand on formality." Lines around the corners of his mouth and an interesting cleft in his chin deepened with his grin.

No, he was more for trying to run her off her land and back to New Mexico more likely. Memories of Santa Fe, distasteful and hideous, lodged in the hole in her chest.

"In that case, Payton it is."

"I believe you were going to explain some quandary you're in with a fellow you don't know. I get the impression you don't truly wish to be here. So why do something you might regret, something that may bring you to rack and ruin?"

Ruination wouldn't be hers if she could help it. Wait until he got a look at what she'd packed inside her valise.

The waiter arrived at that moment to take their order then retreated with a huff after they'd only wanted coffee.

"We'll get to that." She stared deep into his eyes, her fingertips massaging the back of his gloved hand. "First, let's enjoy the moment and these beautiful surroundings."

"I agree. The Amarillo Hotel is magnificent. My boss, Mr. Sanborn, sure has an eye for high living. He built one of the finest establishments north of Austin." Payton released a sharp breath when Amanda removed her fingers to idly trace the swirls on the tablecloth.

Good. She'd lured him further onto the patch of quicksand.

Payton's hand shook slightly as he raked back a thick lock of hair. She flashed the biggest smile in her arsenal.

"You know, I think you're the first man I've seen who doesn't wear a Stetson. Most everyone sports one of some sort. I have this old floppy straw hat I wear on the ranch."

"Lost mine. The darn thing blew away in a wind storm and I never found it. Probably in Louisiana by now. Before I head back to the Frying Pan today I have to go by the mercantile."

Blew away? Amanda lifted the water glass to hide the jolt.

If the hat she'd found belonged to Payton it no longer bore the shape of one. And Fraser seemed to like his new dish.

"Odd, isn't it, how things do tend to disappear?" She clutched the napkin and drew it down the length of her throat in an excruciating crawl. The green gaze widened, following the sliding, downward waltz. "It's rather warm in here."

With abrupt impatience, Payton peeled off the gloves and wiped his palms on the tablecloth. "Indeed it is. Very hot."

Suddenly Amanda's stomach whirled.

A crescent birthmark marred the back of his right hand.
What had she done?

Chapter 4

Payton's attention strayed from Amanda's come-hither pose when Joe entered the dining room. *Damn!* The friend brought nearly every last hand of the Frying Pan with him.

Shenanigans of the rotten kind swirled. Payton shifted in the chair. Whatever they were up to reeked to high heaven.

Joe grabbed the empty seat at their table, making himself at home. Payton didn't care much for his friend's goofy grin or the way he stared at Amanda.

"Don't you have anything better to do besides bother us, Joe? Cows to brand? Chickens to feed? A wife to cajole?"

"Boss gave us the day off. Thought we'd come watch."

Twisting and turning in Payton's gut made him dizzy. Watch what? He wasn't some bug under a light. Romancing a charming, beautiful woman didn't call for an audience. But, maybe that was it—they wanted to see in action someone who shied away from things of the heart. Lord knows he scoffed at it often enough. How in Sam hell did they know Amanda would be at the hotel though? He had some square pegs that wouldn't fit in round holes. One of the mismatched pegs became crystal clear however. He smoothed his mustache, the cold knot in his belly tightening.

"Wyness wasn't supposed to meet me, was he? You're up to no good. What have you done now?"

"I swear to my time, Payton, you're not a Pinkerton man at a train holdup. Relax." Joe winked at Amanda. "Miss Amanda, I declare you're prettier than a speckled pup. Always a treat."

Employees of the ranch—Bert, Amos, and Felipe— watched from the next table, grinning like squirrels eating ripe acorns.

Payton didn't enjoy the niggling suspicions. He turned his attention to the pretty lady who'd swept into his life. "You know each other? Don't tell me this is the fellow you came to meet." If so, he'd gladly whoop the tar out of Joe for free.

"Not hardly." Amanda frowned. "Joe wouldn't have any reason to write me letters."

"Letters?" A sinking feeling made Payton weak.

"Notes someone keeps tacking to my door. The writer signed the last one with the initials P.M. You wouldn't know anything about that, would you, Payton McCord?"

He did a double take with the sudden switch. Where had the beguiling smile gone, the soft curve of her jaw? He could almost see a layer of frost form on her lashes. And why was she accusing him of things of which he had no knowledge?

"Don't look at me." He had a sick feeling.

Joe's grin became more smug than goofy. "Miss Amanda, maybe you oughta fill Payton in on the nature of your ranch."

The sooty brown of her gaze became pitch black. "Tell him yourself." Her sudden shove freed a path from the table. She jumped to her feet. "It's just as I suspected. You won't make me the butt of your jokes."

"Fair enough. But could I trouble you for the love letters Payton wrote? He's my friend and I gotta protect him."

"Love letters? I didn't write any . . . ." Payton's voice trailed, remembering Joe and his secret doings. He felt the blood drain from his face. Amanda's wounded gaze hurt worse than a gut full of buckshot.

"Don't look so innocent, McCord. I can prove it." She

whipped out a crinkled paper from her handbag and pitched it at him. "This was the first. I burned the others."

He read the script. *The brightness of your smile puts the sun to shame. The pleasing curve of your fair lips makes my heart flutter. I will one day advance my cause and you will know I speak these words in good faith. Until that time I remain your humble servant.*

What a bunch of hogwash. Then, the magnitude of Joe's deceit began to sink in. *Good God Almighty!*

"This isn't my handwriting. I promise." But he could damn sure pitch a silver dollar on the one it belonged to. And what about poor Lucy? He ought to horsewhip Joe.

"No use denying true feelings, Payton. Loving someone ain't nothing to be ashamed of," Bert kidded with a wink.

Amos and Felipe's snickering added to Payton's misery.

"Yeah, unless she happens to raise sheep," Joe tossed in.

"Sheep?" Payton's heart lurched.

"Yes, sheep." Her face, with its high, sculptured cheekbones tilted in defiance. "I own a sizeable flock of the wooly creatures as if you didn't already know." Amanda's glare aimed a flurry of cartridges and the box too at the narrow space between his eyes.

"You're *that* Amanda?"

How was he supposed to know what she looked like when he was fairly new to the area?

Tears sparkled in her gaze before glinty steel hardened them into bullets.

The hint of rosewater tickled his nose when she propped her hands on each side of him and leaned over, her feathery breath rumpling the hairs of his mustache. "Darling, I made sure everyone saw you in the company of a lowly sheepherder and obviously very delighted. You know how fast that shoots a respected cattleman's reputation. I had nothing to lose because the good citizens of Amarillo already revile me. Gentlemen, you best remember that the next time you try to make a fool of me. And trespass on my property again, I'll fill you so full of holes you'll have to give up bathing to keep from drowning."

A flash of her skirts left Payton reeling. His chair turned over when he stood. "Amanda, wait. I can explain."

"Appears she's not of a notion to listen," Joe drawled.

Payton swung with fists clenched. "I oughta beat you like a rented mule. That was the meanest, low-down prank you've done. What happened to let bygones be bygones? We shook hands."

"You should know better than trust a fellow you've wronged. My marriage was the best part of me."

"Don't think I'm going to forget this."

"Expect not. But the shock on your face is something to tell around the campfire." Joe's chortle drew curious stares from nearby tables. "You were lovin' right up to her when we came in. Had prunes in your voice and everything. Looked like you were damn near fixin' to kiss her."

"I was admiring her . . . eyes."

Those full curves had pulled the fabric tight across her chest until he thought her embellishments might pop out accidentally. Imagining the weight of them in his hands didn't take much effort. Fragrance that spoke of warm nights and full moons promised things he would sell his horse and saddle for.

His lungs swelled with a sudden rush of longing. Damn, Amanda was a bundle of gunpowder and satiny curves. But, she took him for nothing more than a desperate, lonely cowboy who had nothing better to do than write mushy words of love.

Truth to tell, she hit the nail on most of those heads except he wouldn't depend on paper and pencil to do his talking if he had anything to say.

And then there was the matter of her sheep.

Not exactly a big thing in itself. Not if they were in the heart of Scotland. It was, however, an unforgivable sin when it happened in cow country on cow land. He couldn't have anyone think for a minute he was a lamb-licker. They'd laugh him plumb out of Texas. In fact, they'd probably already started a petition to bar him from participating in any Cattlemen Association affairs. Amanda was right about the whole town seeing him in her company.

Spit fire!

Joe leaned back and hooked his fingers in the waist of his britches. "Yep, I could see you were certainly admiring that part of her anatomy. Someone oughta teach you to lie better."

Payton slumped weakly into the chair. It wouldn't do any good to tell him to lower his voice. The damage was done.

They'd fixed him good. He couldn't live this down.

"Your lady is *muy bonita*," Felipe said. "I think maybe she like you. And you have this look of love on your face."

"Looks more like the dry wilts to me," Bert said dryly.

They appeared as satisfied with themselves as pigs in clover.

"Keep your horseback opinions to yourself." Payton wished he could turn back the clock. He would definitely undo the prank that started all this. Talk about rack and ruin.

"Learn to baaaaah before you go courting." Amos picked up the valise Amanda had left behind in her hurry and fiddled with the catch.

"Give me that." Payton jerked the case away before they opened it up in the hotel dining room. That's all he needed. Lord only knew what would jump out. If she had come hoping to spend the night with the writer of the love letters, which technically meant him even though he hadn't written 'em, the valise would hold yards of frothy lace and things of dreams. Things that would show every inch of her big . . . eyes. He flushed, glancing around the dining room.

But the latch had come loose and an assortment of ropes, handcuffs, and . . . leg irons? flew into the air. The devices came down amid a spilled cushion of lacy apparel fashioned of little more than illusion.

Hell and damnation!

Chapter 5

Amanda stomped up the street to Diggs Grocery and Hardware, mindful of the stir her presence in town created. However, judging by the far more than usual whispers and stares, the traveling gazette that carried a whole budget of local gossip from lip to lip must've already began circulating the sordid details of what had just taken place at the hotel. Her plan to ruin Payton McCord's good name appeared to have met with resounding success. It should've pleased her.

Darn it, why didn't it? No one ever claimed war was fair. In fact, it was dirty business. But at what price had winning come? She hadn't expected this murky gloom. In a way it compared to having someone up and die on you.

Maybe they had. Maybe she had. Maybe a dream had.

Deep in thought, Amanda nearly plowed into Hank Harris, a mountain of a man, who stepped from the barber shop onto the wooden sidewalk. His size intimidated. Not that she was afraid of him. She simply felt like a sapling next to a mature oak.

"Ma'am." Hank tipped the brim of his hat to her and kept walking before she could utter a word. She'd heard womenfolk made him ill at ease and it certainly appeared the case, which explained why he'd remained a steadfast bachelor so long.

His ranch wasn't too far from hers, with a huge house as impressive as his height sitting smack in the middle. She guessed he built the enormous structure to keep from knocking himself silly when he stood upright. But, Hank had a good heart and was known for helping people in need. She just tried not to ever need. It was best that way.

Pushing through the mercantile door, she almost collided with Opal Duncan who cradled her newborn son as if he were a fragile egg. It didn't take much to make someone grasp something with such fierce determination when they'd lost their farm and livelihood. Amanda saw her own weary confusion reflecting in the woman's gray eyes.

"I'm terribly sorry. Are you all right, Mrs. Duncan?"

"You just startled me. You're Amanda Lemmons, aren't you?"

Prickles crawled up her back. "Yes, ma'am."

"I just want to tell you to hang on to what's yours. Don't ever let anyone take it away. Fight." Then she whispered, "Talk to my husband if you ever want to sell any of your sheep." Tears swam in Opal's gaze before the woman hurried out the door.

Amanda watched the proud carriage with sorrow. Offer to buy her mutton came unexpectedly. It took brave souls to cross the Association. And Milford Duncan was as strong as they came.

The clock inside the store chimed, reminding her to hurry. She jerked up a sack of sugar and gallon of vinegar and stacked them on a section of the counter. Payton would be making tracks to buy a new hat and she wished to avoid another run-in with the rugged cowboy. Especially one itching to get even. No doubt thick frost would now coat his deep, pleasing baritone.

But, he'd earned what he got for belittling her. In the end he was like all the others. How could she have thought P.M. would stand up when it came time to be counted? The moment came and went and he sat on his California Levi's. There had been no defending her. No apology. No shame. He was nothing but a cow-lover who trifled with a lady's feelings. He scoffed her and her sheep.

Her face burned with remembrance. She fretted in vain over damaging him with her plan. She prayed he never forgot how it felt to be an outcast.

"May I assist you, Miss Lemmons?" Jeb Diggs stood beside his wife, Mary Carol. Both wore shocked expressions that said she was awfully bold to help herself like she owned the store.

The sack of flour Amanda was about to sling onto her pile sank to the floor. She'd just committed another unspeakable sin—that of waiting on herself. Truth was she'd been in such a hurry she forgot the social rules and how they applied to her.

She apologized and told the couple her needs, adding a box of cartridges to her list for good measure. Never could have too many bullets, her father always said. He should know. He'd outlasted blue northerns, encroaching cattle barons, and a sour puss of a second wife who tried her best to kill him before she ran off with a snake charmer from a traveling sideshow.

Amanda blinked back sudden tears at the reminder of what it cost to survive and stared at the small mountain on the counter. She must've been out of everything.

Thank goodness she'd thought to leave the wagon in front of the mercantile when she arrived that morning. Wouldn't have far to carry the supplies. Pray tell that a tad of the mutton smell would rub off or someone would see the Diggs's aiding the enemy.

A fashionable, very pretty woman approached, clutching a pad and pencil of all things. "Miss Lemmons?"

The large feather protruding from the hat perching on the woman's head indicated wealth, no sympathy for the naked bird she'd stolen the tail feathers from, or both. No one in the Panhandle wore such trappings so perhaps she came from far away and therefore wasn't part of the mud-slinging. Still, the question made Amanda bristle.

"Who wants to know?"

"Oh dear, I've done it again." The woman stretched out her gloved hand. "Kaira Renaulde from Boston. Well, actually I'm a new reporter for the *Panhandle Herald*. I only need a moment."

"I'm sorry." The striking newsmonger could peddle her papers elsewhere. "Maybe another time."

Payton McCord should be opening the worn, leather bag Amanda deliberately left behind right about now. All hell would break loose when he discovered the contents.

"I promise to be brief. Please allow me to explain. Somehow, I've gotten myself in a bit of a pickle and promised my boss, the editor, I'd get an article for the paper."

"I really can't. Now, if you'll excuse me."

Kaira brushed aside Amanda's brusque dismissal. Her hand poised to write. "Although I'm from back East I hear it's quite unusual for a born and bred cowboy and a sheepherder to consort. But I must say it's quite romantic. Is there any truth to the rumor Payton McCord of the Frying Pan Ranch met you this morning at the hotel, and that he's written you love letters?"

The perfect opportunity to destroy what was left of Payton's reputable name fell into Amanda's lap. What better artillery than a newspaper to finish him off good and proper?

Except, she'd seen integrity in his gentle soul.

"I do apologize, Miss Renaulde. It's a private matter that I have no wish to air either with you or the entire town. Perhaps you'd have better luck asking the gentleman."

Without a doubt he could fill the woman's column for her. But would he? The assortment she'd packed into the valise crossed her mind. Amanda swallowed a lump. Oh yes, he'd definitely want revenge.

"I understand." The brash reporter broke into her train of thought. "But, in case you change your mind . . . I'll be very discreet. I promise."

"Like I said, it's between me and McCord."

Jeb Diggs spoke up. "That'll be $4.75, Miss Lemmons."

Amanda winced and counted out the change from what remained of last year's wool profit. Money dwindled fast. She'd have to begin shearing tomorrow. To her amazement, the Diggs's son toted the purchase to the wagon while she followed.

Kaira Renaulde of the *Herald* stood waiting outside. "If you ever want to talk about anything I'm available."

"Now I know you're new." Amanda gave a short laugh. "Evidently you haven't gotten the latest issue of the Amarillo Scuttlebutt."

"A cardinal rule in reporting—I don't listen to gossip. Remember what I said. Everyone needs somebody."

Indeed they might, but they rarely got what they needed.

Sudden commotion erupted outside the hotel. It appeared some sort of noisy parade. Amanda gulped.

In the center of the maelstrom strode the tall, purposeful figure of Payton McCord. He stalked toward the mercantile, his face the color of ripe beets.

Oh Lord, he'd opened the valise.

"Excuse me, Miss Renaulde." Amanda clambored onto the wagon seat. "I really mustn't dawdle. Have a nice day."

A fleeting glance over her shoulder reminded her of a story she once read about the folly of awakening a sleeping lion.

This lion didn't have a bit of sleep in his eye.

Chapter 6

Blood thundered in Amanda's ears as Amarillo faded like remnants of a dusty dream under the speeding wagon wheels. The sun bore a tad more heat than ordinary. But to be honest, she couldn't lay the blame for moisture pooling between her breasts solely on the warm rays.

An unfamiliar feeling rippled, the intensity choking her.

Something indescribable had changed. Her life had taken a totally unexpected turn. Good, bad, or indifferent—it shook her to the core.

The cloudless sky appeared a vivid turquoise instead of simply blue. Crows flitted and dipped through the air in some sort of odd bird promenade. Perhaps they, too, sensed this odd awakening of sorts.

For once she'd bested the buffle-headed land-grubbers. McCord should understand she wouldn't abide any cheap tricks.

Although he denied writing the love letters, and perhaps she could believe that without too great a stretch, he hadn't stood up for her. He hadn't stopped the ridicule. He hadn't seen beneath the surface. Disgust for her chosen profession had colored his minty gaze a shadowed tint of purple nightshade.

The man could be dangerous in a way she'd never known.

Before she reached home, a sobering thought crossed her mind, one she didn't particularly relish—McCord would insist on returning the valise. Putting the assortment of imprisoning devices in the case made certain of that.

She'd have to see him again.

Sudden recollection of the sinful curve of his mouth rocked confidence that she could handle the visit. A horde of locusts seemed to have made a nest in her stomach.

From the wagon bed, the gentle slosh of vinegar against the sides of the bottle added to the floundering in her brain.

At least she had all the ingredients for a vinegar pie. Didn't hurt to have one ready to throw in McCord's well-chiseled face. The concoction would serve the conniving jularker right.

She crested a rise and the adobe dwelling she called home came into view. Her breathing returned to normal. She was back on her land where she knew the workings of things, where she didn't have to pretend, where she could be who she wanted without worry or fear of reprisal. Her dog and her flock provided all the security she needed even though it did get a bit dreary at times. Give her that any day to a piece of the world that saw and judged people unfairly.

The familiar sight also served to remind of her distaste for cattlemen. Something she needed to bear in mind next time she encountered the broad-shouldered Texan. She welcomed the pain if only because it drew horns on P.M.'s handsome head. And anyone else who chose the path to her door.

Movement in front of her home brought skitters of alarm until she saw long braids on the man who eased from the weather-beaten willow chair. Her old Navajo friend, John Two Shoes Running Deer, always seemed to know the precise time for shearing, although he had no use for printed calendars. He marked the days in his head and by the seasons, as his culture had taught for generations. She pulled the horses to a stop and set the brake.

"John, it's wonderful to see you."

"I'm here every spring." He helped her down. "Or are you surprised I didn't freeze over the winter?"

"Your skin is about as tough as alligator. I doubt you felt the cold. Besides, your hogan is probably warmer than the inside of Hades. I'm just glad for the company."

Now let McCord come calling. She wasn't alone.

"Only a fool would refuse the offer of a new wool shirt in exchange for shearing a few sheep." John's eyes twinkled. "Your handiwork is some of the finest. You spin and weave in the old customs. If I didn't know of your heritage I'd believe you had Navajo blood."

Amanda scowled. "With a Spanish mother and Scottish father, I'm afraid I'm a sorry mixture."

The blend of nationalities was the kind that aroused prejudice and misgivings. The kind that destroyed chances of a normal life. It seemed men couldn't look beyond the surface to see how she ached to fit in.

John peered into the bed of the wagon. "You've been to town. It explains the burrs under your *serape*."

"Can't hide much from an old war-hide like you."

"People will continue to shun if you keep adopting the ways of the Indian. Your moccasins remind of your stubbornness."

"Who said I want to be a horn-tossing hypocrite? My feet are happier in these moccasins than heavy boots." Images of cold stares, the sneers of some of Amarillo's finest, created a brittle hardness inside. "Those buffoons wouldn't accept me no matter what I do."

"Pain in your heart says this time was worse."

She side-stepped the unpleasant subject, casting an eye to the sun's overhead position. "We're wasting time flapping our gums. If we hurry we can get a few sheep done before dark. I'll fix a place for you to bed down until we finish the job."

"I sleep outside under the stars."

"As you wish."

"It is." John lifted the sack of flour, threw it over his shoulder, and carried it into the house while Amanda gave a sharp command for Fraser to round up the flock.

Sight of the collie marching the sheep toward the fold like fat, little soldiers banished raw feelings. She could count on the animal to do his job with skilled perfection. Unlike people. Bitterness rose. Years had flown and yet certain events ate at her sanity. . . .

Argus Lemmons's abandonment upon the heels of her mother's death opened wounds that had scarred with age. Sure, he'd left Amanda in the care of an old aunt. But he did his daughter no favor, considering the woman forced her to stand on the street and pretend blindness so passersby would toss a few coins in her cup. Not that she got to keep any for herself. Dear Auntie made her strip and scrubbed her thoroughly for any hidden tokens.

"Worthless stray mutt," Aunt Zelda would call Amanda, wrinkling up her nose. "Argus shoulda drowned you."

Amanda turned fifteen before she got up enough courage to set out alone for Santa Fe to start a life that had to be better than lying, begging, and starvation.

Except new surroundings didn't improve Amanda's situation. A few years later, her fancy suitor left her at the altar after he made the less than thrilling discovery that she was heir to nothing but a scraggly flock of sheep. He abruptly moved Amanda from the assets to the liability column.

And fighting Argus's second wife for a place in her father's heart had most certainly shown the worst of humanity.

The hollow victory of survival spared Amanda peace in the dead of night. She was still that stray mutt looking for a home.

If the world had a dropping off point, she'd found it on this rocky piece of land in the Texas Panhandle. High winds, dry winters, and low rainfall didn't represent being in high cotton, but this parcel of shortgrass prairie was hers and they'd have to kill her to get her off.

Today she'd almost forgotten the anguish that twisted like

a knife before McCord up and heaped on a lot more. Then, she did the same as she'd always done. She ran.

Well, she wouldn't run again. She squared her jaw. This was the last button remaining on Jacob's coat!

Stashing the supplies, Amanda changed from her finery and hurried to help John. Together they penned the sheep and set up the foot-pump clippers.

Fraser watched over his charges with guarded vigilance. No ram, ewe, or lamb would dare shirk its duty in filling the bags with wool, not with the faithful collie on hand. Amanda rewarded him with a tasty morsel of cured bacon.

"Keep a sharp eye for trespassers, boy. P.M. will be coming."

John's dark stare narrowed. "You expect trouble."

"Doesn't hurt to be prepared."

"Who is this P.M.?"

A man who'd given her hope, who walked with purpose, and who snatched away airy dreams with the lift of an arched brow.

"No one much."

"And yet, you are sure he will come."

Oh, yeah. The awakened lion would definitely ride her way

"He's just another two-bit cowboy who fills Amarillo's establishments. Works for the Frying Pan. I turned the tables on him and he's madder than a frog on a hot skillet at being bested by a woolie."

"Whatever happened he earned. He comes, we scalp him."

"Now John, no reason to get out the bows, arrows, and tomahawks. I can handle one measly nuisance. I am grateful to have your company for a few days though."

"Hmph!"

The Navajo flipped a ewe onto her back and began peeling the thick wool from the belly and throat with the clippers before moving to the topside. Amanda stuffed the greasy fleece into a burlap bag to separate later. She'd keep a good portion and sell the rest. What she kept would get a thorough washing before she carded and spun the long fibers into yarn.

She was so busy planning she failed to hear approaching hoofbeats until a low growl rumbled in Fraser's throat and the hair on his neck rose. She jerked around and her spit dried.

McCord sat astride a spotted appaloosa. Sparks in his gaze betrayed the easy slouch that might've suggested he'd stopped for a moment to discuss nothing more than the weather.

Steel strengthened Amanda's spine. "Get off my land."

"Not very hospitable. I recall you seemed pretty friendly when you were dragging a man's life through the muck. What did you do with that woman? She was soft and . . . obliging." A lazy smile crinkled the corners of his eyes.

"If you came out here to discuss my qualities or the lack thereof I'm afraid I have no time."

With a quick motion, he untied the worn leather valise and held it out. "Thought you might need your *equipment* before nightfall. The assortment appears well broken in. Must get regular use I figure. Lord only knows why a handsome woman would have to depend on restraints to hold a man. Seems you're awfully insecure of your abilities."

Amanda gritted her teeth, becoming rigid at the suggestion she had to hogtie a man for his company. McCord bedeviled in a thousand impossible ways and every last one of them irritated beyond belief. Every fiber prodded for attack. So she blocked out the sight of his sandy, sun-streaked waves ruffled by the wind, and the mustache that drew attention to the firm shape of his mouth. Amanda met the dangerous glint in his eyes head on.

"Begs to ask why you pried into personal belongings."

"It wasn't by choice, believe me. The damn thing flew open and everyone in the hotel and hell's half acre saw the contraptions. Made me a laughingstock. I hope you're happy."

"Not yet, but close."

John Two Shoes Running Deer released the freshly naked ewe and stood to his full six feet. "Ahhhh, this must be P.M. Can we scalp him now?"

Chapter 7

Waning light bounced off the glistening coat of a border collie as it danced around Payton's horse, Domino, threatening to tear the strapping animal limb from limb. Leave it to a woman who played with torture devices to keep a dog with the temper of a rabid coyote.

Had he heard or imagined the threat to scalp him?

Good God! He should've had better sense than ride out alone. He didn't know who was crazier: Amanda, the Navajo, himself, or the dog.

The woman had seemed perfectly normal back at the hotel. He never would've mistaken her for a lunatic.

It must be the sheep. Those God-awful, smelly sheep.

They would make anyone lose their ever-loving minds. Payton scowled at the sneaky cotton-balls-with-eyes, shifting to the critter the Navajo had just stripped bare. One problem with the animals—besides the fact they weren't cows—was they either looked like scrubby, puffy clouds or so spindly a gust of wind would blow them away. Cows looked the same day in and day out. They were hefty on their hooves and their bellering could lull a man right to sleep. He'd have to stick something in his ears and a clove of garlic under his nose if he had to put up with this damn baahing.

"I can't relieve you of your loathsome burden right now." Amanda raised palms that were greasy from handling the wool and pointed to the ground. "Drop it there and I'll get it later."

He stiffened in the saddle. "Since you're up to your elbows in mutton, I'll set the bag inside your door. Just call off your dog. I'd like to be gone before your friend gets out the scalping knife."

Annoyance and open irritation pinched her kissable lips into a narrow line. He'd like to believe he saw the makings of a smile, but that appeared merely wishful thinking. Lush willingness he'd glimpsed in the hotel had given way to a tough-as-almighty-steel banshee.

"Fraser, enough!" The collie ceased yapping after Amanda's stern order, but sat on his haunches and watched with distrust.

Payton adjusted the brim of his new hat that didn't fit quite right yet, slid from Domino's back, and ambled toward the adobe structure.

Three sets of eyes followed his every move.

A string of curses rolled around his brain but they remained unsaid in case the threat to lift his hair had been more than idle words. But damn, if he'd wanted to pillage and plunder he would've chosen some place more lucrative. This sheep farm didn't have a blessed thing worth taking. Except maybe the lady who owned it. In spite of all, he found her a worthy opponent if not someone he could share a life with.

He pushed open the door and bent to set the worn piece of leather inside. Raising up, he spied a circle of black felt on the floor with a handful of boiled carrots smack in the center of it.

His gaze narrowed. It appeared a hat of some sort although it'd been flattened almost beyond recognition. Taking two steps forward, he determined it had indeed once been a noble Stetson.

Furthermore, a piece of rawhide stuck off to one side, the same kind that had served for a band on the hat he'd lost. He inched closer and gulped.

It was his hat.

Crumpled and smashed like a piece of trash.

His hat . . . used for a dog dish.

Hell and be damned!

Payton whirled as Amanda flew through the door with the dog at her side. "What in hell have you done to my damn hat?" he exploded.

The way her spine instantly tensed let him know he was in for a heck of a fight. A reasonable man might back off, but who said he was reasonable? Some things were sacred to even a rough-around-the-edges cowhand like him.

"What makes you think I'm to blame?" she huffed.

"It's here isn't it?" It was hard to keep his finger steady; it shook when he pointed to the dog dish. "That belongs to me. What the hell did you do? You've mutilated the hat until I barely recognized it as wearing apparel."

Spite in her eyes told him the place he could go and he'd recognize it by the fire and brimstone.

"Why are you snooping in my house in the first place? You violated the privacy of my belongings and now dare come into my home, my place of refuge, to raise your voice, accusing me of all manner of things. You were merely to set the bag inside. I didn't tell you to barge in and make yourself comfortable. I should've known better than trust a smooth-talking rawhider."

"I'm a sight better than someone who stomps the guts out of something and treats it like a bad haircut."

At least she had the grace to color. But nothing excused her. In his estimation she didn't have a leg to stand on to explain the deliberate destruction of a piece of him. The treasured piece of felt was like family. No, it was better than family because it never nagged, gave reproach or grief. The Stetson had been with him through thick and thin, rain and shine, hay and grass.

"Maybe it used to be yours. Don't think you'll waltz in here and take it back. The hat's mine now."

"The hell you say."

From the corner of Payton's eye he saw Fraser mark a course for the mangled hat. The dog took a bite of carrots then looked up with a satisfied gleam as though gloating that he'd staked his claim and he'd not budge. Payton cringed at the rank dog-breath odorizing the felt circle. He took a step, intending to rectify the situation. But Fraser growled and bared his teeth, ending those grand ideas.

"If you wanted the bonnet so bad why didn't you glue the darn thing to your head?"

Payton jammed his hands in his pockets and shifted his glare from the bandit dog to Amanda. "It figures you'd try to shift the blame. And don't belittle my Stetson more than you have. It's a hat, not a bonnet. The thing blew off while I had my hands full with a few thousand pounds of snortin' cowhide. I've searched the Panhandle over for it."

Anyone with half sense knew how blessed tiresome the wind on the Panhandle got. Old-timers claimed barbed wire was the only divider between this stretch of land and hell. He wasn't about to apologize for something beyond his control.

Amanda shrugged her shoulders. "Guess not hard enough. I didn't have any trouble finding it."

Payton struggled with desire to strangle someone. "A dog dish? You thrashed me in town and made sure to finish the job out here." His gaze narrowed dangerously toward Fraser, who responded with spiked bristles. "What did I ever do to you? As far as I know we've never met before today."

"We haven't."

"Then would you care to enlighten me? I think you owe it."

Her tongue took a slow turn around her lips. "For the record, I didn't plan a personal attack."

"Couldn't prove it by me."

"I meant to aim the hat, the shackles, and the name-smearing at the faceless author of some love letters. I was positive, whoever the anonymous man was, he intended to use the notes as some sort of vendetta. I finally got tired of the slurs, the laughter, and everyone trying to force me into leaving. So I decided to fight back." Amanda caught her bottom lip between her teeth.

"I didn't know you were an innocent bystander caught up in Joe Long's prank."

"Would it have made a difference?"

A wry grin tugged the corners of her mouth. "Perhaps."

"What did you think I planned to do? If I had written the letters, of course."

Amanda shrugged. "The usual. I thought you'd stand up in the middle of the hotel and chide me for believing anyone could love a mutton puncher. Then, the whole blamed town would have a huge laugh. They already shun me as it is. I wouldn't have been able to trade there after that, to sell my wool or any excess sheep."

He caught the slight tremble of her chin before she clenched her jaw. The woman carried deep hurt. Would she love as desperately as she fought to keep what was hers? He'd bet his life on it.

"I've never publicly ridiculed anyone."

"Oh, but you did." Her voice lowered barely louder than a whisper. "Sometimes silence speaks with a clear voice."

Yep, he guessed it certainly did. He'd participated without being aware of it. To his credit, shock in the hotel kept words from forming, not disgust for who she was. The facts coming out the way they did spun his head like a top and it hadn't stopped yet. Still, Amanda was right. He should've set Joe and the whole Frying Pan bunch straight.

"I don't know a man who doesn't have a passel of regrets. To clear the record, Joe didn't mean the love letter joke for you. He wrote those to get back at me." Payton told her about their jokes and Lucy and the saloon girl.

She folded her arms. "I don't blame his wife. You both need strung up."

Fire in Amanda's gaze that had threatened to burn him to a crisp seemed to lose a bit of its spark, although he knew it still smoldered beneath the surface ready to leap into a bonfire at the least provocation. After all, his mama didn't raise a fool.

Heifers and steers were unpredictable. Each led you to believe one thing and did the opposite.

Look at how soft and seductive she'd been in town before she turned into Chief Sitting Bull on the warpath. A trick.

Not that she wasn't appealing now. The plain russet dress she'd changed into had been patched so many times it bore similarity to a quilt. But, it added toughness to her. He admired a woman with grit and sass. Miss Amanda Lemmons had plenty of both and she earned it the hard way from the looks of things. Whatever had happened to form the granite layers must've destroyed her softer side. The desire to hold and protect her from ill swept past the ache in his bones.

Payton shifted his feet, lowering his gaze. "The sun's winding down. Guess I'd best get back or Joe'll send out a search party."

"You've likely missed supper. I could offer you a spot at my table to help make up for what I did. Will you stay?"

The thought of sharing a meal with her made his blood rush. However maddening, she was the most desirable woman he'd ever met. He didn't have far to go from that to thoughts of taming some of the wildness from her and kissing her until neither had breath or willfulness left.

But, she had said "could offer" as if it was something she felt obliged to do instead of coming from true sincerity.

He shook his head. "Appreciate it, but keeping company with you won't do either of our reputations any good. We're on opposite sides of the fence. It's best if I don't."

Amanda bristled. "Then don't let me keep you."

He gave the new dog dish a long scowl before he turned, colliding with the solid weight of Navajo fury.

"Need help with this *gringo*, Amanda?"

"He's just leaving, John." The door probably would bear the imprint of her grasp. She didn't seem to understand he'd turned down the supper invite to save her.

"Hmph! Scared of my knife, huh?"

THE LOVE LETTER 247

Amanda followed Payton to his horse. "I admit you got the short end of a pitchfork today. And I apologize for the hat."

Despite the words, the Mutton Madam's somber expression wrapped in axle grease said she didn't regret the shambles she'd left him in for a minute.

"You must really despise cattlemen."

"Don't know the half of it. Do you blame me?"

"Can't say that I do. I'd likely feel the same if someone had it in for me." He put a foot in the stirrup and threw his leg over the saddle. "You're a strong woman, Amanda Lemmons."

The dark-eyed shepherdess had a will of iron and the disposition of a riled bull that had his manly parts cut off.

Taking the long way back to the ranch seemed a good notion. He was in no hurry to take the derision he'd get. Besides, he had a bit of thinking to do that required peace and quiet. Amanda had wiggled under his skin and he didn't think he'd ever be the same.

Under all the hardness he'd glimpsed a lady who had her heart stomped on too many times. Someone had done her wrong and made her fighting mad.

And that the cattlemen were up in arms over her sheep didn't improve the situation. If he had anything to do with it, they wouldn't succeed in forcing her out. Pitiful though the ranch looked, it belonged to her. And the adobe house didn't have enough room inside to sling a cat, but it was hers.

A woman tended to arch her back when she was trying to hold on to every ounce of self-respect she had left. Payton knew a little about facing down a group of people who wanted to destroy him. Oh yeah, he definitely knew that feeling.

Tugging the brim of his hat low, he tried to forget the pain that thickened in his chest, trying to starve him of air. He hadn't won, but maybe Amanda Lemmons would. He hoped so. She deserved a shot. He didn't think he'd ever hear himself argue equal rights for sheepherders, but that's what it boiled down to. Long as he didn't have to see or listen to the dumpy critters, they could go on their merry way.

Yep, the wooly rascals had better stay on their own side of the fence if they wanted to get along with him.

Payton was a born and bred cowman and nobody, not even the sassy hat-mauler in sheep's clothing, could change that.

Amanda watched until Payton McCord became a speck in the distance. She hadn't meant to rub his nose in his misfortune with the hat. But, damn him, he shouldn't have come borrowing trouble. It was best she told him right off how things were. Saved time.

"Nice man," John said softly. "Nerves of steel. Wasn't a bit afraid of my knife."

"You old crow bait, you've forgotten any such skills. Been too many moons ago since you scalped anyone, if you ever did. You only said that to get his attention. And since when did you develop a liking for high-struttin' cowboys?"

"I have nothing against anyone. Maybe you should try to understand 'em instead of running 'em off. You are a beautiful woman and way too young to be so soured on life."

"I'm perfectly happy this way. I can live without the likes of McCord. I have my flock to occupy my time."

"The bleating of sheep cannot compare to a human voice whispering in your ear. Or have you forgotten the warmth of a touch? You need companionship. The Great Father didn't mean us to live life all alone. Surely you desire for someone to share your days. And nights."

She thirsted and pined for such a man. If John's Great Father meant for things to be different why had he given her an extra helping of solitude and despair and left off masculine, comforting arms to hold her?

"I'm not going to let myself get taken in by every two-bit hustler."

"You do not trust this man?"

Truth be told, it was herself that Amanda didn't dare trust.

Payton McCord had awakened too many unbearable fancies she'd buried long ago in Santa Fe. The man tempted her to forget the pain of believing in people who let her down.

She would steel herself against temptation.

And she would put her faith in no one ever again.

Chapter 8

Early the following morning Payton threw a blanket over Domino, stealing a sideways glance at the lone figure standing in the barn door, staring moon-eyed toward the little cabin across the compound. Payton felt sorry for Joe despite being angry enough to cuss a blue streak over the stunt his friend pulled with the desirable Miss Lemmons.

"Ever think maybe you should pick Lucy some flowers, Joe?"

A heavy sigh filled the space.

"Reckon it couldn't hurt none."

Joe stalked toward yellow blooms that scattered down the fence row. Payton grimaced when the man yanked the stalks from the ground by the roots and marched toward his former home like General Grant bound for Richmond.

Lucinda evidently kept one eye trained on the window because she waited until her husband got within a few feet of the porch before letting the first boot fly. Joe skittered back out of range of her pitching arm.

"I picked you posies, sweetheart." Dirt fell from the handful of plants he held out.

"Get your bony, flea-bitten rear end back across the yard. And take your weeds with you. I'll tell you when you can call."

"Dammit, Lucinda! I cain't apologize if you won't let me."

Payton whistled a tune, focusing on cinching the wide band around Domino's girth. His attempt to keep a straight face failed. Luckily, he wiped off the grin before his glum friend noticed. "That Lucy sure can sweet talk a fellow."

Daggers in Joe's eyes could've slain a den of man-eating bears. Payton ducked his head, grateful he had things to do that spared watching his best friend's misery.

"Anymore bright ideas, McCord?"

"Nope."

"Then I suggest you get busy with the branding. I see the boys have rounded up the herd and headed this way. They'll have 'em in the corral before you can get a good fire built."

Domino pranced as though anxious to get to friendlier ground. Payton was about to swing up when their boss's wife, Ellen Sanborn, opened the door of the Frying Pan's sprawling ranch house to shake a blanket. Ellen hummed a pretty hymn, so that must be a good sign Boss's health had improved.

A solid thud behind him made Payton whirl. Joe had hauled off and kicked the tar out of a half-full rain barrel. Water sloshed up to the rim. Payton hoped Joe didn't break a toe to add to his list of misfortunes. He wasn't about to ask though.

"Any word on Mr. Sanborn's bout with the grippe?"

Joe hobbled to the workbench in front of the barn. "Doc said if the missus can get enough of Golden's Liquid Beef Tonic down Mr. Sanborn's gullet he'll be up and around soon. Now get out of here and quit being so nosy."

This mess with Lucy sure had Joe in a dither.

Payton was suddenly overjoyed he only had a bunch of cows to worry with—anything that wasn't connected to women or sheep.

He rubbed his bum knee and set off to meet the cloud of dust. His mind wasn't on the task at hand, but on the bunkhouse that burst at the seams with the addition of Joe. A dozen men trying to keep out of each other's hair had gotten harder. To make it worse, their foreman persisted in grinding his teeth and fiddling with every blooming thing even if it didn't need fiddled with.

"Domino, I'm going to have to take matters in my own hands with Lucy if any of us are to get a minute's peace."

Besides, he had a more important reason now. The longer this thing dragged on, no telling what Joe would hatch up next. He didn't need his life complicated further. He had enough to try to sort out as it stood.

For one thing, Amanda had already lumped him into the category of skunk oil salesmen and riffraff. And Lord only knew when he could repair the damage done in town. He could testify that he had grief by the dozens. Too bad he couldn't crate it up like eggs and sell it. He'd be rolling in money.

A few hours later, Payton separated a calf from its mother. He swung the lariat, caught two hind legs, and tightened the rope around the horn. He leaped off Domino and, with a twist, flipped the protesting calf onto its right side near the branding fire. Bert and Amos rushed forward. One anchored the head, the other the feet.

Payton removed the rope and gave Felipe room to press the brand smoothly against the flank.

Scorched hide greeted Payton's nostrils. Everything he ate for the next month would likely bear the taste. He took a swig from his canteen to whet his whistle and watched the bewildered baby shake his head and bellow for his mother. Mama Cow charged over, checking her calf from head to tail. Then, giving Payton a disagreeable eye, she nudged her offspring away from the rest of the herd. Seemed his popularity with females had spread.

Riding herd involved hard work, long hours, and short pay but Payton loved the freedom of the range.

A man had plenty of fresh air out on the panhandle. Endless prairie land rose up to kiss the sky like a jealous lover, creating a breathtaking landscape.

Life seemed pure here—unblemished, uncrowded, and unappreciated by some. City folks didn't know what they missed. He poured a cup of coffee from the pot on the fire and joined the others who took a break.

"Hey, Payton, ever think about doing anything else?" Amos cut a plug of tobacco with his pocketknife and stuck the brown chaw in his mouth.

"Nope." He came into this world a cowboy and that's how he'd die.

Amos leaned back on his heels. "Sometimes I wonder what walking in a banker's shoes would be like."

Bert laughed. "Stiff and squeaky. Ever hear them walk?"

"*Si*," Felipe joined in. "I don't want no banker's shoes."

"Me either." Amos wiped his mouth. "Squeaky shoes are for stuffed shirts. The damn things would drive a man batty. Reminds me of the time—"

"Oh hush!" Bert tossed a handful of gravel. "Everything reminds you of some time or another."

"Many days I wish for a pretty *senorita* though."

Payton eyed the half-breed. "And what would you do with her, Felipe, my friend?"

"Love her."

That word again—love. Among a batch of confirmed loners the declaration was like an elephant that everyone saw but pretended it trampled harmlessly an ocean away. Because to admit such existed meant they'd have to think about what their lives didn't have in it. Like the rest, he didn't cotton much to changing his ways.

"From what I've seen, loving a woman takes a heap of work and patience." Payton took another swig of water and corked the canteen. The sinful curve of Amanda's lush mouth crept into his thoughts. Upon the heels of the warm recollection, kissing and cuddling crossed his mind. *Damn!* She'd probably sic her dog on him if he tried. But, to have her in his arms might be worth getting chewed to bits by a mangy, sheep-smelling animal.

"Shoot, with my luck the woman would turn out like Lucinda

and have a God-almighty pitching arm," Amos replied. "No thanks, I'm satisfied with loving and leaving 'em. Saves on blood and bruises."

"You couldn't find one to have you anyway, you old coot."

"Bert, I'm tempted to make you eat those words."

"You and what army?"

Through the drone of their banter, Payton tried to quell panic that generally visited only after the sun went down and the day ended. He wasn't getting any younger. His bones creaked and ached, compliments of breaking horses and wrestling mean steers. One day he'd wake up all alone with only the ornery longhorns for company. No one wanted a broken down has-been. In a couple of years he'd be forty. His time had passed.

"Hey, Payton, you never did say what happened when you toted the bag to Amanda Lemmons." A twinkle lit Bert's eyes.

Payton should've known he hadn't heard the last of that. They'd given him hell last evening until he finally marched out to Wild Horse Lake and counted the bullfrogs until he ran out of numbers. When he'd gotten back they were all snoring pretty as you please, which suited him just fine.

Amos's bushy beard twitched. "You don't leak when you drink so I don't reckon she shot you. A case of bad aim? Or did by some miracle a brave soul pour ice water on her to put out the flames before you got there?"

"Nothing happened. Not one thing."

Other than he found his hat that had been smashed and filled with boiled carrots.

And he'd learned the value of a woman's pain.

"I bet you boys anything she invited ol' Payton in for tea and crumpets," Bert said. "Or maybe she handcuffed and fed you mutton stew."

A growl rumbled in Payton's throat. "That's enough."

"You can tell. We won't breathe a word," Amos promised.

"No one here but the cows and they don't gossip," Bert teased.

They'd badger Payton to death until he told them something. He had to nip this thing in the bud before someone
got hurt. He sighed, tossing out the grounds in the bottom of
his cup.

"I returned her property. She thanked me and I left. Now
let it drop. If I hear anyone say a word out of line about the
woman you'll answer to me. She has a right to her own business whatever that may be. You'll respect her or you'll wish
you had."

"I swear the man's got it bad."

"Amos, I warned you. Shut up before you're sorry."

Felipe slapped his thigh. "I think he like her. Maybe she
kiss him."

"For the last time, let it be." Through a narrowed squint
Payton noticed a rider kicking up a dust cloud. He made out
Joe Long as he drew closer.

Damn, the friend still acted downright strange!

Reminded him of the time Joe stuffed some mutton under
the cantle of his saddle. Took him a week to find the source
of the stench and the damn thing still stank to high heaven on
a warm day. Just like he'd done back then, Joe went around
sniffing, wearing a quirky grin.

Payton had better get things squared away with Lucy and
pretty pronto.

Chapter 9

Payton didn't have long to wait for Joe's next move. The sun squatted on the horizon by the time the hands called it a day and rode back to the ranch. They'd had a particularly hard day that left Payton's butt dragging in the dirt. All he wanted was a hot meal and his bunk. He'd also have settled for a bath, but that wouldn't happen until Saturday.

His spurs jangled as he stepped inside the bunkhouse. Thoughts of his material welfare froze in his brain. Someone had tied a ball of white fluff to the foot of his bed. When it saw him, the cotton ball opened its mouth and bleated.

"Who the hell put that blasted thing in here?" he thundered, looking around for the culprit. He'd wring Joe's neck. But the foreman had vanished.

Bert laughed so hard he rolled on the floor. The black scowl Payton shot him could've singed the hide off a greased pig. The look certainly seemed to get the laughing hyena's attention. Bert stood, covering his mouth to hide the grin. "Looks like you have a new bed partner, McCord."

Felipe untied the creature and cradled it in his arms. "I like him. My father was a sheepherder many years ago."

"Is this the start of your new herd . . . uh, I mean flock, Payton?" Amos roared until he had to sit down and catch his breath. Tears ran down the old man's rough bristles. He didn't pay the murderous glare Payton leveled on him a speck of notice.

"What you gonna do?" Felipe patted the soft head.

"Before or after I kill Joe? I'll have to take the damn thing back I suppose. No, don't look at me with those sad, brown eyes. We're not keeping it. It doesn't belong here. We're respectable cowmen."

The door opened and Joe stuck his head inside. "Aw, dad-burn it! I missed the fun. Was he surprised?"

With a growl, Payton lunged and tackled his friend before Joe could block the attack. "I oughta rub your nose in the smelly ball of yarn. Surprised? Yeah, I'm overjoyed."

Joe grinned in the headlock. "I thought you would be."

"Leave things alone or you'll see what other surprises I have in store for you."

In a heartbeat, Joe sobered. "You can't make my life any more worthless. On her worst day, Lucinda is my one and only. Losing her took my reason for waking up in the mornings."

The gray, forlorn misery crawled inside Payton. He released Joe and motioned him outside for more privacy. "You haven't lost her. Don't ever think that. Lucy hasn't given up squatter's rights on your house, which tells me she's planning on staying."

"You reading a crystal ball or tea leaves?"

"I know that when a person decides to end something for good they pack up and leave. So Lucy isn't finished."

"Never looked at it that way."

"Give her a few more days and she'll beg you to come back."

Come daylight, after Payton got through, Joe would be out of the doghouse one way or another. He'd had it. Someone would listen to reason or else.

"Reckon I ain't got nothing but time."

"Then you can cart this lamb back where you got it."

Joe's eyes widened. "Can you be a good friend and do that? I don't feel so hot."

"Skin your own stinking skunks, don't look at me."

"Will you do it if I promise to lay off the foolishness?"

Payton wouldn't fall for that trick. "No."

"I can't leave tonight. Mr. Sanborn wants to see me after supper. Probably wants a tally of the branding. After the business part is done he'll want to play poker. You know how he gets being cooped up with womenfolk all day."

"Get one of the others to cart the thing back then. It's not my problem."

"Are you forgetting how I saved your life when you first hired on? You owe me."

Payton's mind drifted back to winter and the blizzard that wiped out a third of the herd. He'd ridden with the men to try to get a bunch of cattle out of the icy creek bed down in a draw before they froze to death. Domino lost his footing on the ice and went down. The horse was all right, only scared. He got up and ran, leaving Payton buried in the snow with an injured leg. Payton thought for sure he'd freeze to death before someone found him. And he would have if not for Joe, who scoured the drifts looking for him.

Yeah, he owed a debt for sure. But enough to take a bullet?

"I shouldn't, but seeing how down on your uppers you are with Lucinda and all I guess I could take pity this once. Need I ask where you got it?"

"Nope. Amanda Lemmons will be less than thrilled to see you. I sort of borrowed it."

"Figured as much." If the Navajo was still there, Payton might find himself losing his hair. He didn't relish returning to the scene of the crime. Surely, the woman wouldn't be too mad though since he'd be wagging the dumb lamb home.

Domino gave him a walleyed stare when Payton lifted the saddle and slung it again on the horse's back. He draped the bellowing sheep across his lap and set out.

Twilight fell by the time he crossed onto Amanda's ranch,

and it got darker still before he saw the glow from the adobe's windows. It seemed welcoming if a body didn't know better. Unease twisted his gut. The pitch black was eerily still.

Payton figured on quietly putting the lamb into the fold with the rest of the scrubby clan and leaving with no one the wiser. Only the noisy ball of fluff had other ideas. The blessed animal evidently got a whiff of its mother because Payton never heard such a ruckus from a small mouth. Then the collie started barking as if the world had come to an end and he had to alert everyone. Payton let loose a string of cussing.

The hellacious racket outside the house aroused pinpricks in places Amanda didn't know they could crawl—like her brain and her heart. Something or someone was out there. Her feet hit the floor. She grabbed the shotgun and burst out the door to see a spotted appaloosa standing near the pen. Atop the animal sat the silhouette of a man bold as could be. A lamb draped across the saddle bellowed its head off.

The dirty, rotten thief! And he had the audacity to linger even after she'd caught him.

Fury swept past reason. With a squeeze of the trigger, orange flame spat from the killing end and sent hot lead whistling past the interloper's ear.

"Move and I'll make you regret it, mister."

The scoundrel's hands lifted. "This isn't how it looks."

Amanda stepped closer. Recognizing the proud profile of the man who had seemed to have integrity riddled the strength she wrapped around her. Payton McCord had shown her quiet respect. He'd even done the unimaginable—made her question her hardened opinion of cowmen. And now he was taking her lifeblood. A firm clench of her jaw stilled its trembling.

Damn McCord! Why did he have to go and prove again how easily someone with an honest twinkle in his eye and sinful way with words could take her in?

"From where I stand I see a sheep-thiever. That lamb didn't hop up there on your lap by itself."

"Confound it, I'm returning the darn thing." Danger rumbling in Payton's throat said he wasn't a man to cross, but she was too busy trying to salvage her pride to heed.

"A likely story." He could've thought of a better lie. Disappointment and tears blurred the figure. Her palm tightened around the stock of the rifle.

"I'm not used to being falsely accused. Why would I want one miserable little piece of mutton? Ask yourself."

"Retribution for the hat? Or a reason more ominous. You work for Henry Sanborn. He wants my land. Maybe he hired you to take the sheep one at a time? That way I wouldn't miss them until too many had disappeared. I don't care. I caught you red-handed."

"Put down the damn rifle before it goes off again. I can explain."

She waved the weapon toward the fold. "Leave the animal where you found it and get off my property."

Payton slid to the ground with the lamb in his arms. Fraser nipped at his pant legs as he marched to the stone sheepfold and gently returned it to its mother.

"I'm sorry you think I'd harm you." He swung into the saddle. "Good night, ma'am."

Just like that? She was supposed to let him go free? He'd moseyed by and killed her dream with no thought of recompense. Amanda meant to exact something. Making sense of the turmoil would be nice. Short of that, she'd take snapping on the leg irons that her father had pilfered off a convict wagon and feeding him mutton until he puked. That'd even the score.

She raised the rifle barrels. "What do you think you're doing?"

"Getting the hell out of here."

"You owe me that explanation and I will have it."

"That's great. Now you're going to shoot me to keep me *from* leaving?" He didn't appear afraid, resting an elbow on the saddle horn. "Make up your mind. You want me to stay or go? I can't do both."

Amanda's knees sagged. Which order did she want him to obey when she didn't know herself? She propped the Winchester against the side of the house. It didn't make much difference. Nothing did. She still lost whether she trusted or not. How much could a body take? The futility of it all was too much.

"Do whatever suits you. Take the whole darn flock if you want. Be doing me a favor. I'm tired of trying to make something from nothing."

She barely noticed that his boots made little noise when he climbed back down, or that he covered the space between them in a few long strides, until the deep timbre of his voice cut through the everlasting misery that wore like a second skin.

"You don't mean that. Owning land has meaning. I don't know why you chose this life, but you can't quit swimming in the middle of the stream." He touched her cheek with a calloused thumb, the warmth melting the edges of ice layering her heart.

"I'd prefer drowning over this slow, torturous death."

"Nothing worthwhile comes easy. You have far too much courage to give up. I've never met anyone with more grit."

With a shaky breath, she brushed a weary hand across her eyes. "You make it sound simple. Want to come inside? Looks like you can use some cider. I know I can."

Payton shifted his weight. "This isn't an ambush is it?"

"Don't be ridiculous. I only shoot buzzards." *And thieves who plundered her good sense,* she vowed silently. Amanda resisted the thought of the striking figure being in either category. McCord offered a ray of hope in her despair. He said he could explain. She wished to believe in miracles. At what cost would another mistake come? Still, she needed to think this cowboy had possibility. She liked the way he held the door for her, the light hand on the small of her back with his broad shoulders keeping the ghosts of the night at bay. She felt safe.

Fraser scooted between Payton and Amanda, racing to stand guard over the sorry piece of felt. The collie bared his teeth at Payton. Amanda gave the dog a pat and told him to shush.

"Don't pay Fraser any mind. He gets cranky occasionally. We're not used to visitors. Have a seat. I'll get the cider."

From the corner of her eye she watched Payton perch stiffly on the chair, gripping his new Stetson with both fists. He acted as though she'd rip the hat from him any minute and stomp it. How utterly ridiculous. She'd only mangled the other one because she assumed it came from the head of a cattle baron, not anyone she might fall in love with, which she hadn't of course. Nothing wrong keeping company with a man who made her feel alive and protected.

Her supple leather moccasins scuffed softly against the planks as Amanda bustled to the small kitchen corner.

"I hope you don't mind blackberry. John Running Deer has quite an affinity for apple and emptied the crock."

"Whatever you have is fine. Don't want to put you out."

"It's no trouble." She plunked down two glasses and a jug.

"Where is your Navajo? Thought I missed someone."

"He only comes to shear once a year. Usually he stays until we finish, but he got word his wife had taken very ill."

"What will you do if he can't return?"

"I'll manage." She bit her lip. "Always have."

"Shearing a flock of sheep is too hard for one small woman, however wiry she is."

"You think I can't take care of my own affairs?" Anger returned in full force.

"Unload your slingshot. I'm saying I admire you."

"Oh." She sniffed.

Payton took a sip of blackberry cider. "Quit getting your back bowed. I'm not picking a fight."

"Didn't look that way skulking around in the dark."

"So now we're back to thievery."

"What were you doing? You never gave that explanation."

"I don't want your damn sheep." His dark glare would make an outlaw head for cover. "Joe pulled another prank on me. Had the lamb tied to my bunk when I got in off the range. You want to nail someone's hide to the wall, go after him."

"Must get God-awful wearisome using Joe as an excuse for everything."

A tic developed in Payton's jaw. "Damn, woman. Lord knows I have my faults, but I don't lie. Or steal. Joe's mad because Lucy still throws a hissy fit if he so much as glances at their cabin, and he blames me."

"I guess I have no choice but grant the benefit of the doubt since I vowed not to step foot on the Frying Pan. If it's true, Joe Long has both of us paying dearly."

His face darkened. "Not for long. I intend to rectify the situation after daybreak."

"Good luck. Women tend to carry grudges a long time."

"Does that warning pertain to you, too?"

Amanda's chin rose defiantly. "I don't bother anyone and I expect others to mind their own business. If trouble comes I handle it, but I don't go looking for it either."

"What happened to fill your voice with barbed wire? Your fight with the cattlemen can't be all. Someone dug a hole and tried to push you in." A soft tone crept into Payton's drawl. "Had to be someone you trusted to dry up every bit of softness."

"I didn't know it was so apparent."

"Only to a man who's been there before."

Amanda measured the man next to her. The brush of his hand earlier against her cheek seemed to carry his brand as if to say he claimed her. His leather gloves were tucked under his belt. She vaguely remembered him taking them off right after he put the lamb into the fold. Did he think they smelled of mutton? Or simply to better curl his fist around the new hat? Not that she'd think of stomping it—unless he gave her provocation.

But she'd never do that to someone who loaned hope and buoyed her will to survive.

His hands fascinated her. They were calloused and strong enough to tame a wild stallion but gentle enough to wipe away tears. Such tender strength could hold a woman close and never let her go. She closed her eyes for a brief second and pretended that Payton would see more than what she truly was and be satisfied with it. She had captured his fancy in the hotel when he thought she was someone else. Could she again? Or would he find disappointment when he looked beneath the layers of resentment?

Rugged power radiated from Payton's nearness, robbing the need for words. They could feel the other's thoughts. In the silence she knew he'd suffered and lost something dear. A subtle shift in her chair moved her even closer. She could easily touch him—if she wanted.

What was his story? Life evidently hadn't been kind.

"Amanda, if you'd rather not tell me I'll understand."

"What happened? Plenty of people dug that hole—my father, stepmother, aunt, and my beau. Take your pick. I mistakenly trusted them all."

"I should've guessed a pretty woman would have beaus."

"Just one. It was one too many. The rogue jilted me at the altar. I didn't realize how much it hurt to be reviled by a man to whom I had given my heart." Amanda raised her gaze and fell into minty green depths. She would accept no pity. "Isn't that what you wanted to know? Go ahead and laugh."

He took her cold hand between his warm ones. "Whatever you say stays here. I would never betray you. Besides, I have secrets I've not told anyone either."

Tingles from his touch ran up her arm and thawed a little more of that ice encasing her heart.

"Doesn't do any good to talk about things you can't change. But I'm a good listener. Anytime you get ready to spill your secrets you know where I am."

"I'll bear that in mind." Payton rose. "Appreciate the cider . . . and for not shooting me."

"Well, there's always a next time. I'll work on improving my aim."

Amanda regretted the granite wrapping her words. Sarcasm was a habit she couldn't seem to break. It had been years since she even wanted to. Walking beside him to his horse, she was mindful how blessed tall he was next to her slight frame. She breathed the night air and wondered when she started to care so much about a saddle-weary cowboy.

Payton's mustache twitched when he winked. "Keep that Winchester loaded. I'll be back."

Now what had he meant by that? Was it a threat or a promise? She squashed the rising heat before it became full blown. But not before hope rose that he'd soon find his way to her door again.

That human voice whispering in her ear had possibilities unless she mistook the wink as lint in his eye.

Perhaps it wasn't too late for her.

But just as the thought came she saw herself on that street corner, pretending to be blind. Could she ever be anything more than a pretender?

A crop of tears blurred the impressive form atop the horse as he headed toward the Frying Pan.

No one in the state of Texas sat a horse quite like Payton McCord.

Chapter 10

The sun still slumbered when Payton rolled from his bunk and rustled up some coffee. He needed time to go over the case he intended to make to Lucy Long. But speak his mind he would. He had to find his balance again—the sooner the better.

Putting the pot on the fire to boil, his mind strayed to the events of last evening.

Moonlight had played across Amanda Lemmons's sensitive features, revealing the glisten of moisture in her gaze, and in the midst he heard the shattering of her heart. As the sound punctured the silence, he knew something he never thought to witness—the piss-and-vinegar woman who grabbed life by the horns and hung on, stood mighty near to getting thrown.

That hadn't set well. Holding on and riding like hell for as long as a body could stand took principles and grit. She had all that and more, and it seemed his duty to remind her. At least by the time he'd finished, the woman who mauled perfectly good hats had returned. Her sort of strength grew on a man.

Amanda made him think of all kinds of crazy things like marriage and trying to get back what he once considered forever lost or impossible.

Six years ago he had a parcel of prime land and a nice herd of longhorn—a near-to-perfect life.

Then, it all changed in the twinkling of an eye. The railroad company rooked him out of acreage that had been in their family for two generations. When he refused to sell, they had their shyster lawyer forge a bill of sale. A part of Payton died when the judge upheld it. They booted Payton off his land with nothing but Domino and the clothes on his back. He knew what it meant to lose a life, a hope, and the starch from his soul. He shriveled inside the day they stole his pride and left him nothing to live for.

Payton closed his eyes and recalled how Amanda's skirts whispered around her ankles in a crazy sort of lullaby that could sing a man right to sleep. Somewhere between admiring the trim curves and wondering at the warm flesh that lay beneath, he'd had a thought. Amanda Lemmons was a downright prissy woman. A grin teased his mouth. He liked priss and fuss, especially when the lady didn't have the business end of a Winchester pointed at him.

Maybe he wasn't too old for some of that stardust he'd contemplated a few days back. And a devious man could always wrestle a pack of mangy wolves. The grin widened. Amanda called for lots energy. And patience. But he had more now than he ever did.

Yep, he'd see her again. He'd crawl through a hail of gunfire on his belly to do it.

Payton put the memories and hope in safekeeping and poured himself a cup of brew. He had a passel of planning to do.

The lid of the coffeepot banged loud enough to wake the dead. Amos raised his head and sniffed. "You're up mighty early. Making plans for that mutton ranch of yours?"

"Go back to sleep, you old gopher."

"After I smelled coffee? Nope. Besides, I'm raring to hear about your adventures with the sheep-grower. Gotta get up and see how bloody you are. Was she mad?"

"Yep."

"Accuse you of thievery, did she?"

"Yep."

"Can't you spare a few details?"

"Nope."

Payton had no desire to discuss the beautiful Miss Lemmons. She belonged to him. Not like cows or land, but like the sun, moon, and stars which guided a man on a journey. Amanda gave him a sense of direction that he hadn't had in a long while.

He opened the bunkhouse door and stepped into the fresh air, leaving Amos's grumbling behind him. He stared toward the Long's cabin, surprised to see a light coming from the window.

"Might as well get this over with."

With a firm grip on the coffee cup, he strode across the combat zone to the front door and rapped.

"Payton, how nice to see you," Lucy greeted, wiping tears from swollen eyes. The woman evidently hadn't seen a wink of sleep in a while, judging by the haggard look.

"Can I come in? We need to talk."

An hour later he emerged much lighter. Lucy had confided the emptiness of her bed was too much to bear and she'd welcome Joe back home. Thank God things could return to normal.

He could've sworn Joe wore a smile the entire day, even after the branding commenced and the fire put out enough heat to stoke a freight train across the tops of the Rocky Mountains.

Payton's thoughts kept turning to the proud shepherdess despite every effort to avoid the subject. He wondered how she'd manage to get all that sheep wool peeled off the critters without another pair of strong shoulders. She was too small to wrestle rams and ewes. The image of those soft hands cut up and bleeding made him wince. He threw the lasso and missed the steer he aimed for by a mile.

"What's wrong with you, McCord? Sun get in your eyes?" Joe slapped a layer of grime from his hat before he jammed it back on his head.

Nothing in his eyes except a film of stardust, but Payton didn't share that with the rest.

"Have a few things on my mind. Got distracted."

"Yeah, I'll bet we can guess who's to blame. You've been keeping saloon hours the past few days," Amos chimed in. "If I didn't know better I think you've taken up baaahing lessons."

Bert leaned against the corral post. "If it walks like mutton and talks like mutton, it's mutton. Thought I recognized that peculiar sound this morning."

"Glad I could give you boys something to chew on besides the coffee Felipe made." Payton slid from the saddle. "Keep it up and you'll be sorry."

"Leave him alone. McCord saved my marriage," Joe growled.

"Did the *senorita* kiss you for taking back the lamb?"

"Felipe, my friend, I'll never tell. You boys keep on mining an empty gold shaft. Speculating is risky business. Never will strike pay dirt." Payton turned to Joe. "Is it all right if I quit a little early? I have to be somewhere."

"Will wonders ever cease? The man's going courtin'."

Payton shot Bert a warning glare. "I'm no porch-warmer. And I'm not saying another word."

Of course, it'd be right rude to refuse an invite to sit on her porch—if one popped up. It might be sorta nice to sit and watch the sun fade, count the stars, and listen to the sound of her heart beating.

Amanda stared at a hefty ram and told him in no uncertain terms what she expected him to do. Then she grabbed a leg and the neck, gave a heave, and tried to flip him over with the quick motion John had. But she lacked the muscles to wrestle the five hundred some-odd pounds. The ram balked, digging in his heels and she ended up with her back-side in the dirt with the animal giving her a lesson in the finer points of bleating. The ram took in a huge breath, expanding his stomach, and let out an ear-splitting *baah* that seemed to last forever.

She sat there a moment getting her second wind, fuming that she hadn't had the good sense to keep going when she located her father after all those years. Argus Lemmons didn't leave her anything but a bunch of empty dreams. She grabbed a handful of sand and threw it. The ram would've gotten the same treatment if the blessed animal didn't weigh as much as a small horse.

Fraser cocked his head to one side and then the other—a pretty good indication he thought she'd gone off her rocker. Maybe she had. Suddenly the dog growled, his ears perking up.

Her breath caught when she spied the black and white horse in the distance.

McCord had returned like he said.

And here she sat on her rear in the middle of the corral. Amanda jumped up. Something wet stuck her skirt to the back of her legs. She needn't imagine what it was. The evidence lay all around her. Tugging and brushing her clothes the best she could, she smoothed back her hair. She must look a mess. What she wouldn't give for a second to run to the house and get presentable for callers.

How stupid that would be though. Most likely McCord came for a million other reasons and none of them pertained to wanting to ride her way on purpose. She put up her hand to block the sun. No sign of another lamb with him.

Remembrance of last evening made her groan. It hadn't been her finest hour. She'd nearly killed the only person who made the pulse in her throat explode into a million stars.

The man rode straight to the corral and dismounted. Fraser didn't even bark, which flabbergasted her given the fact he tried to eat up everyone who came on the property. The dumb traitor-dog was even licking McCord's hand. Next Fraser would be climbing into the cowboy's lap and trying to moo.

"Afternoon, Amanda." For a brief moment the corners of Payton's mouth lifted beneath the trimmed mustache before settling in a firm line. "Got that rifle loaded?"

"It stays that way. My cider draw you back?"

"Nope. Came to help if you'll let me. I see you need extra hands."

A jolt of surprise wound through her.

"John came by this morning to say his wife is bad sick and he won't be able to finish the shearing." She tried to block the pleasure that insisted on sneaking into her chest. It'd do to keep this strictly business. Saved on heartache. "Can't pay much, but reckon I won't turn down your offer."

"Not looking for pay."

"What is it you're looking for, McCord?" Her breath went soft so that she barely knew her chest rose and fell. His minty gaze full of principles had that effect on a woman regardless of her intention to keep fancies in check.

"You know, I admire directness. Indeed I do. And you deserve an answer." He pushed back his hat with a forefinger. "It's simple. I need to know at the end of the day that something I did made a difference, maybe eased someone's burden in a small way or helped a pretty lady forget about the people who betrayed her for a moment."

"That's a lot of need for one man." A tremble went through Amanda. She inhaled the scent of worn leather and unmistakable desire. His Adam's apple bobbed when he swallowed.

"Yes, ma'am. But there's more. I also hanker for the company of a handsome woman, I guess. One who has enough guts and spirit to fill the empty spaces of an old bachelor's heart."

"You think you might find that here I suppose? Could it be you suffer from delusion?"

"I've heard that a man who risks everything to stand up for

something can never be wrong. The whole of a life is greater of the sum of its parts."

"My heavens! You're a philosopher in boots and denim."

Payton grinned. "I've kept quite a few things secret."

There was that word again. What secrets, pray tell?

Heat rose to Amanda's face. Her cheeks must match the crimson of her dress. She wasn't herself. Perhaps she had a fever and imagined McCord and his need.

A suitable reply fought for room in her mouth. "Thought you were skittish that being here will sully your name."

"Concern was for you, not me, I reckon. A certain pretty hat-stomper shot *my* reputation all to hell." The lopsided smile deepened the creases around his mouth and the cleft in his chin.

Amanda's heart lurched. "And the sheep? You hate them."

"A few things are worth abiding I'm told. Even rhubarb, which I share no fondness for, but that's another story."

Thoughts flew to the pie she'd baked that morning, wondering what he had against the delicacy. No need to worry about something he'd never know. He'd come to work, not eat.

"Indeed. We don't have to love something to tolerate it."

Payton's hand grazed her cheek in a slow sweep that left warmth in his wake. He must've felt her turmoil. "You had a streak of dirt on your face. You're far too comely to let a speck of anything mar the beauty. I hope you didn't mind—"

"No, I'm indebted."

Thank goodness he didn't know the shambles he made inside. She could get used to a saddle-warmer if he promised to hold her close and banish ghosts of the past—and maybe assure her she wasn't a worthless, stray mutt.

But love?

Who knew what that was? She doubted it existed.

He picked up the clippers where they'd fallen in the dirt, his smoldering gaze wrestling with hers. "Are we done getting things straight? If so, I suggest you let me get to work. Show me how to work these damn things."

Chapter 11

Amanda welcomed the task of explaining equipment that must be as foreign to Payton as roping and bronc busting were to her. She dare not examine his presence too closely for fear of what she might discover . . . or have it vanish like a desert mirage that existed solely in her mind.

Had she gone stark raving mad from living so long with nothing but animals and the howling of wind for company?

McCord certainly looked real enough. And the shoulders that brushed hers felt like no figment of anyone's imagination. She could never design a dream like this from mere yearnings.

But had he truly said he hankered for the company of a handsome woman?

"All right, I think I have the hang of these god-blessed contraptions." Payton's wry nod suggested an executioner at a hanging who gave the order to spring a trap door. "I'm ready to try 'em out. Send the first bag of wool this way."

She opened the narrow chute and nudged a ewe inside, quickly fastening the gate behind before the animal could get other ideas. Then she hurried to help Payton subdue the scared creature he'd already flipped onto its back. Just as Amanda tightened her arms around the thick neck to keep it secure, the ewe flailed the air with powerful feet, jerking and twisting.

Losing her balance, Amanda stumbled against Payton, sending them both to the dirt. When she got her bearings, she found herself pinned beneath him, staring up into a pair of devilish green eyes.

"I . . . You're on top me." The hard chest pressed into her bosom, the virile scent of the man taunting her good sense made it difficult to form lucid thoughts.

"Do tell."

The sinful curve of his lips began a slow descent, arousing tingles of longing from places long dead.

Perhaps she hadn't moved too far from the little girl who begged in the streets those years ago. She still held a tin cup and took whatever she could get, however she could. Except she didn't pretend to be blind. No, her vision was quite clear.

The faint whisper of his breath feathered tendrils of hair at her temple.

Amanda's heart skipped. She had no inclination or will to stop this delicious fantasy. To feel his lips, taste the musky desire, was a power that nothing on this earth could stop.

Payton's hand, calloused from years of hard work, trembled as he caressed her cheek. A feathery brush of her eyelids, then the curve of his mouth gently touched hers with the barest of pressure and she knew she'd surely die a happy woman. She wouldn't ask for more than what she got. It was enough. It'd have to be. She'd learned the value of necessities and how to make do.

His mustache tickled her lip exactly as she'd suspected it would. Her mouth parted slightly and she savored the hunger that Payton had evidently denied himself for a long time.

The kiss that began with a mere brushing of lips grew into one of heated urgency. Amanda felt as though Payton had awakened her from a deep slumber and brought life seeping back into the crevices.

This was the first time she could recall feeling totally safe and protected . . . and loved. For a moment she didn't have to fight anyone and that in itself was pretty amazing. She relaxed into his arms and rode the wave of warmth.

Just as she gave herself fully to the idea of blessed happiness, Payton pulled away and scrambled off her.

"I didn't mean to do that. I'm sorry."

"Don't apologize." Unshed tears formed, creating a lump in her throat. He hadn't truly wanted to kiss her. It had been an accident. He'd only dropped a nickel in her cup because he felt sorry for a blind girl. "Please . . . don't."

"Damn, did I hurt you?"

Amanda bit her lip to stop the quivering. "I'm fine."

Payton jerked off his hat, ran his fingers through his hair, and jammed it back on. "From the very first second you came through the door of the hotel I knew I wanted to kiss you. I just didn't intend to do it today." He gave her that lopsided grin that stole her breath. "I meant to let you gradually get used to the idea beforehand. I've never been . . . I'm used to wrestling longhorn, not females who require a gentle hand."

Confusion muddled her brain. She thought he just confessed to kissing her on purpose.

Accepting his hand, she got to her feet. "Damn, McCord, I'm no piece of fragile china. I have no regrets."

A rush of air left Payton's mouth. "I'm glad. I sure thought I'd messed up. Thought you were going to hand me my hat and run me off. Or reach for your trusty rifle. You don't have it hidden somewhere do you?"

She wouldn't let him know how deeply he'd shaken her. It paid to be cautious in any case. Maybe it was a ruse, some new tactic. She'd not give anyone leverage to use against her if she could prevent it.

"Run you off before you shear my sheep? Are you serious?"

"And afterward?" Payton arched an eyebrow. "When you have little need of me you'll tell me to climb on my horse and not look back?"

The gaze that saw things in shades of green twinkled, giving birth to a new set of problems—like how to keep the clusters of tingles from reaching her heart, because once they did they'd release the hope she'd imprisoned so long.

"Perhaps. I haven't decided yet."

"An unscrupulous man would drag this out."

"What would an honest man do?"

"Work like hell and count his blessings." The grin flashed, revealing even teeth.

Good heavens, he could sure charm a lady. How could she ever have thought him befuddled? Seemed outlandish now. The teasing, assured cowboy who stood braced to the wind had kissed her and acted like he enjoyed it. A flush rose. She turned away, casting a gaze to the far distance.

"Looks like Fraser rounded up the escapee." She pointed toward a ravine. The dog was herding the ewe toward them. "Ready to have another go at this business?"

"A range rider never cries uncle. Always figure I have no choice but get back on the horse that threw me."

Under Amanda's tutelage, Payton learned the ins and outs of sheep shearing in record time. She watched the compassion he showed her animals. And when he took a break for a cool dipper of water, she caught him watching her.

Memory of the kiss created waves of heat that threatened to scorch her. She could spend the rest of her life wrapped in his arms with no stretch of the imagination.

Except, she didn't dare allow herself to bank on a flash in the pan. Her cowboy was a tender of rawhide, not wool. He would help her now, but when it was over he'd be gone like a breeze full of lavender, leaving nothing behind but the scent of his passing.

As dusk approached she could see Payton's weariness. Muscles that had been taut and firm in the beginning began to give out with the last ram they'd shear this day. He struggled to contain the weight and the shears at the same time.

Despite Amanda's help, the ram gave them a tussle. She recognized the grinding sound coming from Payton's mouth. That would be the gnashing of teeth. She'd heard that noise a lot through the day. That he did something he truly abhorred elevated his character to near sainthood.

"Hell and be damned, you ornery piece of stew meat! Be still or you'll end up in a pot."

Amanda smothered her laughter. A pleasant glow of happiness had spread through her and had been there since Payton accepted the supper invitation. She didn't dare serve him mutton though. Or the rhubarb pie she'd baked that morning. Smoked ham she'd gotten from Jeb Diggs would do and a jar of apples from the root cellar. Get him in a good frame of mind and maybe he'd share those secrets he'd mentioned. She wished to know everything about the man who braved ridicule, reprisal, and rhubarb to come to her rescue.

Payton's arms ached as he dropped the bucket into the water well on Amanda's property and hauled it up so they could wash. The day had held a lot of surprises. He never imagined that he'd find contentment and belonging here. In fact, he'd have told anyone that he most definitely abhorred the little beasts. He was a cowman. Still was, but he was beginning to see where there might be room for both sheep and longhorn.

Maybe it had a lot to do with a beautiful brown-eyed woman whose pliable curves and winsome smile had spoken to his heart.

"Don't hog all the water, McCord." Amanda jostled him aside, trying to reach around him.

He held the bucket over his head, daring her to come closer. "That's some way to treat a hard-working man who slaved over your ornery flock. Besides, I'm a guest, remember? Mind your manners and I'll think about it."

The light from Amanda's eyes shone past his empty days and nights all the way to the center of promise. "You're right. It's fair I let you wash first."

"A lady of reason always sees the error of her ways." He lowered the bucket.

But Amanda was quick. She dipped in her hand before he knew what she was doing and flung water into his face. Payton blinked and set the bucket down, calmly wiping the droplets that dripped from his mustache. She watched him carefully with a hand covering her mouth; probably to hide laughter was his guess.

"I didn't mean to do that. I truly didn't."

"This is war, lady." Payton dumped the entire bucket over her head, leaving her sputtering and gasping. "Now we're even."

"That wasn't nice."

"I know, but it sure was fun." He hadn't enjoyed himself this much for a long while. It might've been the first time since he grew up and became a man. Lord, it felt good. He wished he could bottle it up for when life wasn't being so kind.

Payton brushed Amanda's hair from her eyes, hoping she wasn't mad. But the mischievous twinkle hadn't faded. She evidently yearned for a moment of carefree foolery, a time when the weight of the world didn't weigh her down. He reached for the towel she'd brought from the house and gently dabbed the parts he dared, trying to ignore the swell of her breasts clearly outlined by the plastered dress.

Amanda's breathing stilled as if she were waiting for something. "McCord, you're a wicked man."

"I know."

She leaned to kiss his cheek. "Thank you."

"For what?"

"Showing me how wrong I was and for making me feel like a woman again. I'd forgotten how it nice it feels."

By the time he left that evening, his stomach was full to bursting and so was his heart. Though his muscles protested, he had a most satisfying day. Yes, indeed.

He'd learned a lot about Miss Amanda Lemmons, who put on a good show of pretending not to care when she really did. The glistening moisture in her eyes, slight quiver of her lip, and hope hidden behind the rough texture of her voice gave her away.

And he'd learned some things about himself.

Surprisingly, he discovered shearing sheep wasn't much

different from branding cattle. He hadn't minded working with the scrubby cotton balls. They were sure heavier than they looked. And they didn't stink as bad as he thought either. Maybe his feelings for Amanda must've perfumed the air.

The feel of her breasts cozying up to him when he'd landed on top of her was something he could take extra helpings of—as many as she wanted to heap on his plate.

Her soft lips that kissed like an angel didn't raise any argument either.

Amanda Lemmons excelled in almost everything. Her cooking left a little to be desired, but if someone tended the sheep so she could devote more time to the art, she'd take to it like a duck to water. He'd bet anything on it. He saw her expertise with the spinning wheel and a few bags of wool. Cooking had to be a snap compared to the difficult chores she did regularly.

Yes, he could visualize spending the rest of his days with Amanda. She was everything a man would be proud to claim. Now to get her defenses lowered until he convinced her of the fact.

The breeze suddenly died and a whiff of his clothes reached his nose. There'd be hell to pay from Amos, Bert, Joe, and the boys. He'd never live it down. But that wasn't the worst part. If Mr. Sanborn found out how a self-respecting cowman shucked the cattle for sheep, Payton could lose his job.

Where would he go then? He was tired of looking for a place to light. Longings for permanence rumbled in his chest—a home all his own where he could live out his days in peace.

Old memories of what had been ripped from him nagged.

He'd stop by the horse trough and dip himself to get off some of the stink before he bedded down in the bunkhouse. That'd keep a lid on his secret until he could figure how to sweet talk Amanda.

Chapter 12

Payton struggled to keep his thoughts on his job the next day. He saw Amanda's face in the short prairie grass, in the lazy clouds that drifted overhead, and strangely in the patterns ingrained in the longhorns' hides.

She totally absorbed him. He couldn't remember what his life was like before she entered it.

No one had said a word about where he'd been yesterday, although the boys did give him some curious stares. They might suspect, but if so they put a lid on any speculating. That they were capable of keeping their mouths shut surprised Payton.

"Will you be back tomorrow?" Amanda had asked.

"Can't promise when, but I'll be here," he'd replied. "Might be late afternoon. Can't say."

Rounding up strays with some of the other range riders far out toward the property line, Payton straightened in the saddle and cast a casual glance toward Amanda's property as he'd done a million times since breakfast.

An uncomfortable jolt traveled the length of him.

A wisp of smoke rose from where her house stood. A brief play of light on some object? Had to be either that or some dirt had blown in his eyes. He blinked but it didn't go away. In fact, the smoke grew thicker.

Maybe she decided to burn some brush. But with the wind gusting this way? Even standing directly over the flame, deliberately lighting dry tinder would be foolhardy.

On her worst day no one would call Amanda anything but careful and smart. Alarm skittered up his spine. Trouble brewed in the air. Thick, black trouble.

Fire . . . Amanda's place was ablaze.

Payton spurred Domino and raced toward it, vaguely aware of the shouts behind him. He didn't waste precious seconds to explain. The valiant, sensitive, captivating woman who clung to the small section of land by her fingernails stood to lose everything. Just like him.

The closer he got the angrier and grayer the sky became. He didn't dare think of her lying still and lifeless.

Lord, give Domino more strength to run.

He rode from the ravine near the adobe structure and saw flames leaping from the bales of hay in the corral. A quick glance located Amanda in front of her home with legs firmly planted. Fraser poised beside her, prepared to battle to the last drop of blood for his mistress. Amanda pointed the rifle in her hands at a group of undesirables—Payton counted four. He slowed up and slid to the ground, yanking his Winchester from the scabbard.

They hadn't seen him yet, which fit into his plan.

No one had better hurt his beautiful lady. Payton guaranteed that. He gritted his teeth and sneaked forward.

"You can't shoot us all, Miss Lemmons. Besides, there's more left to take up the fight than you can get rid of," one man shouted. "And we have the Association to back us up. What do you have but a bunch of scraggly mutton, a worthless hound, and a shack? We oughta put you out of your misery. It'd be the humane thing to do."

If they did it'd be the last thing they'd remember before he blew them off the face of the earth.

Answering the threat, Fraser lunged, aiming to take a chunk out of the attacker's leg. The man kicked at the dog, missing.

Amanda squeezed off a shot, barely missing the assailant's toes. "You hurt my dog and I'll send you back to town dragging a bloody stump."

They might not believe her capable, but Payton knew she delivered no idle threat. The scrappy woman was tough as rawhide.

"Your mangy sheep are ruining land meant for cattle," yelled another varmint. "We aim to take it back."

"You won't take back a God-blessed thing," Amanda answered with steel in her voice. "This rifle will make sure of that. Who gives you the right to trespass onto the property of a law-abiding citizen and give me orders? I want a name."

Payton crept behind the foursome. If one sneezed it'd be too bad. He'd gladly bury them at Boot Hill.

"We have a long list of people who want you gone by whatever means. Maybe we'll just hafta kill you," the ringleader sneered.

"Kill her and get ready to kill me, too." Payton pumped a cartridge into the rifle with an abrupt up and down motion. The men whirled and Payton recognized them as skunk bait from the Amarillo Belle saloon. "You'll discover you have a big job in doing either."

"McCord, you cross to her side now? Thought you stood with the cattlemen." The man Payton knew as George Anders glared.

"The only sides here are right and wrong. I'm proud to say I'm on the right one at last." He met Amanda's brown, liquid gaze and winked. Relief and happiness shone back, though she had the situation under control. Except for the bales of hay that were too far gone to save. They didn't pose a risk to the house, thank goodness.

The mob exchanged shiftless glances, revealing their change of heart before George started sniveling. "We was only having some fun. Didn't mean to cause no harm."

Amanda's features remained stone cold. "Pitch your weapons to the ground. Now!"

"What're you gonna do?" George whined, obeying.

She stalked to a satchel leaning against the stone corral and pulled out the leg irons, manacles, and handcuffs. Payton grinned at the fear on the trespassers' faces. She'd finally found a use for the devices after all—and they weren't going to keep the men bound to her, but to tote them to jail.

He helped shackle the scoundrels to the fence and left Fraser to stand guard. "Can I have a word with you, darlin'?"

Amanda wore a questioning scowl, but followed him into the small shed that housed the wagon. Once inside, he turned on his heels and captured her face between his palms. With tender passion, he drank his fill of the wild determination that was his to claim.

The arms that stole around his neck bore no hint of a woman who'd almost given up on life on one moonlit night. His lady had strength to fight for what she wanted. He only prayed she wanted an old, broken-down cowhand with two cents to his name.

They were meant for each other, her with a past riddled with disappointment and misery and him . . . Well, he figured she might just need someone around to remind her occasionally that life goes on no matter if a person gets busted and bruised all to hell. He was an authority on that subject.

"Marry me," he whispered against her mouth when he caught his breath. "I want to spend my days and nights loving everything about you."

"You don't know what you're asking."

"I absolutely do. There are givers and takers, lovers and leavers." Payton leaned back so he see clearly eyes the color of rich cocoa. Questions in her stare made it hard to form the words. "I have a heart bursting with love for you. I'm a giver and a lover. I want to give you so much love I don't know where to start. And I damn sure will never leave. When I pledge something, it's for good."

"I've trusted before and lived to regret it."

His thumb caressed the hollow in her cheek. "Darlin', I

wish I could take away every bit of hurt people have dealt you. I'd be lying if I said I could. I reckon we just have to live by faith, one day at a time, until each festering sore heals."

"You have any other reasons to give up your freedom? Seems you're pretty set in your ways to think of change."

If he mentioned getting naked and exploring every curve, hill, and valley, would she cart him to jail along with the trespassers? Bold excitement filled him. He'd better save that for later.

"The next time someone comes gunning for you I want to be here. It's the only way I can keep you safe—the only way I can sleep at night."

"You think one man can even the odds?"

The wink was lazy and deliberate. "I know the secret handshake."

"Awful sure of yourself."

The smile that crinkled the corners of her eyes gave hope. Payton pushed back his hat with a forefinger. "I promise if I cause you pain I'll load the gun and stand still so you can shoot me. Can you beat a deal like that?"

"It's a fair offer." Her chin raised. "But, I won't be pressured. A decision this big deserves thought."

"Just so you know . . . I'm not going away. I'll badger you like a dog chasing a possum."

"Damn, you're romantic, McCord."

Payton grinned. "I see you found that out."

At that moment, something whined, brushing his leg. He glanced down. Fraser sat on his haunches, his tail wagging furiously. Amanda's watchdog and faithful companion grinned with the old mangled Stetson in his mouth, obviously pleased with the token he offered.

"I swear, Fraser's burying the hatchet? Even the rabid animal has a tender spot for me."

That afternoon in Amarillo, Amanda strolled down the street, humming a tune and planning a wedding that she hadn't committed to in anything but theory. It didn't matter. She knew she would when the time was good and proper. She'd already given her noble cowboy the key to her heart and a map of how to get there.

Nearing the Amarillo Hotel, her steps slowed, recalling the day they met. It would always be a place of significance.

Her chest swelled with happiness and contentment. They had things still to iron out in this newly formed arrangement, but she harbored no doubt that they could solve any problems.

All of a sudden a lean, handsome figure with a certain swagger, wearing a brand new Stetson, exited the hotel in a hurry. She ducked into the shadow of a doorway. Not that Payton McCord stood any chance of seeing her with the voluptuous Mavis Harper plastered to him. No, he wasn't paying anything any mind except the hussy in his arms and the lust in her gaze.

Shock and hopelessness knocked the wind from Amanda.

Tears swam in her eyes. Against better judgment she'd put aside each old fear and trusted someone again. How could Payton betray her this way and so publicly? It was evident he had no trace of the honor and integrity that he'd projected in his declaration of love a few hours ago. He took her for a fool. An utter, stupid, blind fool with a tin cup.

Well, she'd not cower in the shadows like some waif. She'd stand up and show the man for the conniver he was. Amanda took a deep breath and stepped into their path.

"You double-crossing, two-timing rat! I thought your word meant something."

Payton hadn't expected to get caught, judging by the bobble of his Adam's apple as he tried to swallow and instead choked on his spit. Mavis Harper's garish mouth formed a silent *O*.

"This isn't what it looks like, darlin'," Payton began.

Bitter disappointment scalded the back of her eyelids.

"Don't darlin' me." Amanda hauled off and kicked his

shinbone. "I'm only glad I found out how far you'd love and cherish, and with how many others, before the ceremony."

Payton hopped around in a circle, holding his ankle.

"What ceremony? You wrote me a love letter," Mavis insisted. "She's right, you are a two-timing rat." Delivering a kick to his other shin, Mavis flounced toward the *Panhandle Herald* office with revenge evidently in mind.

"Wait just a cotton pickin' minute. This was all Joe's doing. Mavis, I didn't write anything. And Amanda, I promised if I caused you pain I'd load a gun and let you shoot me." Payton jerked his Colt from the holster. "Before I hand this over, grant a dying man a last request."

Even as anger coursed through her, she wondered what kind of man would barter with his own life.

One who had nothing to lose or one who had everything to gain? Her brain whirled. She couldn't spill his blood no matter how furious he made her.

He'd spoken of love and kissed like the prince she dreamed would stand by her side and whose arms would be strong enough to withstand the buffeting winds of the cattlemen's greed. She had to consider in all fairness that Payton gave more than he took.

Too bad she misjudged his honor.

"Make it quick with this request of yours. I have . . . I . . . Damn." Tears clogged her throat. This was worse than standing at the altar alone in Santa Fe because she'd gone into it knowing another betrayal would strangle the very life from her. And this time it would be a permanent condition.

"Give me one kiss."

"A kiss? One?" It came out squeaky and not at all the way she wanted.

"Yep. That's it."

Amanda didn't dare agree. The rugged cowboy's kisses were addictive. One kiss would simply fuel the fire for more. And if she gave in to that, he'd murmur those words of endearment against her lips and she'd be forever lost.

"Seems an odd thing to ask of a scorned woman."

Heavy sorrow in Payton's gaze reached inside her soul. "Have you ever loved someone so much it feels like you can't breathe? And even if you knew the next gulp of air would bury you six feet under, you'd take it anyway if it meant being near them?"

Her voice came soft. "I have."

"Without you I might as well be dead. Hell, I don't want Mavis. You're a million times the woman Mavis is. The woman thought I wrote those love letters. She threw herself on me like a crazed animal that had a gut full of locoweed."

"You weren't working all that hard to pry her loose."

"That's because you didn't see the grip of steel she had on my rear end. I gave up trying to pull her off and focused on trying to outrun her before I found out if the rumor is true." He traced the curve of Amanda's jaw with a finger. The light touch caused an ache in her belly.

"What rumor?"

"The campfire tales of cowpokes who swear that a man can catch something from Mavis that 20 Mule Team Borax can't scrub off."

"That's mean."

"How much more of a reliable source do you need? I don't make up this stuff." The lopsided smile gave his lips a sinful curve and made her heart skitter.

Footsteps sounded on the plank sidewalk and a man politely cleared his throat. "McCord, I hear you're quitting the Frying Pan, gave your notice. Is it true? I'd hate to lose a seasoned rawhider like you. It'll take a while to find someone with your skills."

McCord was quitting his job? Why?

Amanda tugged attention from the heat in Payton's eyes. She recognized the interrupter as Henry Sanborn. Of all the cattle barons he gave her a pretty fair shake. That meant something. Payton straightened with respect.

"Yes, sir, it is true. I had a better offer." His gaze met Amanda's. "That is if it's still on the table."

"Anyone would need their head examined to let the best in the business get away." Sanborn took a cigar from his pocket and lit it. "What are they paying you? I'll match any figure."

"I won't be drawing pay and I don't think you can offer what she is. I'm looking to branch out." The smile that formed beneath his mustache made her stomach do somersaults. "Darlin', I think I might have an answer we both can live with. That north pasture, the buffer zone between you and the ranchers, could be put to good use if you'll let me."

"What are you saying, Payton?" The north pasture was the no man's land where Amanda had found Payton's hat. He must've figured out she left that portion of her land unused to shield her from the cattle barons. If he had plans for it that would suit her fine as long as he stood by her side.

With his eyes fastened on her he turned. "Mr. Sanborn, I'd be willing to help out with the roundup once a year if you'll let me take my pay in cattle."

Sanborn scratched his head, grinning. "Reckon I can. I take it you're throwing in your lot with Miss Lemmons. Smart lady. She can teach you a thing or two I've heard."

"Already has, sir. Cattle aren't everything. I've developed an interest in mutton of late."

"I'm hope you know what you're doing, McCord."

"Yes, sir, I do most certainly know. The way I figure it, sheep aren't anything more than fluffy cows, except maybe a little squattier. The Panhandle has room for both and I aim to prove it. Might want to pass along the word to members of the Cattle Raisers Association that the Mutton Madam has gotten reinforcements."

Amanda watched Sanborn's confident stride up Main Street. Men projected confidence in different ways she was learning. Sometimes that boldness sneaked inside quiet comments that a body could overlook unless they paid close attention.

Had Payton, a dyed-in-the-wool cowboy, spared no thought

to what he'd just done? He'd quit a job that defined who he was. And for what? The line in the sand wouldn't come cheap.

"Did you mean that stuff you said about sheep?"

"Always mean what I say and say what I mean. I love you. I intend to spend the rest of my life making sure you never forget it. My word is my bond."

Joe Long and some of the crew from the Frying Pan rode into town and tied up in front of the hotel. Her stomach sank.

Payton stiffened, tightening his fist. "Hell and be damned! I don't know what they have up their sleeve, but they'd better have their fighting clothes on because I'm not going to stand for any more damn meddling. Sam hell! That's it."

One thing for sure, her future husband knew when to cuss and when to draw lines no one dared cross. A bright man, Payton McCord.

She smothered a laugh and stood on tiptoe. "Quit wasting all that energy on them and kiss me."

No Time for Love

PHYLISS MIRANDA

To the love of my life,
my husband, Bob,
who supported me during the frantic times,
comforted me when I got discouraged,
and celebrated my accomplishments by
bringing me a big Coke every afternoon.

Chapter 1

Spring 1889, Texas Panhandle

Quinten Corbett plucked his watch from his apron pocket and studied the hour. Damnation, maybe time didn't matter to some folks, but to Quin the world revolved around deadlines . . . professional and personal.

"Monk," he barked across the cramped office filled with printing equipment and tables to his old ink-jockey friend. "Where in the blue blazes is the new apprentice? Did they ship him from Boston to Amarillo by wagon train?"

Receiving no response, Quin snapped his watch cover closed. Leaning forward, he returned an extra uppercase type-face to its slot in the tray. He shoved the top drawer into place, and proofread the headlines: *Panhandle Herald*, Killing at Amarillo Belle.

Pleased with the copy, he stood. Stretching to his full six-foot-plus height, he removed his reading glasses and rubbed his eyes.

The monotonous tap-tap-tap of news droned across the wires as James "Monk" Humphrey feverishly translated a Morse coded message. Oblivious to Quin's existence, the ink-spiller stayed focused on his work. The stoop-shouldered old-timer's arthritic fingers scrawled out the final words. Waving a page of script, he eased from the stool and hobbled toward the editor.

Quin glanced over the paper that Monk stuffed in his hand, and shook his head in defeat. "This the best news you can get?"

"I only translate the messages, son, I don't compose 'um."

Snatching up his spectacles, Quin paced the small office, reading aloud: "The juicy watermelon, the odoriferous muskmelon, and warty, git-up-and-dust cucumbers are expected to be in abundance this summer. Men and things change, but every returning season finds the cucumber possessing unalterably the same old characteristics." He flung the paper on the worktable and scooted the wastebasket out of the way with the toe of his Justin cowboy boot. "This is the nonsense I'm expected to use to come up with enough news for two papers a week?"

"I don't make up the stuff, I jest transcribe it." Monk returned to his perch, hunkered down, and prepared to receive the next transmission. "Besides, if it's what the owners back East want, I'm guessing it's what'll be done."

"And they think we can't do it alone, so they send us some wet-behind-the-ears apprentice fresh out of Boston College." Quin consulted his pocket watch again. "And where in the hell is that Renaulde character? I heard the train pull out an hour and forty-two minutes ago. Surely, he had enough sense to get off."

Quin crammed a visor on dark, unruly hair. He jerked open the top drawer of typeface. "Odoriferous! Huh, I've never thought of a muskmelon as odoriferous, but then we don't write the news. Huh, Monk?"

Exasperation rumbled in Quin's chest, but he methodically filled the line bar with one typeface after another.

Memories of how the Boston publishing vultures gobbled up the newspaper when Monk was forced to sell it to pay taxes on the ranch churned through his mind. Frustration wedged in his craw. As the editor, he must work long hours. He would restock his once bountiful spread that sat abandoned north of town.

His gut coiled as thoughts turned to Monk, the only family Quin had ever known. He could hardly handle what the new owners had done to his friend when, after years of running the newspaper, they demoted him to a lowly clerk. All because the old guy refused to print an editorial straight from the president's desk.

But more than anything, Quin fought the demons raging within him. Why couldn't he come to grips with the fact that due to his own reckless behavior he was no longer a free-hearted, spurring rancher?

"Hope the snot-nosed tenderfoot knows the difference between odoriferous muskmelons and warty cucumbers." He wiped his brow, tucking his musing back into the recesses of his mind. "Monk, there are a few things I plan to get straight with this shave-tail before he gets the notion he's runnin' the place."

Receiving only a response from the clinking telegraph, Quinten vented on. "This cub's not a reporter, but an apprentice. And there's one thing for sure, he better not come with that whiny Bostonian attitude that his family seems to have. You know the one I'm talkin' about, Monk? The old coot who makes sure I pronounce Peabody Pee-bid-ee. Completely ignoring the o. Hell, it might be Pee-bid-ee in Boston, but it's dang sure Pea-bawdy in Texas." He strung out each syllable to emphasize his point. "The new guy needs to learn that right off the bat or our townsfolk won't cotton to him in the least." He sighed in resignation. "You ol' hard-of-hearing geezer, have you heard a word I've said?"

Morse code clattered in response.

"It's probably best that he's late," Quin grumbled. "As it is, I'll have to work all night getting this rag ready for Amarillo by morning. Don't need to have him underfoot right now, anyway."

The telegraph chatter ceased.

"Mark my word, we'll get two editions out a week, just like those Yankee squatters want. We'll make this work, and get the money to buy a herd of longhorns. I'll set the rules and he'll abide by them or he can traipse his high-falutin' butt back to Boston."

"Hey, boss. Uh, I think you'd, uh, better, uh—"

"Spit it out, Monk." Quin jerked off his visor, wiped his brow, and reset the hat. "You don't agree?"

"Uh, Quinten, I think you'd better hold up a bit."

"I've already said we're on a tight deadline—"

"I, uh, think your new, uh, apprentice is here."

"Renaulde, you'll just have to wait, I don't have time to waste . . ." Quin pulled to his full height, and turned toward the door, prepared to size up the Yankee wonder.

Quin sized up the new guy okay . . . all one hundred and twelve pounds of ivory skin, onyx tresses piled high on her head, and a scowl that could halt a gunslinger in mid-draw.

When the woman finally broke the silence, she had a voice like a butterfly's kiss, astoundingly light and soft, yet as clear as a mountain stream. "Please go on, Mr. Corbett. I'm eager to hear your rules before I *assure* you that I do not plan to take neither my snotty nose nor my high-falutin' butt back to Boston. So, please set me straight."

Words escaped him, something that rarely happened. Shaking off the element of surprise, Quin recovered sufficiently to take note that the traveling suit she wore no doubt came straight from the fashion plates of *Godey's Lady's Book.* He'd know the look anywhere after being forced to review the magazine during his apprenticeship.

Dang, the black linen bolero hugged her every curve, emphasizing an exquisite figure. An ivory chemisette edged with tatted lace tucked into the low-necked bodice disguised a nice set of . . . attributes.

"I believe you are expecting me, Kaira Clarice Renaulde,

and I'll be glad to relay to my Aunt *Pee-bid-ee* that our ancestors have pronounced their name wrong for centuries."

"I, uh." As though seeking help finding an explanation, Quin turned to Monk, who had sidled up beside Miss Renaulde. "Uh, I'd like to introduce you to my assistant, James Humphrey."

"Much obliged to make your acquaintance, ma'am." The old gentleman tipped his visor, seemingly not unaware of her attributes. "Call me Monk."

"Thank you, Mr. Monk. You're clearly a gentleman." She smiled sweetly, while casting a suspicious gaze at Quin as though to say, "And, I'll reserve judgment on you, buster!"

"Uh, Miss. Uh, ma'am." Blasted! Why was Quin stammering like a young buck signing his first dance card? He'd seen many a beautiful woman. Even courted his share, but never had he known one who just about had sugar and spice oozing from her mouth, while searing him with lavender eyes.

"Mr. Humphrey, don't you have chores to tend to?" Quin snapped.

"Nope. None that I can think of." Monk tore his attention away from the black-headed apprentice long enough to catch Quin's glare. "Yep, for sure, got a bucket of typeface waitin' on me in the back room." He detached himself from the lady and meandered toward the storeroom, mumbling, "All this walkin' sure can make a man poorly." Over his shoulder, he stole another glimpse of their new associate before closing the door behind him.

"Miss Renaulde. I'm . . ." Quin stumbled over the words.

"Sorry, maybe? Wish to apologize?" She pulled one then another glove off. "Take your choice." Slipping out a pin from the headpiece that sported a gigantic feather from some unfortunate bird, she removed her hat and placed it on the counter. Dusting a nearby stool with her hanky, she settled in, making herself comfortable and peering up at Quin.

"Apology?" He groaned, trying hard not to roll his eyes. "That's not exactly what I had in mind. Miss—"

"Kaira Clarice, but K.C. will do fine." In one wide sweep she seemed to survey every crook and cranny of the tiny room.

"I think Miss Renaulde will be more appropriate." His voice was harsher than he had intended. Regrouping, he scuffed the toe of his boot along the planked floor.

"Damnation, lady . . ." He flinched as his curse word caused her to knit her delicate eyebrows together in a shocked expression. "I mean, dern it, ma'am—if we're going to work together, we need to start over again." He studied her, waiting for a response.

Slowly, a lethal calmness overtook her features, and she leveled violet eyes at him. The corners of her mouth relaxed in a teasing smile. "Damn glad to meet you, uh, *Quinten*."

Chapter 2

Sunset cast a shower of golden dust across Quinten's bronzed face, as he stood only inches away from Kaira. So close that she could almost feel his breath against her cheeks.

Deep brown eyes, like chocolate left out on a hot, smoldering day, glared at her. Dark lashes beckoned to explore what lay behind them. A scowl tried unsuccessfully to cloak a tad of a smile.

Quinten rolled his broad shoulders, as though tired of carrying the woes of the world on them. Taking a deep breath, his chest expanded, pressing the buttons on the starched white shirt against the black apron.

Kaira tried to pry her gaze away, but his stance emphasized the force of his tough, lean build. Her pulse quickened, and she fought fireflies that suddenly swarmed in her stomach. She tried to swallow.

Never had she met a man who caught her so off guard and created thoughts that no well-bred Bostonian lady of the *Pee-bid-ee* sort would acknowledge. A man with the heart-throbbing ruggedness of a bronc-buster. A cross between the legendary gentleman-gunslinger, Bat Masterson, and a paramour that Emma Bovary would have taken as a lover, if she existed in the flesh, not in fiction.

And to think mere hours before, her only focus was on teaching her grandfather a lesson for forcing her to come to

Texas. Just because she came from a third-generation publishing family didn't mean that printer's ink ran in her veins.

Now that she'd seen the hot, dry, unwelcome land of the dreamers and schemers for herself, she found it less alluring than on paper. Kaira wanted nothing of it. She needed to return to Boston and embark upon her dreams . . . none of which involved the newspaper business.

Kaira peered back at Quinten.

Although she had set out believing she wouldn't enjoy her assignment, it might be more intriguing than she first thought. She did love a worthy opponent. And Mr. Corbett certainly appeared more than worthy.

What are you thinking, Miss Kaira Clarice Renaulde?

Weariness, exacerbated by the long hours on the train, had to be the blame for her turncoat thoughts. Whiling away the day reading dime novels and daydreaming about the shoot-first-and-ask-questions-later cowboys of Texas probably hadn't helped either.

Her mind felt as fuzzy as a sun-dried dandelion. She tried to pull herself together but faltered. Why did thoughts not fit for a properly reared lady make her feel so warm inside?

Only one problem . . . He still wore that God-awful scowl.

"I must apologize, Mr. Corbett. My cursing was most intolerable and rude."

"I was the one who behaved badly. Maybe we should start over." A gentleman, he waited for her to make the first move.

"Most assuredly." Without considering the unladylike impulse, she offered her naked hand. "Yes, it does call for a new start."

Quinten's fingers touched her with such fire that she inhaled deeply.

"I agree," he said. As if realizing he was a little too accommodating, Quinten stiffened and stepped back. "It's late. I've got a newspaper to put to press, so I'd suggest that you get a good night's sleep and report back to me after breakfast in the morning."

Lost for words, Kaira looked intently at him. Was he not going to at least show her the way to her living quarters? A knot clinched her stomach tightly. He seemed unprepared for her arrival.

Disconcerted, she pointedly looked out the window.

In the west the sun bled onto the prairie, making her painfully aware that little daylight remained, and she had no place to sleep. She gnawed on her lower lip.

"Is there something wrong?" Not waiting for a response, he continued. "You have made arrangements for a room at the hotel or the boardinghouse, haven't you?"

"No." She jerked her attention back to Quinten, taking pleasure in the flicker of surprise that made his dark eyebrows slant into a frown.

"We seem to have a misunderstanding," she stated in her newly acquired unruffled voice. "I have a contract and it expressly states that you will provide accommodations for me."

"Miss Renaulde, I live in the small room above the shop, and when I agreed to those terms, I didn't realize, uh—"

"That I am a woman?"

"Yes, clearly."

"I don't see that it makes any difference. As you so quickly pointed out . . . I am here in the capacity of an apprentice, not as a woman. I don't mind sharing your accommodations." She lightly fingered a tendril of hair that touched her cheek.

"It's nothing but a bedroom and barely big enough for one person. I'd made arrangements for the new hire to bunk with Monk at his place." As though Quin felt uncomfortable discussing her sleeping arrangements, he hesitated before continuing, "And your reputation. A gentleman can't—"

"Precisely my point. You are a gentleman so my reputation will remain intact." She motioned toward the door, where three Saratoga trunks and at least a half a dozen hat boxes sat. "Please lead the way. There's no reason that we cannot be under the same roof and maintain a proper decorum."

"Ma'am, I can assure you that we *cannot* function in those cramped quarters." Quin removed his heavy apron, exposing a mass of chestnut hair peeking out from the neck of his shirt. His muscles rippled under the snug fabric.

Her pulse quickened. "A contract is a contract." She

whipped an envelope from her caba. Opening it, she unfolded a page and handed it to Quinten. "Is this not your signature?"

"Yes. But things are complicated now."

"Because I'm a woman? Please escort me to my room." She closed the French handbag, giving the problem another thought. "Never mind, as you've pointed out, you have more pressing things that require your attention."

Having earlier scouted the office, she observed that the room was big enough to get the newspaper out, yet small enough to feel welcome.

She fetched her hat, and with a springy bounce, she crossed the room. At the foot of the stairs, she retorted over her shoulder, adding a deliberate softness to her voice, "In the event you were wondering why I was so late, Mrs. Diggs at the mercantile has a very impressive selection of bonnets, plus she was most interested in the newest fashions being shown in Paris."

Ascending the staircase leading to his bedroom, she continued, "And the nice waitress at the hotel dining was so very pleasant. Also, Hank Harris said to thank you for helping him out yesterday." She stopped and turned back to him. "They spoke most favorably of you."

Damn, she might as well have added, "And, I have no idea why." Thunder, he expected the owners had sent him an apprentice instead of Miss Dawdle-Butt!

Quin yanked his visor from his head and ran his fingers through his thick crop of hair. Hellfire, it was hard to remain coherent with her around. A sudden twinge of something he hadn't felt in a long time clutched at his gut. No time to explore his feelings. An edition of the paper was due out by morning and his so-called assistant, apprentice, pain in the rear, or a number of other names he could think of, had dawdled away daylight making social calls.

"Monk!" He hung the apron on a wooden peg on the wall. Plucking his watch from his vest, he said, "You ol' print hound, get out here. We've got luggage to carry upstairs."

Chapter 3

Kaira Renaulde had been in Amarillo for a week and still at least one Saratoga, sometimes two, arrived on every train coming through town.

Quin eyed the latest arrivals. "Monk, we need to get those damnable trunks out of our way. Got time?"

"Jest as soon as I finish this transmission."

"How many more of those things do you think that lady has coming?"

"Don't know." Monk didn't look. "But I know one thing for sure, no woman should own trunks that take two men to cart around. And all that climbin's apt to make a man poorly."

Quin glanced out the window, checked the hour, and stuffed the watch fob back in his vest pocket. He tried to pay no heed to Monk's continual mulley-grubbing, but it didn't work.

Monk's grousing interrupted Quin's thoughts.

"Whatcha think she has in those Saratogas?" asked Monk.

"I don't give a tinker's damn. All I care about is getting this blasted newspaper out." Quin rolled his shoulders to relieve some of the soreness that always seemed to creep up around sunset.

"Do you think that calico's totin' a sidearm, son?"

"Doubt it. But if she is, it's probably a pearl-handled, double-barreled derringer." He snatched up his apron. "Why do you think she has to have so many trunks?"

"Maybe to cart around more of those frilly trappin's, you think?"

"Don't know. But I do know that we've got a hundred pounds of trouble and she's upstairs in my bed." Quin pulled the leather protector over his head. "Did you notice how interested she was last night when we were talking about Bat Masterson coming to town?"

"Yep, sure did. She perked those pretty little ears right up like a turkey listenin' for buckshot on Thanksgiving morning."

"Doubt if she even knows who Masterson is."

"Yep, she sure did perk up."

"You know, ol' man, the bonus that gal's grandfather promised me for an interview with the gambler will give us the money we need to restock the ranch and start over, don't you?"

"Sure do. Yep, it'll jest about get that ol' ranch back amongst the living." Monk pulled a bowie knife from the desk drawer and whittled on his pencil. "Son, since you don't need me anymore and I've got a hankering for some of Miss Maggie's corn dodgers and dumplin's with all the doings, I'm fixin' to head that way." Satisfied that his pencil was sharpened enough, he returned the knife to the drawer. "Sure you don't want me to stick around?"

"Nope. Got things under control. That is if *she* keeps her prissy-butt out of my hair. She's been here a week and all she's done is socialize and cause me to waste time having to deal with her."

The old-timer grabbed his weathered Stetson. Shuffling out the front door, he grumbled, "Yep, she sure has. Got us a heap of trouble in that one."

Hours later, a herb moss moon cascaded through the shop's windowpanes, creating cattywampus shadows across the wooden floor.

Quin stacked the last bundle of newspapers near the exit.

Gunfire from somewhere near the Amarillo Belle pierced the air. Another rough night at the popular saloon. Probably a bunch of cowpokes celebrating payday. Or maybe a gambler letting off steam after losing the shirt off his back. Could have been a fight over a soiled dove. One thing was for certain. If there was a serious squabble, there'd be a new digging before dawn.

Gunplay always made for great headlines, but Quin hoped the visiting gentleman, gunslinger, and gambler he needed so desperately to interview wouldn't be the one pushing up daisies. Quin shuddered at what would happen if he missed his opportunity. No sit-down with Masterson. No bonus. No cattle.

Quin checked the time. Three-twenty in the morning. If he caught a few winks, he'd be raring to go by daybreak.

Pulling off his spectacles, he took two steps toward the stairwell before halting. *Blasted!* A sleeping bundle of pure dee ol' womanhood occupied his bed.

He spun on his heels, trudged out onto the porch, and took a deep breath. The balmy night promised to give way to another breezy spring day. As if turning up a lantern, the brilliant moon bleached the buildings white.

Sleeping under the stars hadn't killed him so far. In his drover days, Quin had slept through gully-washers, Blue Norther's that could freeze the hide right off a steer, and winds strong enough to carry the sucker off to parts unknown.

A little reflection didn't hurt either. After all, spending too much time cooped up in a bed could cause a fellow to get all claustrophobic and make him forget his roots.

That beauty upstairs was already proving to be trouble, and spring hadn't even seen its first thunderstorm.

Kaira's heart jumped to her throat as a loud, steely sound rang out in the distance and echoed off the hallowed businessfronts. Gunshots! Just like the ones she'd read about. Oh, she had heard gunshots before but none like these! Real, honest-to-goodness gunfire from the rough and rowdy West. Maybe the sheriff was chasing a bank robber? A murderer?

Yes, a fearless lawman was surely hot on the trail of a fierce, self-willed ruffian who had done some dastardly dark deed. And, all of it happening right below her bedroom window.

Prepared to see her first authentic outlaw barely clinging to life, blood gushing from a wound and him hanging from his stirrups by only the rowel of his spur, Kaira sprang out of bed and rushed to the window.

A midnight black horse carried a rider wrapped in a long ebony cloak. His face hid beneath a wide-rimmed hat, hanging so low that it met his chin, all giving the stranger a sinister appearance. The mischief-maker recklessly fired his weapon into the air as he flew down the middle of town, leaving a trail of dust in his wake.

On his heels, racing to catch up, two more riders carelessly waved pistols, shooting at the moon and yelling at the top of their lungs, "Oooh my dar-lin' . . . Oooh my dar-lin' . . . Oooh my dar-lin' Cle-men-tine!"

Kaira flinched, wanting to cover her ears to drown out the wailing. *Who in the heck is Clementine?*

"You are looost and gooone fooorever, dreadful soooory Clementine!"

That gal wouldn't be lost long with all that ruckus. And where was the sheriff? The good guy?

Could the lead rider, who quickly melded with the darkness, be the infamous gambler, Bat Masterson? The man Quinten and Mr. Monk had been discussing?

A shadow moved on the porch. Kaira squinted to make out the figure.

Quinten stirred and the moonlight gave his dark hair a silvery sheen. His broad shoulders remained squared, as he leaned against the post, gold fob glittering. Turning slightly, he exposed a strong, well-defined profile that any woman wouldn't mind waking up to.

Entranced by the unspoken sadness of his face, she stood silently. An air of isolation punctuated the man's loneliness.

As though sensing her presence, his gaze shifted toward the window.

A vaguely sensuous light passed between them. Hastily she retreated. Hopefully out of his view, she clutched the lacy neck of her embroidered satin gown.

Her curiosity had been aroused; she stepped closer and peeped through the glass.

He was gone.

What was wrong with her? Quinten Corbett radiated a vitality that seemed to rock the ground beneath her, disturbing her in ways she didn't think possible.

Moments later, Kaira eased between the sheets and pulled the still-warm bedding up to her chin. Visions of the good-looking editor played before her eyes as she fought sleep. Sleep that would surely evolve into dreams worthy of the pages of a best-selling dime novel.

This man, the subject of her very wicked thoughts, had to be more complex than he first appeared. Tough, lean, and powerful, an almost stereotypical dime novel hero, and she had to impress him. But how?

She thought back over the days she'd been in Amarillo. Quinten obviously lived and breathed the newspaper, but was more cattleman than editor. If only she had paid more attention to her family's companies. In reality, she had no desire to be a part of their world. Kaira had little talent in publishing that would impress the likes of Mr. Corbett.

Kaira needed to get on his good side—surely he had one—and what better way than to scoop an interview with one of the most famous guns of the West.

Now, where would a lady find a gambler?

Chapter 4

A sleepless night under the stars didn't improve Quin's humor in the least. Feeling like Monk generally acted, about as pleasant to be around as a hide hunter on a hot day, Quin meandered to the potbelly stove and poured himself another cup of coffee thick enough to float an anvil.

The clink of the day's first Morse-coded message drowned out most of Monk's words, as he systematically translated into text the sounds of dots, dashes, and spaces.

Quin paced the floor and tried to ignore the old-timer's mumbling.

In spite of Quin's busy schedule, thoughts of Miss Renaulde intruded into his morning. Eager to get the apprentice busy cleaning a heaping bucket of typeface, the woman's tardiness annoyed him more than he wanted to admit.

Ten o'clock and there still wasn't any movement in the apartment above. As a matter of fact, he hadn't heard a peep since he got back from breakfast around six-fifteen.

What should he do? Check on her? He mulled over the question as he topped off his coffee.

A gentleman would never enter a woman's bedroom without permission. Maybe he should send Monk to see about her? Probably the best idea was to leave the lady alone. At this rate, if he depended on his new associate, the news would be history before he got it in print.

Resisting the urge to check the time again, Quin glanced toward the stairwell and let his mind drift along like a tumbleweed on a windy day.

What would he find if he actually ventured upstairs? The vision of Miss Renaulde standing at the window still crouched in the corner of his mind, waiting for the most inappropriate times to appear. Not able to shuck off the images of the woman bathed in soft light caused a surge of emotion to lash through him.

A rope knotted around his heart and squeezed tightly.

She was certainly a vision of loveliness. Maybe it was her luscious lips beckoning to be kissed that made him feel a wanting. Or ivory skin crying to be caressed; not to mention attributes begging to be touched.

Reality reared its ugly head. She was about as soft and cuddly as a barnyard kitten. She put on a facade of being tame and playful, but no doubt if a man got close enough to touch her, she'd hiss him to death.

Yep, that gal was as hot as butter on a biscuit, yet as tough as hardtack. Maybe a generous serving of boysenberry jam would sweeten her up enough for a man to enjoy.

But Miss Renaulde—guess he could call her Kaira considering the intimate thoughts he'd had about her—was definitely worthy of a second look.

All of his musing about her qualities didn't solve the issue at hand. If she didn't come down soon, he'd have no choice but to leave her in the hands of Monk. It'd put the old geezer in an awkward position to tell her that, as the feared ink-spiller, she was responsible for the muck work.

"Monk," Quin hollered, pulling on his coat. "Masterson got into town yesterday. I've got to go over to the hotel and find him before he begins gambling. I've heard he takes his poker seriously, so I'm not going to be the one to disturb him." He grabbed his Stetson and absentmindedly adjusted the band of woven wire. "If that gal doesn't come down by noon, I guess you'd better go see about her."

"That gal?" Monk repeated, as if he had no idea who Quin referred to. "Oh, she's come and gone. I saw her over at Miss Maggie's having breakfast about sunup."

"What do you mean?" Quin turned away from the door to face the older man.

"Well, if I remember right, I said, 'That gal has come and gone—'"

"I heard that much!"

"Then why'd you ask me to clarify it?" Not waiting on Quin's response, he continued, "I heard her talking to Miss Maggie about Bat Masterson—"

"You don't think she was—"

"Raring to interview the dandy?" Monk quipped. "Yep, that gal sure was." Momentarily drawn back to the telegraph, he glanced its way then back to Quin. "If you'd been listening to me the first time I told you, instead of rambling around the room like a fella finding fault with Paradise, you'd have already known it."

"Damnation and every cuss word I've ever used, I hope I can catch up with her before she fouls up the whole blasted deal." Quin crammed the Stetson on his head and hurried to the door. Over his shoulder he said, "Masterson might be more man than that blue blood is used to handling."

"Don't bet the ranch on that, son," Monk muttered.

"Yeah, Monk . . . that's exactly what I'm doing!"

Quin let the screen door at the Amarillo Hotel slam behind him as he stalked out and crossed the planked sidewalk.

He'd been searching for Kaira for fifty-five minutes, with no luck.

At the mercantile, Mary Carol Diggs hadn't seen her, but didn't miss the opportunity to lecture Quin on the virtues of his new employee. What did the shop owner think? That he had never known a woman besides his mother and didn't recognize his new hire as a classy lady through and through? Aggravation hammered at his heart. Just because he was past his prime at a ripe old thirty-two, and his womanizing days were only memories, didn't mean he had forgotten how to treat a woman.

Worrying about things he had no control over wasn't getting him anywhere. He needed to find Masterson, who had already left the hotel for a day of pleasure at the saloon. But which one?

The Amarillo Belle was the closest, so Quin tramped off in its direction. Eleven o'clock and the sun bore fire on the back of his neck, much like the churning in his stomach.

Quin could put his last buck on Masterson being at the Belle. Enough mounts to stock a respectful remuda were tied to the hitching posts.

He approached the batwing doors. Instead of the expected bustle and noise of the saloon, an eerie quietness fell from within.

His gut clinched tighter . . . This wasn't good, not good at all.

Chapter 5

Not being able to resist the urge to keep time with the music, Kaira patted her foot to the rhythm of the banging piano.

A fun-loving mixture of cowboys willing to spend a little of their hard-earned cash, and flirty dancehall girls more than eager to help them out, crowded the smoke-filled room of the Amarillo Belle.

Using her best persuasion, Kaira smiled sweetly at the bartender. Delicately running her fingers around the lip of her tea cup, she awarded him with a second smile. "Thank you. I presume you don't get many requests for tea?"

"No, ma'am. But I'll let you in on a secret." He leaned across the bar and lowered his voice. "We keep it for our girls. They don't drink, but those cowpokes don't know it."

"That's interesting, Mr.—"

"Wallbrook, but you can call me Wally."

"Thanks, Mr. Wally."

"Sure, ma'am." The bartender turned his attention to a cowboy who'd sidled up to the bar.

Kaira shifted on the stool to get a better view of the table where four men played cards.

Which gambler was Masterson? She'd heard that he was enormously handsome. She took stock of the four players.

She discounted the one facing the bar. He didn't qualify as good-looking. The truth, he was so plug-ugly that his mother would have trouble claiming him as her offspring.

The man to his right reminded her of something she'd read—he definitely had been rode hard and put up wet. He grinned a toothy and used-up smile.

That left two men. Both dark headed, with neatly groomed mustaches. Each looked the part of a professional gambler. Fancy brocade vests, gold watch fobs, and waistcoats sewn from the finest fabrics added to their debonair appearance. From where she sat, she couldn't judge their height, but one man was noticeably shorter than the other.

Kaira tried to spy Masterson's cane or infamous derby hat, but neither was present. Now what could she do? Simply approach the table and ask for him by name? That would put her at a disadvantage. If she had learned anything from her grandfather, it was to retain control of an interview. Never show her inexperience. Proceed professionally and confidently. Never waver and whatever you do, don't ask, "Which one of you guys is Bat Masterson?" Couldn't happen. So, she'd have to figure out another way to get the interview.

Suddenly luck blessed her.

Mr. Plug-Ugly tossed his cards face down on the table, and spouted, "Masterson, you lucky dog."

The man he called Masterson lazily discarded his cards and drew the pot toward him, not bothering to count the money. "Thanks, Ira. I'll take your donation any day."

Fun-loving laughter filled the air.

A sensual smile crossed Bat's lips as he caught sight of Kaira and fixed bold, slate blue eyes on her. Leisurely, he tossed back a shot of whiskey, not breaking their gaze. Suddenly, as though uncomfortable with her brazen stare, he turned his attention back to his game. "Well, you gonna deal those cards today or tomorrow, Shorty?"

Was his perusal interest? An invitation? It certainly justified her approaching him, normally unacceptable behavior for a young lady.

She sipped her tea and continued to pat her slipper against the bar foot railing.

Quinten had made his intentions very clear. The newspaper was his top priority. The quicker she talked with Masterson, the sooner she'd get an interview, prove her inadequacies in business to Grandfather, and return to Boston. But was she doing this to make a point to her grandfather or to garner approval from Quinten?

She'd already been waiting for more than an hour for the players to tire of the game. How long do gamblers gamble anyway? Don't they take a break?

Time had come for her to take control. Seeking courage, she inhaled deeply. Pushing her cup aside, she slipped from the stool.

Realizing all eyes were on her, she adjusted her hat, making sure it sat perfect. After all, she'd taken care in selecting suitable clothing for her first trip to a saloon. Compared to the barmaids, no doubt she was overdressed for the occasion.

Straightening her bolero, she threw back her shoulders to give emphasis to her bosom. After fetching her caba, she strolled toward the table of gamblers, careful not to stir up too much sawdust as she walked.

Silence spread in epidemic proportions over the room as she closed the distance between her and the gamblers.

The piano player stopped midnote.

Are they expecting me to challenge him to a duel?

A wooly cowpoke with a low-slung six-shooter backed out of the door.

Wally dropped a bottle of liquor and let out a profanity she'd only read about.

The noise, or rather the lack thereof, didn't deter the players.

"A wagon wheel to you, Masterson," Shorty quipped.

Bat tossed in a twenty-dollar gold piece.

Beginning to his left, Shorty dealt one card face down to each man, before continuing until each player had five cards in his hand.

Mr. Plug-Ugly barely glanced at his cards before chucking three on the table. Expertly, Shorty slipped him replacements.

"Sonofabitch." Ira threw his hand in the middle of the table, folding.

Masterson covertly peeped at his cards and laid them face down. Slowly, he shook his head from side to side.

Kaira continued toward the players.

Even the quiet got quieter.

Shorty laid an ace of spades face up. "Dealer takes four," he said before replenishing his cards.

"Another wagon wheel to you, Masterson," the dealer said.

It was now or never! Surely the game was coming to an end, since the gamblers were throwing away their cards. Right?

She steeled herself to make her voice casual. "Mr. Masterson, may I have a moment of your time?"

Now that she'd taken the first step, she felt better. Much better.

"Well, uh, Miss . . ." he stammered.

"Renaulde, K. C. Renaulde from Boston—Boston, Massachusetts."

Slowly the man picked up his cards and tilted them up for her to see. "Well, Miss Renaulde, uh, ma'am, not to be rude, but with this hand do you think a wise player would give you a moment right now?" His voice held depth and authority.

"Sir, I honestly don't know. I've not partaken of the game you're playing, but I do enjoy a wicked game of crokinole." With an air of pleasure, she beamed at him. She wasn't sure if the look on his face was the beginning or the end of a smile. "I realize crokinole isn't all that exciting, but one requires grace to position the wooden disks as close to the center as possible. I'm an excellent player."

Though Masterson said nothing, his face spoke for him.

"Okay, so I presume you aren't familiar with the game."

"Well, no, ma'am, I'm not. It's nice to meet you, uh, Miss Renaulde. Now, if I may get back to my game."

"It's urgent that I speak with you. I have a proposition."

The comment seemed to pique his curiosity. His brow shot up. "Darlin', I never shy away from a pretty lady with a proposition, but you'll have to wait until I'm through playing, then I'll be glad to hear you out. Very glad." He spoke smoothly but insistently.

Kaira thanked him and returned to the bar. "I do believe that went well, Mr. Wally. Don't you?" she stated with satisfaction.

The bartender nodded in agreement, and refilled her cup. "Anything else, ma'am?"

"No, thank you." She sipped the tea, trying not to lose focus on her mission.

Kaira fidgeted with the cup. She had come to Texas intending to prove to her grandfather that she didn't have what it took to be in the rag business, but now she suddenly found herself wanting to succeed rather than fail.

Her first step was to get the interview with William Barclay Masterson.

She stole one more glance at the table of players. Another approach might work. With renewed confidence, she stepped from the stool and headed toward the gamblers.

"Mr. Masterson, will it make a difference that I am a member of the Boston Peabodys and my grandfather is running for senator?"

He turned in her direction. Laying down his cards, he pulled to an impressive height. "Gentleman, please excuse me."

Gingerly, yet firmly, he took her elbow and escorted her back to the bar. He pulled out the chair for her. After she took her seat, he leaned down and in the voice only for her hearing, he said, "Miss Renaulde, I don't care if you're a member of the Peediddles of Pittsburg. When a man is gambling, it's impolite to interrupt. So, if you can sit here and busy yourself with some refreshment, when I'm finished I'll spend some time with you. Think you can manage that?" Not waiting for her response, he gave her a friendly wink and strolled back to the game.

Kaira watched him walk away before she took a deep breath. This newspaper scooping was a bit harder than she anticipated. Not letting him get the best of her, she stalked across the room. "I can do that, but may I ask you one itty-bitty question?"

"If it'll make you happy and get you back to your tea quicker, ma'am, I'll be pleased to answer your question."

The look on his face told her he wasn't interested in discussing business.

Her composure was under attack, but she'd come too far to turn back. While not wanting to aggravate the man she had to ask some trivial question. Something that wouldn't upset him. "Fine. Thank you." She shifted the caba on her wrist. "It may seem silly to you, but I've already said that I'm not familiar with the game you are playing, so . . ."

Masterson looked at his cards again, as though checking to make sure the faces hadn't faded away. "Well, ma'am." He put down the cards. "You've got my full attention."

"What is so special about the four queens in your hand?"

Chapter 6

If silence had a voice, the Amarillo Belle was screaming at the top of its rafters. Quin's fingers froze on the batwing doors as he watched bedlam inside the saloon dance to its own tune.

The piano player, dressed in a red shirt with a black garter decorating his right arm, suddenly attacked the ivories as through punishing an evil hombre. He broke into his own rendition of the popular minstrel. "Nobody knows the trouble I see. Nobody knows . . ."

In one wide sweep, the bartender strung out a dozen or more shot glasses along the bar and filled them in one continual stream with nary a drop of whiskey hitting the counter.

Scarlet satin and licorice lace swirled, as dancehall girls scattered like kitties confronted by a vicious hound.

Surely, Quin was going deaf. Had Kaira revealed Masterson's winning hand? From what Quin had heard, the gambler would make short work of sweeping the floor with anyone interfering with his wagering.

Bat Masterson placed his cards face up, scooted his winnings to him, and placed his hands on the table, prepared to stand. A sudden chill veiled the movement.

Quin recognized a bobcat stalking a canary when he saw

one. Feathers were about to fly, and he must protect Kaira. She needed a public flogging, but not by the famed gunslinger.

Like a bogged steer hip deep in mud, Quin stood rooted in place. On the third attempt, his legs moved forward. Picking up speed, he rushed the door, slamming the center with his chest. Both batwings parted and he crossed the sawdust floor before Masterson reached his full height.

In slow motion, Kaira turned in Quin's direction, probably wondering why she hadn't been told a tornado hit town. She blinked in bewilderment.

"Miss Renaulde!" Quin's voice sounded unnatural even to him. "I need to see you outside, *now*." His words echoed in the silence.

"I'm sorry, Mr. Corbett, but—" A crimson flush raced like a fever across her cheeks.

"But nothing. Outside. NOW!"

"Excuse me?" She lifted her chin and threw back her shoulders in defiance, which emphasized her set of attributes to their fullest.

"I didn't stutter." Quin resisted the urge to throw her over his shoulder and exit the saloon. But he had never deliberately embarrassed a woman and didn't plan to begin now. He gulped air. He could almost hear the hemp committee forming for Kaira's public hanging.

Securing her arm with a firm grip, he drew her near. Close enough that the sweet smell of lily of the valley masked the stale scent of smoke, whiskey, and lust.

She shot him a look that could surely send him direct to his grave, and dug in her heels.

"Mr. Corbett, please." She leaned lightly into him, tilting her face toward his.

Bat Masterson took a step forward. "It's in your best interest to get your hands off Miss Renaulde . . . at once."

Quin released her, realizing he could no more move the lady than he could a century-old cottonwood. Yet the thought of touching her in places hidden by crinoline and lace both unsettled and excited him. Where this woman was concerned, he seemed to have nothing but mush for a brain.

Kaira resituated her hat slightly and fiddled with a strand of loose hair that had escaped, but kept her stare glued on Quin, serving to unnerve him more.

While not taking her eyes off her confronter, she addressed the gambler in what was surely her best boarding-school English. "I'm fine, kind sir. Mr. Corbett meant no disrespect. Did you, Quinten?" She smiled sweetly, obviously detecting Quin's uneasiness.

Quin groaned. What's wrong with this gal anyway? He didn't disrespect her as a woman, only her complete disregard for her duties to the newspaper. "Of course not, she's my—"

"His new reporter." She finished the sentence for him. "And we were about to have tea. Are you ready to join me, Quinten?"

Masterson retreated back to the gaming table.

The tar and feather option began to sound better to Quin, as pure dee ol' furor replaced aggravation and rushed through him like a herd of spooked steers. "Do you know when hell is gonna freeze over, Miss Renaulde?"

"I honestly don't know, but I'll ask." She slipped past him and stalked toward the table of gamblers so quick that Quin couldn't catch her. "Mr. Masterson, do you have any idea when hell will freeze over?"

Under a snicker, he answered, "No." He lifted questioning eyes to the card players. "Gentlemen?"

One by one they shrugged their shoulders.

Obviously perplexed with the lack of response, she raised a delicately arched eyebrow to Quin. "Why do you ask?"

"Because that's when I'll start drinking tea."

"Then may I interest you in some spirits while I explain—"

"The only thing that I'm interested in is getting the newspaper out! And on time!"

"I propose to—"

"Drink tea in a saloon in the middle of the afternoon? Surely you jest—"

Masterson broke into one wave of laughter after another, interrupting Quin, until everyone at the table joined in . . . Everyone except for Quin, who was completely buffaloed by the sudden change in Masterson's attitude. Quin studied one person then another.

Kaira cocked her head, as though to say she thoroughly understood the joke. Maybe even knew the punchline.

"This is the best gag that you guys have pulled on me in years." Masterson slapped his hand on his thigh. "A real gut-splitter. And this sweet young thang was so convincing that she didn't understand poker." He gave a loud hey-haw. "Only a pro would know when it was safe to tell what I had in my hand." He winked at Kaira. "And I'd like to hear your proposition."

"She doesn't have one," said Quin, placing his hands protectively on her arm. "Let's go. We've got work to do."

"I'm leaving Amarillo tomorrow, so if you're still interested in discussing your proposition, miss, meet me at the hotel at eight o'clock tonight." With a quirk of a grin he returned to the game, tossing a gold coin in the middle of the table. "Shorty, deal before some tinhorn comes along and wants in the game."

The piano player changed tunes and customized the lyrics to fit the occasion. "Ooooh when a saint—goes marching out. Ooooh when a saint—"

"Saint, my ass!" Quinten groaned.

Kaira squared her shoulders and allowed him to escort her out of the room. *Take control of the situation, Kaira,* she thought. *Don't lose your temper. The man isn't worth it.* Or was he?

Once outside, she indignantly pulled out of his grasp, which seemed to have gotten progressively stronger as they crossed the room and exited the saloon. "Mr. Corbett, I respectfully request that you stop manhandling me immediately."

"Damn it, woman, I'm not manhandling you."

"I don't know what they call it in Texas, but in Boston it is definitely unacceptable behavior." She removed a tatted linen handkerchief from her handbag and fanned her face like a little old lady exposed to risqué humor. "Plus, I had Mr. Masterson exactly where I wanted him."

"Madder than a short-hobbled horse?" He stood there tall, dark, and angry.

"He was laughing."

"Oh sure. Because he was thinking how happy he'd be watching you sitting on a very skittish horse with a tight noose around your neck." He cringed at his sarcasm. "But then, he wasn't really mad at all, only interested in your proposition."

"That is correct. My proposition is the only thing he was interested in."

"And your proposal is?"

"To show you that I can be a reporter and obtain an interview for the newspaper."

"Where did you come up with that hare-brained idea?" A chill ran up his spine. Not sure he wanted to know the answer, his jaw set.

"You and Mr. Monk discussed it last evening. I was—"

"Scooping my interview? Come on." He hooked one arm to his hip. "Either come along gracefully or I'll hog-tie you and carry you back to the office."

Not in the mood to find out what her other options might be, Kaira slipped her left arm through his and secured the brim of her hat with her hand.

As though taking a pleasant stroll after a church social, the pair proceeded along the planked walk. His long stride increased their gait, forcing her to double-time it to keep up with him.

No doubt she was in trouble . . . serious trouble.

Chapter 7

Dozens of pairs of eyes watched the couple walk, rather gallop, toward the newspaper office. Kaira gripped her hat for dear life, afraid if she let go either their fast pace or a sudden gust of wind would carry it away, feather and all. After all, it'd take her months to get a replacement from Paris.

"I need to explain," she huffed.

"There is nothing to explain. You're a royal pain in the butt. You've already gotten into more hot water than one man could get you out of if he began dippin' the day you were born."

"Pain in the butt . . . I am most assuredly not. The way I see it, you're the one who ruined my chances of getting an interview with Mr. Masterson."

Quin partially guided her, practically pulled her into the office.

"Also, don't forget how that nice Bat Masterson almost hit you defending me."

He booted the door closed without comment.

Monk lifted his head. Detecting Quin's testy mood, the old-timer slipped out of his chair and hobbled to the back room, shutting the door behind him.

"Have a seat, Miss Renaulde. It's time we straighten out a few things." The muscles in Quin's neck visually tightened as he stepped to the stove and poured a cup of coffee. Obviously reconsidering his tactics, he inhaled deeply and asked, "Can I get you something to drink?"

"Tea, please." Then she became the one to reconsider. "Silly me." She tried on her best "oops" smile and remained standing simply to make a statement. Although his mannerisms had softened, his stare had not. This was no time to try his patience, so she sat down. "It's much too warm for hell to have frozen over. Right?"

A tiny smile appeared over Quin's cup. "Much too warm."

She wasn't sure but she may have seen a flicker of amusement in his eyes.

Kaira gathered enough nerve, and with as reasonable a voice as she could manage, said, "Quinten, I honestly meant no harm. I thought—"

"You thought! What's wrong with the old-fashioned philosophy that an employee learns their job responsibilities before they go off half-cocked?"

"Half-cocked?"

"Forget it. It's a Texas thing."

She bit her lower lip. "I owe you an apology."

"It seems that's all we do . . . apologize." He set down a cold mug of coffee before her. "Here. Need sugar?"

"No, thanks."

Quin pounced upon Monk's perch like a bullfrog on a toadstool. Pulling out a page of newsprint, he wrote in bold block letters: *DEADLINE. AMARILLO BY MORNING!*

Holding up the paper, he said, "That's *a* deadline. That's *our* deadline. That's *your* deadline." He got up, stepped past her, and tacked the newsprint on the wall. "This is all I'm interested in. Not excuses. Not apologies. Not explanations." He turned back toward her. "I need news, not a gossip column. Understand?"

Kaira nodded, looking up through a fringe of eyelashes like a grammar school girl being raked over the coals for misbehaving. "Perfectly."

"You are an apprentice. That means you do the muck work. Clean typeface. Do what the editor asks you to do. Assist Monk and me." He wagged a long, forceful finger at her. "You're a printer's devil—not a reporter!"

Hasn't anybody ever told Quinten not to point? Deciding that some things are better left unsaid, she let disappointment seep in and muddy her thoughts. Quin's words cut to the core. *Not a reporter!* Do dirty work? No lady she knew would perform such unsavory tasks unless they were the gardener or a stable hand. Rightfully, she should give him a piece of her mind. He had no right. Oh, but he did. Quin had every right but still she refused to be referred to as a devil—even a printer's devil.

Although she'd like the opportunity to soft-soap the rugged, temperamental editor just a bit, no doubt he would not only be amenable to her catching the next train back to Boston, but would cart her trunks on his back to the station to make sure she didn't miss her ride.

Time was ripe to make her move.

"I can see, Quinten, that there is no reason for us to continue our business relationship. I shall return to Boston on the next train." She snatched up her caba, stood, and moved less than a foot toward the stairwell before he stepped in front of her.

"Oh but you aren't, Miss Renaulde. This is exactly what your grandfather warned would happen. And I will not give him the satisfaction of thinking that I can't handle a greenhorn petticoat."

"You know nothing about my petticoats, and you can't stop me."

"Don't think I can't." He moved toward the door, where he filled the frame with his rock-hard body. "Your grandfather ordered me to teach you the newspaper business. And, damn it, lady, that's exactly what I intend to do. So sit back down."

His words assaulted her ears. He meant business and she didn't much like the look in those bold, chocolate eyes that seemed to dare her to challenge him. Screwing up her face, she plopped down.

"Since you dilly-dallied away enough time to make Monk have to clean the typeface for the next run, here is what I expect." Quin folded thick arms across his chest. "First off, you do as I say, and willingly." He relaxed his stance slightly and eased his mouth into a lazy smile.

She felt ambushed by his amusement. A smile that seemed to soften his features, even make the dark stubble on his jaw appealing. Too bad it didn't improve his poor attitude.

Damn, now that her grandfather had intervened, she would be forced to stay in the land of drifters, dreamers, and dance-hall girls. Kaira would much rather perfect the skills she had learned at finishing school, attend cotillions, and use the philosophies acquired at Boston College. Her game of croki-nole needed some work, and she had become lax in her enun-ciation. Back East she could cultivate the ways of the wealthy and privileged and not be concerned with the mundane, day-to-day operation of a newspaper in some unsophisticated, dirty Texas town.

Quin's voice startled her, sending a shiver up her spine. "Are you listening? I'll say it again to make my position per-fectly clear. Leave Mr. Masterson alone." His gaze bore into her. "And since you've wasted most of the day and Monk and I still have to get typesetting done, I have no choice but to send you out again to find some news—"

"And where do you suggest I gather such information?"

"I'd think you would instinctively know the answer."

"I've lived a very sheltered life."

"*Jeeze!*" Obviously his patience had thinned, but he con-tinued, "Look over the wires that came from the *Dodge City Times.*" He deposited a notebook on the table. "Surely there's something more interesting than odoriferous muskmelons and the warty cucumbers."

"Writing instrument, please," she said with smug delight. Quin selected a pencil from the cup on Monk's desk, and placed it in front of her with a thud. "Here. Next go to the undertaker and see who passed. After that, check out the register at the Amarillo Hotel. See if anyone of importance—other than Masterson—is in town. I want something of substance, not who was seen chit-chatting with whom." He placed both hands flat on the table. Leaning into her, the line of his mouth tightened a fraction more and his brown eyes seemed to magnetize her gaze to his. "And, one cardinal rule . . . no gossip."

"But last week at Miss Maggie's I overheard a conversation about two ranch owners meeting at the hotel—"

"No gossip." He warned.

Kaira flipped open the notebook and wrote: No gossip. No odoriferous musk. . . ." Excuse me. Are they mushmelons or muskmelons?"

Obviously exasperated, Quinten forced on his spectacles, opened the top draw of the cabinet, and began selecting uppercase typeface, avoiding eye contact. "That's a reporter's job to find out. It's called research."

"Then I'm a reporter?"

"You're an apprentice." He jerked his head up and sighed in disbelief.

Annoyed, Kaira rose to her feet, grabbed her handbag, scooped up the notebook, and returned the pencil to Monk's holder. "I prefer my own, thank you." She sashayed out the door, not able to resist throwing yet another barb into the mix, "Sounds like I'm a reporter to me."

"Apprentice! Apprentice! Apprentice!" Quin's words rattled the window panes.

Monk appeared from the storeroom. "Yep, sure did set that calico straight, son. Sure did." Mumbling, he shook his head and limped to his workstation.

"If I wanted your opinion, old man, I'd ask for it." Quin couldn't help but laugh, knowing Monk paid as much heed to his sarcasm as he did to the old-timer's grumbling. The duo was like a good ol' pair of work gloves. A perfect fit. One would be useless without the other.

"You only have to put up with her for three months, son."

"That's ninety days—a fourth of the year. . . ." Trailing off, Quin slipped on his cowhide apron and glasses and went to work.

"Less a week," said Monk.

The chit-chat of the telegraph began in earnest. For more than an hour both men worked without muttering a word.

Suddenly, Monk broke the silence. "Yep, that's one thousand nine hundred ninety-two hours." He adjusted his sleeve-protectors and turned to Quin. "It's either keep her here and get the newspaper out like her grandfather said, or kiss that bonus good-bye. Then you can forget restocking the ranch. Choice is yours, Quin."

"I'm at wits end." Quin pulled the visor from his head. "She's so damn frustrating. I've tried to be patient, but it's as if she is bound and determined to make me dislike her and send her packing. Come hell or high water, I'm not breaking the contract. That woman's like a nest of hornets that keep buzzing around me and I can't get them settled down. The worst part, I can't seem to get her off my mind." He absent-mindedly rubbed his aching collarbone. "If she's here she gets me all rattled, and if she's gone I worry about her."

"Yep, for sure. Been noticing that."

"She's gotten under my skin and I can't shuck her."

"Maybe you shouldn't try. Jest play the cards you've been dealt." Monk shifted his weight and massaged his thigh. "But you've got to be powerfully patient with her. She's like a bad rash that sure does hurt to scratch but feels mighty good when you're through. You gotta make a newswoman out of her."

"How do you profess I accomplish that?"

"Lengthen the lariat you have around her neck. Give her space. Gotta teach her come here from sic 'um. She's no nitwit, jest wants to see how long she can beat you around the stump before you send her home. Then it'll be all your fault she failed. No sir, for sure. That gal is no dummy."

"Patience and a loose lariat will do it, you think?"

"Yep, sure do."

Although it would be a stretch, Quin could try to be more patient, but wasn't all that keen on the giving her space idea.

Quin had tried to allow Kaira to find the news on her own, but all she'd managed to come up with was that a ranch hand on the Frying Pan had bought a new Stetson, and a lady sheep rancher had come to town for supplies. Mrs. Diggs at the mercantile had ordered a new array of bonnets from Fort Worth, and ol' Ira was complaining about Amarillo needing a good gunsmith.

Flipping his watch open, Quin checked the time. She'd been gone for nearly two hours and he couldn't help but wonder what pickle the sassy-butt had gotten herself into. Damn, he hadn't known her long enough to worry about her, but he did.

The thought barely had enough time to wane before Kaira burst through the front door, as though chased by a rattler in the outhouse.

"You'll never believe what I just heard!"

Chapter 8

Astonishment painted their faces as Quin's and Monk's gazes followed a blur of feathers, crinoline, and ivory lace rushing in one door and out the other.

On her way through, Kaira halted, unpinned her hat, and dropped it, along with her handbag and notepad, on the deacon's bench.

Quin held back a smirk and studied the bonnet. Dubiously, he shook his head. "Damn, that hideous thing looks like a confused bird made a nosedive for Miss Renaulde's head and got all tangled up in that netty stuff," he said to no one in particular.

The back screen slammed, echoing throughout the room.

A sinking feeling hit Quin as he drew his attention away from her bonnet and back to her words: *You'll never believe what I just heard.*

"Lordy, Lordy, did she ever have a bee in her bloomers," Monk snipped and turned back to his desk. "Someone needs to tell her we don't have the only privy in town."

Quin leaned back in his chair and thoughtfully tapped his index fingers together. "You do it. I don't have time to figure her out." He stared at the note on the wall . . . *DEADLINE!*

Interrupting his thoughts, Kaira rushed from the back room,

fetched her belongings and headed toward the stairwell, before turning back to the two men. "I have a few things to take care of before I tell you the—"

"Gossip?" Quin finished her statement. "I've already cautioned you—"

"Oh, fiddle-faddle." Kaira seemed unaffected by the warning as she continued, "Mr. Monk, may I bother you for a hammer and a few nails?"

The ol' codger scrambled to a small workbench that clung to the south wall and selected a claw hammer and half a dozen Wagon Box nails. He smiled at her like she was a hot apple pie. "Anything else I can get you, ma'am?"

"No, and thank you. You're such a precious man." She accepted the items. Proceeding to the stairs, she flung over her shoulder, "This will not take long. I'll be down shortly and tell you the, uh, news."

And she was gone.

"What do you think she wanted the hammer for?" Monk nonchalantly asked, as though giving a lady a hammer and a handful of nails wasn't out of the ordinary.

"Don't know. You seem to be the expert on the lady's needs, not me."

What could Kaira, who on one hand seemed to be helpless, yet on the other requested a hammer and nails as though she were a carpenter, be up to? The thought barely had time to formulate when thunderous pounding rocked the walls from the ceiling to the planked floors.

Thud. From the reverberation, no doubt Kaira had dropped the hammer. Rapid-fire raps ensued, quickly followed by one abrupt bang.

As sudden as the noise began, an eerie quietness cloaked the building. Nothing could be heard except Monk's labored breathing and Quin gulping air. Even the telegraph stopped to listen.

"For Pete's sake, what did she do, find a mouse and beat the confounded creature to death?" Quin wondered out loud.

"Musta got him with that final splat." Monk never looked up from his task.

Time passed in silence until lithe footsteps sounded on the stairs, drawing both men's gazes upward. Dressed in a no-nonsense taupe skirt, topped by a plain ivory blouse accented with rows and rows of ruffles that hugged her . . . uh, attributes tightly, Kaira descended.

"Wearing sensible shoes, I see," Quin muttered beneath his breath, figuring Monk couldn't hear him anyway.

"Yep, for sure. She looks like she's ready to get down to work," the old man quipped.

"And it could even be newspaper business." Quin resisted asking Monk why he seemed deaf to some things and turned all ears when it came to Miss Renaulde.

Coming within hearing distance, Kaira met Monk's smile, passed over the hammer, and thanked him for his kindness.

Damn, if she didn't make the ol' hip-shot broncbuster blush.

"Miss Renaulde, if I'm not interrupting your day, I'd appreciate knowing about the news you gathered." Quin nodded toward an oaken library table. "That is your work area, remember."

Kaira carefully opened her notebook, flipped over several pages, and poised her pen as though prepared to take notes. "And what precisely do you wish to know?"

"What you found out!" Quin inhaled deeply and exhaled, trying desperately to corral his annoyance.

"Well, Payton McClain—"

"McCord not McClain. From the Frying Pan—"

"Payton McCord," she repeated, as though she had used the right name in the first place, "and a lady named Harper came out of the Amarillo Hotel, and Payton's intended, Amanda, uh . . ." She flipped through her notepad.

"Lemmons." Quin provided the last name. "She inherited a little spread up near the Canadian River and raises sheep—"

"Oh yes, Amanda Lemmons, I ran into her at the mercantile shortly after I arrived when you assigned me the task of finding a story. A lovely woman. Evidently, the sheepherder wasn't too happy finding McClain—"

"McCord—"

"With another woman and she kicked him in his, uh—I've heard it's called his . . . well, his delicates." She referred to her notes, as if she'd find the answer on the pages.

Monk suddenly reinvested himself in the conversation. "You mean Amanda kicked him in his—" Meeting Quin's frown, the old ink-jerker hushed, clearly realizing his support wasn't appreciated.

"Yes, Mr. Monk, his shins. Miss Lemmons proceeded to give a rather vicious kick he won't forget for a while. I'm not sure what they said, but Miss Harper turned on him and booted him in his other shin. The ladies were somewhat brutal, and left him jumping around like a boarding school mistress at a cotillion. Talk has it that—"

"Miss Renaulde—"

"It's not gossip."

He folded his arms across his chest and leaned farther back in his chair. "So, tell me what you know as fact."

"Payton McCord was wearing a new Stetson. Looks a lot like yours . . ." Apparently his look of disapproval made Kaira realize this wasn't the kind of fact he needed.

"I saw, uh." She hesitated. "Well, the altercation involving McCord, wasn't that his name?" Seemingly proud that she remembered his name correctly, she looked directly into Quin's face, who nodded. "And Miss Lemmons and Miss Harper, whatever her first name is—"

As if compelled to respond, Monk added, "I hear that Mavis Harper gal with them cow-patty eyes and swingin' hips is as flighty as a strumpet on nickel night, but then I've only heard that—"

"Gossip! Give me news!" Quin was more angry at allowing Kaira to trap him into asking questions about the incident than Monk's intervention.

"That being said"—she flipped over another page—"as I recall, one of my assignments was to learn the difference between muskmelons and mushmelons." Her eyes brightened with pleasure. "I do believe the correct term is muskmelon. Although Samuel Clements, you know, Mark Twain . . ." She hesitated, as though waiting on Quin to challenge her. "Anyway, he referred to them as mushmelons in *The Adventures of Huckleberry Finn.*"

"That melon story, as stupid as it was, is already in those stacks of newspapers you nearly stumbled over coming in." He tipped his head toward the door.

"To be more exact, it was Huck using the word mushmelon in chapter twelve—"

"I don't care about mushmelons or muskmelons, Samuel Clements or Mark Twain, I need news. What about that paint that went loco, got himself unhitched, and went to find his owner in the Amarillo Belle last night? Did anyone get hurt?"

"I didn't ask. They probably—"

"No probably. I want facts!" He darted from his chair and towered over her.

The shocked look on her face confirmed his speculation that she had used up the afternoon most likely rereading Mark Twain. "Here's the deal, Kaira—"

"You called me Kaira—"

"That's your name, isn't it?" Damn, his glib response slipped from his mouth like marbles played on shale. He had intended to keep their relationship professional, and referring to her as Miss Renaulde was more appropriate than using her more intimate given name. "Uh, yeah. Yes, I did. If we're going to work together—anyway, back to the issue at hand. You will sit here until hell freezes over, or until you write me three articles for the newspaper. I don't give a rusty rat's ass which one you do. I want something printable, factual, and newsworthy."

Quin placed both hands on the table and leaned into her. "I got my interview with Masterson. Where is yours?" He tried to shut out the faint smell of sweet lily of the valley and ignore her softness, but all he could think about was the sense of excitement growing within him, penetrating the stone center of his heart.

Kaira watched him intently, not giving an inch. A single thread of respect and understanding began to form between them.

Damn, he didn't need a woman in his life. Any woman, much less some beautiful, spitfire Easterner who made his temper flair and his blood boil.

Where was Monk when he needed him? Now would be a perfect time for the ol' codger to dispense some sage advice, but it seemed that he had disappeared, probably to find Mavis Harper and see if she needed consoling.

"Uh, Miss Renaulde." Quin straightened and looked down on the most generously curved parted lips he'd ever seen. The sudden need for air strangled him. "I'm going out." He grabbed his Stetson. "When I get back, I'll expect those stories written, ready for me to typeset."

A drink suddenly sounded good. A stiff drink . . . one stiff enough to make Ol' Glory stand at attention!

Hooking up with Ira, Shorty, and Monk, Quin played five card stud and chased whiskey with beer until the pain in his shoulder subsided. Winning enough to order Monk a comfortable chair helped his mood, but the liquor didn't begin to chase away thoughts of Miss Dawdle-Butt.

Images of her lavender eyes following him out the door waltzed across his mind. They were closer to violet, like a field of primrose on a misty morning. Her eyes brimmed with passion and half-filled promise.

Such an attraction could be dangerous. He mustn't forget the purpose of her employment. If he failed to teach her the newspaper business, he'd lose the bonus. In turn, he'd break a pledge to himself and Monk. His ranch was at stake, yet the memories of her presence stoked a rampart fire in his gut. Illogical sensations couldn't define the source, but the feelings continued to erupt.

Quin had a growing need to check on Kaira. He'd been pretty tough on her earlier. Maybe he should apologize.

Hell no.

If there were any apologies heaped out, she'd do the spooning. What did he have to apologize for—because she riled him up so much with her beauty and sharp tongue? Humbug! He ordered a final shot of whiskey and tossed it back, hoping to get rid of the nagging question marks.

Quin slid his glass toward Wally and pitched some extra coins on the bar. As an afterthought, he turned back to the bartender. "You got any of that tea left over?"

After some good-hearted ribbing from Monk, and with thoughts of Kaira still thickening in his head, Quin tucked the crock of warm tea in his arms and headed toward the shop.

Off to the west, soundless lightning flickered against the night sky. He pushed the print shop door open, and the quietness that welcomed him was as noticeable as the lack of thunder. Dying lamplight caused gray shadows to dance against the walls.

Sitting down the crock, Quin noticed Kaira slumped forward, resting her head on her folded arms, as though protecting a secret. She had removed the ornaments holding her ebony hair high on her head, making her locks cascade around her shoulders. She snored softly.

He drew closer, halting behind her.

Quin tried to look away. He wanted desperately to keep his arms to his side, but as though a magnet drew his fingers to her, he stopped short of caressing the patch of soft, ivory skin exposed at the nape of her neck. An utterly enticing and very kissable part of her body. No Texas-born male could resist touching her. Gingerly he laid one finger, then three, on velvety skin. The feel of naked flesh against his calloused fingertips reached across the years to rouse emotions he had kept buried . . . until today.

Kaira stirred only slightly, as though enjoying a tender

moment. A tender moment! He wasn't being tender . . . he was being selfish and manhandling a defenseless woman.

Jerking his hand away, he caught sight of three papers neatly penned with a woman's flourish. Each had separate headings.

He shook off the unexpected sensations and picked up the articles. Taking the pages to his desk, he turned up the lamp, put on his glasses, and began to read.

"Poor Chicken: The Pan Handle has a curiosity in the shape of a chicken which has only one leg. It was hatched that way, is about a year old, and seems as happy and contented as though it had two legs."

Doesn't she even know, Panhandle is one word? Tossing the story aside, he continued to the next headline:

"Apples Quickly Taken: An itinerant-looking man with very small mules was selling apples here Wednesday. They came from Wichita Falls. They retailed at four bits a dozen, and were quickly taken."

The apples or the mules? Maybe both! Groaning while cutting his eyes toward the sleeping woman, he went on to the next story:

"Christening Scheduled: Briar Ebenezer Duncan, infant son of Milford Duncan and his wife, Opal, will be christened on Sunday."

Damn it! Quin slapped down the page with purpose and jerked off his spectacles, frustrated for almost forgetting the upcoming event, and all because of Miss Peabody-of-Boston!

He made a mental note to swing by the mercantile tomorrow to check on the silver rattler he had ordered. Maybe he should have selected a more practical gift than what Monk had suggested. Being a godfather to a little tyke was a momentous obligation. There were dozens of well-respected men more qualified than a washed-up cowboy. Joe Long, the foreman of the Frying Pan, and his wife, Lucinda, would be better godparents, particularly since she couldn't bear a child. Quin had helped birth a heap of calves, so why would the thought of being a godfather to little Briar Duncan make his chest fill with pride?

Quin leaned back in his chair. Making steeples with his fingers, he watched Kaira sleep, obviously unaffected by the light or shuffling of papers.

"Miss Renaulde," he little more than whispered.

She didn't stir.

"Kaira," Quin said louder. Pulling out of his chair, he walked toward her. "Hey, wake up. You need to go to bed."

She moved her head slightly, but remained still.

Tarnation, he had two choices; let her sleep or rescue her from a crick in her neck. She was an investment, and if she couldn't walk tomorrow because of sleeping sitting up, she couldn't find any news at all, worthless or not.

Quin owed her. After all, she had probably saved him from a public tar and feathering by reminding him of little Briar's christening.

Gently, he lifted her into the cradle of his arms. He could feel her soft breath against his neck as she snuggled into his shoulder. The sweet scent of lily of the valley once again shrouded him. "Kaira, I'm taking you to bed," he whispered so close to her ear that he could feel his own breath.

"Good." Kaira's voice was barely audible.

Quin felt the words more than heard them, her lips feather-touched his neck, arousing his passion once again.

She nuzzled closer, like a newborn kitten—needy and hungry.

Taking the stairs two at a time, he quickly reached the landing without waking his charge, and pushed his bedroom door open with the toe of his boot.

Outside, the night sky blazed with angry blue-white lightning, setting the room aglow. Fat raindrops splattered against the windowpanes as cannon-blasts of thunder echoed in the distance.

Protectively, Quin tightened his hold on Kaira.

His breath caught in his throat and his heart missed a beat, not from the electrical storm, but from what he saw in his bedroom.

"What in the hell?" He almost dropped Kaira on the wooden floor. "What in Sam Hill did you do?"

Chapter 9

Shocked beyond belief, Kaira steadied herself and watched Quinten Corbett stalk down the stairs. Never had she been treated in such an undignified fashion. He hadn't quite dropped her, but had unceremoniously plopped her on her feet. Quinten shot her a glare that would melt a horseshoe before he walked—rather, stomped—out, leaving her staring at the south end of the northbound pigheaded editor.

Kaira flounced to the window, pulled back the lace curtain, and watched lightning arc from cloud to cloud.

Why the sudden change with Quinten? And, just when she had come to enjoy the feel of his forceful hands as they cupped her posterior. A rock-solid chest that held a heart that sounded like it was trying to beat its way out of his chest cavity. Muscles of iron protecting her against the raging storm, and his tenderness . . . was a trait she hadn't expected in the big man.

A rambunctious clap of thunder caused her to jump.

Could it be that Quinten recognized that she only pretended to be asleep? Or that she played an innocent shenanigan on him by copying some old articles that she knew would catch in his craw? After all, isn't April Fools' Day a time of trickery? But then, he probably hadn't noticed and she hadn't had a chance to remind him. Kaira enjoyed a good prank every now and again, especially one that held promise. But this one had failed miserably. She ended up the fool.

Oh, Kaira had no intentions of allowing Quinten to touch her inappropriately, or do anything unacceptable to a lady. Nothing she didn't want him to do.

A flash of light lit up the room again.

She would not be treated so shabbily. She had done nothing wrong. He had suddenly turned coat and stomped away. He couldn't touch her the way he did, setting off sensations that no well-bred Bostonian lady should feel, and get away with it. By daybreak, she might be on the next train back to New England, but she deserved an answer from Mr. Corbett. He might be a handsome, rugged cowboy with a fiery, white-hot touch, but he would not trample on her emotions.

After taking a moment to pile her hair on top of her head and reinsert hairpins, she straightened her blouse and tinted her lips. Throwing her shoulders back, she headed downstairs to locate the jackass.

Quinten was nowhere in sight and the office was dark, except for soft light slithering from beneath the door of the back room, which served as storeroom, a place for the type to be cleaned, and a small corner kitchen.

Cautiously, she touched the closed door. Detecting the rush of water hitting a basin, she tested the knob. Unlocked.

Uncertainty knotted in her soul. Quinten was no doubt still angry for reasons she couldn't phantom. Kaira swallowed her misgivings, knowing she mustn't allow an innocent joke to turn into something it was never meant to be.

She wanted to help Quin succeed, while learning journalism herself. Kaira realized that the whole thought of being taken sincere was foreign to her. She had never thought of herself as a journalist or anything except a product of an affluent family who gave her the best. From a French nanny to an education at the elite Boston College, she was given everything her heart desired and more. So why the sudden need to have Quinten's approval?

Easing the door open, she made less noise than a scampering mouse in a cotton field. She caught sight of Quinten's magnificent near-naked body with nothing on but his unmentionables. Her heart leaped to her throat, and she felt sparks burst into flames and shoot directly to a place where such sensations were alien to her.

Never had she seen anything as shocking, or riveting. Kaira tried to quell the awareness flittering in her body.

Quinten leaned over the washbasin and splashed water on his face. Picking up the pitcher, he doused himself with cold water, leaving his hair shimmering in the soft lamplight.

Kaira wondered if he was trying to wash away his anger. Her gaze froze on his tall, beautifully proportioned body.

He shivered as the cold stream hit, making his muscles ripple like skipping stones on water.

From powerful thighs made for a pair of tight jeans to the slimness of his hips, she studied every muscle, every inch of the man that exuded masculinity in every breath. He shifted his weight, exhibiting a forceful body better fit for a saddle than a desk.

Her gaze stopped below his right shoulder. Numerous pitted pockmarks were lodged around a deep, purplish, and jagged scar plowed into his back. Suppressing an outcry, Kaira covered her mouth and closed her eyes. Not from repulsiveness, but from being unable to bear thoughts about a man carrying such a horrid disfigurement. What horrible accident had caused the scar?

Composure held a fragile shell around her. Kaira opened her eyes but continued to stay fixed on the painful-looking, long-ago-healed wound. Her stomach knotted. Taking a deep, unsteady breath, she grabbed the doorframe for balance.

Quinten whirled.

Kaira stood frozen. His physique was even more impressive face on. Since he had already seen her, she might as well make the most of the opportunity. After all, she'd never seen a man in his unmentionables before. In boarding school a floozy described a naked male body to her, but it paled in comparison to this magnificently built man.

She took the liberty to study his features. From his chiseled jaw covered with a smidgen of dark stubble, past angry lips and stormy eyes raging with furor, to that God-awful scowl he seemed to reserve just for her.

"What in the hell?" A muscle clenched along his jaw. He grabbed his shirt. Pulling it over his shoulders, he left the front open, and took a decisive step toward her.

But not before she got a good look at his memorable front side. As she had suspected, beneath his shirt he had a broad chest with a massive triangle of dark hair that disappeared somewhere beneath his flat stomach, short of his unwhisperables. His nipples formed perfect peaks on the swells of muscle. He looked magnificent, as though created from some novelist's imagination.

Bewildered at his outburst, and not sure whether it was a question or profanity, Kaira refused to respond and stood rooted in place, unable to pry her stare off the man.

What she was doing was simply unacceptable, yet she couldn't help herself. Unsuccessfully, she attempted to transfer her gaze to his feet, but that didn't help once she got midway down his exquisite, scantly dressed body.

Hypnotized, she boldly held a fortuitous stare on Quinten, shocked to think that as a well-bred lady she had such an overwhelming desire to reach out and boldly touch him. To see if his skin was as warm and strong as his fingers, if his muscles would harden beneath her touch, if the heat that filled her body like a prairie fire would flame hotter yet.

"What in the hell are you staring at?" He furiously snatched his pants from a nail. "I can't even have any privacy in my own place! Get the hell out of here."

"Well, I'm not leaving, so go ahead and put on your trousers—"

"Jeans—" His angry retort hardened his features.

"Jeans, trousers . . . you still put the same, uh, necessaries in them as any man, don't you?"

Not expecting a response, she inventoried the room as Quin turned his back, tucked in his shirt, and buttoned his fly.

A massive worktable anchored the room, allowing for little furniture. A stove, washstand, and cupboard in the corner made for a makeshift kitchen.

"You just don't seem to be able to follow instructions. I said get out." He ground the words between his teeth.

"Not until you terminate me or we get things straight between us." She spoke boldly, matching his ire.

"Don't tempt me. You have no idea, sweetheart, just how close you are to being thrown to the wolves . . ." Quin pushed past her and headed for his desk. "And they love fresh meat.

"You're not cut out for this business. I'll send a telegram to your grandfather advising him that you are on your way back to Boston. I don't know why in the hell he sent you here in the first place, but I bet he had a reason."

Uncomfortable with his accusations, Kaira flinched at the words spearing her heart. Grandfather did nothing without a reason. He told her he'd chosen Texas to send her to learn the business, but was that the only reason? She responded in a firm, decisive voice. "I'm not going anywhere. Besides, we have a contract."

"Yes, a contract that says you'll work here as an apprentice for three months. In exchange for your help, I'm to teach you the rag business. Something you don't seem to take seriously."

"Why are you so angry?"

"Why not?" He shoved the trash can aside and jerked open a drawer. "You take over my bedroom. Interfere with my work. Refuse to do yours. And, in general, you are more trouble than any man deserves."

"Are you irritated because I had items shipped from Boston and changed a few things in the bedroom?"

"A few things!"

"It's the lace curtains, isn't it?"

"No . . . Yes. It's the, uh, everything. The frilly, girlie stuff everywhere I turn. That damnable ugly hat you wear. The prissy china basin and pitcher. Soft and velvety pillows and the bedcovers. What in the hell did you do with my quilt?" Not waiting for her answer, he vented on. "Why all that satin and lace on *my* bed?" He thrust the drawer closed with such force that it knocked over his pencil holder.

"Your bed?" The cussed man made her madder than—than her grandfather. "I believe it's mine. As I recall, my contract states that you will provide me with suitable accommodations, and to be comfortable—"

"Where did it say that you can wreak havoc on my life? And I want that quilt."

"It's in the Saratoga." She stepped toward Quinten, almost afraid of his response. "Why is the quilt so important to you?"

"It's personal." His tone softened. "My mother made it."

Although he lowered his voice to a midrange roar, the annoyance on his face didn't slack, yet the underlying sensitivity of his words captivated her.

"Quinten—"

"Don't call me that."

"But you called me sweetheart."

"I was thinking about Mother." He stomped into one boot then the other and bolted upright. "Miss Renaulde, let's get one thing straight. I am your boss and you are my student. Nothing more. Not now, not earlier, not ever. Do you understand?"

His stubbornness unleashed something within her. "Sit back down." Triumph flooded through her when he winced at her words.

"I'll do nothing of the sort."

"Then I'll tell everyone in town that you forgot your own godson's christening."

Shocked, he crossed his arms and planted his feet apart,

which only served to call attention to his pigheadedness. "And how do you know that?"

"First off . . ." She eased onto Monk's stool, feeling a bit like a fawn facing a Winchester. "Mrs. Diggs asked me if I'd remind you that the baby rattle you ordered had come in. You'd been by the mercantile several times of late, and hadn't inquired about it, so she was worried."

"Learning about the christening wasn't hard. It's no secret. What about the other two articles?" He snatched up his watch and looked at the face, as thought he was clocking her.

"The truth—"

"That'd be nice, wouldn't it?"

"I wrote them. Every single, solitary word. Well, with the exception of—"

"How much is four bits?" he asked smugly. "And how did you know the man selling apples was from Wichita Falls?"

She shrugged off his first question, but became frazzled with the second. "I checked out each fact—"

"No, you didn't." He proceeded back to his desk, tore open a drawer, and tossed a newspaper at least two years old in her direction. "That story came straight from the *Dodge City Times* and we've already run it. And the chicken story sounds faintly familiar, except for the age of the critter. How many one-legged chickens make the newspaper?"

"Are you going to thank me?"

"For what? For intruding on my privacy, inserting yourself in my life without being asked, for nearly getting my chops busted by Masterson . . . for—"

"For saving your hide! If I hadn't jogged your memory, you would have missed the christening."

"Not on your life."

"You never answered me. Why are you so angry?"

"Why are you so nosy?"

She frowned, not sure if his question was rhetorical or not. This was her opening. Maybe the last opportunity she would have to set the record straight.

"I think you're angry because you're scared."

"I don't recall asking your opinion. I asked why you're nosy."

Kaira didn't hesitate and rushed past his comment. "Scared that a woman will be attracted to you, then repulsed by your scars. Scared you might show your tender side. Which, by the way, you did this evening when you rubbed my neck. First one finger, then three."

"I knew you weren't asleep!"

"No, you didn't, or you would have never touched me. You are frightened of living, don't think you deserve being happy, and so many things that I couldn't even keep count. You make a job of making folks think you are insensitive and tough." She needed to take a breath, but couldn't stop long enough, afraid the words would stop flowing. "I came into town prepared for you to put me on the next coach back to Boston. I was afraid, too. Afraid of succeeding. You made me see that I don't have to be afraid any longer. Ever since I can remember, I followed in the footsteps of one powerful man after another. My grandfather, his father before him, my dad, at least a half a dozen uncles and twice that many cousins. I had to go to the right school, use proper etiquette, speak and act a lady, everything I wasn't. Everything I didn't want to be. Everything . . ."

Somewhere between the second and third "everything," or even as early as her reference to her grandfather, Quin lost his train of thought. One that was heading for a huge pileup any moment.

Why am I so angry?

Not for any of the reasons she had named. He was angry for reacting so badly to her seeing him undressed, reaching in his soul and massaging an ache. Resurrecting feelings he tried much of his life to hide.

Quin hooked a chair with the toe of his boot and slumped into it. He closed his eyes, not giving a flying fig if Kaira noticed. After all, she was too busy flouncing around the room, performing a soliloquy.

Anger was all Quin could remember feeling. First was hugging his father good-bye when he went off to war, never to return, then watching his mother grieve herself to death. Later, Quin was shipped from one family to another until Monk took him in and taught him the worldly ways of living.

If it hadn't been for his mentor, Quin would have lost the ranch before he was old enough to play with roly-polies. Settling in at the old homestead, Monk taught Quin how to ride with the wind, follow a trail while covering tracks, and how to hunt and fish for survival. Drink whiskey like a man and play a decent hand of poker. To take care of his body and mind. Quin went to school, something many young men his age didn't get a chance to do. Readin' and numbers, as Monk used to say, were what would make a man successful. That and having general smarts, he'd always add.

Quin couldn't help but smile at his wandering thoughts. The ol' cowpoke had taken him to church every time the door opened, except during roundup time. Then they'd hook up with an outfit and take a herd of cattle up north to market. Once Amarillo became a rail town and stockyards became a plenty, Monk bought the print shop, like his father before him, and trained Quin in the newspaper business. The ol' buzzard had taught Quin everything a young man needed to know, except how to keep his heart from being broken.

Kaira's rambling cut through his musing. "And then I arrive in Amarillo and . . ."

Quin watched Kaira. Every time she stopped for a breath and her eyes met his, his heart turned over. When she wasn't watching, his gaze traveled over her face, then moved down her body slowly. The very air around her seemed electrified and wrapped him in invisible warmth, sparking feelings in him that had nothing to do with reason.

"Plus, today is April Fools' Day, so I thought you'd enjoy a joke." She stopped and looked up and his heart lurched madly. "Any red-blooded man enjoys . . ."

"The last I heard, April Fools' is on the first day of April, so you're either early or late, depending on which you prefer."

Kaira's brows arched mischievously and she twisted her pretty little lips, as though giving the whole idea plenty of thought. "I rarely look at a calendar . . ."

Or a watch, either, Quin thought.

Damn, that woman was so compelling, with a magnetism potent enough to rivet him in place. He veered away again, thinking about velvety skin concealing an inner strength bordering on stubbornness like nothing he'd ever experienced.

Monk had taught him everything, but somewhere along the line he'd failed the class on how to handle a woman like Kaira.

"Do you want to know what happened to my back and shoulder?" Quin wasn't sure where the words came from. Maybe it was her magnetism after all.

"I barely noticed a scar."

And I barely noticed your attributes looking as though they are crying to be caressed, to come fully awake, Quin thought.

Torn by conflicting emotions, he began. "I was foolishly young, invincible, I thought. Rode the range when I wasn't on my ranch, near the Canadian River." He cleared his throat, pretending not to be affected by his pounding heart. "Monk and I hired on with an outfit taking a couple of thousand longhorns up to Dodge City. Moses, the lead steer on the drive, was hoofin' it along between me and Monk, since we were riding point. We had our eyes on a young, feisty bull closing in on Moses. I knew if they began to fight, Moses would kill the maverick and we'd be gathering up strays for a month. Like an idiot, I thought I could distract the ornery critter, but not before Ol' Moses turned and decided to put the bull in his place. They hooked horns and somewhere along the way, I got into the fracas."

"Which one did you say was the head cow?"

"Lead steer, and it was Moses."

"You and Monk didn't hurt either of the cows, did you?"

"Steers! No, between me getting gored and Monk getting me the hell out of the way they forgot their differences and the bull ended up at the railhead. Ol' Moses had to sluefoot his way back to Amarillo with the drovers. If it hadn't been for Monk, I'd be dead."

Before he knew it, Kaira kneeled before him. Taking his hands in hers, she kissed one then another. "It must have hurt, Quin." She cooed like a mourning dove, throaty, soft, and meaningful. "Can I do anything for you?"

"Try giving that tongue of yours a rest, sweetheart." Not knowing what possessed him, he lifted her into his lap.

Hungrily, his mouth covered hers, sending spirals of ecstasy through him. He intended to kiss her gently, but when she returned his kisses with such reckless abandonment, he turned demanding. Quin masterfully taught her new ways to use her tongue. Learning fast, she amorously responded, arousing him fully.

Blood pounded in Kaira's brain, leapt from her heart, and made her knees tremble.

Quin's mind told him she'd slap him all the way to Goliad and back if he went further, but his body refused to listen to the warning. He slowly moved his hand under her skirt to skim her hips and thighs. She was stunned at the unharnessed desire that his gentle touch sent throughout her body, her own eagerness to touch him, accept, and return each passionate kiss.

Before she completely tossed out any semblance of logic and let Quin have his way with her, Kaira had to tell him the truth. She couldn't sleep with a man she lied to. She slid her arms from around his neck, splaying her palms against his chest. Looking into his eyes, she knew the moment might pass, and Quin would withdraw as he did earlier in the evening, but she had to take the chance. He had to know everything. "I have something I have to say . . ."

Quin rolled his eyes. She always had something to say, but why right now? He tried to pull her back into his embrace.

"You have five seconds, starting right now." He pointed toward the shelf clock and smiled. A very wicked, sensual smile.

"I need to say this. I feel so sorry for you—"

As quickly as their kisses turned to passion, he pulled her arms from around his neck and set her upright, allowing the hem of her skirt to fall into place in the process.

Quin came to his feet. "I'm not your charity case. I don't want your pity." He ran his hands though his hair. "Your grandfather sent you here for a purpose, and taking me on as a charity case wasn't it."

"You're not a charity case. I meant—"

"You seem to think the words 'I meant' will correct whatever ill-conceived remarks that flow from your mouth. Do us both a favor and do the job you were hired for—get me some news." He pulled his slicker and hat from the coat tree. "I'm not your project or your lackey. Don't feel sorry for me." He stormed outdoors bareheaded, carrying the raincoat.

Intense lightning flashed, followed by a deafening clap of thunder that split the air and seemed to reinforce Quin's furor.

Kaira yelled into the darkness. "You'll have an editorial tomorrow that you will never forget—*Mister* Corbett!"

Chapter 10

Kaira kicked the door shut with picture-rocking force. The reverberation disturbed the only shelf on the wall, which held a mantel clock with some God-awful mythological creature reclining on top.

Settling her hands on her hips and pursing her lips, she studied the newsprint that Quin had nailed up—*DEADLINE, AMARILLO BY MORNING.* Good judgment replaced childishness, and suppressed her desire to rip the ludicrous reminder into a zillion pieces, bake it in a pastry, and serve the rascal some humble pie.

In fairness, maybe she had created chaos in his tranquil existence. She'd taken over his bedroom, spiffing it up to make it to her liking. But, in turn, his touch had set off wild, unleashed sensations within her, feelings reserved only for soiled doves.

Why had she even attempted to apologize to the knot-head for Grandfather Renaulde saddling him with a wet-behind-the-ears, snot-nosed tenderfoot? She didn't think she'd missed any of the idioms Quin had tagged on her as she'd waited outside the door on her first day, summoning up enough courage to face the unpredictable, big man with a bigger reputation. Now she understood why her grandfather said that Quin and three Philadelphia lawyers would make a good match for the devil.

From the moment she stepped into the newspaper office, she had recognized a restless rebellion in Quin's every move. His forced demeanor failed to mask an underlying wildness. Definitely a man who gave women the desire to tame. He portrayed independence much like her grandfather. Mulling it over, she counted the similarities between the two obstinate, bullheaded men.

No! Quinten doesn't deserve my apology. The turkey could stay mad for all she cared. Then reality nudged her—aside from being a comely Texan who any woman would enjoy spooning in the moonlight, Quin was the editor and her boss, so she had no choice but to respect his position.

Kaira dropped into the editor's chair and steadily rocked back and forth.

Spitfire and brimstone—bring on the matches, the whole room smelled like him. Woodsy, layered with leather and printer's ink, as bold and appealing as the man himself. The one scent missing—coffee. Monk always had a pot brewing.

After making her way to the makeshift kitchen in the back room, Kaira fed the cast-iron stove two small logs—a new experience for her. Proudly, she poured water into the coffee pot and added a generous amount of Arbuckle's. Not sure how much she should use, and considering its dark, rich color, she tapped in another cup or so of grinds. She then replaced the tin in the cupboard beside a bowl of peppermint sticks.

On the battered sawbuck table she spied a crock that she didn't remember seeing before. Lifting the lid, the aroma of tea waned as it filled the air. A smile tickled her lips. Had hell frozen over?

Hot tea and honey sounded irresistible. After preparing a cup, Kaira found her way back to the front office. Pacing and blowing on the mug to cool the hot liquid, she kept an eye on the window. Sunrays radiated out into a vivid tapestry of copper washed with indigo. Morning approached rapidly.

With little sleep, except for the wink or two she caught waiting on Quin to return to the office, Kaira hurried to her room and selected an ordinary, blue muslin day dress. She missed the luxury of her indoor bathtub at home, finding drawing and heating water quite annoying.

She eyed a hatbox. Considering the windy, dusty weather of the Panhandle, her beautiful, hand-fashioned trappings served no purpose but to be bothersome. Her starched, Bostonian friends would be appalled at her lack of style, but at least it'd give Quinten one less thing to find fault with.

On her way out, she laid aside two dime novels and picked up a leather-bound book from the highboy.

Refreshing her tea, she returned to Quin's desk and opened an etiquette book considered the boarding school Bible. She thought back to the hours her headmistress had forced each girl to practice becoming a lady. Kaira flipped through the pages and began to read, taking in each word with new meaning: "A false admiration of man will change an angel into a demon. A misguided blow of the mallet will shatter all the efforts of years of training to learn to become a lady . . ."

Hearing the familiar sound of Monk shuffling into the office, she sprang from behind Quin's desk and slipped the book beneath her notepad on her worktable.

Appearing unconcerned with Quin's absence, Monk muttered a shy hello before exchanging his jacket and Stetson for an apron and visor.

Monk knew Quin better than anyone. Maybe he could tell her why Quin seemed angry with her more times than not. She needed guidance, and the seasoned gentleman seemed long on candid advice.

"Are you too busy to have a cup of coffee?" Kaira asked, taking a chance that he wouldn't decline.

"Sure would be a pleasure, ma'am. I'll fix us both a cup." He started for the back room, his limp more profound than usual. She recalled her nanny saying that the wet after a storm stirred up her "rumatiz" something fierce.

Monk returned with two chipped mugs, gave her one, and headed to his desk. Taking a sip, a stunned look caught on his face, and his cheeks swelled up like a squirrel carrying a walnut. From across the room the dastardly, thick, ill-smelling concoction assaulted her nostrils.

She considered taking the trash can to him so he could spit out the unsavory stuff, but he swallowed.

"Mighty fine coffee, ma'am. Yep, mighty fine." He set the cup aside.

"Do you know where Mr. Corbett might be?" She followed his example, and slid her cup out of the way.

"Reckon I do, ma'am, sure do. He's over gettin' all duded up, he is." He pulled on a sleeve-protector.

Good! That would give her time to talk with the old man.

"You know Mr. Corbett better than anyone—"

"Raised the boy since he was knee high to a grasshopper, sure did."

She caught herself glancing toward the door, realizing her misgivings were increasing by the second. "I don't know exactly how to ask this—"

"Spit it out, ma'am. Jest say what's on your mind. Keepin' somethin' stuck in your craw will make a man poorly."

"Good advice. Thank you." For once, she felt uncomfortable speaking her mind, but Monk made it so easy. "Has Mr. Corbett—"

"Call him Quin, he never took a likin' to being called Mister."

"Okay. Has Quin always been— let's call it a tad testy?"

"He ain't a tad testy, he's about as out'a humor as a prairie chicken headin' for a skillet. Jest depends on how the wind's blowin'."

Well, this might be easier than she first thought, considering Monk normally protected Quin like a nanny goat with her kid.

"Did it all start when he got hurt?" She hesitated, realizing Monk didn't know she knew about Quin's injury.

"Figured you found out . . ." He picked up his cup then set it back down, probably remembering how horrible the coffee tasted. "Considering what a sore mood that boy was in over at the livery stable last night, pert near midnight. Yep, he sure looked like something the dogs drug in outta the rain. Growled like one, too. Yes, ma'am, he sure did look unhappy."

"I guess it's my fault."

"No, ma'am. It's not your fault. It's mine."

"I don't understand." Kaira took a quick, sharp breath of confusion.

"There's a lot of things you don't understand, ma'am. A man like Quin ain't fond of being fenced in."

"And, I'm fencing him in?"

"Nope. The work is. He was born to ride the range and be free. His back is jest part of what's eatin' him."

Kaira sat back and listened to Monk tell her about Quin's father dying in the filth and neglect at Andersonville Prison. Too tired and frightened from fighting the Indians, his mama grieved for the past. Unable to continue managing the ranch, she allowed the few head of cattle not rustled or slaughtered to wander away. Finally, all her hands took their measly pay, what they hadn't already stolen from her, and headed off the ranch, never to return. Nothing gave her hope, not even her son, Quin.

Step by step, the ol' codger told every aspect of Quin's growing up, including how Monk came upon the little feller burying his ma under a big old cottonwood tree not far from a withered field of wildflowers. How he watched the youngster pick a few stalks of limp Indian Blanket and some sort of a daisy and stick them in the mound of dirt that he had so carefully packed over his ma's grave . . . as firm as any nine-year-old could.

Tears trembled on her eyelashes. More slow, hot tears wet her throat and threatened to spill out of her eyes. Faced with the harsh reality of how helpless and frightened Quin must have felt, she closed her eyes, allowing the links of his life to fit together one after another, until it formed a beautiful chain depicting the whole of Quinten Jon Corbett.

"I talked the kid into letting me stay on as a ranch hand for the winter. He paid me what he could until the money played out, then we took to droving to make ends meet. We had our good times, and some not so good 'uns, too." Monk stood and picked up his cup. "Want more coffee?" he asked as though he'd drank the whole pot.

"No, thanks." Kaira covered her face with her hand, trying to sort out everything she had learned about the mysterious editor.

But the most astonishing revelation came after Monk returned from putting water on to boil. He never complained about her coffee, just started another pot.

"We'll have us more Arbuckle's before we know it." He returned and hitched himself upon a stool. "After he got hurt and couldn't hit the trail, I didn't feel right about going off and leaving the kid behind, so I took the little money I'd horded, bought this print shop, and ran it until I sold it to your grandfather."

"He bought the shop from you?" Stunned, she repeated what he said. Kaira attempted to mask her inner turmoil with a deceptive calmness. "I'm confused."

Her grandfather had told her unequivocally that he had purchased the shop from Quinten.

Kaira cleared her throat, more shaken than she wanted Monk to know. "Then how did Quin end up with the business? He does own it, doesn't he?"

"Yep, he sure does. I don't think you'd appreciate the story, so let's jest leave it be. The shop belongs to the boy, not me."

"I believe I'd surprise you."

"No ma'am, nary another word. It'd only disappoint you." His tone was apologetic, yet left no room for discussion.

"Quin owes you for everything he is—everything he has?"

"No, ma'am! It's me who owes Quin. He saved me from

sure death when that ornery lead steer and a bull filled with pizz'n'vinegar got into a scrape up around Dodge City. If the boy hadn't been brave—not to mention foolish—enough to get me out of the way, I'd been pushin' up daisies somewhere on the range, with nobody but a bunch of buzzards for company."

"So that's the real reason Quin doesn't want anyone to know about his injury. He doesn't want anyone to know the truth . . . that he was hurt being a true hero."

"No, ma'am, Quin don't wanna be nobody's hero 'cause heroes only get their hearts broken, and that boy's been hurt so much that he's bound and determined not to let it happen again." Monk shifted uneasily in his seat, probably realizing that Quin would be furious if he knew they were discussing him in such an intimate fashion. "Yep, for sure, the man's fightin' with all his might to make sure he won't get hurt no more."

Thoughts whirled in Kaira's head as she tried to separate emotions from reality. Why had her grandfather deliberately kept from her the truth about who he bought the shop from? She thought him a lot of things, but a liar wasn't one. Why the deception? Did he want the newspaper to fail? And, if so, for what purpose?

Determination coupled with a streak of inbred defiance took over. Kaira had no intentions of allowing the ol' toad back in New England to take away the only thing Quin had left—the *Panhandle Herald.* Whether Quin wanted her help or not, she was in Amarillo to stay. The newspaper would succeed. She'd focus on nothing but learning the rag business, maybe even enough where Quin could be free to spend more time at his ranch—go back to doing what his true calling was . . . being a cowboy.

By George, if Grandfather wanted to play a game, she'd best him this time.

Monk interrupted her thoughts. "I gotta take next week's newspapers over to Jeb Diggs cause we never know when

Coop will be pulling in here to pick 'um up to cart over to Mobeetie."

"Mr. Monk, before you leave, may I ask you something else?"

"Yes, ma'am, reckon you can." He removed his visor and fingered the bill, as though he'd answered about all of the questions he planned to.

"I need your help."

Panic settled over the old-timer's face. "Yes, ma'am. You know I'd do most anything for you——"

"I mean, I need your advice."

"Yep, for sure, got lots of that."

"Will you teach me the newspaper business?"

"Yep, can sure do that." He held onto the visor for dear life. "Yes, ma'am, I'd be plumb tickled to help you out."

"Thank you. You won't be sorry." She picked up her cup and walked toward Monk's desk to retrieve his. "Another question. What can I do to make the newspaper successful?"

"Do your job, ma'am. Quit playin' games with Quin. Teasing the boy. He's had enough of that to fill a lifetime. Pardon me for saying it, but—"

"I haven't taken any of this seriously, is that what you're saying?"

"Sorta, ma'am." He hung the visor on the peg. Shuffling over to the stack of papers, he effortlessly lifted a twine-tied bundle over his shoulder. "One more thing, Kaira, you're not a dimwit. You gotta make him believe in you. You know what the boy needs, jest give it to him."

"Beginning with an editorial he won't forget?"

"Yep. And, a good ol' pot of sonofabitch stew and biscuits wouldn't hurt either. Don't got many fixin's in the cupboard, but we got credit with Jeb Diggs, so get anything you need." Not bothering to take off his apron or sleeve protectors, Monk grabbed his hat and headed toward the door.

Stopping and slightly turning her direction, he said, "Quin loves them Maryland Beaten Biscuits, and a good ol' larruping tongue pie would cheer the boy up."

Once Monk was out of sight, Kaira seized Quin's weighty, black apron and heaved it over her head. She laughed good-heartedly as it fell heavily over her breast, almost taking her breath away. She stretched. Having to put her arms in positions unaccustomed to her, she finally got the waist tied.

Oh, Kaira was taking this serious . . . nobody knew how seriously!

Chapter 11

Quin watched Monk exit the newspaper office like a short-tailed bull in fly season as he headed toward Diggs Grocery and Hardware. The bundle of newspapers balanced on Monk's shoulder seemed weightless as he scurried along, dragging his leg slightly.

"Afternoon, Miss Harper." Quin tipped his hat to the woman who had appeared beside him, damning himself for poor timing. Another twenty paces and he'd made it to his office without her catching up with him. He kept walking until Mavis Harper latched onto his arm, making it impossible to continue. At least he was squarely in front of the window of his office, and hopefully Kaira would come to his rescue. On the other hand, she might gleefully watch Mavis eat him alive.

Half-heartedly, he listened to Mavis rave about his new reporter. *Reporter my ass!* Nodding in agreement every now and again, he let her sing Miss Renaulde's praises, while his thoughts seemed to focus mainly on Kaira's, uh, attributes.

Surely the woman had cooled down by now.

Quin had. He'd had plenty of time to adjust his attitude and think things through on the cold, wet trip to his ranch.

Once the storm moved out, a full moon showed him the way. Quin had checked on the barn and the house to make sure no saddle tramp had taken advantage of his absence. Satisfied, Quin led his buckskin, who he unimaginatively had named "Buckskin," to the barn where he unsaddled the gelding, rubbed him down, and turned him out in the corral.

Too restless to sleep in the house, Quin found his secret corner of the barn and stretched out on the dry, dusty hay. Unsettled, he tried to shuck memories of hiding in the barn, praying he was invisible, being scared of strangers who happened onto the ranch. Terrified of what they would do with a young child alone if they found him. Fearful for his life, but more afraid of being forced on yet another family who viewed him as nothing but a nuisance and an extra mouth to feed, since he hadn't been big enough to work in the fields.

Sleep came sparingly.

At daybreak, having spent a chilly, fitful night, Quin rambled his way up to the house. Not bothering to start a fire, he found some beans and ate them straight from the can. That would be enough nourishment to last until he got back to town and had a good meal at Miss Maggie's.

Saddling the gelding, Quin made his customary stop under the cottonwood trees. A weathered cross with the words REBECCA KATHLEEN CORBETT—MY MOTHER burnt into the wood and bent by years of wind and rain served as the headstone.

Quin cleared the area of dead limbs and winter's brush. Pleased that the Indian Blanket had bloomed, he picked a few.

While Quin worked, the sun came alive and burned off much of the haze, casing a shadow over his shoulder. A sense of serenity veiled Quin as he placed the wildflowers on the grave still glistening with dew. As though someone touched his soul, he shivered. He had to be going loco because he was certain he had heard his mother's voice. "Live my son. Live for me."

Quin laid his head on the grave. A tear dropped silently on the wildflowers. He knew it wasn't manly to cry, but maybe he should have done it years ago.

Swinging into his saddle, Quin headed Buckskin for Amarillo, with thoughts of Kaira heavy on his mind.

He'd never experienced such heated passion as he did with her. She brought out both the best and the worst in him . . . the beast in him. She seemed to find perverse pleasure in challenging him to protect her. Every curve of her body spoke defiance, with a hint of maddening arrogance. Quin loved the way she had prickled up when her anger turned to scalding fury. She had hurled words at him like stones. Damn, he thought he might be in love with her. A gal to match him tit-for-tat. He'd seen salty women in his life, but none like Kaira Clarice Renaulde.

"Quinten Corbett." Miss Harper's voice penetrated Quin's thoughts and brought him back to the streets of Amarillo. "I do believe I lost you for a moment." She smiled, her big eyes blaring in excitement.

"No, ma'am. I heard every word. Would you excuse me?" Quin made his getaway before she could grab his arm again.

Quin virtually slammed the door behind him. He took off his Stetson and hung it along with his slicker on the peg, mumbling a sheepish hello to Kaira, who sat at her desk reading.

Out of habit, he checked the time. Three sixteen. Damn, he'd missed dinner and supper wouldn't be served until five o'clock. Miss Maggie never varied her schedule an iota.

Walking to his desk, he caught sight of Kaira tucking wayward strands of hair back into place. She seemed flustered and a bit nervous as she pulled at the cuffs of her sleeves, barely glancing up.

"Are you getting sick?" He noted the beads of perspiration on her forehead, and a shimmering of blush that ran across her neckline and downward toward her . . . attributes.

"No. I'm . . . fine." She sounded winded.

"Did you have a good morning?" Quin retrieved his apron from the back of his chair.

"Yes, thank you." Her blush deepened to crimson.

Quin was certain he'd hung the apron in its regular place when he left, but then he'd been pretty angry and might have forgotten to put it up.

He slid the protector over his head, surprised by the warmth left over from being recently worn. It was Kaira's warmth, and dern if he didn't think he smelled her—lily of the valley on the cowhide. But why had she worn his work apron?

Kaira watched Quin pull a stack of handwritten pages from his center desk drawer. He carefully sat them on the typesetting table.

Uncertainty clutched at her heart.

Quin flashed a brief, arresting smile that dazzled against his sun-drenched skin. He was even more stunningly virile than ever. Blasted, he was so charming when he smiled.

Clenching and unclenching her hands, Kaira squirmed in her seat, wishing her uncomfortableness would subside and she could scrounge up the courage to ask him where he had spent the night. But then it wasn't any of her concern.

Dern it! The man looked better than any French pastry she'd ever tasted. A delicacy that once you are introduced to, you can't do without. Although still unruly, Quin's dark hair was shorter and he was freshly shaven, smelling of soap, leather, and a hint of lilac aftershave.

"I ran into Monk last night. He's been working too hard, so with you here to help, I told him to take the rest of the day off. He's picked up enough news off the telegraph to put together a decent paper next week."

"Do you still need a piece?" Although Quin had typeset most of the next edition, she knew he still had white space, something not profitable to a publisher.

"I could use it. Got one?" A flash of humor crossed his face. "One that doesn't have anything to do with melons or apples. No fruit at all."

"And no Mark Twain?" Half leery of his good humor, she flashed a tentative smile. Fully prepared for him to quill up at the notion that she had a serious story, she said, "Yes, I have something. It isn't gossip. It's a peace offering to prove my renewed commitment to the success of the paper."

"Then for once, we're both plowing in the same direction, huh?" He spoke in a kind, jesting way. "Did you put it in the drawer with the others or do you have it on you?"

"I have it in here." She reached for her caba, hesitating slightly. "Before you start typesetting it, we need to talk."

"Kaira, generally you do the talking and I do the listening, so why don't you start and I'll catch up with you." He went back to his desk and sat down.

"Why did Monk sell the newspaper to my family?"

"The ol' coot didn't tell you?" Quin looked surprised and a bit hesitant to say more.

"No—no, he didn't and I need to know."

"He sold the newspaper after I got hurt to pay the taxes on the ranch. We'd depleted most of our funds, and the money we were suppose to receive for the few head that did make it to market never got back to us."

"I didn't know. So, how did you become the editor-in-chief?"

"He didn't tell you that either?" Quin didn't wait for her reply. "It'll only disappoint you."

"That's exactly what Monk said, so tell me the truth . . . all of the truth."

"Let's just say he and your grandfather didn't see eye to eye. Didn't share the same philosophies. Monk pretty much wanted to stay low-key and not disturb folks. Renaulde wanted big changes that most of the new frontier wasn't prepared for. Monk was bound and determined not to give in and they fired him."

"Fired him!" She was appalled. The cold and heartless cad. Terminating someone because they didn't share his opinion.

"Yep. I stepped in and agreed to become the editor, only if they'd leave me be, let me hire my own assistant, and pay his wages out of my own pocket."

"That is an atrocity." She wasn't sure that the soft spot she had for the old man wasn't responsible for much of her ire. She opened her pocketbook and retrieved two envelopes that she had carefully protected all the way from Boston to Texas.

"Quin, I know I haven't appeared to take my employment very seriously, but I want to begin. I want to learn. I'm well educated and have something to offer. Here is a piece I brought with me." Carefully, she avoided saying a piece that her grandfather had given her in return for her promise that she'd get it into the newspaper. "It's an editorial."

"We don't do editorials." He smiled, backing off. "But let me read it."

"Grandfather said that they are what makes a newspaper sophisticated, gives it respect, and increases circulation."

Kaira took a deep breath, thinking back to when her grandfather had given her the article. How he explained that she would know when the time was right to give it to Quin. That it was the kind of piece that would set a journalist apart from a reporter. Not some silly writing about the patent dispute over the flexibles. As he had pointed out, paper matches would never replace stick ones.

He warned her that she didn't want to spend all of her career reporting on events such as the new drinking straws that they were sure would catch on. Or the Atlanta druggist who was peddling his new concoction, Coca-Cola, right out of his store. There might be a story there if the two got together; otherwise, she'd spend her career trying to create a name for herself out of drivel and other's troubles.

Grandfather had promised the editorial would make him proud of her and she would be a real journalist. A reporter who could make big money selling her stories to *McClure's* and *Ladies Home Journal*. She'd be somebody to reckon with.

"Are you going to give the article to me or do I need to hogtie you to get it?" Another arresting smile appeared.

Kara handed both envelopes to Quin and returned to her chair. Facing him, she fidgeted in anticipation. She visualized the pleasure on his face after he read the story.

Grandfather said it would put the *Panhandle Herald* on the map and everyone would be talking about the story.

Quin placed the thinner envelope in his desk drawer. "Bonus for the Masterson story," he said. Carefully he unsealed the thicker one.

Leaning back in his chair, he slowly, methodically read the editorial, occasionally peering up at her over his glasses.

Once finished, he returned to the first sheet. After rereading each page, he turned it face down on his desk and continued on. He read each word, almost too carefully. His jaw clenched tighter and tighter as he read further. His eyes became stormy, and his brow furrowed into a frown. Apparently, he wasn't as enthralled with the story as she thought he'd be.

Quin laid the editorial on the desk. He removed his glasses and wearily rubbed his eyes. Opening his pocket watch, he checked the time and closed the gold cover.

Kaira fidgeted in the quietness, feeling a black cloud hovering overhead. The spirited editor's attitude had changed, dampening the air with gloom.

He gathered the parchments in a bundle, folded them neatly, and tapped the edges on the desktop, apparently weighing his words carefully. "You didn't write this." Quin's voice was uncompromising yet oddly gentle, quickly turning rigid. "I would have thought that coming from a publishing family you would know that plagiarism is the worst breach of ethics." He set his jaw and continued to tap on the table. "Maybe presenting something old and contrived is acceptable in Boston, but it isn't in Texas. At least not while I'm the editor."

"I didn't write the damn thing, Quin."

Seemingly unaffected by her confession and her profanity, Quin asked, "Have you even read it?"

She thought she might cry. "No."

"Then let me read an excerpt for you." He took a deep breath before beginning. " 'For decades it has been the goal of the federal Indian policy for containment on the Indian. About six years ago, a group of social reformers and government officials met at Mohonk Lake, New York—'"

"My grandfather instructed me on the details. Even our nineteenth President, Rutherford Hayes, attended. The Friends of the Indian movement has opened dozens of off-reservation day schools and boarding schools for the sole purpose of re-educating the Indians and make them better citizens."

"Do you realize that all of the participants were from the East and only two had ever laid eyes on an Indian?"

"No, but, Grandfather Renaulde said—"

"Malarkey! He's like so many other Easterners who are scared out of his wits about the political power growing in the West. They want it stifled."

"And you truly believe that?" She didn't wait for his response. "Grandfather and Uncle Christian sat me down and went to great lengths to explain the movement thoroughly, focusing on how it would benefit the Indians."

"Kaira, you are naive to their motives. Have you ever heard of yellow journalism?"

"I'm familiar with it. It's sensationalism in order to drive up circulation."

"I recognize that you've been shielded from the realities of life. You've been protected from the ugly things that have happened." He waved the pages through the air. "This piece all by itself can open wounds that are still very fresh in this part of the country." He put his hands on either edge of the desk and leaned forward. Defiantly, he said, "I refuse to publish it, so take the damn thing back to Boston and tell the great Renaulde where he can shove it. . . ."

"Grandfather is an influential man. He's running for the Senate and has powerful people backing him. He won't let this go without ramifications."

"Don't tell me about how cruel your grandfather is."

His words made her bristle. "I didn't say he was cruel—"

"I've been down this path before, and I know how ruthless he can be. Right after Monk sold the newspaper to your family, they tried to push the same editorial nonsense down his throat. That's why they fired him."

She shook her head in disbelief. "And you kept him on. Grandfather allowed it?"

"Only after I convinced him that it was in their best financial interest to let me keep Monk. It wasn't anything out of his pocket, after all, I had agreed to pay Monk's wages." Quin leaned closer. "Money seems to pique your grandfather's interest. He and I haven't been on the best of terms since."

"I had no idea, but wouldn't it be better to publish the damnable thing than to antagonize Grandfather again?"

"Do you think it's right to force someone to change their heritage?"

"Say what you mean. To force the Indians to take on our customs? If it betters them, possibly."

"This group professed to support the Indian and be their friend, and it's doomed to fail."

"I don't believe my family would support any type of renegade movement. Quin, maybe you aren't keeping an open mind."

"An open mind? Have you ever heard of the Red River War? Battle of the Washita? Adobe Walls?"

He frowned, but didn't stop. "Do you think the old Navajo who befriended Amanda Lemmons's father years ago and who still has to come to her place in the dark of night has a problem with Colonel Ranald Mackenzie slaughtering over a thousand Indian ponies at the Battle of Palo Duro Canyon?"

As hard as she tried to weigh his words, she could only stare at Quin. Slowly the pieces fell together. Her grandfather had used her, hoping she'd influence Quin into running the editorial. Fighting for words that refused to form, she shook her head.

"No, you wouldn't. But I can assure you that folks around here remember. Remember being terrorized, having their cattle butchered, their homes burnt to the ground. Some of our town's folks watched their whole family die because of the disagreements between the Indian and the government."

"I had no idea, Quin. Honestly." Tears welled in her eyes.

"Now, do you think I'd jeopardize my reputation and turn against my friends and neighbors by publishing an editorial on how much headway the government is making on molding the Indian into something they don't want to be? And the Indians aren't the least bit fooled by what the government is trying to do."

"To make them into someone they aren't?"

Quin slipped the pages back in the envelope. Retrieving the second one, he pulled to his feet and handed both to Kaira. "I've got to get over to the hotel to see Hank Harris, but I won't be gone long." He walked toward the door, grabbed his hat, then turned back in her direction. "I know this is distressing and makes you sad." He tilted back his Stetson with his thumb, as though making sure she could see his eyes. "That's why I don't want what's in the second packet. It's a bonus for the Masterson interview. Renaulde used you, and I'll never accept his blood money."

"You know Grandfather will fire you, and you need the money."

"No, it's little more than a bribe, and it could never make me happy. Monk and I can live without this job. We've done it before and we can do it again. He'll be happier out at the ranch, anyway. I've saved up enough to take care of us until I can find something else."

"You need to restock the ranch. The money means nothing to Grandfather, so take it." She shoved the white parcel in his direction.

Quin stepped forward, stopping in front of her. Studying her, he casually lifted her chin with his thumb, bringing her eyes up to meet his. "I know Texas isn't the life you are accustomed to. So go on back to Boston. I can't hold you here." He lightly kissed her lips. Taking her hand, still clutching the envelope, he lifted it to her breast. Covering her hand with his, he whispered huskily, "Take this with you. Return it to your family."

He turned and walked out in silence, taking part of her heart with him.

Kaira fought nausea. Tears rolled down her face. Quin was right. Grandfather had used them both, planning to force his personal views onto the world. Probably, just as Quin warned, as a way to create havoc on the strengthening politics in the new West.

How could she pressure Quin into keeping the money, or at least try to, by showing him how he could take it without compromising his values and her sincerity? Maybe she should enlist Monk's help, getting him to talk some sense into Quin. After all, they had gotten the interview with Bat Masterson.

She didn't know how much the draft was for but figured it was in a sufficient amount to buy a herd of cattle. Not trying to sort cows from steers, she walked to the archived newspapers, remembering that Quin had published something recently that had the price of cattle listed. She leafed through the pages.

Idea after idea formed and like bubbles on a windy day, bursting before they were fully developed. If there was enough, Quin could buy some of the new barbed wire and fence off part of his acreage for a vegetable garden or for flowers and roses.

Monk promised to teach her the printing business, and once she learned enough to run the newspaper, he and Quin could spend their days on the ranch. Or maybe Quin would spend the nights with her in the big four-poster bed upstairs.

But how much money would it take to stock a ranch? She thumbed through a few more pages. She had to convince Monk to take the cash and buy cattle.

Kaira resisted looking at the draft long enough. After all, Quin had given it to her, so technically it belonged to her. She hurried to the door and locked it, hoping Quin or Monk wouldn't return before she finished. She opened the envelope.

The draft fell to the floor as she saw her Grandfather's familiar calling card with a note scrolled in his masculine flourish.

This draft is for the Masterson interview. One in a like sum will be yours if you keep that twerp of a grand-daughter of mine in Texas and out of trouble until the election is over. After a period of three months, I will transmit a ticket for her safe passage to Boston. FJR

In despair, she grabbed the deacon bench and eased herself down on the hard wood. She tried to will her body to quit shaking, but it wouldn't cooperate. She fought tears of disappointment, but her sense of loss was beyond tears.

Quin was right—her grandfather was cruel, more cruel than she could ever imagine. She had always been spirited, even her nanny said she marched to her own drummer, but she had never caused her family any embarrassment, at least not enough for him to banish her from his life so he could hold public office. Was she that easy to discard?

A fleeting thought made a brief appearance. Not for a second did she believe Quin knew the true reason her contract called for her employment of three months. The contract was clear that Quin would receive extra pay for teaching her.

The shimmy of the doorknob penetrated Kaira's clouded thoughts. Determined to shuck her pensive mood, she smoothed her skirt, and wiped her eyes with the back of her hand. Standing tall, she gathered her wits and unlocked the door, coming face to face with Jeremiah Cooper.

"Sorry, Mr. Cooper, I didn't realize I had locked the door." She hoped her voice didn't show her emotions. "Neither Mr. Monk nor Quinten are here at the moment. May I help you?"

"Miss Kaira, I came for the newspapers to take up to Mobeetie."

"I'm sorry, Mr. Monk took them to Jeb Diggs a while ago."

"Thank you, ma'am." He tipped his hat. "I best catch up with him."

"Mr. Cooper, you deliver items for hire, don't you?"

"Yes, ma'am."

"Could you take some luggage to the train station this afternoon?"

"Yes, ma'am. I'll be back after I pick up the papers and make my delivery to the mercantile. Did Quin get his story on Bat Masterson? You know he fought at Adobe Walls and was a surveyor over at Mobeetie, don't you?"

"Yes, he did. And no, I didn't."

Kaira followed him to his colorful wagon with gilded scrollwork and painted scenes on the side panels. It reminded her of a gypsy wagon instead of one belonging to a drummer. Mr. Cooper asked to be called "Coop" and introduced her to his pretty, pregnant, red-haired wife, Deidra.

Standing on the wooden boardwalk, Kaira watched the peddler's wagon move toward the Diggs Grocery and Hardware, stirring up a ribbon of dust behind.

With a heart as heavy laden as Deidra Cooper's fruitful body, Kaira hurried upstairs. Removing her lace and satin Paris fashions from the wardrobe, she placed them in a Saratoga. Gingerly, she packed her hats. Once she finished, resisting a look, she closed the door and walked the long stairwell leading down to the office.

Coop returned and loaded the trunks.

Assured that her baggage was safe, Kaira strolled back into the newspaper office. Picking up Quin's apron, she pressed it against her breasts.

Quin would be back before long. She still had a lot to do and not much time.

Chapter 12

The etiquette book Kaira had opened as a ruse, so Quin wouldn't know she had been wearing his apron, still remained on her desk. She jotted down an excerpt that caught her eye. "It is most necessary for a girl to have a motive placed before her—one no more than the making of bread . . ."

She had come to Amarillo for a purpose. To take her apprenticeship and learn to be a journalist. Whether Mr. Quinten Corbett liked it or not, she was there to stay. She would help him keep the newspaper until he had enough money to restock the ranch . . . and she'd do so without her grandfather's piddling crumbs. Quin might be a turncoat at the drop of a hat, but she wouldn't. Maybe she couldn't write worth a dern, but she'd learn to be indispensable in his life.

Kaira turned back the etiquette book another two pages "A misguided blow of the mallet," she read. The idea formed with "the making of bread" and developed into a full-fledged mission.

She'd become indispensable, and the beginning . . . cook Quin dinner. After a hot meal, the intriguing cowboy would surely be more receptive to her theory on why he should keep the money. Maybe he'd let her stay around. Maybe he'd accept her lack of punctuality. Maybe he'd let her love him the way a woman should love a man.

Love! She nearly jumped out of her sit-down-upons. She had in mind stew, biscuits, and a pie . . . not making a home, making love, and making babies.

"I'll start with cooking supper." She shook off the wicked thoughts that had taken hold and pulled Quin's apron over her head. This time it was much easier to tie.

On the way to the tiny kitchen in the corner of the back room, she thought about her expensive dresses and hats she'd shipped to Boston. She didn't need anything that had been purchased with Grandfather Renaulde's money. Damn him . . . damn his hide to hell!

Forcing disquieting thoughts to the recesses of her mind, she turned to the matter at hand. Now what in the heck was she going to cook? Although trained to someday become the lady of a house, she could barely boil water, much less prepare a meal. Where would she begin? A recipe book would help.

Searching the cupboard, she realized Monk was right. There weren't many *fixins* but she'd make do. About to give up on finding a cookbook, she unearthed a well-worn one with a wooden cover, etched with a cattle brand she didn't recognize. But then, she wasn't familiar with any cattle brands, so why would that surprise her.

Written on fragile parchment she found recipes. Some were so faded that she could barely make out the quantities.

"There really is a Sonofabitch Stew!" she declared, immediately discounting that as an option. Touching a dead cow's, or steer's, brains and heart, even if she could find them to buy, made her stomach do somersaults.

And sure enough there was a tongue pie. Her throat went dry and she could hardly swallow, but she read through the recipe. Women actually scraped a cow's tongue! And adding cinnamon and raisins would make it taste better? Not in her lifetime.

Maryland Beaten Biscuits, that's what Monk called them.

She ran her finger down the list of ingredients. Although she had no idea what the equations of a tad, a lump, a smidgen, or a handful would translate to, she had watched the cook make biscuits before. She could do it by guess and by golly. It hadn't looked too difficult. A might laborious, but she remembered how scrumptious the biscuits turned out. Quin would be thrilled. After she got the bread made, she could decide whether he might like ham and eggs or biscuits and gravy. Bleakly, she discounted the gravy, not having the slightest idea how it was made. She was pretty sure she'd need cream of tarter or soda, but not sure which.

The biscuit recipe looked simple enough. She followed the recipe exactly. "Take one crock of warm water, not too hot, put in a smidgen of salt, a lump of lard, and the amount of flour you think the size of the family may require." She stopped and rubbed her nose with the back of her hand.

Now, we aren't a family. So, that means not as much flour as I'd use if I were making biscuits for a bunch, she thought.

She added a couple of handfuls of flour and read on. "Make it into a paste, douse it with flour, and beat the batter with a rolling pin until its workable, right at thirty minutes. If one doesn't have a rolling pin, a solid mallet or ax will do."

Thirty minutes! Kaira looked at the recipe again. Not wanting to soil the page any further, she didn't touch it. Surely, it was three minutes, not thirty.

She proceeded to pour the gooey mess out on a tea towel. A little watery, but it did say paste, she thought. Kaira sprinkled it liberally with flour. No rolling pin to be found. A mallet? Isn't a hammer the same as a mallet? She knew exactly where Monk had put the claw hammer.

Hurrying to the office, a trail of flour followed her. She found the hammer, and glancing at the clock she realized she had to hurry, and hot-footed it back to the kitchen.

With the hammer posed over the puddle of flour and water, Kaira gave the whole procedure a second thought. The pointy end would take too long. She examined the flat side of the tool. Fairly flat, and it would speed up the process. If only she had an ax, not that she knew what one looked like, but she did know that it was much larger.

Taking aim, she drew in air to reinforce her misgivings. She closed her eyes and thought through the process. Yes, she'd done exactly as the recipe had called for, and the biscuits were truly a delicacy that would tempt any man's taste buds. Even Monk appreciated them.

Using both hands, she lifted the hammer high above her head and proclaimed silently that she wouldn't stop until she had beaten the dough for thirty minutes.

One second. Two seconds, she counted.

Splat! Water and flour shot through the air with lightning speed. She reared back and made contact again. And again, trying desperately to convince herself that with a few more beats, her biscuits would be perfect.

Slam! She'd make the newspaper a success.

Slam! Make her grandfather sorry.

Slam! Make Quin happy and give him a life he deserved. One he didn't have to pay for by compromising his values.

One hundred twelve. One hundred thirteen . . .

"Sweetheart." Quin's voice split the air and caused Kaira to jump as though he'd caught a black widow guaranteeing her inherence. "I hate to bring it to your attention." He laughed, full-bodied, whole-heartedly. Once he controlled his hilarity, he came to her and took the hammer from her hand. "I think you've beat that damn thing to death."

Quin laid her assault weapon aside and turned only to chuckle again. He couldn't believe his eyes. There stood Kaira Clarice Renaulde, astounded member of the *Pea-bawdy* family of Boston, covered from head to toe with flour, lard, and water. Dribbles of paste dripped from wet ringlets around her temple. His apron, now a shade of gray, hung well below her knees and no doubt she had dough in places he only dreamed about touching. Even her nice attributes were dusted in white.

"I'm sorry, Quin." She bit at the corner of her mouth. "I think I made an error with the amount of water I was supposed to use." Then she joined him in his merriment, not stopping until tears ran down her cheeks.

Pouring water from the kettle, he wet a cloth and began helping her clean up. He swept and mopped the floor, while she picked dried dough out of her hair and tried to wash off his apron. He made a mental note to tell Mary Carol Diggs to buy two new aprons. One extra large and one tiny.

While the floor dried they sat on the worktable, legs dangling as if they sat on a dock. They sipped tea and laughed. Laughed and sipped tea.

Quin wasn't sure exactly how he ended up drinking such a dainty, wimpy concoction, unless of course hell had frozen over.

"Quin, I've had a lot of time to think today. You gave me valid reasons why society shouldn't try to make people into something they aren't. Isn't that exactly what you are doing?"

"I don't see how I'm forcing—" He drained his cup and set it beside hers.

"No, you aren't forcing others. You are forcing yourself. You are a cattleman who needs to be out on the open range, not cooped up in a newspaper office." She moved her thigh, so it fit more comfortable against his, enjoying the feeling of his warmth through his Levi's. "That's why you stay angry, or did until today." She rested her fingers lightly on his arm. "It isn't because of the losses in your life . . . but that you've lost your life."

"Then tell me why you want to be someone you aren't, too."

"Ah, there's where you are wrong. That's my problem. I didn't conform to society, so Grandfather shipped me down here, so far away from Boston that if I spoke my mind the election would be over before New England got word of it. He wouldn't have to take a chance on me embarrassing him and costing him the election."

"So what are you going to do about it?" He leaned into her, nudging her shoulder with his.

"My ball gowns and those ugly hats you seemed to detest have already been shipped to Grandfather. I don't need anything bought with his money. I want to be myself. Enjoy life. Enjoy a good prank. And enjoy . . ." She looked up at Quin. The smoldering flame she saw in his eyes startled her. "Enjoy kissing you."

"Then what in the heck are you waiting on, sweetheart?" He swung her into the circle of his arms. "You know I have nothing to offer but a passel of love and a broken-down cowboy with no cows."

"You mean steers?"

"Smart aleck."

"Quin, I'm not in love with your cows, your steers, or your body. It's your heart."

Quin feathered warm kisses over Kaira's lips, and she quivered at the sweet tenderness of his touch. Kissing the corner of her mouth, he nipped at her lower lip, sending sensual anticipation down to her soul.

Slowly, he outlined her lips with the tip of his tongue in leisurely exploration. All rational thought fled her mind. Not being able to stand the torture another minute, she claimed Quin's mouth with hers. Kisses that had begun as soft and sensual became hungry, demanding.

Quin's hands roamed freely over her body, allowing his fingers to touch as much skin as possible. He nestled her against him, the cradle of his hips welcoming her, and he didn't try to hide his excitement. His tongue delved into her mouth, meeting hers, tasting, savoring the familiar and longed-for sweetness. She showed him how seriously she had taken his lessons on kissing, as she pleased him again and again.

Kaira circled Quin's neck with her arms, inching her fingers into his tousled black hair. The smell of musk lingered. Quin's breathing was rough, ragged as he moved to trail a ribbon of kisses along her throat and slipped his hands under her skirt, finding her warm, delicate thighs and hips. A vision only in his memories. Her bosom was crushed against his chest, her soft curves molded to his heated, aching body.

She answered the demands of his lips but wanted more, all of him. Desiring to touch him freely, she whispered, "Do you think we have time to make love?"

"I don't know, let me check my watch." He pretended to reach in his pocket.

Kaira caught him hand. "Not now you don't."

Quin angel-kissed her nose. "To answer your question, until now, making love to you never crossed my mind."

"Liar." Kaira unbuttoned his shirt, one button at a time, until his chest was fully exposed. "Don't forget we have a newspaper to get out." Burying her face in his chest, she breathed a kiss there.

"Hush." Quin eased his hand from beneath her skirt, and lifted her head to where they were eye to eye. "I've got most of the work done. Monk can finish it. If you think you can behave yourself until Sunday, maybe Reverend Hicks can marry us right after my godson's christening."

"Quin, I want to be part of your life, and promise to make the hurt go away." Her vow was sealed with a kiss.

"Don't ever make it go away, sweetheart. I hurt so good right now that I don't know what to do." Sweetly draining all her doubts and fears, he kissed her again, until her body began to vibrate with liquid fire. "Just keep it up. Keep making me hurt this way."

And she did, until dawn approached when Quin fell asleep in the big four-poster bed upstairs, holding Kaira.

Curled into the curve of his arm, she felt the velvety lace of the comforter they laid on. She pulled Quin's mother's quilt up to his chest and snuggled deeper against his side.

Kissing him good night, she whispered, "Sleep tight, my cowboy. I promise we'll get the newspaper out to the folks of Amarillo by morning, and still make plenty of time for love."